STAR TREK

PREY

Book 3
THE HALL
OF HEROES

JOHN JACKSON MILLER

Based on *Star Trek* and
Star Trek: The Next Generation®
created by Gene Roddenberry
and
Star Trek: Deep Space Nine®
created by Rick Berman & Michael Piller

POCKET BOOKS

New York   London   Toronto   Sydney   New Delhi

Pocket Books
An Imprint of Simon & Schuster, Inc.
1230 Avenue of the Americas
New York, NY 10020

First Pocket Books paperback edition December 2016

POCKET and colophon are registered trademarks of Simon & Schuster, Inc.

For information about special discounts for bulk purchases, please contact Simon & Schuster Special Sales at 1-866-506-1949 or business@simonandschuster.com.

The Simon & Schuster Speakers Bureau can bring authors to your live event. For more information or to book an event, contact the Simon & Schuster Speakers Bureau at 1-866-248-3049 or visit our website at www.simonspeakers.com.

Manufactured in the United States of America

10 9 8 7 6 5 4 3 2 1

ISBN 978-1-5011-1603-2
ISBN 978-1-5011-1606-3 (ebook)

For my father

reH DuSIgh vavlI'
"Your father is a part of you always."

Historian's Note

In late 2285, Commander Kruge died pursuing his life's mission: opposing the Federation at all costs (*Star Trek III: The Search for Spock*). His young protégé, Korgh, launched what would become a hundred-year quest to seize control of his mentor's house and accomplish Kruge's dream.

In 2385, Korgh hired an illusionist to impersonate a resurrected Kruge and trick a group of discommended Klingons into becoming a fanatical cult: the Unsung. These violent puppets were deployed in early 2386, allowing Korgh to seize control of the House of Kruge.

Over the weeks that followed, Korgh used his trumped-up crisis to rally Klingon opposition to the Khitomer Accords, even as Starfleet engaged in an all-out search to find the Unsung and preserve the agreement. The Klingon Defense Force, seeking revenge for its slain warriors, attempted to wipe out the former exiles—unaware that the Unsung held two presumed-dead Klingons as their prisoners: Commander Worf and the clone of Kahless the Unforgettable. Taking advantage of the schism, Shift, a Breen agent, sought to use the Unsung crisis to aid the forces of the Typhon Pact.

The main events of this novel begin in April 2386, several years after the *U.S.S. Enterprise*-E's 2379 confrontation with the Romulan Praetor Shinzon (*Star Trek: Nemesis*). The overture takes place in late 2382, after Andor's secession from the United Federation of Planets (*Star Trek: Typhon Pact—Paths of Disharmony*).

Tout est perdu fors l'honneur.

"All is lost, save honor."

—*Misreported version of a line
from King Francis I, 1525,
later invoked by Napoleon
after the Battle of Waterloo*

OVERTURE

2382

One

"**Y**ou should've seen it. I shot that Breen right in the snout!"

T'shantra winced as she heard the jubilant whoops out in *Dinskaar*'s hallway. The other Orions were still chattering about the battle, as short-lived as it was; such engagements were the high points of their lives. For a pirate, no day was better than one following a successful capture of a hapless vessel.

And few days were as hard on the slaves those pirates owned.

The emerald-skinned beauty had seen it many times. Once the killing and the looting were finished, the pirates always celebrated nonstop. Drunken revelers emptied the ship's pantries and damaged its mess halls, making life miserable for galley workers. It was worse for T'shantra and the others like her: despite being Orion, she was a slave required to provide "entertainment" to such louts and brawlers. Often the weeklong post-battle binges resulted in more casualties than the engagements they were celebrating.

Dinskaar's latest capture, a Breen shuttle ambushed while creeping alone from Kinshaya space toward neutral territory, normally would have portended another unpleasant week for T'shantra. Instead, it had gone wrong for Wogan, keeper of the weapons stores and her latest master. Insensible, Wogan lay bleeding to death on the floor of his office, his favorite jewel-encrusted dagger sticking out of his back. The yell he had made when T'shantra plunged it in had sounded like just one more celebratory cheer.

The dark-haired young woman glanced back at him with indifference as she packed her satchel. While she had never killed before, T'shantra had lived surrounded by death and found little objectionable in it. At least she had not had to suffer Wogan's company one day more; Leotis, *Dinskaar*'s boss, had only traded her to him three days earlier to settle a gambling debt. Leotis had pulled that stunt twice before, winning her back each time. She would not give him another chance.

Her bag stuffed full of food pilfered from the galley and weapons liberated from Wogan's arsenal, she turned and looked toward the door. Nobody had missed the weapons master yet. T'shantra quickly knelt and rifled through his pockets. She found several gold-pressed latinum strips, more than enough to make it worth leaving the bloody dagger right where it was. She shoveled the currency into her pouch—and after a thought, she fished inside the bag for something else. She would leave it as a gift for those who found Wogan.

T'shantra slipped out into the corridor, sealing the door behind her. No one bothered her as she made her way to the deck with the docking port. Everyone aboard was headed away from *Psocath*, the Breen vessel, arms full of plunder. Leotis had ransacked the ship first, as was his right, followed by his favored minions. Watching the raucous looters filing past her, she could tell her timing was right. No guards at the airlock meant little was left to steal. Looking both ways, she took a breath—and slipped into the hallway connecting *Dinskaar* with the Breen shuttle.

A trail of fallen Breen warriors led to the top level. Past experience had told *Dinskaar*'s crew there was little of worth inside the creatures' armor. It was useful, but only to the Breen, who appeared to be more of a social construct rather than a single race. Only they were able to make sense of their gear's complexities.

Hearing motion as she approached *Psocath*'s bridge,

T'shantra anxiously drew her weapon-stuffed satchel closer to her. Someone was lying on the deck behind the captain's chair, working at the furnishing with a spanner. She tensed. A green face peeked over the armrest and smiled broadly at her. "Hey, beautiful!"

T'shantra let out a breath of relief. "Hi, Tuthar."

Bald and skinny, Tuthar worked in *Dinskaar*'s supply room. While his station was higher than hers—*whose wasn't?*—he was lowliest among the pirates, meaning he got last pick of the loot before Leotis moved to dispose of the captured vessel by sale or scrap. Tuthar had never presumed to impose himself on her, and T'shantra found him mildly amusing. "You're stealing a *chair*?"

"It's a nice chair," he said, standing up. He gestured to three bodies, piled in the corner. "Those Breen have to live in those suits all day. You've got to figure they need their lumbar support."

"Are they all dead?" she asked.

"I wouldn't be here if they weren't." He clapped his hands on the armrests and gave the chair a good tug. "My father always said people overlook the real treasures in plain sight."

"Your father sounds like a smart man."

"Not smart enough to be rich."

T'shantra's father, Fortar, had been *very* rich—trafficking in everything, with love for no one. He had sold her to Boss Leotis as if his daughter were just a second-rate good from his Azure Nebula warehouse. In retrospect, she should not have been surprised. Her mother had left the family—a malapropism, *family*—in the same way, only to die as collateral damage in a syndicate war.

She couldn't waste time. "Here, let me help," she said. She stepped beside the chair and helped him pull at it. With a groan, it snapped free from its moorings.

"Thanks." Tuthar hefted the chair. "What are you doing here? I wouldn't think Wogan would let you out of his sight."

"I was . . . looking for him." She turned to the command interface, now minus one chair. "Do the systems still work?"

"I think so. We just gave the shuttle a few love taps. The Breen weren't expecting us."

Something had happened recently in Kinshaya space, according to the bits and pieces she had been able to gather from Wogan. The Holy Order, the scripture-spouting outfit that ran the Kinshaya government, had just lost political control in some kind of coup. The Episcopate's Breen allies had unwittingly triggered the uprising by participating in a massacre of dissidents on Janalwa, the Kinshaya's new capital planet. The backlash had driven one religious sect from power—and it had also sent the Breen packing in a hurry.

That included whoever was aboard the shuttle *Psocath*. Ordinarily, the Breen traveled the local spaceways with confidence, protected by their warships and privateer vessels. This was no ordinary time. *Psocath* was the second easy picking the Orions had found during the exodus.

Tuthar heaved his bulky prize toward the exit. "I guess I'll see you later, T'shantra. Big party tonight."

"And tomorrow. And the next day."

Tuthar laughed. "Wogan's a lucky man. Maybe *I'll* win a dance from you one day."

She smiled back at him primly, and he departed. She had thought to tell him to avoid the *Dinskaar* deck that held the arsenal. But Tuthar was no different from any other pirate on the ship. Some were monsters; others were monsters in training. It was time for her to be rid of them all.

T'shantra struggled to make sense of the controls. The Breen language was unknowable, whether spoken or written; the creatures' obsession with opacity was infamous.

In three minutes of searching, she had figured out how to seal the airlock and nothing more. She was running out of time and options. Closing off the ship would certainly draw attention; Orion forces could reboard *Psocath* at any moment. She rustled in her bag for a disruptor pistol—

—and then she saw him. One of the Breen warriors that had been piled in the corner was very much alive—and advancing across the bridge toward her.

"Stop!" she shouted, whipping out the weapon. She did not understand the squawks and squeaks coming from the gray-armored figure, but the Breen apparently understood her, stopping halfway across the deck and lifting his hands in the air. The Orions had at least remembered to strip the Breen bodies of weapons, even if they had been less than thorough in guaranteeing all their foes were dead.

The Breen chattered more. T'shantra didn't know much about the Breen, but the creature seemed less fearsome than the others the Orions had faced. And more rational: a Klingon wouldn't play dead. If that was the case, she thought, then perhaps there was a deal to be made.

"Do you understand me?" she asked. "Squawk once if you do."

The Breen gave a low electronic snort.

"I'm not one of the people who attacked your ship. I'm trying to escape them. Do you understand?"

The Breen's head tilted sideways a little. Then, another chirp.

She gestured to the interface. "I can get us away—but I need your help to activate the ship's systems. You can help me—or I can shoot you." She adjusted the disruptor. "This is on full power. It will chew through whatever you're wearing."

Her prisoner simply stood and watched. Was he ignoring

her? Calculating? Was "he" even the right pronoun? There was no time to wonder. Hammering sounds came from beyond the hallway—and out of the corner of her eye, she could see images from the sensors. The Orion guards had noticed *Psocath*'s closed hatch, and were trying to get back in.

"You see?" she said, gesturing to the screen. "They're going to get us both, unless you help."

The pounding grew louder. She shook her head. "I'm wasting my time."

Just as she aimed the disruptor, the Breen responded by reaching for his helmet. A hiss of air escaped as the seal opened. The naked face that looked at her was furry and golden, with a lupine muzzle and short fangs. Dark oval eyes darted between her and the screen. "I will do as you say," he said in a rasping voice not much louder than a whisper.

T'shantra allowed the unmasked Breen to access the interface. The Breen touched the controls once before pulling back. He looked over at his dead comrades in the corner—and then at her. "This is futile. We will not escape the Orions' tractor beam."

"Leave that to me," she said. She reached into her pouch and withdrew a handheld communicator. Composing herself, she pressed a key. *"Leotis!"* she cried out. "Leotis, it's T'shantra. Please answer!"

"What is it?" replied an irritated Orion voice. *"I'm busy. Someone's messing around aboard the Breen ship—they've locked the hatch. And you shouldn't be using Wogan's comm unit, my dear. Unless you're ready for me to buy you back from—"*

"Leotis, Wogan is dead! Come quickly!"

The unmasked Breen studied her as she recited the

lines she'd practiced. "I'm scared, Leotis. Please, hurry!" She raised an eyebrow, confident her performance would convince.

It did. *"I'm sending the sentries on that deck to you. Be careful, T'shantra."*

"I will," she said. She deactivated the comm unit and threw it away. "I just wish the bastard was going to look at Wogan himself." She pointed to the Breen. "Hurry and start the ship. Don't worry about the tractor beam."

Puzzled, the Breen touched more controls. *Psocath* shuddered, its engines coming to life. "What was the meaning of your call?" he asked as the ship wrenched away from the docking clamps, turned, and lurched forward.

"They're about to find Wogan. And when they try to move his body—"

Psocath shook violently, struck from behind by something metallic. The helmetless Breen grabbed at the interface with both hands, steadying himself. "I told you this wouldn't work," he said. "They're shooting at us!"

"No," T'shantra said. "Look."

As *Psocath* cruised in a wide arc away from the pirate ship, the pair spied *Dinskaar* through one of the starboard ports. Several decks of the larger vessel were ablaze, with others venting to space.

"As I was saying," she said as the Breen gawked, "moving Wogan triggered the grenade I tucked underneath him."

"Just one grenade?"

"Did I mention his office was in the armory?" She looked outside with a canny smirk. "I suspect the magazine's gone up. It won't destroy the ship, but it'll buy time to get somewhere." She just hoped her stunt had taken out Leotis too.

The Breen regarded her, clearly impressed. After a moment, he asked, "The other Orions. They mistreated you?"

"You could say that. So I'm leaving." Her grin faded. "I—uh, haven't figured out where to go yet."

"That I can help with," he said as he turned back to the interface. "My people have . . . a *facility* near here."

"Aren't the Breen from the Alpha Quadrant?" T'shantra looked over his shoulder at the map display. She had seen plenty of maps in her father's operations center as a child, and the Breen's statement didn't make sense to her. "I didn't think you controlled anything around here. What kind of facility?"

The Breen said nothing. T'shantra filled in her own answer: *The kind of facility no one knows about.*

She grew anxious as her prisoner set the heading. "Who said I wanted to go to this place?" She fingered the disruptor trigger. "Listen, I'm not trading one prison for another. I just want to get away."

"It is no prison, you will see." Intelligent eyes looked back at her. "And among the Breen you will never be harmed again—one way or another."

Two

The Breen had told the truth: their destination was no prison. Neither was it like anything T'shantra had ever seen.

The system—Jolva Ree, according to the star map—had no worlds hospitable to life. The Kinshaya ignored it, even though it was deep within their territory; there were no souls there to save. Leotis's gang had avoided it, too, figuring its asteroids were of little use to anyone.

Anyone save the Breen. T'shantra had looked on with curiosity as her Breen prisoner directed *Psocath* toward a largish rock—and then in wonder, as hidden spacedoors opened to allow the vessel entry. Inside, she beheld dozens of armored Breen jetting in zero gravity around the shells of several colossal spherical vessels.

"A starship factory in an asteroid?" she asked as she looked out.

The Breen didn't respond.

T'shantra stepped closer to the starboard port and stared outside. The Breen had more people at work than she'd ever seen, even including at the bazaar on Chelvatus III. The Orions she'd known had never built anything. They'd only taken. And what wasn't worth taking, they abandoned or destroyed. To see so many beings laboring together toward a common goal was alien to her.

But something was odd. "Those aren't Breen ships." She looked back. "Are they?"

"The less you know," the Breen replied, "the more options you will have later."

T'shantra thought that a puzzling response. As *Psocath*

nudged toward a firm lock between one of its undamaged ports and the docking gantry, she waved the disruptor. "You said I wouldn't be a captive here."

"You don't have to be. But my people have a right to be cautious about you. Your people did attack mine—"

"I told you, they're not my people."

"And I believe you. But even the Kinshaya don't know about this facility. You have come to a very secret place."

"A secret place you must have been in a big hurry to leave, if Leotis was able to catch you." She thought for a moment. "Or were you trying to reach it?"

The Breen looked at her. His eyes narrowed and he nodded. "Wait a moment." He strode to the corner where several of his dead comrades lay. "You will be more comfortable if you wear a helmet where we are going."

She stared at the headgear. "What, will I not be able to breathe?"

"That's not the problem. All Breen are expected to wear helmets in public. And it will help with communication."

T'shantra understood. She had never seen a Breen unmasked before that day. She watched as he knelt over one of the corpses and unlocked the snout-nosed helmet. "You may not like the smell inside this," he said, "but it is for the best."

"Wait," she said, stepping over. The corpse's exposed head looked nothing like that of her fur-faced companion. The being had no nose at all—and a pale, scaly complexion. "He's Breen too?"

The hairy one looked back at her, fully expecting the question. "The Breen are not a single species—but, rather, a confederacy of several peoples with somewhat similar anatomies. I am a Fenrisal. Poor Jaan here was a Kalystarian. Our vocoder units translate our voices into a common tongue that only those wearing the helmets can understand."

He handed her the fish-face's headwear. She retreated to the far side of the bridge, where, keeping the disruptor within easy reach, she put the helmet on. The smell did not offend her, but she saw nothing whatsoever. "What's the idea?" she said, only to be startled to hear macabre squawking coming from the helmet's public address system.

"Just a moment," she heard the Breen say. "I will have my armor transmit an authorization code so you may use Jaan's helmet."

T'shantra waited—and within moments, the space inside the helmet came alive with light and sound. She saw the bridge around her in sharp detail, with various glowing captions in a strange language hovering near various things within her view. Including the form of her companion, who donned his own helmet.

"Speak normally," he said, his voice repeating clearly inside her helmet. *"The systems will recognize your language and translate appropriately."*

She did speak—and as she did, the characters in the captions before her eyes made sense. "Thot Roje," she said, reading the inscription by the Breen's figure. "Is that your name? Thot Roje?"

"Roje, yes. Thot is my title."

"This is amazing." She thought the helmet would be stifling, but the longer she wore it, the more the environment adjusted. "The air's fresher inside than out."

"We spend a lot of time in them. It helps to be comfortable."

She heard a familiar sound: that of someone trying to open the sealed airlock downstairs. But inside the helmet, she heard it with such sharp clarity she felt as though she was in the same room, not a deck above. She gave a start as Roje moved toward the exit.

"I must open the hatch," he said. *"Discard the weapon and I guarantee your safety."*

"What good is your promise?"

"I am head of Beta Quadrant operations for the Breen Intelligence Directorate. At least, I was yesterday."

"You might not be now?"

"I go to find out."

They had not made her a prisoner, but neither did T'shantra entirely feel like a guest. The quarters she had been assigned were nicely appointed and quiet, with her only visitors a number of interviewers asking about her life. She had continued to wear the helmet in their presence, and the conversations had gone easily. She had as many questions about her armored hosts as they had about her. As time went on, their reticence gave way to more candid responses.

The helmet interface had already answered one lingering question for her: how the Breen told one another apart. It also alerted her to something when the spymaster returned to visit a few days later.

"I see you are still *Thot* Roje," she said.

"For the moment, yes." She could not see the Fenrisal's expression inside his helmet, but her mind's eye filled in the slight smile. *"Was I wrong about your stay, T'shantra?"*

"No. Nobody has harmed me."

"And you have learned much about us, I take it."

"I have." The Breen, she now knew, were the ultimate egalitarian organization. Not only did their armor put members of species with different physiognomies on the same footing, but it worked within races, as well: no one seemed to have any advantage or disadvantage over another due to birthright, physical malformation—or even basic attributes.

Even seemingly positive attributes, she knew, could be a liability. Her beauty certainly had been. Among the Breen, she was just another being.

Or not. *"My people have liked what they have seen in you,"* Roje said. *"Strong aptitudes in several key categories."* He was apparently reading from something before his eyes inside his helmet. "Extremely *strong scores."*

T'shantra nodded. She knew even during their conversations they were testing her. "I know I can do things, Roje. I'm a good watcher. I learn fast. I've just . . . never had the chance to do anything important."

Roje nodded. *"Let us walk."*

He led her through the rooms that had been her world for the past week and into a long corridor. At the end, they entered an observation area looking out onto the massive hidden shipyard.

"Same number of vessels," she said, looking out. "But where are the people?"

"I have spent this week winding down construction." Roje stood off to the side, head low and arms crossed. *"What else do you notice?"*

"Weaponry. Those are warships."

"They were to be Kinshaya Fervent-*class combat vessels."*

She blinked. "You're building them for the Kinshaya?"

"We were," Roje said, shaking his head. *"There should be hundreds of workers out there, T'shantra. But the Kinshaya revolution cast all of that into doubt."* He joined her beside the observation port. *"I was returning here from Janalwa when your associates attacked."*

"They're no friends of mine."

"I know that now."

She'd had no reason to lie—though she was very good at that, if it came to it. Still, it felt good to be trusted. "You were helping the Kinshaya against the Klingons?"

"That was the intention. The Kinshaya failed to hold H'atoria and Krios last year following the Borg Invasion, when their chances were optimal. Now that we're allies in the Typhon Pact, our plan was to construct improved warships for them, with Breen officers aboard as . . . advisors, shall we say, to help them hold what they took next time around."

"Why can't they build their own?"

"The Kinshaya waste too much time in religious observances when they should be strengthening their military. They lack our drive. But these battlespheres aren't ready and never will be, now that we have lost all control over the Kinshaya."

"Control?" She looked at him, not understanding. "Why do you need that? They told me Breen considered all creatures equal."

"The Breen are not the Federation, seeking others to join us. Nor are we the Borg, seeking to make others just like us. The Breen are the galaxy's elite. A place with us must be earned." He waved dismissively. *"The Kinshaya are too mercurial, too untrustworthy. We ally with the Kinshaya through the Pact— and we channel their aggressions where it aids the Confederacy. But that is as far as it goes."*

She nodded. An Orion pirate's life was full of partnerships of convenience. "What will happen now?"

"I leave shortly to report to Domo Brex, who is certain to relieve me of command. And we will destroy this facility." He turned to her. *"Soon it will not be a secret worth keeping. That's half of why I didn't fear to have you see this place."*

"What's the other half?"

"You helped me."

T'shantra studied the mammoth spherical frames outside. Something occurred to her. "Wait a moment. How long would it take to finish these ships?"

"Construction of this fleet was projected to take three to four years."

Three to four years! Nobody T'shantra had ever known had such patience. "If the Kinshaya weren't going to be able to use the fleet until then, what does it matter if you've lost control of them now? You just have to get it back when you're ready."

Roje seemed startled by the thought. *"We could be building them for nothing. I would not like to lie to Domo Brex about my prospects."*

"You're not. You have one plan to build ships—and you make another plan, to get control back. As long as you're honestly working on each track, there is no lie."

Roje looked back out at the darkened construction area—and then nodded. *"We've invested much,"* he said slowly. *"It's worth considering. But there's no guarantee of success. There are many Kinshaya factions in play, more than we understand—but it's clear Breen are no longer welcome on their worlds. It will require many agents, and I have few in this sector who are willing to sacrifice their Breen equality for as long as it would take to operate undercover."*

"I've never known any equality," she said. "I've had to shift allegiances every day of my life, from one owner to the next. I'm good at figuring out what's what." She looked back at Roje. "Could *I* earn a place with the Breen?"

He appeared to study her. *"Perhaps,"* he said, after a long moment. *"If you pass further tests, I have the power to admit you to the Confederacy. We have an orientation program for someone with the right abilities and outlook. There could be intelligence opportunities for you, in time."*

The thought excited her. If she never saw another Orion again—or her own face in the mirror—it wouldn't bother her at all. The fact that the Breen had been known to target her former slavers was a happy bonus. "T'shantra of the Breen," she said, trying it out.

Roje laughed. *"You would never be allowed such a gaudy name among the Breen. Our names are short, communicating our equality and function. For an intelligence agent, a name might bespeak of a trait or talent."*

She thought for a moment before it occurred to her. "You want me to change people's allegiances—and my own," she said with a smile that only she knew about. "Call me Shift."

ACT ONE

THE WAY OF WARRIORS

2386

"The dust of exploded beliefs may make a fine sunset."

—Geoffrey Madan

Three

I hate this place, Captain Ezri Dax thought as *Starship Aventine* went to red alert. *Every time I come here, something crazy happens.*

Another photon torpedo detonated several kilometers to starboard, its blast merely kissing the *Vesta*-class vessel's shields. A subsequent flash dead ahead was closer, triggering the main viewscreen's brightness filters and shaking the bridge crew.

"Evasive action," Dax ordered. The black-haired Trill captain had ordered shields raised moments after the first attack. "Back off—and keep hailing until you get someone!"

If they *could* hail, that is. Weeks earlier, *Aventine* had gotten what all aboard had longed for: the chance to do some serious exploration, taking advantage of the quantum slipstream-capable vessel's unmatched speed. Dax's crew had spent many weeks exploring a stellar nursery in the Zalkon Sector, far beyond the Romulan Star Empire. It was expected and understood that *Aventine*'s proximity to the intense radiation sources would keep it out of contact with Starfleet Command.

What wasn't expected was that ionization damage to her vessel's subspace transceivers would keep the ship incommunicado during its return through warp space. Her crew was still feverishly trying to bring the system back online. "Lieutenant, who's out there?"

"*D'pach*. Klingon battle cruiser, *Vor'cha*-class," declared

Lonnoc Kedair. The security chief's green, scaly fingers quickly worked the controls on the tactical interface. "She started firing as soon as we came out of warp. Aim's not improving. I'd say they're warning shots."

"*D'pach*," repeated Sam Bowers, her first officer. "Captain, we saw her on our last visit to No'Var Outpost."

Our last visit. Maybe that explains it, Dax thought. "We've got an itchy trigger finger over there—or someone with a grudge. Put some distance between us, so they'll see we meant the outpost no harm. And hail them with everything we've got."

Aventine had a past with No'Var Outpost, and not a good one. Several months before, in what had become known as the Takedown Incident, a foreign power had used *Aventine* and its weapons to damage the outpost's communications array. No one had been injured and *Aventine*'s crew had been faultless. Dax had routed their return here as a goodwill gesture, intending to offer her technicians' services if any more repairs needed to be made.

The captain had acted as the codicils to the Khitomer Accords had directed; with subspace comms down, *Aventine* had dropped out of warp far from the asteroid-strewn neighborhood of the space station. That hadn't been far enough for *D'pach*'s captain, evidently. The battle cruiser wasn't taking a refusal to engage as an answer.

"They're pursuing, sir," Kedair said.

So much for goodwill, Dax thought. It didn't make sense. The Klingons were the best about threat assessment. "We're not going to—"

"Comms back up," Mikaela Leishman announced from her station.

The instant *Aventine*'s chief engineer finished her sentence, a broken-toothed Klingon behemoth appeared on screen.

His voice boomed across the bridge: *"—repeat, Starfleet vessel NCC-82602, this is Thagon, acting outpost commander. Drop your shields and surrender!"*

Bowers looked at her, astonished. "Surrender" wasn't the greeting of a friend. But neither were photon torpedoes. Dax stood and addressed the screen. "Commander, our shields are only up because you fired on us."

D'pach answered with another photon torpedo, aimed wide over *Aventine*'s bow. It passed without detonating. *"What's your business, appearing unannounced?"*

"We're visiting a friend and ally," she replied. "Our subspace comm systems were down."

Thagon snorted. *"More Starfleet incompetence. We're on high alert, based on reports that the devils you let out were in the area."*

"Devils? What devils?"

"Don't play the fool. I have half a mind to—"

"New arrival from warp," Kedair interrupted.

Dax rolled her eyes, wondering if the new ship would make things better or worse. "Identify."

"Another *Vor'cha*," the Takaran said. *"Gur'rok.* General Kersh's ship."

That's your boss, Dax thought as she saw Thagon's surprised reaction on screen. She took the chance that Kersh would be reasonable and ordered a hail to *Gur'rok* on the open channel *D'pach* was on. "General Kersh, this is Captain Dax of *Aventine.* Your sentry has been firing on us!"

"The Aventine. *So there is no end to the plagues on our people,"* said a gravelly female Klingon voice Dax had heard before. *"Stand down, Thagon—now!"*

On screen, Thagon looked flustered. *"General, they arrived without warning, just as they did before."*

"I remember," Kersh said icily. She was on duty when

Aventine had made its controversial first visit to the outpost. *"Follow my command, Thagon. For what little use they are, we are still allies."*

"I'm glad to hear *that*," Bowers said under his breath.

Thagon went stone-faced—and made a hand gesture to his crew off to the side. *"I do not regret defending my post,"* he said. *"You lost control of your ship before, Captain Dax. It could have happened again."* He vanished from the screen.

"D'pach peeling away," Kedair said. "It's dropping shields."

"Drop ours," Dax ordered. "Full stop."

Now the dark-skinned general appeared on screen. Kersh's tone was acidic. *"You must be mad, Captain, showing up this way. You are not on Thagon's list."*

Dax explained about *Aventine*'s comm system issue, and their intentions in visiting. But then her eyes narrowed. "Wait. *List?* What list?"

"The list of expected visitors—of approved travelers in this region."

"We're a Starfleet vessel, General. The Khitomer Accords guarantee reciprocal free transit between our peoples." She stared at Kersh. "One doesn't look over the shoulder of a friend."

Kersh wore a wry expression. *"Even a friend who has disappointed us in the past?"* The Klingon woman shook her head. *"Thagon was within his rights to worry. There are enemies of the Empire on the loose—and they have shown they can beam through your shields. Thagon feared your ship had been commandeered—again."*

That nearly left Dax speechless. "Enemies? What enemies?"

A tone sounded—and at ops, Oliana Mirren spoke. "Subspace hail from *Enterprise* for you, sir. Priority one."

Kersh let out a disgusted sigh. *"I'll let them tell you. I am tired of thinking on it."* Her frown returned. *"Do not test my hospitality, Captain. I have a hunt to return to."* The general disappeared from the screen.

Bewildered, Dax composed herself and sat back down. "Dax here, *Enterprise*."

If the sequence of events since arriving in Klingon space surprised her, the familiar Vulcan voice speaking over the comm simply added to it. *"This is Commander Tuvok. What is your status,* Aventine?"

"We're fine. Just a misunderstanding with the Klingons," Dax said, blinking. "I'm sorry, Commander. I was told the *Enterprise* was hailing us, not *Titan*." She shot a puzzled look at Mirren, who shrugged.

"There is no error. As a result of the crisis, I am currently stationed aboard Enterprise. *We have just heard about your arrival there from the chancellor's office."*

Dax's eyes bugged. She looked at Bowers, who said, "Someone already told the chancellor?"

Tuvok evidently heard the comment. *"The occupants of No'Var Outpost sent the message when you entered their system unexpectedly. Chancellor Martok contacted Admiral Riker, who contacted us."*

"That's fast," Dax said.

"We are on high alert," Tuvok said. *"You were not on the Klingons' list."*

The *"list"* again, Dax thought. She hoped her officers weren't watching as she gripped her chair's armrests tightly and let go to release tension. Forcing a polite smile, she asked, "Commander, we've been out of communication for a few weeks. Could you please fill us in?"

"That is my intent. But there are portions of it we should discuss privately, on a secure channel. This matter is of the utmost seriousness."

"I'll bet." Dax stood. "Stand by, Tuvok."

"Standing by."

The captain headed to her ready room as Bowers moved to take her chair. "Never a dull moment, huh?"

Dax responded with a look that made the ones she'd gotten from the Klingons seem pleasant.

Four

"I don't think I heard you right, Commander." Her fingers on her freckled right temple, Dax struggled to focus on the face on her screen. "You're telling me that in the time we've been out of touch, the Federation's relationship with the Klingon Empire has started to fall apart—and that Emperor Kahless and Worf have been *killed*?"

"Presumed killed, in Commander Worf's case," Tuvok replied. The Vulcan's expression did not change. *"I regret being the bearer of this news, Captain Dax. I know that one of your symbiont's past Trill hosts was married to Worf."*

Her throat suddenly dry, Dax forced a swallow. She struggled to register Tuvok's next words: *"Aventine is now attached to the Starfleet task force searching for a Klingon terror cult known as the Unsung—along with most of the other vessels we have in Klingon space."*

Worf. Kahless. The Unsung? Much had changed in her absence. *Too much.* Dax's eyes narrowed. "Why am I not hearing this from the admiral?"

"Admiral Riker has been called to Qo'noS to deal with the ongoing political crisis," Tuvok said. *"The admiral asked that I brief you."*

Dax nodded. On her padd, the official order from Starfleet Command appeared. It lacked detail—but quite a bit more was to be found in the reports that had just populated her device following the reestablishment of *Aventine*'s subspace comm capabilities.

"I take it there's a cult threatening the Klingon Empire, Tuvok. But if the general public knows about it, why all the cloak-and-dagger?"

"*Because certain elements would be damaging to Klingon domestic tranquility, Chancellor Martok has asked that those facts not be shared publicly.*"

"All right. Tell me everything."

Tuvok laid out how Starfleet had agreed to stage a celebration on Gamaral, in Federation territory, for the Klingon nobles of the House of Kruge. Arriving aboard a squadron of Klingon birds-of-prey known as the Phantom Wing, the Unsung struck the event and killed the guests—embarrassing Starfleet, as the *Enterprise* was in charge of security. They had also kidnapped Worf and Emperor Kahless, the clone of the ancient founder of the Klingon Empire, who had served in recent years as figurehead emperor.

The Unsung had retreated, with their prisoners, to the Briar Patch. To a planet, Thane, that had been their place of exile for a hundred years. "*The Unsung descend from a group of discommendated officers loyal to Commander Kruge. Their birds-of-prey once belonged to him. Their strike at the nobles was an act of revenge for what they see as the wrongful shaming of their families. So, too, was their broadcast execution of Kahless.*"

Dax was sorry to hear of the emperor's fate. The grisly images of the murder were in one of the reports that had appeared on her padd. "How do we know all this?"

"*Commander Worf told us.*"

Dax raised an eyebrow. "I thought you said he was killed."

Tuvok said, "*When the* Enterprise *tracked the birds-of-prey to Thane, the Unsung escaped capture—and Worf escaped them. He told us—and this is classified—that the Unsung had been urged to violence by their new leader: an imposter posing as a hundred-forty-five-year-old Commander Kruge. A Klingon who is most certainly dead.*"

Dax suppressed a dark laugh. "I'll say. Captain Kirk shoved him into an ocean of lava—or that's how I heard it."

"*Your information is correct. The Unsung knew this, too, but the imposter convinced them otherwise. I now believe he did so using technology that . . .*"

The Vulcan paused. Ezri knew that look. Dax's hosts had seen it many times. Someone that knew Dax before the revelation that the Trill were a joined race was remembering how every Trill had lied to their allies for generations.

"*Technology,*" he began again, "*that you and I became familiar with in our first meeting, long ago.*"

"Wait." Her mind raced back. "You mean aboard *Excelsior*?"

"*Captain Sulu's command. Curzon Dax visited as a diplomat, to deal with the Kinshaya on their onetime capital world of Yongolor.*"

Dax struggled to recall. "Niamlar, the Kinshaya war god. There was a prankster posing as a deity and riling them up." Her eyes narrowed. "Did you ever find out who that was?"

"No. But I formed a theory then as to *how* they did it—and I believe it explains events on Thane," Tuvok said.

Captain Picard, Tuvok explained, had encountered a technological trickster named Ardra nearly twenty years earlier. "*The support ship Ardra used to generate her illusions,* Houdini, *is alongside* Enterprise *now. We used it to detect the hoaxer who was deceiving the Unsung: a Betazoid, Buxtus Cross. We believe he may have impersonated Kruge. One of his confederates killed him—an Orion woman. She fled—as did the* Blackstone, *the ship that was helping him perform his illusions.*"

"She boarded *Blackstone*?"

"*We do not know if she transported aboard that ship or a different one. There was another unidentified vessel in the area.*"

"If the imposters were out of the way, shouldn't that have ended the Unsung threat?"

"*Unknown. Before we reached Cross, the Unsung attacked and wiped out the Klingons stationed at Spirits' Forge on H'atoria. Then they struck the Klingon outpost at Ghora Janto—where we believe at least half the Unsung force was destroyed.*"

"By the Klingons."

"*A joint force of Klingons and Starfleet vessels, but also ships from the Romulan Empire and the Breen Confederacy.*"

One surprise after another, Dax thought. "Romulans and Breen—in Klingon space? Who invited them?"

"*Chancellor Martok, under pressure from Lord Korgh, the new leader of the House of Kruge.*"

Korgh, Tuvok explained, had no apparent love for the Typhon Pact powers—but he vociferously blamed Starfleet for the fate of the members of his house on Gamaral. He also accused the Federation of having given the exiles a haven in the Briar Patch a century earlier.

"*He seizes upon any chance to undermine the Federation's special relationship,*" Tuvok said. "*That is why Admiral Riker is on Qo'noS, even as* Titan *continues its search for the remaining Unsung ships. The Khitomer Accords must be saved.*"

"The Klingons we ran into here were definitely on edge," Dax said. "I thought it had to do with the Takedown Incident, but this is worse than I'd imagined."

"*General Kersh is a member of the House of Kruge. We do not know if she shares Lord Korgh's views, but she does want to see order restored—as do we. Starfleet must find the remaining ships of the Unsung squadron, the Phantom Wing, as quickly as possible. Their controller may be dead, but while they are free, a near-century of friendship is endangered.*"

"Worf, Tuvok. What happened to Worf? You said he escaped them."

Tuvok spoke in even tones. *"I was coming to that. He felt responsible for what happened to Emperor Kahless—"*

"He would."

"—and Commander La Forge and Lieutenant Šmrhová considered themselves culpable for the Gamaral Massacre. They devised a plan to transport an away team aboard one of the cloaked Unsung vessels above H'atoria."

"And naturally Worf went." She shook her head. "Alone?"

"That was not the intention, but that is how it transpired. A weapon belonging to him was found in the wreckage of one of the birds-of-prey at Ghora Janto. We suspect he may have been a prisoner aboard."

"He wouldn't have been taken captive again if he could've helped it." She took a deep breath. "Worf performed a heroic feat to get Jadzia into Sto-Vo-Kor. He could have been trying to do the same for Kahless." The captain bent her head, damp blue eyes closed.

"His devotion was admirable. Captain, I grieve with you."

"Thank you." She lifted her head and opened her eyes, saying, "What do you need from *Aventine?*"

"You are to join the search for the Unsung, for as long as Starfleet vessels are permitted free movement in Klingon space."

"We could lose freedom to travel? It's that bad?"

"If Lord Korgh accomplishes his aims, yes. Starfleet must find the fugitives first. Admiral Riker believes that Aventine's *speed would be most helpful."*

He's felt that way before, Dax thought. She and the admiral had disagreed over his use of *Aventine* in the past—but clearly the stakes now were much higher.

"I will send you the specifications we have on the Phantom Wing, along with information on sectors to be searched."

"Thank you, Commander. *Aventine* out."

The captain stared at the blank screen for a long

moment—and then sat back in her chair. She looked at the blackness out the observation port and wondered what Worf's final moments were like.

I hope you died in battle, she thought. *And if you didn't, I now have a favor to return.* She rose and headed back to the bridge.

Five

"I am Kahless, clone of the Unforgettable—and I have returned!"

Worf stared, slack jawed, at the figure before him in the mess hall of the bird-of-prey—and wondered if he was delirious from lack of air. Moments earlier, he had been surrounded by the Klingon cultists of the Unsung as they attempted to strangle him with chains. Now the clone of Kahless stood beside him—and Worf was reliving, after a fashion, one of the most important moments of his life.

Years earlier, the same clone—created from DNA purportedly belonging to Kahless the Unforgettable, legendary ancient ruler of the Klingon Empire—had first appeared to Worf on Boreth. Then, it had been in a blaze of supernatural effects, intended to make the clone seem like a visitor from the afterlife. Clerics at the Boreth monastery had created the clone as a ploy to unite the Empire's quarrelsome factions. The truth had been revealed, but with Worf's help, the clone assumed the ceremonial role of emperor, offering spiritual guidance to many.

All that had come to an abrupt end in the Briar Patch, where Worf witnessed the clone's execution by the Unsung. They had acted under the orders of someone claiming to be Kruge, the feared Klingon commander who had been killed a century earlier by James T. Kirk. The false Kruge was dead, so far as Worf knew. But the clone of Kahless stood beside him, very much alive.

This time, Kahless's arrival required no technical artistry. The emperor had burst through overhead access panels. He landed on the makeshift dais where Worf, captive of the cultists, had been standing in judgment. Clad in the Unsung's own black sensor-foiling armor, Kahless started freeing Worf from the chains binding him. The emperor snarled at the Klingons on the deck surrounding them. "I have returned—*and I will see who here is worthy!*"

Amid sounds of astonishment, Valandris, one of the Unsung's great hunters, stared at the clone. "We—we saw you *die*! We killed you, back on Thane."

"You killed *someone*," Kahless said, detaching another chain from Worf's neck. "But it was not I." With a strong heave, he wrested the chain from the Klingon holding the other end. Looping it around his hands as a weapon, he whipped the loose end against the platform once with a loud clang.

Two members of the Unsung closed in from one side. Kahless lashed out, snapping the chain in their direction. Metal struck flesh. The young Klingons backed away, bruised and bleeding.

The emperor held the chain over his head, swinging the loose end around in a circle and turning so all in the room could see the fire in his eyes. "You may try to kill me again— if you dare. But you will not imprison me. Never again."

"I, too, have tired of it," Worf added, rubbing his neck. The Unsung had jailed him multiple times.

"Worf, there is a blade at my hip," Kahless said, edging toward the commander. "Take it."

Ducking the whirling chain, Worf grabbed the *d'k tahg*. Looking around, he realized that the Unsung were making no offensive moves. Indeed, they almost cowered—and not because of any threat from himself and Kahless.

"It was no phantom," declared wild-haired Harch, whom Worf knew from the ill-fated *Rodak*. "I stabbed you, clone. Back on Thane!"

"As did I," said another Klingon, "at Lord Kruge's command."

"Many of us stabbed you," whispered a very pregnant Weltern. "And you, Valandris—you marched him to his executioners."

Valandris seemed stupefied. "You saw it happen, Worf, just as we did. How could this be?"

Worf didn't know—but the question angered him. "*Now* you question, Valandris? You blithely accepted Kruge when he appeared to you. The 'Fallen Lord,' you called him. You let that pretender talk you into committing murder—into striking against your own people in the Empire. You knew Kruge had died a hundred years earlier, plunging into a sea of flames." Worf glared at her. "You believed *him*. Why would you not believe Kahless?"

"There was a body!" someone shouted.

"Who said this?" The emperor looked around.

"Dublak." One of the older males in the group stepped forward. "I dragged you—I mean, I dragged *the corpse* to the pit to discard it. The body was real. It was yours."

"It only *looked* like mine," Kahless said. A portable light sat at the edge of the crawlspace above them, casting rays down on the emperor. "You simple-minded fools. You have been tricked! Deceived, by a pair of illusionists."

Worf's eyes widened. "Illusionists?"

"Actors. They used technology—holography—to portray Kruge and his priestess, N'Keera. A Betazoid man and an Orion woman is what they really were. They used their fakery to make it appear that I had died."

A clamor rose from the dozens of Unsung warriors in the

room. Valandris called out. "We are not fools! No one could make illusions that good."

"Yes, they could," Worf said, thinking. "*Enterprise* faced someone who had those skills. Her name was Ardra."

"I heard them mention her," Kahless said. "They spared me on purpose, to learn more about me and impersonate *me*, someday." He smiled in the light, his teeth gleaming. "But I outwitted them and escaped into the bowels of the ship."

Worf studied Kahless. The clone seemed thinner than when Worf had seen him last, his beard longer and more ragged. "How long have you been between decks?"

"Too long," Kahless said. "I have known only darkness and noise, living in the crawlspaces and looking for a way to the weapons lockers, so I might arm myself. After the last battle you were in, I decided I had wasted enough time." He stepped off the makeshift dais. Cracking the chain against the deck, he glared at those surrounding him. "If you would fight, strike me now!"

Valandris extended her arms, waving her people back. "I would know more about these tricksters."

"You would, would you?" Kahless smiled darkly. He brought the chain to a standstill. "Find your 'Lord Kruge' and his priestess. Bring them to me. I would delight in showing you who they really are."

No one responded. Kahless looked about, confused. Worf stepped off the tabletop toward him and touched his arm. "Then . . . you do not know?"

"What?"

Valandris looked around at her companions before speaking gravely. "N'Keera killed Lord Kruge before all of us on Omicron Lankal. Then she beamed away."

The emperor frowned. "Did she take his body with her?"

"Yes."

Kahless snorted. "Then he is no more dead than I am—and he was certainly never Kruge. His name is Buxtus Cross. The woman is called Shift. They had been speaking all along about abandoning you when they accomplished their aims—whatever they were."

Worf looked about warily. There was no appetite for combat—not when the room was still thick with wonder. Dublak scratched his head. "This makes no sense. There *was* a body on Thane. It was no illusion." He displayed his hands. "The blood covered me."

The emperor's expression changed. "Oh, yes," he said, his voice solemn as he paced near the perimeter of the platform around Worf. "There *was* a person they made to look like me. I heard them say who it was." He crossed his arms in judgment and laughed. "You colossal fools. You have slain many who did not deserve death—but you unwittingly included one of your own. It was the warrior who founded your colony. You killed General Potok!"

Six

"Potok?" Valandris said. "That's impossible!"

Worf remembered the blind old man, onetime devotee of the true Commander Kruge and founder of the discommendated colony. He faced Valandris. "Yes . . . it very well could be. You were holding him prisoner in the same kennel where you were keeping Kahless. Just before I escaped I sought him out—but he had vanished."

"The imposters transported him away," Kahless said. "He was made to look like me, using their tricks. I heard Cross describe how, after the fact. Then they returned him to this vessel—"

"Where I marched him down the ramp," Valandris said, voice nearly catching in her throat, "to his death."

Worf looked around. Some of the Unsung were just as shaken as she was; others, more. Dublak stared at the deck, shaking his head in silence.

Kahless's eyes widened in the low light. "Yes. Yes, you see it now. You killed the father of your people," he said, "at the command of a charismatic liar who said pretty things."

Someone shouted, "We didn't know it was Potok!"

"You did when you imprisoned him in Kruge's name," Worf retorted. "Do you not see the shame in what you have done?"

Valandris shook her head. "Potok made our lives miserable, Worf. *He* is the one who shamed *us*."

"That does not forgive what you have done!" Worf said. "The general was blind, barely in his right mind. You jailed him, hung him from a hook like a carcass."

Kahless laughed. "Worf, you do not give them enough respect!" He strode defiantly around the perimeter of the clearing that had formed around them. "Behold the great and powerful hunters before us! They defeated a general of a hundred fifty years. That must be worth killing five generals of thirty!"

Murmurs arose again. Beside Valandris, Weltern slowly sank to her knees. Kahless's words had shaken the Unsung to their very beings.

"That's impossible," Valandris repeated, clutching her hair with both hands. "All impossible. They were with us for a year—knew everything about us. We were not, *could* not have been tricked so completely."

"Is that so?" Worf strode to face her, fearing nothing from her comrades. "What is easier to believe? That a Klingon who fell into a sea of lava could return a century later?"

"Your people believe stranger things," Valandris said, looking up at him. She was shaking. "Like you told me, Worf, about how the true Kahless is supposed to return from the dead." She pointed to the emperor. "You all believe that. How is what happened with us any different?"

"Kruge was no Kahless," the clone said, his voice dripping acid. "But let us say he was telling the truth. If someone did return from Sto-Vo-Kor, why in the stars would he visit *you*, over all the worthier Klingons in the universe?"

"We are worthy," Weltern said, rising. "It is what Kruge—" She stopped. "It is what our leader told us!"

"And that is why you followed him," Worf said. "Because he told you that you were worth something, after Potok convinced you of your uselessness. But deeds secure a Klingon's honor."

"Correct," Kahless said, a devilish smile forming. "Tell me, Worf, what do you think of these people's deeds so far?"

"They would not want to know."

Silence fell across the room. The commander surveyed

the Unsung, who had been ready to kill him minutes earlier; confusion and grief was all he saw. Worf was uncertain what would follow—

—and when a klaxon sounded, everyone present nearly jumped.

"Proximity alert," Valandris said. "Stations!"

Klingons started quickly filing out of the room. Worf looked at the many Unsung members still present—and then at Kahless. "Come. We will follow."

Dublak objected. "You cannot leave!"

"Stop us," Kahless said, shaking the chain still clenched in his fists. "I have been living inside the skin of this vessel for too long. I would see where we have been all this time."

The Unsung were already at their bridge when Worf and Kahless arrived, followed closely behind by the other warriors. Outside, Worf saw a rocky, lifeless landscape—but no gun turrets port or starboard. *Chu'charq* was cloaked as it sat on the floor of a canyon. Looking at one of the displays, he could tell that the other three Phantom Wing vessels were parked and cloaked nearby. He looked to Kahless. "Only four of their birds-of-prey survive."

"I have only seen one, and too much of that," the emperor replied.

"Contact spotted," announced Hemtara. "Vessel passing through the system. Likely another search party."

"Put it on screen," Valandris said from the command chair. She looked to Worf and Kahless—who now stood amidst the Unsung. "Don't try anything foolish."

"Would you be the judge?" Kahless asked.

The magnified image that appeared on screen wasn't anything Worf was expecting. "A Breen cruiser." He looked around. "Where are we?"

"Cabeus, in the Empire," Valandris responded.

"A Breen vessel—in Klingon space?" Kahless was flabbergasted. "Some nerve they have, trespassing in—"

"New contact arriving from warp," Hemtara said. The view on the screen adjusted. "Klingon battle cruiser, moving to intercept the Breen. Identification reads *I.K.S. Gorkon.*"

Kahless nudged Worf. "Captain Klag! Now you'll see something. He won't suffer these cretins."

Worf's eyes narrowed. He didn't know what the Breen ship was doing here, but he hoped that *Gorkon* would scan for the presence of the Phantom Wing vessels. There was little chance of an Unsung ambush, as the command crews of the other ships were all aboard *Chu'charq.* Valandris seemed willing to wait and watch as the ships closed.

"No shields, no weapons powered up, either side," Hemtara said.

"This makes no sense!" Kahless looked to Worf. "What goes on here?"

"Listen for hails," Worf said.

Valandris looked back at him impatiently before nodding to her companions. "Do it."

"They're on an open channel. Easy intercept," Hemtara soon said. "Here it is."

"*—Breen vessel,*" called a powerful Klingon voice, "*this is Captain Klag of* I.K.S. Gorkon. *Where is your escort?*"

Nonsensical Breen warbles came in response.

"*You know the terms,*" Klag said. Worf surmised that the *Gorkon* captain had access to translation capabilities that the Phantom Wing ships lacked. The captain sounded enraged. "*The Empire permits Breen and Romulan search parties, but you must have a Klingon escort!*"

Another meaningless reply from the Breen.

"*You've got an escort now. Follow us to the border—and do*

not return until you learn to abide by an agreement. End transmission!"

Kahless gawked as the Breen vessel changed its heading to match the *Gorkon*'s. "What is this? Klingons cooperating with Romulans and Breen?"

Worf frowned. "Things have changed, Emperor. The Unsung have struck against many different parties—including the Romulans at H'atoria. *Enterprise* was present when that happened."

"The attack on the Romulans wasn't our intention," Valandris protested. "That was Zokar's doing."

Worf believed her. The rogue Unsung ship captain, now dead, had been following through on a grudge. "It does not matter how it happened. The result is that the Romulans and Breen were fighting alongside the Klingons and Starfleet at Ghora Janto. I take it that they have been allowed to join the search for you, as well."

Kahless was stunned. "I refuse to believe it. Martok would never accept aid from those fiends—not in our territory!"

"When I was last free, the Unsung attacks had been empowering the chancellor's enemies on the High Council," Worf said. "It seems that was just the start." He looked around at the Unsung bridge crew, his eyes full of disdain. "See the chaos you have wrought—all on the orders of a charlatan!"

His listeners buzzed with words of self-defense—none of them particularly full-throated. It fell to Valandris to speak for all. "I still don't believe this story," she said. "If it's true, then we really *are* nothings. No—we are worse than nothings. We are fools." She shook her head. "Whoever this Cross person is, he has much to answer for."

Worf frowned at her. "So do you, Valandris. So do you all."

Seven

Aboard the *Reikin*-class fast-attack warship *Sustax*, Shift looked through her Breen helmet's visor at the fearsome Klingon cruiser off to starboard. "So that was the great Captain Klag," Shift said, her helmet transforming her words into a series of squawks. "When I saw him, I thought we were going to have to fight it out."

"*There was never a need for concern.*" Thot Roje stood in front of his command chair. *Sustax* was his flagship, the place from which he worked his mischief in the Beta Quadrant. "There are currently twenty-six Breen ships in Klingon space assisting with the search for the Unsung. It was under that cover that we were able to look for you."

Shift was glad to have been found. She'd had her fill of Klingons over the last months. "I was afraid Klag had found out about the Defense Force bird-of-prey you destroyed back in Cragg's Cloud."

"*The nebula hid our presence—and our circuitous departure route means there is nothing to connect us to that.*" The armored spymaster joined her at the port. "*There is no reason for concern. You have already survived far worse dangers, Chot Shift.*"

Chot. The Orion woman delighted in hearing her Breen title again. Since the onetime T'shantra had rescued Thot Roje from *Dinskaar* four years earlier, he had made good on his pledge to see her made into a proper member of the Confederacy. She had returned the gesture by learning everything Roje was willing to teach her about intelligence work. Before long, Shift had become one of the Breen's top field agents, risking execution and enduring imprisonment as she worked against her new people's enemies.

And why not? They were her foes too. The Orion crime lords who'd made her life miserable had worked the zone between Klingon and Federation territory for years. Either power could have eliminated the brigands with a concerted effort, but neither did. Starfleet's obsession with exploration—who cared about *that*?—meant its devotion to patrolling neutral space was less than absolute. The Empire, meanwhile, saw the Orions as a nuisance; Klingon warriors were more interested in conquest than police work. Both powers had earned her disdain—and her best efforts in opposition.

The Breen would control the entire Beta Quadrant one day. And the Orions would never enslave anyone again.

This project had been her masterstroke. Shift's infiltration of Buxtus Cross's team of truthcrafters had taken the most time of any of her intelligence operations. She had spent well over a year working her way into the insufferable mimic's confidences. She had played the part of his girlfriend so well he had made her his apprentice—after which she had helped him fool the discommendated Klingon exiles of Thane, portraying High Priestess N'Keera to his aged Commander Kruge.

Both masquerades had ended, with Shift killing the sniveling Cross before he could seek immunity from the Federation. That act—accompanied by *Sustax*'s timely destruction of a Klingon warship threatening her—had yielded the very prize she had worked so long to acquire: *Blackstone*, the wondrous ship that had allowed Cross to work his illusions.

It, too, was outside the starboard viewport, invisible to

Shift and—critically—to Klag and his Klingon warriors aboard *Gorkon*. Her Breen comrades were aboard the illusion-generating ship, repairing battle damage to its cloaking systems from its engagement at Cragg's Cloud. Having visited Cabeus before on one of her training missions with the Unsung, Shift knew it was a system the Klingons didn't frequent; a safe place for repairs. It was pure luck that the cloaking device was working again when *Gorkon* happened by. The Klingons had yet to detect it. *Sustax* had already destroyed a bird-of-prey in order to acquire *Blackstone*, but it might not be able to succeed against the better-armed and ably crewed battle cruiser.

"We're supposed to be here searching for the Unsung," she said. "Do you think Klag noticed that we weren't scanning for cloaked vessels when he found us?"

"The important thing is that Klag wasn't scanning," Roje said. *"He might have noticed our prize. The cloaking device aboard* Blackstone *isn't exactly state-of-the-art."*

"We can fix that," she said. "It's what else the ship is capable of that makes it so valuable."

Roje readily agreed. Shift had already shown him some of what *Blackstone* could do, to the extent that she could operate the equipment. It offered the Breen intelligence community a capability it hadn't had access to since it allied with the Changelings of the Dominion: the power to impersonate an adversary without fear of detection. For someone trained as an agent provocateur as Shift was, it was more valuable than a starship full of gold-pressed latinum. Indeed, the Breen had left latinum behind, taking *Blackstone* instead.

Roje strode over to the officer at the comm station. *"Contact the team aboard* Blackstone *and tell them to get under way, regardless of their condition.* Gorkon *intends to escort us to the frontier. And that is where we wanted to go all along."*

The officer sent the message—and then beckoned for Roje's attention again. *"Coded message from Domo Pran."*

"Send it to my helmet display."

The domo? Shift's eyes widened as Roje read words only he could see. In the years since the Kinshaya revolution ruined his plans for the fleet at Jolva Ree, her mentor's star had fallen. She'd worried during her assignment whether Roje still had his office. A call from the leader of the Breen Confederacy was a good sign.

Or not. Roje communicated to her privately on a channel only their helmets could receive. *"The domo demands an immediate conference."*

Shift took a breath. "I hope it goes well for you, my friend."

"Spare some hope for yourself. The domo wants to speak to you, too."

PHANTOM WING VESSEL *CHU'CHARQ*
CABEUS

"The Breen and the Klingon are halfway to the system edge," Harch said, pointing to a screen on the bridge. "We should take the other ships and strike, while we can!"

"Strike?" Standing alongside Kahless, Worf stared with incredulity at the brash Unsung member. "Why?"

"They killed our brothers and sisters at Ghora Janto," Harch said, bushy black eyebrows forming an angry chevron. "They killed Zokar!"

"Zokar killed Zokar, by slamming his bird-of-prey into a Klingon cruiser," Worf replied. "Is that what you intend? Suicide?"

"What else are we supposed to do?" asked the youthful

Raneer from *Chu'charq*'s helm station. "Our home is gone, as are most of our people."

"Only because you struck at the Empire," Kahless said. "At your so-called lord's command."

"Yes. We struck at our lord's command," said Valandris, who had been standing far forward looking at the viewscreen. She turned and walked back toward the command chair, her arms sagging. "And if our lord was what you say he was, they all died for nothing."

Harch appealed to her as she passed him. "Would you have us simply decloak and show ourselves? Give ourselves to their justice?" He pointed at Worf and Kahless. "Trade these two for survival? Then we might as well be in chains."

Valandris took her seat and looked over to Worf. "Isn't that why you beamed yourself aboard Zokar's ship? You wanted us to decloak."

"I wanted to stop your rampage," Worf said. The Unsung needed to be prevented from further violent acts, and the deaths of their victims demanded justice. But the Unsung weren't attacking anyone now, and he wasn't sure of his next step—especially now that he knew of the deception involved. "I . . . am not sure revealing yourselves is wise. Captain Klag is honorable, and I believe I can reason with him. But tempers are high. His crew might think otherwise. And I cannot guarantee what the Breen will do."

"Decloaking could be the same as attacking," Valandris said. "Suicide." She thought for a moment. "Do your ancient texts talk of a ritual suicide?"

"Yes," Kahless said. "*Hegh'bat* for the warrior who can no longer stand to face his enemies. That does not apply. *Mauk-to'Vor* is a path open to those whose honor is irretrievably lost. But I would not give this gift to you, and neither would Worf. You never had honor in the first place."

"Because our families were discommendated?" someone shouted.

"Because of how you have conducted yourselves. It does not matter what you were taught, or not taught. You have Klingon blood. You should know your actions were wrong. You feel it in your bones."

Worf studied Valandris. She had been wavering, questioning, since his time with her on Thane—and perhaps before. She had kidnapped him from Gamaral, against the false Kruge's orders, in the hopes that he would join them. If the charlatan's word was all she needed, what purpose could that have served—except to suggest to her that another path was possible?

For the sake of those still with the squadron—especially those, like the little orphan Sarken, who were blameless, Worf had to find an answer. And that required time. "Wait," he said. "We will find a solution."

Before anyone could react, Harch rushed Raneer and shoved her from her seat at the helm. "Madness!" he declared, initiating the engine startup sequence. "Our people must be avenged!"

Chu'charq's systems rumbled to life. Raneer rose and grabbed at Harch, even as the larger Klingon drew a dagger. Valandris bounded from her seat, enraged. "Back away, Harch! We will decide this together, or not at—"

A shrill alarm interrupted her—along with a festival of flashing lights on various stations. Raneer, struggling with Harch, looked past him at the console. "Power loss. Emergency shutdown sequence!"

At the engineering station, Hemtara called out. "Dilithium damage," she said. "We'll lose the cloak if we try impulse power. And I don't think warp speed is possible at all."

Worf approached the engineering station. Hemtara

looked at him with suspicion. Valandris, hearing her starship's engines whine and die, gave permission for him to step in.

"You have exhausted your dilithium crystals," Worf said, checking the readout. "You have been running under cloak almost constantly—and Commander La Forge told me the modifications you have made to your transporter systems required significant energy."

Within a few moments, *Chu'charq* was hailed by the skeleton crew aboard *Klongat*, one of the other vessels on Cabeus's surface. "They're reporting the same thing," Valandris said. "I will tell *Cob'lat* and *Krencha* to run checks as well."

"They will find the same thing," Worf said. "If not now, then soon. Commander Kruge's own bird-of-prey, a hundred years ago, encountered a similar problem."

"What did he do about it?"

"Nothing. Montgomery Scott fixed the problem, by using particles from a primitive nuclear reactor."

Harch looked out at the canyon beyond. "Where are we supposed to find something like that?"

"You will have to depend on yourselves." Worf stepped back and crossed his arms.

Valandris looked about the bridge—every one of her people, clueless about what to do. Then she approached Worf. "Outside," she said gruffly.

Worf shot a glance at Kahless before following her into the privacy of the corridor. There, she spoke to him in hushed but urgent tones. "This is real? Not a trick?"

"I do not do tricks."

"But it's what you want, isn't it? If we decloak, we're found by the next ship that passes over this canyon. Or perhaps you would have us call for help?"

He said nothing.

"It will not happen that way," she said. "These people will do something worse. You saw how they felt before Kahless appeared. Now, knowing what he has told us, I cannot predict how they will act." She looked at him urgently. "If we do nothing, the children on these ships starve—or worse."

Worf considered her words. It was true that there was no telling what the other Unsung would do. He needed to keep them from resuming their rampage. Without hope here, the situation could quickly deteriorate.

"I think there may be something aboard that can help," Worf said. "Come with me."

Eight

It's a hell of time to be having a conference when a Klingon battle cruiser is looming less than a kilometer away, Shift thought. But Roje was confident of the encryption of the comm in his private office.

Shift had done most of the speaking. Any nervousness at addressing Domo Pran had melted away as she provided a concise yet spirited description of her activities in Cross's employ. Now Pran knew everything she had done. She had described *Blackstone* and its technical magic first. Its crew sat in *Sustax*'s brig, still deciding if they would cooperate. Onscreen, Pran sat silently, unmoved by her enthusiasm. Roje had calmly gestured for her to move on.

The Unsung were a juicier topic. Shift had been there at the very beginning, when Cross had first tricked the discommendated Klingon exiles of Thane into thinking he was Lord Kruge back from the dead. She detailed how Cross had transformed them into a fighting force. She spoke of how Cross manipulated the Unsung into attacking Gamaral and H'atoria. Then, finally Ghora Janto, where he sent his thralls, no longer needed, to their presumed destruction.

That piqued Pran's interest. *"Four Unsung vessels are unaccounted for, Chot Shift. Where are they?"*

"I do not know," she said. "Cross had a detection algorithm aboard *Blackstone* that allowed him to find the Phantom Wing vessels when cloaked; it's how we traveled with them without their knowing it. He was about to give

the secret of the algorithm to Starfleet when I killed him."
She paused, suddenly doubtful. "I was afraid the Federation
might capture them and take the credit."

*"Your instincts were correct. Every day the Unsung are at
large, the alliance between the Khitomer signatories suffers. If
anyone should catch them, it should be the Confederacy."* Pran
paused. *"You have the algorithm. Why do you not have the
Unsung?"*

Roje interjected, *"It no longer works, Domo. The algorithm
on Cross's padd and in the* Blackstone's *systems lost its ability
to detect the Phantom Wing ships at almost the exact moment
they were fleeing the battle at Ghora Janto. Whatever system
was permitting the tracking has been shut down."*

"Inconvenient. You have no idea as to where they would hide?"

"Almost too many, Domo," Shift said. "I had provided
the Unsung with the locations of more than a dozen bolt-
holes in and around Klingon space—locations my Orion
slavers used to frequent. Cabeus, where we paused to repair
Blackstone—they knew of as well." It momentarily amused
Shift to think that the Unsung might have been cloaked and
hiding in the same system where the Breen had fixed the
cloaked *Blackstone*, with neither party the wiser. But that
was unlikely.

"We cannot go looking for them now," Roje said. *"And that
is not our mission."*

"Agreed," Pran said. *"They have done their damage to the
Klingon Empire's relationship with the Federation. We need
not worry about them."* With that peremptory dismissal, the
domo demanded that Shift move on to the last, and most
shocking, section of her report.

She did so with zeal, knowing how explosive what she
had learned was. By the time she was finished, Thot Roje sat
back in amazement. And he had already heard it.

"Korgh hired Cross and his truthcrafters. He supplied the Phantom Wing birds-of-prey. He chose the targets—and when he was done, he ordered his pawns' destruction. And he would have destroyed *Blackstone* and her crew had *Sustax* not arrived to destroy his minions." She snapped her fingers. "There is yet more. While Korgh is now the leader of the House of Kruge, he is not Kruge's heir. He had the truthcrafters fake the vid of his adoption ceremony."

"*Astounding!*" Roje was excited. "*Think of what we have here, Domo.*"

"*Blackmail?*" Pran seemed reserved.

"*At a minimum. We could have control of a leading member of an important Klingon house,*" the spymaster said. "*We could know all that went on in the High Council. The House of Kruge compound on Ketorix produces many of the Klingon Defense Force's most advanced warships. Korgh could channel all that technology to us.*"

"*You are mistaken,*" Pran said, "*if you think this Klingon would agree to that.*"

"*We could reveal his complicity in the creation of the Unsung,*" Roje said. "*If that were to get out, Korgh would be destroyed.*"

"*He would be of no value to us destroyed,*" Pran said, "*and he would know that. Your weapon is one you cannot use.*"

Roje froze. Shift noticed his body language—and cautiously nodded. "I admit I am also concerned by something, Domo. Korgh is fiendishly clever for a Klingon—he must have Romulan blood, somewhere—there are just too many angles for him to consider. He might not be able to keep everything hidden much longer." She frowned. "The Korgh card must be played quickly, if it is to be played at all."

"*Card? I do not understand the expression.*"

Shift shrank a little. "An Earth game I learned from

Cross. If we wish to take advantage of what we know about Korgh, we might only get one chance."

Pran growled in frustration. *"All this effort, Thot Roje— and I am not sure what you have. A ship that produces phantasms and a Klingon fraudster, both of dubious value. Why didn't you seize the treasure ship, the Ark of G'boj, when you had the chance? Latinum would have been useful to our other operations."*

"There were Starfleet officers aboard," Roje said. "Had we remained on the scene, we might well have found ourselves outmatched." The armored Fenrisal shifted in his chair. *"Domo, because of this operation, we are on the verge of a major realignment of powers. Korgh wants to sever the Empire from the Federation, perhaps even realign it with the Typhon Pact—"*

"Have you heard his speeches, Thot Roje? He and his supporters would insist the Empire be first among any allies. This search for the Unsung has been a model for it: a Klingon operation with all the outsiders following their lead." Pran shook his head. *"No, this could go very wrong."*

Roje's voice rose in agitation. *"Domo, it must be better than what we have now."*

"You should have your visor checked, Roje, because you speak as one blind. The Romulans already treat the Confederacy as junior partners. The last thing we need is another ally lording over us. We must ever be the puppet masters—as you intended back in your plot on Garadius IV or with your accursed Jolva Ree operation. I can't believe you've talked me into keeping that going. Yet another Thot Roje waste of time and resources!"

"I knew you would bring that up," Roje said. Jolva Ree, with its stillborn Breen fleet project, remained a sore point between him and the domo. *"I also know you sent Chot Dayn there to report on me. If you want me to resign, Domo, you may—"*

Shift raised her gloved hand before Roje. "Wait." She looked at Pran on screen. "Comrades, I have an idea . . ."

PHANTOM WING VESSEL *CHU'CHARQ*
CABEUS

"—to recrystallize dilithium crystals while still in the warp chamber, use the following procedure—"

Worf had guessed correctly. The tutorial padd he had found on *Rodak* existed in large numbers aboard *Chu'charq*, as well as the other three surviving birds-of-prey. Each contained the same files, explaining how to do various duties aboard a bird-of-prey—many of them involving advances—like recrystallizing dilithium—that had developed in the hundred years since the Phantom Wing's construction.

The same flinty-voiced person narrated many of the files.

"Do you recognize this woman's voice?" Worf asked as those in main engineering listened to the recording.

"Yes," Valandris said. She looked at the padd with interest. "There was an old Klingon. She came to visit us on Thane, always beaming down to the hut of Lord Kruge—or whoever he was. She never told me her name, but she was the smartest person I have ever met. She delivered us to where the Phantom Wing was hidden—and then trained us in the ships' functions."

"If she was with the tricksters, she may not have been Klingon," Worf said. "She might even have been Cross or Shift in disguise."

"No, I saw the three of them together. But you are right. She could have been another pretender."

"I think there were only two," Kahless said, arms crossed

as he rubbed his back against the column he was leaning on. The clone had stripped off the jacket from the sensor-muting uniform he had been wearing for days, an act that had given him great relief. "Cross never spoke of a third actor. But she could have been one of the people aboard his ship."

Valandris shook her head. "I doubt that." She asked Worf, "You said the ship had to stay close to us for the illusions to work, right?"

"If it was like what I saw in Ardra's case, yes."

"This woman accompanied me on several training flights that Kruge and N'Keera weren't on. She went with us to the Hunters' homeworld, beyond the Bajoran wormhole—that's where she stole the technology behind our transporter systems."

Worf's eyes narrowed. "You said she was old?"

"Yes. Maybe even as old as Potok." Valandris reflected for a moment. "Actually, I was with her when I first came to this place. Cabeus was a stopover—she had us practice landing in a cave near here. So she must have known about it."

Hemtara, who had been studying ahead on her own padd, looked up. "I think we may need that cave. The protocol she describes will work, but we will need to shut down everything on the birds-of-prey—including life support and the cloaking devices."

Valandris frowned. "We would have to do it on one ship at a time—and just transfer everyone off."

"There is risk," the engineering expert said. "From what the other ships have told us, their dilithium crystals are equally decayed. If any one should lose their cloaks, the next passing ship could target us."

"This cave," Worf said. "Is it possible to fly there?"

Valandris called up to the bridge for a surface map. "The

thrusters should get us to the cave," Hemtara said. "But I wouldn't wait to move."

Standing at the back of the gaggle, Harch spoke out. "More hiding?"

Valandris's head snapped back. "Yes, Harch. The ships are dying. What do you suggest?"

"Why do you take suggestions?" Kahless said, a snarl in his voice. "Do you not lead this rabble?"

She glared at him, impatient. While not exactly prisoners, Worf and Kahless had never been left alone. Valandris clearly thought his comment unwelcome. "There are no leaders among the Unsung. There was only Kruge. And before that, only General Potok."

"A fine thing. Nothing to aspire to." Kahless put on a jacket someone had handed him. "Die arguing if you wish—but I need food. I have been living in the ship's hull on runoff water from compressor coils and the few scraps I hid while I was hostage."

Several in the room departed for their own ships, intending to rendezvous at the shelter. Valandris left, but not before speaking with a few Unsung. They remained in engineering, making sure Kahless and Worf did nothing to escape or sabotage the vessel.

That wasn't Worf's intent. Rather, he took advantage of the first quiet moment since Kahless's arrival to clasp arms with the clone in a heartfelt greeting. "I am glad to see you, Emperor."

"And you, Worf, son of Mogh. I heard Cross say you had escaped the Unsung on Thane." He studied the taller Klingon. "Why are you here?"

"I intended to—" Worf said, before he stopped. "I came back," he finally said. He decided it was better to leave it at that.

Kahless nodded, seemingly understanding. Then he

grinned. "You see? Still, no meal. I expect better treatment from my assassins."

Worf smiled back. "You have lost weight, Emperor."

"I do not recommend the diet." He clapped his hand on Worf's shoulder. "Come, let us see what swill there is to be found."

Nine

Kahless the Unforgettable lifted his *bat'leth* high into the air for all to see. Then, in a swift motion, he brought it down against the weapon held by the tyrant Molor. The villain struggled to remain standing—but Kahless's might was too great. Molor dropped to one knee and cried out for mercy.

Those watching the fight called out, jeering at Molor and chanting Kahless's name. There were hundreds in the audience, perhaps more than a thousand, all gathered on the spacious grounds of Azetbur Square. Constructed following the Borg Invasion of 2381, the column-lined plaza provided the First City with a large meeting ground, perfectly suited for a *Kot'baval* Festival. While the actors reenacted the ancient Kahless's triumph on the main dais, fire dancers entertained on other stages—and all around, Klingons ate and drank.

Lord Korgh stood just behind the main stage and smiled for the first time since the deaths of his son and grandson, days earlier. Staging the fete had been a stroke of genius. Chancellor Martok would never have permitted a political rally of any kind on public space, and certainly not an event criticizing the Empire's Federation allies. But *Kot'baval*, usually observed on the anniversary of Molor's defeat, could be celebrated whenever the people's spirit needed boosting. Martok could not possibly object to an event designed to remind Klingons about honor's meaning—especially not when the scurrilous Unsung had spread terror.

In fact, Korgh had secretly created the Unsung for the express purpose of shaking confidence in Martok and the Empire's alliance with the Federation. That their trumped-up threat had made the gathering possible was an irony that delighted the old Klingon. The fact that he didn't have to pay for the event was even better.

"A great turnout," said a Klingon dressed in a rich robe. "Your people did amazing work, Lord Qolkat."

"I spared no expense, Lord Korgh." The ruddy-skinned Qolkat stroked his finely coiffed beard. "Our High Council colleagues could do no less to honor your son and grandson. I am glad it pleases you."

As long as you all keep trying to curry favor with me, Korgh thought, *I will be happy.*

The allies Korgh had made in his brief time on the High Council were a gallery of the thwarted. Nimoe, Grotek, Satevech: all feared to challenge Martok directly, but would happily hide behind the robe of Korgh, their new and popular front man. They stood behind him now, ready to ascend to the dais with him so that they might be seen with the man of the hour. The new lord was the perfect vessel for their aspirations, a tragic newcomer able to rail against Martok's policies without fear that the chancellor would challenge him to combat. There was no honor in fighting a Klingon of a hundred and twenty. Martok would never make that mistake.

Qolkat, with his vast wealth, had been Korgh's most important new ally. His father, Qolka, had long been an influential critic of the alliance with the Federation. While serving as *gin'tak* for the House of Kruge, Korgh had quietly cultivated the family's friendship through business dealings. Qolka died defending the capital during the Borg Invasion, after which Qolkat had assumed his father's title. But he lacked his father's gravitas and political skills, and had been little more than a thorn in Martok's side until Korgh joined the High Council.

Qolkat's support had allowed Korgh to sublet a good portion of his political machinations. Qolkat had put his family's name and fortune behind the *Kot'baval* Festival here on Qo'noS—and into similar events happening simultaneously across the Empire. Attendees there would hear the simulcast of Korgh's remarks in Azetbur Square, greatly amplifying his message.

"I wonder if the Unsung will strike at this event," Qolkat said. "I would welcome the chance to break their necks."

"So would I," Korgh replied. Qolkat, of course, had no idea of Korgh's role in the Unsung's creation. None but Korgh knew that the puppets' strings had recently been cut. The cultists' job done, Korgh had sprung a trap to destroy his cat's-paws and the evidence of his treachery. The wretches had slipped free, killing his son General Lorath in the process. One-third of the Unsung's forces were still at large aboard four birds-of-prey. Korgh had no idea where to find them. Now he was just as interested in their destruction as everyone else in the Empire.

No, *more.*

And he had no clue what had become of the collaborators of the illusionist Buxtus Cross. According to reports from Starfleet, Cross had been betrayed and killed by his Orion companion, Shift. She was missing, as was Cross's technical crew and their ship, *Blackstone*. Korgh was certain they had a role in the death of Bredak, his grandson, but there was nothing he could do about it.

He had House of Kruge investigators openly searching for both the Unsung and the killers of Bredak; there was no need for secrecy. No one would doubt he had a right. But while the Empire was already scouring the stars for the Unsung, he had a particular interest in making sure the illusionist's crew was wiped out. Shift knew who he was and what role he had played in turning the discommendated exiles of Thane into the Unsung. She had to be eliminated.

For now, Korgh could only wait—and continue his crusade, which grew ever more popular. After his son's and grandson's deaths, he could have surrendered to despair and suicide, or he could redouble his efforts against Martok and the Accords. He had chosen the latter—and it had given him a reason to go on.

The historical pantomime ended, he climbed to the stage to raucous cheers. "*Korgh! Korgh! Korgh!*"

Korgh! Protégé and heir of Commander Kruge, the great and unfairly maligned conqueror who sought to protect the future of the Empire against the likes of his eventual murderer, the Starfleet thug Kirk.

Korgh! The savior of the House of Kruge, the dutiful caretaker who had loyally defended his mentor's estate for fifty years without ever once seeking wealth or glory.

Korgh! A noble example for the age—and a connection to a time when the Klingon Empire was unrestrained by constricting alliances.

All these things, the master of ceremonies said—and it was no mistake that the speaker was the actor playing Kahless. The actor turned and presented his *bat'leth* to Lord Korgh. Grasping it with both hands, the old man thrust it over his head.

Korgh, heir of Kruge! Protector of the Empire's honor!

Korgh reveled in the adulation for long moments, remembering every year of the hundred that had brought him to this place. Then his arms dropped, and the crowd hushed, anxious to hear the speaker who had taken the High Council by storm.

"I will not thank you for coming," Korgh said. "For it is we who have given you a gift, showing you, on this stage, the unforgettable acts of honor which made our Empire great. There could be no better time to remember the true Kahless than in the wake of the assassination of his clone, our emperor."

Cheers for the emperor—louder and more passionate than those he had received. Korgh hastened to continue. "You all know what happened at Ghora Janto. After all the fumbles by the chancellor's regime and his Federation cronies, we have finally begun to avenge the emperor. My son Lorath, the great general, gave his life in destroying most of these outcasts, these Unsung. We have culled their numbers—the rest are on the run!"

Now the chants were of Lorath's name. Korgh listened with satisfaction. "My son fought alongside many valiant warriors. He led a force attended by ships from the Romulan Star Empire, the Breen Confederacy, and, yes, Starfleet." Catcalls and hisses greeted each name—but Korgh was quick to turn the point back on the crowd. "We did not accept aid out of weakness. Rather, they were eager to follow our lead—which is why our attack was successful." He raised an eyebrow. "It must have been educational for Admiral Riker to see what a victory looked like!"

Korgh got the laughter he wanted, and more. If any members of the Klingon public had not previously known of William T. Riker, the old lord and his comrades had remedied the situation. In High Council sessions after the Gamaral massacre, Korgh had hammered Starfleet's performance, making capital of every one of its shortfalls, real or manufactured. After the Unsung attack on Spirits' Forge, where Riker was present, Korgh had brought his criticisms to a wider audience—and zeroed in on his chosen scapegoat. Riker had been convenient, but anyone would have done.

His message had gotten through. "Curse the Federation," called one listener. "Praxis is past! Damn the Accords!" said another.

"*The Federation stands with the Empire!*"

Korgh scanned the crowd for the new voice. "Who speaks?"

"Alexander, son of Worf!" The gaggle parted to allow the young Klingon to be seen. He stood strong before suspicious eyes. "Starfleet vessels fought alongside your son at Ghora Janto, my lord—and our forces search for the Unsung with the Empire now. These are the acts of a loyal ally!"

Several Klingons in the crowd shouted approval; others, derision. Korgh could not have been more delighted at the speaker's identity—and the dais with its address system gave him the advantage. "We have among us today the ambassador of the Federation, *Alexander Rozhenko*." Korgh drew the name out long, knowing just how alien it would sound to his listeners. "Welcome to our event, Ambassador. I am sure this celebration is quite novel to you—as you are a visitor to our Empire." Guffaws rose from the crowd.

"I know the *Kot'baval* well, Lord Korgh. My father took me to see it on Marenga IV when I was a child."

"I see. And what are you now?"

More laughter.

"A comrade, in battle and peace!" Alexander looked around. "My father escaped the Unsung once, yet he volunteered to face them again in order to protect the Empire. He is missing, and may have given his life. Yet he—and I— would give no less for our valiant friends."

Korgh pursed his lips and contemplated a response. He

had heard through channels that Worf had vanished. "The two of you are Klingons," he finally said, deciding on a tack. "We would expect no less from you. How, then, is this an example of *Federation* loyalty?"

"The Federation's loyalty equals ours. They have been the Empire's friends for nearly a hundred years!"

"When you have lived nearly a hundred years, young man, perhaps you will see things more clearly." Korgh paused. "Or perhaps not. This is why I have called for the *chavmajta*—a record of our joint accomplishments with the Federation—to be recited before all."

Many in the crowd voiced surprise. The ritual Korgh and his allies had demanded had not been public knowledge— but it was now. "I have challenged Admiral Riker to speak for his people in the rite. If the Federation is truly worthy of our future trust," Korgh said, "let them demonstrate how valuable they have been in the past."

The crowd rumbled with excited conversation. The *chavmajta* was the unhappier cousin of the *ja'chuq*, a similar ritual performed during the Rite of Succession. The difference was that it was not an application for a high office. It meant that one ally had failed another and had to justify their continued partnership. For the Federation, it was a dressing-down. For Korgh, it was another stepping-stone.

He quieted the throng. "Many of you here—and listening across the Empire—have fought alongside Starfleet officers against the Dominion, the Borg, and others. I honor your service. In fact, I believe that under scrutiny, under questioning, we would find that the heroics were all Klingon. Just as we found that the Federation lied to us, in providing a haven for a hundred years to the dishonored trash who now threaten us—the Unsung!"

The cheers rose again as Korgh retreated from center

stage, drowning out the ambassador's shouted response. Korgh looked to see his council allies grinning. And for only the second time in days, he smiled too.

"Well played, Korgh," Qolkat said.

"Agreed," said Grotek, the scarred loudmouth. "What next?"

"Things will take their natural course," Korgh said. "And certain things will receive a push. Grotek, I will tell you what I need you to do . . ."

Ten

"**H**ere's one," Riker said, studying his padd before the firelight. "General Korrd once worked with Spock to rescue Kirk beyond the Great Barrier." He looked up at the chancellor. "That took place before the Accords, but it's cooperation, for sure. Should we include it?"

"We have gone over this already," Martok said, letting his frustration show. "Spock assisted the exiles who became the Unsung. It is better not to mention him."

"Understood." Riker didn't accept the premise, but it was late and there was no point in pressing the matter. Sitting in a room littered with Klingon historical texts, the admiral shook his head. It was folly, trying to tell of the early days of the Federation/Klingon friendship without somehow mentioning Spock, Kirk, and the rest of *Enterprise*'s crew. Yet that was the needle he was being forced to thread.

The *chavmajta* was the Klingon equivalent of a call for a no-confidence vote: he and Martok had to put on a defense. An audience of High Council members would listen to the litany of valorous acts and judge the partnership worthy, if Riker and Martok did their jobs right. But Lord Korgh, who had skyrocketed to prominence, would be prosecuting the case against them and would no doubt leap on any mention of Kirk's *Enterprise*. The same went for the *Enterprise*-E, which was seen as responsible for failing to stop the massacre at Gamaral. How did one spin tales of heroism without mentioning the heroes?

"I will speak of the Battle of Cardassia," Martok said. "It would be better coming from me. But I think we should move Narendra III to the end."

"Is there a problem including that?" Riker said. "An *Enterprise* was involved there too."

"Captain Garrett gave her life honorably. If Korgh's cronies do not like hearing the ship's name, let them choke on it."

Riker had grown ever more concerned during recent days over Martok's political situation. The ascension of Korgh to the control of the House of Kruge, combined with the Unsung crisis, had put the chancellor in a bind. His rivals said the Accords were contrary to the interests of the Klingon Empire. In Riker's experience, Martok had been direct and honest: a warrior elevated to chancellor, he was not always cognizant of the intrigues of the ambitious people around him. Riker's official mission was to preserve the Khitomer Accords, not to protect a valued personal ally. But he felt loyalty was important—and no one doubted what a Chancellor Korgh might do if given power.

The admiral could not let it come to that. They had decided to stage their preparatory meetings at Martok's private office at his residence, just behind the Great Hall in the First City. The chancellor had an official workspace in the hall, but pointed out there would be fewer difficulties if they met in private.

However, one expected visitor belatedly arrived, accompanied by one of Martok's aides. Riker set down his padd and looked back at the doorway, astonished. "Ambassador, are you all right?"

"I am fine." Alexander Rozhenko walked inside, favoring one leg. His face was bruised, and his diplomatic uniform was torn and dirtied. "The wounds will heal. But I am angrier than I have ever been."

Martok and Riker stood as he approached. "Who did this?" Martok said, boiling. "Who attacked you?"

"It was not so much an attack as a riot. I was at the *Kot'baval* Festival—the one Qolkat staged on the square."

"A riot!" Martok grabbed his aide by the arm. "Why is this the first I have heard of a riot?"

The burly aide looked shaken. "You told us you wanted to hear nothing about Qolkat's celebration, my lord."

"Get out!"

The aide retreated. Lord Korgh was getting under Martok's skin. Riker cleared a space amongst the books for Alexander to sit. "How did it happen?"

The ambassador described the event, which had turned into a rally against the Federation, as well as his confrontation of Korgh. "One of the other speakers took the stage after Korgh left—Grotek."

"Bah!" Martok growled. "Now it becomes clear. Grotek is a walking sonic grenade."

Alexander rubbed the side of his jaw. "He started railing against Azetbur." The daughter of Gorkon, the square was named for her. "He said it was wrong for her to agree to the Accords—and wrong that the Empire ever made her chancellor."

Riker's eyes widened. He looked to Martok. "That's bold."

Martok waved it off. "The more reactionary councilors have held that grudge forever. They say a male would never have sought peace."

"Really?" Riker replied. "Have they met any Klingon women?"

Martok laughed. "It is an old belief that dies hard. Qolkat's father fought me, hammer and tong, when Kurak, daughter of Haleka, sought to lead the House of Palkar."

He snorted. "Would that I had only given Kruge's house to General Kersh, as she had asked, Korgh would not vex me today."

I wouldn't be so sure, Riker thought. "Then what, Ambassador?"

"Grotek started in about the Unsung, and discommendation," Alexander said. "He blamed you and chancellors past, my lord, for not simply putting dishonored citizens to death. He railed about the Federation, and how Spock had given aid to Potok's people. He said that my father should not have recovered his name. He suggested that because of that, I feel sympathy for the Unsung." Alexander paused, gritting his teeth. "Then he suggested my father had given them Kahless—and that he had run away to join them!"

"Oh," Riker said. He was hoping there hadn't been a diplomatic incident—but clearly matters were past that. "Who threw the first punch?"

"I tried to head for the stage, but someone in the crowd blocked my way. My supporters—veterans, I think—pushed back." Alexander rubbed his forehead. "I'm not sure who struck first. Once it started it got very confusing."

Martok was beside himself with anger. "You are my honored guest on Qo'noS! Any attack on you is an attack on me!"

"I don't think they cared," Riker said. "This is why you had us stop work on the Federation Consulate—the protesters outside have made proceeding . . . difficult."

"*Morath's blood!*" Martok declared. "I will not be pushed by this old man and his mob. Korgh's allies are little better than the nobles who ran the House of Kruge before him."

"Ne'er-do-wells?" Riker asked.

"Some never do *anything*. Others, like Grotek, only do the wrong thing. Korgh had been manipulating such people for years as *gin'tak*. It has taken him only weeks to become their champion."

After a pause, Riker looked again at Alexander. "Why *did* you go to the *Kot'baval*? You knew what it would be like."

Alexander sat silently for a moment. He looked up once at Martok before speaking. "This assignment is an honor. But these weeks . . . have been a trial."

Martok chortled. "The Klingon Empire concurs."

"The emperor was slain. My father has gone missing— *twice*—and I have been able to do nothing." Alexander shook his head. "But Father took me to a *Kot'baval*. I thought that going, and hearing the words of Kahless, would revive me."

Riker nodded. "Did they?"

Alexander looked up. "I was reminded of his tenet, 'Leave nothing until tomorrow.'"

"He also said we should seek adversity and face it directly," Martok said. He curled his fingers into a fist. "I have had enough. We will show Korgh we have no fear—and we will start with this: he may have demanded the *chavmajta*, but he is not able to dictate where the event takes place."

Riker looked at Alexander—and then back to the chancellor. "You don't mean—?"

"We will stage the event at the Federation Consulate. Your expanded, completed consulate—which will be finished by Klingons in honor of our fellow warriors in the Federation. And those Klingons will march proudly into the facility—*not* transported—accompanied daily by an honor guard. If anyone would assault them, they had better like the sight of their own blood."

The ambassador smiled. "It would certainly send a message," he said. "A High Council meeting on Federation soil. Chancellor Martok, we would be honored."

"A way to convey our mutual trust," Martok said.

Realizing what the idea entailed, Riker was hesitant. "I'll need to bring in a team to put together an event that size."

"You have such a team on *Titan*," Martok said, "which is already in our space. The team that saved the fortress at Spirits' Forge. It is right that they should have the honor."

And it would further tweak Korgh, Riker thought, *who has been casting Spirits' Forge as a failure for both the Federation and the Empire.* Riker agreed. "I can have Lieutenant Xaatix organize a team and take a runabout here. I want to keep *Titan* in the search."

"Fetch them yourself," Martok said, his expression wry. "I know you have been restless to be a part of the hunt."

Startled, Riker gestured to the padds and documents. "Chancellor, this is my place. Here, preparing for the *chavmajta*."

"The decision to stage the event in your consulate buys us time," Martok said. "You can study on *Titan*. It would show you have no fear of the ritual."

"Go, Admiral," Alexander urged. "I can coordinate with the chancellor. I will enjoy preparing the consulate for our honored guests. It is something important to do."

Riker scratched his beard. "It would be good to be up there," he said, nodding. "Should we capture or stop the Unsung, would there still be a *chavmajta*?"

"Yes," Martok said. "But it would surely be a capstone for our argument." He smiled toothily.

"You've sold me," Riker said. At that, he picked up his padd. "But as long as I'm here, there's more to do. If you're willing to lend a hand, Ambassador, we could use a section on the Borg Invasion."

Eleven

Sarken knelt and picked up a pebble off the smooth floor. "Are all caves this big, Worf?"

"A few," he said. His words did not echo; the chamber was that large. When Cabeus had been closer to its star and more volcanically active, the lava tube had been the source of an enormous outflow, creating the fanlike golden shield that spread beyond the cavern's opening. Inside was more than enough room for four birds-of-prey to park—and for children who had been cooped up aboard ship to run.

Not young Sarken, who lingered by Worf's side. She had protected him while he was on *Rodak*, and he had saved her life when the ship was destroyed. The orphan seemed fascinated by the golden world around her.

"Where does the fire come from?" she asked, pointing to the pillars of flame venting upward, providing light and heat to the space.

"Gas from beneath the surface." On the flight here, he had seen the smoke venting through natural fissures above the landform—a common sight on Cabeus. No one would suspect the cave hid the squadron, unless they took a very detailed scan.

No guards watched him. There wouldn't have been any point. The birds-of-prey were all dead, their systems offline while the Unsung's engineers struggled with the dilithium recrystallization procedure. Their comm systems were of no use to him, and he and Kahless could not commandeer a bird-of-prey alone. Nor was there any place to run.

While no one was watching him, he was hardly alone—not with most of the population of the squadron in the cavern. He marveled at the contrasts before him. As children dashed about, exultant at having room to roam, the adults were far from happy.

Some quarreled. He recognized Harch, deep in intense argument with several companions as they stood around one of the fiery plumes. He could not hear what they were talking about, but they kept looking back at the birds-of-prey—and occasionally at him. Several other small gatherings were similarly occupied.

Yet most of the exiles were morose. Some silently went through the motions of setting up camp; others milled about, staring into the flames or at the walls. As with the belligerent groups, Worf knew the reason was the same: the truth that he and Kahless had brought to them.

And in a far alcove, Kahless stood unmolested, sharpening his dagger on a boulder. He had shown no interest in the other Klingons since the two of them exited *Chu'charq*, and the Unsung had seemed reluctant to approach him. The clone seemed to be an object of some superstition after his miraculous appearance and he had not minded the solitude it provided in the least. The emperor had found little good to say about the Unsung.

"Did your friend really live in the hull of the ship?" Sarken asked.

"He did."

"I used to think those places were scary, but not anymore. Not after you went with me into the guts of *Rodak*."

"It is how we learn not to fear, Sarken. When you are older, you will brave new places alone."

"I guess. Still, I'm glad you were there."

Off to the side, Worf heard footfalls on *Chu'charq*'s loading ramp. Valandris emerged from the dark opening.

"It is under way," she reported. "They do not know how much time it will take."

Sarken looked back at the ship and scrunched her nose in distaste. "All the lights are out in there?"

"They are," Valandris said. "Do not go back in, if it frightens you."

"I'm not worried. I can go with Worf."

Several running children dashed through their midst, catching Sarken's attention. She followed them, joining their game of hiding around the landing gear assemblies. Valandris looked up at Worf and smirked. "At least one of us has not tried to kill you."

Worf said nothing. But when she started walking away, he joined her.

"I have taken a count," Valandris said. "Of the three hundred or so people we began with, only a hundred twenty-three remain—and only because we stopped fighting at Ghora Janto to transport survivors. There are forty-six children, as we would have considered them on Thane."

"You do not have a Rite of Ascension?"

"No. No rights conferred to adulthood because no one had rights. The only determining factor was the ability to produce offspring—hardly a privilege when those children would be born discommendated." Valandris frowned. "A hundred eighty of our kin died at Spirits' Forge and Ghora Janto—including fifty children."

Worf blanched. *So many.* Fully half the future of a people that barely had a future to begin with.

"That has left enough adults to operate all four ships,"

Valandris continued. "Which is convenient—as there are four camps regarding what to do next."

Worf's interest was piqued. "Tell me."

"There are many who are bereft beyond reason. True believers in Lord Kruge who feel lost—and those who feel guilt over what we have done. One group, I fear, would destroy themselves. Dublak, whom you met, is one. Weltern represents another group, which would look for another place of exile."

"Either choice is cowardly."

"Then you will like the next group." She pointed to the Klingons quarreling by the fire. "Harch's mind, you know. He served with Zokar, looked up to him. He would throw the last of us against our enemies—go out in a final battle."

"What enemies?" Worf asked. "Without the fake Kruge to lead you, whom does he think to oppose?"

"That is what they argue about. But I know what the answer will be: *Everyone but us.* Our people have lived generations as dirt. Before we die, Harch would have us muddy those who are unsoiled."

Worf shook his head. "Madness." Then he looked keenly at her. "And the fourth group, Valandris?"

"Right now," she said with reluctance, "it is just me."

"And what will *you* do?"

"I do not know," she said. "But I am beginning to favor surrender."

Worf raised an eyebrow. "To Klingon justice?"

"I dispute that it exists." She shook her head. "No, it is about making the best, final end for those who survive. That is why I have decided to take all the children aboard *Chu'charq* for safekeeping. I would not have them die in a mass suicide or a foolish act."

Her statement surprised Worf. He looked out to the rest. "The others would agree to let you take them?"

"Our children are raised communally—I would not expect parents to object. And if any challenged me, I would fight them." Valandris's eyes locked intently on his. "I read enough of the original Kahless to know that he looked down on acting simply for survival. He said that honor made Klingons more than beasts. Perhaps I am a dumb beast, for I have no honor. But I would rather the children survive in your world than be massacred—or be forced to live in a hole, as Weltern would have it."

Worf was impressed. "There is more honor to that choice than you may think. It is the best path—and can be for all." He looked to the disparate gatherings. "How can you bring others to your way?"

"I can't," she said. "You already know we have no leaders."

"I think you do."

"Going in different directions. No. We had Potok, and then Kruge. We need a unifier. We need you."

It was something they had discussed before, in a different context. "I am not the best choice."

"Why not? You've filled my ears with how your traditional Klingon ways are best—with opinions about what we should be doing. Are we too soiled, too corrupt to be worthy?"

"That's not it. I met a group of Klingons once who had been detached from their heritage, and I was able to teach them. But continuing to ask for a leader from outside keeps your people from becoming whole. They first much choose to seek a better way on their own, as you have."

"But I didn't do it all on my own. I told you I had help from the words of Kahless. What you told me—and what was in his book."

"You mentioned that. Where did you read the *qeS'a*?"

"In Spirits' Forge." Her brow furrowed. "Zokar burned

that book. Kruge, or whoever he was, had us destroy and delete the other versions on board."

"Not every one," Worf said. He gestured to the emperor. "A complete record of the word of the Unforgettable stands before you."

Valandris cast a jaded eye toward the clone, who was using his freshly sharpened blade to cut into a bolt of leather-like material he had found aboard *Chu'charq*. "I forgot. He was created to speak Kahless's wisdom." She snorted with derision. "He is nothing *but* words."

"He is himself. An individual, a warrior in his own right. He knows much."

Staring across the space at Kahless, she chuckled. "I can't see trading one false dead leader for another."

"The emperor is not false. You know who and what he is. There is no deception in him, beyond what it took to escape Cross. He lives," Worf said, pausing. "But I do not know what he would think about helping you."

"No one asked him," she replied tartly. "And I am not surprised. He feels the word of Kahless is too good for us."

"That is not what I meant." Worf watched the emperor, singing as he worked at the material. "For his entire existence, others have forced leadership on him. I certainly urged him to become emperor. His frustration with that role drove him to retire—only to find that without it, he lacked direction and confidence. Before you kidnapped him on Gamaral, he was at a crossroads." He considered for a moment. "At the time, I would have said Kahless would have been unlikely to counsel you—especially given what you have put him through. But now I am no longer sure."

Tentatively, Valandris asked, "If any of us were interested in learning from him, would you ask him? On our behalf."

"He would not respect an indirect plea. You have spat

upon our heritage. If you would have it now, it must be you to make the appeal—and accept his judgment." Worf let out a deep breath. "If he does choose to counsel you, I will help as best I can."

Valandris studied him—and nodded.

She turned on her heel, ready to head back into *Chu'charq*, when Worf added, "There is one more thing."

She looked back at him. "Be quick about it."

"I understood that you do not have a mate."

Valandris looked puzzled. Then she laughed loudly. "Son of Mogh, you pick a fine time to ask. I am too busy to consider it."

Worf scowled. "That is not why I asked. Your cousin Tharas—he was father to the girl Sarken, correct?"

This question startled her too. "That's right. Her mother was killed on a hunt we were on. I have seen the girl from time to time."

Worf nodded. "I understand the way your people raise children. But blood is strong. It means something to a Klingon."

"Even a discommendated one?"

"Yes." Worf looked again at the running children. "Whether or not Kahless becomes your guide, you should become hers."

Valandris exhaled and shook her head. "I never had time for children. Unless things change, I'll be watching over all forty-six."

Twelve

"Listen, friend, I appreciate the whole inscrutable-warrior thing," the Ferengi prisoner said to the Breen jailer. "I really do. It works for you. It's a good look, effective. But if you'd just speak words I can understand, you could do away with the electric prod. I assure you, I am eminently reasonable."

The Breen responded by giving Gaw another shock from his weapon. The Ferengi squealed from the touch of the wand and bolted backward with a spryness he hadn't known since hitting middle age. Gaw sought a far corner of the cell, featureless except for a meter-high cube that passed for a bed. "I told you, cut that out!"

Gaw was the chief of *Blackstone*'s truthcrafters, the technicians who had generated illusions for Buxtus Cross. As the ever-changing public face of the group, Cross was by tradition considered the band's leader—but his sudden and mysterious death had pressed Gaw into the role. The hiding place he had selected for the battle-damaged *Blackstone*, the tail of a comet in the Atogra system, had not protected them from discovery by the Breen. He had been imprisoned ever since and permitted no contact with any of his companions. Were they even on the same ship?

Neither had he seen the person he held responsible for *Blackstone*'s capture. A friend, he had thought; a friend turned traitor. Worst of all, they had taken his prized pince-nez. The parade of indignities seemed endless.

The door to the chamber opened, and another Breen entered. The Breen warriors all were the same size and shape; Gaw had not found a way to tell them apart. Not that it mattered. They had all been hostile to him, only speaking words he understood when they wanted answers he could not give. One wall, he was sure, was transparent on the other side; Gaw imagined he was being watched constantly.

The two Breen began conversing in electronic gibberish. "Oh, great. A conference," Gaw said. The Breen with the prod departed, leaving behind the new arrival. "Okay, so it's a shift change."

The remaining Breen looked at him suddenly and voiced something like a garbled chortle. Removing the helmet, the Breen stood revealed as Shift, the Orion woman who had worked with Gaw's team before betraying the truthcrafters to the Confederacy.

Gaw knew he should hate her but he had always been fond of Shift, and anyone with a face was a relief. Especially hers. "Welcome to my little palace," he said. "I'd offer you a chair, but these people aren't big on amenities."

Shift smiled gently. "Sorry I haven't been down before. I've been busy."

"I'll bet. I imagine it's hell for you guys deciding what identical suit to wear each day."

"They tell me you haven't been very cooperative."

"We never are," Gaw said, pacing the chamber. "Sweetie, you were with us long enough to know. Truthcrafters never tell. It's our way. If we told people how our tricks worked, we wouldn't be good for much."

Shift nodded. "You won't be good for much if the Breen kill you."

Gaw gulped. "Is that likely?"

She shrugged. "I am not in charge. They could kill you.

They could interrogate you in ways that you wouldn't recover from. Or . . ."

"Or?"

"Or they could break all of you up and send you into service as Breen warriors. On the front lines, wherever the Confederacy is fighting."

"Joy." The Ferengi nervously kicked at the deck. "This is how the Breen negotiate? Choose bad-bad or worse-bad?"

"The Breen don't negotiate, Gaw. They want to know how to operate the systems aboard *Blackstone*, but Cross never told me his passphrase. We can't even get the imaging chamber open without breaking it."

"It would take you forever to figure it out, if you even could."

"And that's why they can't offer you your freedom. Whatever happens, the Breen will require your assistance to use the ship."

"Use it for what?"

"That's not important. What matters is the Breen Confederacy needs your help. They'd be happy if you gave your help willingly—but if not, we'll find a way to get it."

"*We'll* find—?" The Ferengi stared at her for a moment before shaking his head. "I just don't get any of this. Why are you with the Breen?"

"Because I believe in them. In what they stand for."

Gaw waved his hands. "Who can tell *what* they stand for? With that whole *snork-squawk-gawk* they do, I can't tell whether these guys want me to eat my dinner or sing an opera." He looked out through the doorway at the guards. "If they *are* guys, that is. Those suits hide everything." He looked back at her. "It's a damn shame, in your case."

"That's one reason I believe in them," Shift said. "Cross was only interested in me because of what I looked like—

just like every other person in my life." She gestured to her armor. "Be honest, Gaw. Would Buxtus have taken me on if I were wearing this?"

"No. But he knew you were smart, Shifty." Gaw's expression softened. "You were different from his other apprentices. You, he thought, could become a practitioner. 'Maybe another Jilaan,' I heard him say. He thought you were that good—a natural."

Shift took that in. "And what did *you* think?"

"I thought you were better than he was—and he was the best I've ever worked with." At the thought, Gaw's brow furrowed. "What happened to Buxtus?"

Shift looked startled. The question wasn't one she was expecting. "What do you think happened?"

"Our sensors saw his life signs end on *Ark of G'boj*—but we didn't know how it happened."

"Ah." She thought for a moment—and then put her helmet back on and called out into the hall. Another Breen entered, delivering a rectangular object wrapped in a protective opaque covering. The newcomer placed it on the large cube in the center of the room and departed. Shift removed her helmet again. "I'm not supposed to show my face in front of the others while on duty."

"Their loss," Gaw said. "Or maybe not. What do the rest of them look like?"

She ignored him, gingerly sliding the large object out from its wrapping. Inside was a hefty book with an ornately detailed cover. Gaw recognized it immediately. "That's from Cross's room. That's a copy of the *Annals*."

"The official record of the feats of the Circle of Jilaan, as presented at the secret association's convocations."

Gaw rolled his eyes and groaned. "You didn't tell the Breen about the society, did you?"

"No, they crossed Klingon lines and destroyed a bird-of-prey just to get to meet you," Shift said. "They're very interested, Gaw. Try to keep up."

Gaw crossed his arms and gave the book a sidelong glance as she opened the massive cover. The gilded type caught the harsh light of the cell, glistening as her fingers turned the gossamer-thin pages.

"There's a particular story here I'm interested in," she said. "One of Jilaan's big ventures, from nearly a century ago."

"Uh-huh."

"She's very interesting—I can see why she was Illusionist Magnus for so long." Shift reached a particular page, marked by a multicolored ribbon. "I've read the account thoroughly—but I was looking for some better images of the character she portrayed."

"Is that right."

Shift studied him. "You know, if you cooperated, I could see that the Breen freed you—after you helped us. Everyone on your team." She raised an eyebrow. "Including Cross."

Gaw's mouth dropped open. "*What?*"

"I don't know what your sensors picked up, but he's alive—and in our custody."

"You're lying!"

"The Starfleet officers on *Ark of G'boj* stunned him—but he hit his head when he fell. *Sustax* beamed us both off at the same time. He's in a pretty bad shape, but he should pull through." She locked eyes with Gaw. "Help us, and they'll help him—and you can all go when we're done."

Gaw looked at her—and then at the open doorway, outside which he could see Breen milling about. "If he's here, let me see him."

"No. That would be a waste of time. I could show him to

you, but then you'd say he was a hologram we'd created. We may not be as good as you truthcrafters, but we at least have that technology." She returned her attention to the book. "You have my offer; that should be enough."

He stared. "I thought you said Breen didn't make deals."

"I was an Orion—old habits die hard. Do we have a bargain?"

Gaw thought. Telling tales outside the Circle broke the organization's cardinal rule. But he and Cross had first helped each other escape capture by the Federation nineteen years earlier, and in the years since they had gotten each other out of countless scrapes. If Shift's offer was real and it was a one-time thing, Gaw considered that it might be worth it. He cleared his throat. "What was your question again?"

"The pictures." Shift ran her fingers across the page, which seemed to glow with her touch. "The drawings here of Jilaan's feat are very stylistic, made to look like a fairy tale."

"That's what they do in the *Annals*," Gaw said. "But there's also the ribbon."

"What's that?"

"The bookmark." Gaw gestured between the pages. "Take it in your hand."

Shift took hold of the length of shimmering ribbon. One end was attached to the volume's binding.

"Say, 'Show me.'"

"Show me." Seemingly responding to her command, it came loose from the volume. She ran the ribbon back and forth over her hands. "That's odd."

"Those are microfilaments in the bookmark, encoded with data," Gaw said. "The books of the *Annals*—they're not just histories. They're truly spell books. If you board *Blackstone* or *Houdini* or *Minerva* or any of the truthcrafter ships and run the ribbons through the scanner, the imaging chamber will show you the characters the practitioner played."

"What, holos of them?"

"More than that. The full characters Jilaan inhabited. All the modeling work—it's all there. That's why it's such an honor to get your feat into the *Annals*. It's more than just bragging rights. You're contributing to a library of stock characters that all the practitioners of the Circle can draw upon."

"Wait. I thought you said you never shared your tricks . . . how you did things."

"With outsiders, no. But among colleagues, well, it's an addition to the art. And besides, most people aren't likely to ever use the same trick again. But if I'm helping my practitioner put together an act and I need a fat Gorn that walks with a limp, I'd much rather snag a character that Ardra's people designed a quarter century ago."

Shift closed the book and showed him the cover. "What about this? Could you help me do this?"

Gaw read the title—and his eyes narrowed. "Are you serious?"

"I may be."

"You're crazy. You're looking at generating a very large illusion—huge. Much bigger than *Blackstone* can handle."

"But the characters are already on the ribbon, right? You wouldn't have to do any of the programming work."

"Yeah, but the projection demands are immense. Jilaan could do it because *Zamloch* was enormous. *Blackstone* would need computer cores with another fifty thousand gigaquads to feed the emitter. I don't know where we'd get that—or where we'd put it."

"We'll figure it out," Shift said, placing the ribbon in a

utility pouch. "Don't go anywhere," she said as she put her helmet back on.

"Is that a joke?"

Shift answered with a squawk, took the book, and hurried for the exit. As Gaw watched her go, he wondered what she had gotten him into, and why anyone would bother caring about something that had happened to the Kinshaya ninety-three years ago.

Thirteen

It was enough to make one dizzy, thought Jean-Luc Picard. There were approximately five hundred sixty thousand major comets orbiting the brown dwarf named Atogra, and over the last two days, the *Enterprise* had visited every one of them.

Actually, he knew that was an exaggeration—because he could hear the running count. "Nearing close approach to Cometary Body Atogra-878," announced Lieutenant T'Ryssa Chen from flight control.

"Scanning," came the response from the science station.

Picard scarcely gave the luminous object on-screen a look. It had been a marathon session for flight control, wearing down multiple shifts; Chen had taken over for Lieutenant Faur, who had been fighting exhaustion.

"No trace of visitation on the surface," Science Officer Dina Elfiki said. "No signals from cloaked vessels."

"Log Cometary Body Atogra-887," Picard said. Realizing his mistake, he blanched. "Correction. *Eight-seven-eight*." He looked up with a weary grin. "My apologies."

The moment brought a welcome chuckle to the bridge crew, which proceeded to record its observations of a comet nobody had ever bothered to look at before, and which no one was ever likely to examine again. Least of all the Klingon Empire, which possessed the star. The *Enterprise* had not even been able to get basic charts of the planetless system; they were using the Federation Astronomical Survey's name for it.

The only thing about the place that had *ever* been of

interest was that at some point in the recent past, a very peculiar starship had activated its cloaking device in the system. Distant Klingon surveillance satellites had captured fleeting signals from the illusion-generating starship *Blackstone*'s imperfect cloak not once but twice over an eighteen-hour period, both episodes suggesting the ship had lingered near Atogra for some time.

And that made Atogra significant, or so Picard hoped. Across the Empire, other ships were hunting for the better-cloaked ships of the Unsung, who were suspected of having four operational birds-of-prey; Christine Vale's *Titan* was leading several vessels in the Starfleet portion of the effort. *Aventine* had joined the search, having been recalled. *Yet more explorations denied*, Picard thought.

Enterprise's quarry was different. First detected by his chief engineer, Commander Geordi La Forge, *Blackstone* had initially been sought as a potential clue to the location of the Unsung; however, *Blackstone* had apparently parted ways with the Klingon cult. But finding the ship, he hoped, would shed light on the Kruge plot, if not point the way to the remaining Phantom Wing ships.

The most aggravating part was that Picard had two members of *Blackstone*'s crew in his brig: a pair of Bynars named 1110 and 1111. Since their capture by Commander Tuvok and Lieutenant Šmrhová during an incident at Cragg's Cloud, they had refused to respond to a single question. That was consistent with the behavior of Ardra, the technological illusionist Picard had tangled with nineteen years earlier; neither she nor her engineers had ever talked about their schemes or capabilities.

But that hadn't stopped Picard's crew from using something of Ardra's in the search. "Give me a view of *Houdini*," he said to his ops officer.

Houdini appeared on the main viewscreen, its two big nacelles forming a triangle with a large, third spire stabbing forward above the hull. Originally piloted by Ardra's accomplices, *Houdini* had been pulled from storage by La Forge and Tuvok in the hopes that it would have its own means of detecting *Blackstone*, its twin in function.

"Hail Commander La Forge," Picard said. "Let's see if he's got anything we're not able to detect."

"Aye, Captain."

"*Enterprise, this is* Houdini," La Forge said over the comm a few moments later. *"No change in emissions detected by the ship's sensors."* He paused. *"At least, we think. It'd sure help if our Bynar friends could teach us a few things about the controls."*

Picard nodded. Perhaps they hadn't found the right pressure point yet. "How is she handling, Geordi?"

"Like she's been sitting in dry dock for nearly twenty years. Have any further signals been detected outside the system?"

"None, I'm afraid. The trail ends here. Which is why I'm hopeful *Blackstone* is holed up in or around one of these bodies." Picard knew he was wishing out loud.

"Another possibility is they realized we tracked them to Cragg's Cloud—and fixed their cloaking device once and for all."

Picard took a deep breath. "Stay positive. *Enterprise* out."

"Beginning approach to Cometary Body Atogra-879," Chen said. The view of *Houdini* onscreen was replaced by another oblong comet. This one wasn't in a state of eruption. "Three minutes until rendezvous."

Hearing the doors opening behind him, Picard looked back to see Joanna Faur exiting the lift. "Permission to resume my station, sir. I'm feeling better."

He glanced at Chen. "You're relieved, Lieutenant. Thank you for pitching in."

Chen rose, seemingly reluctantly. As Faur took the station, Chen headed up the steps to the captain's platform, beyond which lay the turbolifts—only to pause and look back at the comet for several long moments.

Picard noticed her. "What can I do for you, Lieutenant?"

Distracted from her gaze, she withdrew. "Nothing, sir. Good hunting."

The captain suppressed a sigh as he heard the doors close behind her. His crew's zeal for redemption following the Gamaral massacre had propelled them a long way. But the inconclusive end to the Battle of Ghora Janto—plus the seemingly conclusive proof of Worf's death aboard one of the birds-of-prey—had taken the wind out of everyone, himself included. Ennui had replaced eagerness. He was out of ideas.

"Nearing Cometary Body Atogra-879," Faur announced.

"By all means, let's have a look," he said. He wondered if comets understood sarcasm.

Fourteen

Kahless put down the knife and flipped over the mud-colored material he had been working on. He lifted it with both hands and looked at it in the light from the ignited gas vent nearby. Thick and rugged—the hide of some beast the exiles had skinned on Thane. It would serve, he determined: a breastplate to wear over the vest he had already carved. He set it down on the flat-surfaced boulder he was using for a cutting board and went to work shaping a belt.

The clone had worn the same sensor-baffling uniform for days inside *Chu'charq*'s crawlspaces, but he had little desire to change back into his tattered robes. They stunk of the sewer pits of Thane. Nor had he any inclination to wear the clothing of his captors: he had already stooped to using their gear once and would not do so again.

He had learned to make his own clothes while living alone on Cygnet IV. While the new wardrobe might not fit perfectly, just looking at it made him feel refreshed. It also gave him something to do.

All around him in the great cavern, the Unsung went about their business—if their business was moping or quarreling like children. That is how Kahless saw them, regardless of the fact that many had drawn breath for more years than he had. He could not hear what they were arguing about, and neither did he care. All he knew was that his friend Worf had advised waiting—and while it was not Klingon to delay action, the stoutest heart could not force a dilithium crystal to repair itself any faster.

Ahead of him, two males in their twenties came to blows over their disagreement. One was named Nelkor; Worf had earlier described defeating the brash Klingon when he served as a guard on Thane. Kahless barely looked up as the two charged at each other, each shouting epithets as he sought to bowl his opponent over. Locked together, the pair tripped and slammed to the rocky floor, where they wrestled as they rolled. Onlookers hooted as the combatants tumbled in the direction of the boulder Kahless was using for a worktable.

"You are doing it wrong," Kahless grumbled.

His words were barely audible over the din—yet Nelkor heard and looked in his direction. That gave his pinned opponent the opening to break free, and the struggle was renewed. Kahless watched with only the vaguest interest as Valandris approached the fight.

"What was this about?" she demanded of the young Unsung after the fighting ceased.

"They cannot agree whether it is better to kill themselves by knife or hammer," Kahless said, before going back to work on his belt.

"I would have won," Nelkor said. On his hands and knees, he pointed in Kahless's direction. "The clone said something a minute ago. He distracted me."

"I said you were doing it wrong," Kahless said, carving at the material. "You seek to make a point—but you do not attack as though you intend to prove yourself right. This is play." He gestured off to the side. "Go join the children, if you must do this."

"I do care," Nelkor said, flustered. "We were arguing about whether we should attack the Empire or go back to Thane."

"I say you do not care. Your opponent does not bleed and neither do you. Your blades remain sheathed." Kahless nodded to a cluster of rocks near the site of the scuffle. "You even had those stones in easy reach—yet neither of you went for them. The matter between you has not the slightest value to either one of you."

Both scrappers looked at him, bewildered. "This is my friend," Nelkor said. "I would not hurt him."

"You bring shame to the concept of battle," Kahless said. He put down the belt and looked up. "It is one thing to fight over nothing while drunk. We celebrate high spirits. Our honored dead battle one another for sport in Sto-Vo-Kor. But combat is a gift to the Klingons. Sober people do not waste it on insignificant disputes."

Valandris glared at him. "What happens to our people is not insignificant."

"So you say." Kahless returned to his labors.

Valandris continued to stare at him for a moment, before turning to address the pair. "Go back to your ships and see if they need your help in engineering."

Nelkor sneered. "You do not rule us. What makes you think you can order us around?"

"Because I make sure my opponents bleed," Valandris replied. The young Klingons looked at her for a moment and then retreated to their separate ships.

Valandris lingered, watching Kahless. He was aware of her presence. "What now?"

"I am watching you work." She gestured to the garments. "I thought you were an emperor, not a common laborer."

"Who made the clothing your people wore, before the false Kruge gave you modern gear?"

"We made it. Out of necessity."

Kahless laughed and made another cut. "*butlh ghajbogh nuv'e' yIHo'.*"

Admire the person with dirt under his fingernails. The

expression appeared to amuse her—but it was how he said it that prompted her next response. She repeated his maxim and said, "Your Klingon is . . . different from ours."

"Your accent is strange to me. Mine is the proper form."

"General Potok only wanted us to learn as much as we needed to communicate," she said. "The rest of our vocabulary we took from the exiles who came to join us."

Kahless glanced up from his work. "I do not understand this Potok. He told you of Kruge in loving terms—and he taught you in the use of starships so your descendants could leave one day, once their honor returned. Yet he would not give your children the customs they needed to live again as Klingons?"

"He was more open about that—once. But as the years passed and survival on Thane became difficult, he grew colder." She looked down. "He forbade the teaching of many things. He thought language was a gift we did not deserve."

Kahless scowled. As he understood it, Potok's response to his people's discommendation had in some ways been honorable. But in other ways, the man had clearly failed. It was possible to take things too far. "Wretched business," he finally said.

Another fight broke out across the cave floor. Valandris looked back on it and sighed. "I must go." She turned back to Kahless—and, after a moment, added, "Perhaps we will speak about language again."

She started to walk away. She was several meters away when he called out. "Songs," he said.

She turned. "What?"

"Songs," he repeated, not looking up from his cutting. "That is where Klingons learn to speak as the ancients did. Where you will hear *tlhIngan Hol* as it should be spoken."

Valandris's head tilted. "We have no songs."

He glanced up. "I am not going anywhere."

She looked at him for a long moment—and then departed to quell her outbreak. As Kahless ripped through another section of hide, he started to sing to himself.

Fifteen

"Welcome, my sons," Korgh said as he stood by the open door to the house residence. "You look good to an old father's eyes."

In fact, Tengor and Tragg looked about as they always did to him: disappointing. The lamented Lorath had been an imperfect vessel for Korgh's ambitions, but he had been the firstborn. By the time Tengor and Tragg were added to the family, Korgh was so deep into playing his role as Galdor, *gin'tak* of the House of Kruge, that he had little time to spend shaping their characters.

Not that it would have helped. Middle son Tengor loped in as he usually did, all arms and legs, saying not a word. He was so solemn some thought him mute, seldom opening his mouth except to fill his bottomless pit of a stomach. When he was younger, that, combined with his great stature, suggested the makings of a stoic general. But where height among Klingons usually coincided with great physical strength, Tengor had bad knuckles and all the coordination of a blind *bok-rat*. Few had been willing to fight alongside him.

And when he did open his hair-shrouded mouth, it was hardly worth the wait: "Have you eaten yet?"

"In time, Tengor. Patience." Korgh turned to his youngest son, who needed no prompting to deliver a proper embrace. "How fares Tragg?"

"Well, Father." A smile permanently affixed to his face,

Tragg looked down the long hall in amazement. "I have not visited the palace since you were *gin'tak*. Reminds me of when I was a boy!"

Which was about fifteen minutes ago, Korgh thought as he detached himself from his shorter son. At thirty, Tragg was amiable but dim, always trying to earn approval by working toward the advancement of others, but never accomplishing anything on his own. In the company of friends, he had too often found himself talked into abandoning his and his family's best interests.

Korgh had reluctantly forced himself to realize that his younger sons would not come to much. Both had entered the Defense Force, like their elder brother, but neither Tragg nor Tengor had made their marks. In the last decade, when Korgh had more control over the house's assets, he had seen them both appointed to leadership roles in factories. Tragg got on well enough with the weaponsmiths he supervised, but Tengor's lack of interest in his work had proved a problem again and again, requiring repeated repostings. Before Korgh took control of the House of Kruge, he had worried he was about to run out of places to send Tengor to.

The problem was that with Bredak's death, the generation following consisted of six daughters fathered by Tengor—whose success in finding a mate Korgh considered a miracle worthy of story and song—and the late Lorath. None were old enough for responsibility, and in any event it would be difficult to campaign for their advancement when he had used General Kersh's gender to thwart her control of the house.

But Korgh would see the long row of offices filled by members of his line—and it had to start with the blood that remained. Knowing he had no chance of his words reaching Tengor's brain before dinner, he had escorted them back to the dining hall, where he had a simple meal of *gagh* ready and writhing.

It was over bloodwine at the end that Tragg remarked on the emptiness of the suites. "You should have slaves to feed you, Father, and to keep the place."

"I lived in this home for nearly fifty years as no better than a slave," Korgh replied, "minding the affairs of absent lords. I would not be tended to by outsiders who could whisper and scheme." *Which was exactly what I did,* he did not add. "Before that, I lived by my wits. I learned to feed myself. That is all any Klingon needs."

"Maybe not for Tengor," Tragg joked, watching the lanky senior brother lick the inside of an empty bowl.

Korgh shook his head and got to business. "You are here because I want to share with you that which I never had the chance to tell Lorath."

That got even Tengor's attention.

"In the past month, I have been setting the affairs of the House of Kruge aright. I think it has been done."

"Because of your hard work for years," Tragg said. "You made the lords listen to you."

"Yes," Korgh said, waving his hand in indifference. "The more important thing is that in my short time on the High Council, I have found that the Empire is in disarray—far more so than the house was, when I first went to work here."

Tengor nodded. "Damned Unsung."

"The discommendated wretches were just the final crack in the dam—an unsteady one built by Martok and those like him who placed too much faith in outsiders. It has burst, and we have seen the flood."

Tragg and Tengor nodded. Korgh was not about to give his whole stump speech to his own blood, but it was important that they understood where he was taking the family.

"You have met some of the allies I have developed on Qo'noS. They feel as I do—as *we* do. It is our intention to make a move."

Tragg's eyes widened—and despite the fact that the whole floor of the structure was empty except for them, he spoke in a whisper. "You intend to challenge *Martok*?"

"Challenge him—and defeat him." Korgh pushed aside his cup and clasped his hands on the table. "This is how it will proceed. I have asked for the *chavmajta*, and Martok has called for it to take place in the Federation Consulate in the First City. This was an attempt at a tactical delay. Let him have it. Unrest only grows while the renegades are at large."

"Agreed," Tengor said. Korgh was glad they were following so far.

"The *chavmajta* will commence, and I will make my charge against the Khitomer Accords. Riker and Martok will rise to defend them. But before Martok speaks—"

Korgh rose from the table suddenly, causing the feet of his chair to squeak noisily against the floor. "—we will all rise," he continued, "our brother councilors walking from the room, led by me. It will be seen across the Empire as it happens. We will go to the streets to rally the people. And when Martok emerges from the consulate, it will be to resign."

Tragg and Tengor stared at him. Then Tengor reached across the table for a jug that had something left in it and drank. Tragg gawked at Korgh. "You are sure he will step down? He will not seek battle?"

"In private, he might challenge another. But an old man—one now thought a hero—is another matter, especially when I will be carrying through on a principled objection. He cannot defend the failings of Starfleet and the Federation. He will fall on his sword—or someone else's."

Korgh began to pace around the long table. "I tell you this because there is a strong chance my allies will support me for chancellor. I am seen as a compromise by the hotheads—someone not expected to live long enough to bar their own accession. For the sake of stability, I must show everyone that the House of Kruge deserves not just to have leadership, but to keep it."

He reached the midpoint of the table between his sons and slapped his hands on the surface. "That is why I am immediately placing the two of you back into military service," Korgh said. "We must have their support."

Tengor gawked—and Tragg was wide-eyed, dazzled. "The Defense Force?" Tragg asked.

"Tengor," Korgh addressed his elder son, "you will immediately enter with the title of commander, the same as the great Kruge. The battle cruiser *Lorath* will be yours." He had just renamed one of the family's home guard ships in Ketorix's dry dock.

Tengor blinked. "I do not want to return to the Defense Force, Father. I did not do well there."

"You only suffered because you thought you stood in the shadows of your brother," Korgh said. He walked over and put his hand on Tengor's shoulder. "Then you were the son of a loyal retainer. Now you are the elder son of the lord of the House of Kruge. You will command respect. No, *demand* it. Kill any warrior who does not obey you."

"That is the problem," Tengor said, shifting uncomfortably. "I have aged. Four children and a factory job. It has been too long since I have had to fight for my place."

"In your position now there will be even more who will take up your fights for you. Do not hide behind them. Act like a Klingon!"

Tengor straightened, or tried to. "Yes, Father."

Korgh turned to face his youngest. "You, Tragg, are hereby appointed head of the planetary guard here on Ketorix," Korgh said. *The better to keep an eye on you*, he thought. "This makes you a general. The rank comes with the duty."

Tragg was flabbergasted. "I was nowhere near that rank when I left service!"

"You are the son of the lord of the house. Ketorix is the seat of the house's holdings. This is only right." He pointed at Tragg. "It is *your* right. Claim it."

Tragg stood and pumped his fist against his chest and saluted. "I will do my best, Father."

It took several seconds for it to dawn on Tengor that he should stand as well. Korgh looked on him with a wan smile and dismissed them. He left to find another bottle of bloodwine—this one for himself. One could only build so much with wet sand.

Sixteen

"Four suspect birds-of-prey, rising from the surface," reported Ranul Keru, standing in for the absent Tuvok at tactical. "That matches the number of Phantom Wing ships remaining, Captain."

"Stay sharp," Christine Vale said from the center seat. "We might have finally caught a break. You see them, Dax?"

"We've got a read on them, Titan," Ezri Dax said from *Aventine,* hundreds of kilometers off *Titan's* bow. "They won't get past."

"This could be it," Admiral Riker responded from his position standing at the rear of the bridge. "Martok's people just confirmed no Klingon craft are currently supposed to be here."

Vale's heart raced. *Titan* had chased the Unsung for so long, both before and after Ghora Janto. Her crew deserved to bag them, but being in the moment felt otherworldly—like a gift had come from above. And with Riker returned from Qo'noS and observing on the bridge, it couldn't have come at a better time.

For her, for him—for the Federation.

"No aspect change on the contacts," Melora Pazlar, science officer, reported. "Definitely birds-of-prey. We've got some leaky cloaks over there."

"If it's who we think it is, they've definitely been through a lot," Vale said.

Starfleet had been chasing the appropriately named

Phantom Wing across the farthest reaches of the Klingon Empire. With the House of Kruge's home guard defending the already-searched frontier territory, *Titan*'s attention had turned to a lead developed by Chief Petty Officer Dennisar. Looking into the pattern the Unsung had followed of hitting pirate strongholds in and near Klingon territory for resupply, Dennisar had found a goldmine of information in Tuthar, a prisoner transferred from *Enterprise* at Ghora Janto. The two men, both Orions, stood on the bridge to the captain's right. Chief Dennisar was minding his prisoner; Tuthar was so nervous about being an informant that she was afraid he might soil himself. But as much as he feared his own people, he feared going to a Klingon prison more.

"That settlement they came from," Vale asked Tuthar. "You're sure it's a pirates' nest?"

"Um—yeah," he said, fidgeting. With the blood drained from his face, Tuthar's skin was pale olive. "Theta Thoridor's a safe house. The Empire never bothers us out here."

"They're not backing off," Keru said. *Titan* had been at red alert with shields up since the first detected signal. "Orders?"

Vale resisted the urge to glance back at Riker. As sector commodore, it could be his show if he wanted—but he had let her make the play. "Photon torpedoes, full spread to their port. *Aventine*, can you do the same to their starboard?"

"Affirmative," Dax said. *"Box them in."*

"Torpedoes away," Keru announced. Vale watched as they lanced out from *Titan*, accompanied by a flanking spread from *Aventine*. The warheads detonated, forming an emanating ring of destructive force bubbling outward—and inward, where energy coruscated over unseen spacecrafts' shields.

I count four, Vale thought. "Attention, unidentified vessels. Decloak immediately and drop your shields! I repeat—"

"What right have you?" an enraged Klingon voice screamed over the comm. An instant later, four birds-of-prey shimmered into view—all still crackling with energy from the warning shots. *"We are Klingons—in Klingon territory!"*

"You are not authorized to be in this system," Vale said in her sternest voice. "This is the *Starship Titan*, with the joint task force seeking the Unsung. I repeat, drop your shields!"

"Not authorized? By you?" A visual from aboard the lead bird-of-prey appeared on the main viewscreen. A hairy eye-patch-wearing male sat on a bridge that had seen better days, even before *Titan*'s and *Aventine*'s love taps. *"We are no discommendated scum. You have no right to fire on us."*

"Your chancellor says we do."

At ops, Lieutenant Ethan Kyzak whispered, "Captain, we have a priority one message. Starfleet Command. Admiral's eyes only."

Vale's eyes went wide. She looked over at Riker, who was similarly surprised. "That's fast even for the complaint department," he said.

"Take it in my ready room, Admiral," Vale said, and watched him leave. Several times before during their search of Klingon space, locals—particularly those conscious of the recent strains in the relationship between the Federation and the Empire—had wasted no time in making their displeasure known, including protesting to the chancellor. But this was ridiculous.

"Identify yourself and stand down," Vale said.

"You stand down!" One-Eye replied. *"I refuse to recognize your authority. This alliance is finished, haven't you heard? Lord Korgh will make things right, as they should have been!"* He clenched his fist. *"Leave, before we fire on you!"*

Tuthar, who had been breathing heavily since before they opened fire, let out a squeak that sounded like the start of a statement. "Yes?" Vale asked.

Tuthar pointed to a figure in the background behind the Klingon captain. "That guy. I know him," he said unevenly. "He's a trafficker—sells Klingon hardware to the Orions down on the surface."

One-Eye heard Tuthar's voice and scowled. *"You have a filthy rodent on your bridge,* Titan. *Perhaps I should help you with extermination."* As Tuthar cringed, the Klingon turned to command his cohorts. *"Ready weapons!"*

"Proximity alert," Keru declared. "Arrival from warp. Klingon battle cruiser."

Now what? Vale wondered. But it soon became clear from One-Eye's alarmed reaction that the visitor wasn't expected—or welcome.

"Birds-of-prey beginning to move," Keru said.

A new voice came over the comm—an audio transmission from the battle cruiser. *"This is Captain Klag of* Gorkon. *Attention, birds-of-prey: attempt to cloak or flee and we will blow you out of the stars!"*

The new arrival's words nearly drove the Klingon on screen into a panic. *"We are Klingon tradespeople,* Gorkon. *This Starfleet trash was harassing us—"*

"You will watch who you call trash," Klag said, *"you in decrepit vessels you should not have. Surrender or die!"*

The bird-of-prey cut its communications link with *Titan,* and One-Eye disappeared from the screen. Klag remained on audio. *"Give them a moment,* Titan. *They cannot operate their controls while they are shaking with fear."*

"Birds-of-prey are dropping shields," Keru said. "They are powering down. *Gorkon* is beaming forces aboard their ships."

Vale leaned back in her chair and took a deep breath. *Not the Unsung, after all.* Some of the life seemed to go out of the bridge, she thought—literally in the case of the relieved Tuthar, who would have hit the deck had Dennisar not held him up.

The approaching *Gorkon* appeared on screen just in time for Riker to emerge from the ready room. "Did I miss anything?"

"Is that Admiral Riker I hear?"

"Klag?" Riker, stunned to hear a familiar voice, smiled. "How is the son of M'Raq?"

The Klingon he had served with during his exchange program experience aboard *I.K.S. Pagh* appeared on screen with a toothy grin. *"My old sparring partner,"* Klag said. *"Martok sent me this way. What have you found?"*

Riker looked to Vale for the answer. "We think they're here to sell to the Orions below."

Klag winced. *"It is time we ridded the frontiers of these places—and the dishonorable Klingon curs who sell to them. Perhaps this Unsung business will set that in motion. We were returning from escorting a Breen ship to the border when we took Martok's hail."*

"Breen? On the search?"

"Wandering around lost, as near as I could tell. Over at Cabeus, the middle of nowhere." Klag shook his head. *"They are unfit as searchers, much less allies."*

Riker nodded. "It is good to see a friend, Captain."

"Always. Though passion may have strained, it must not break our bonds of brotherhood. Gorkon out." The transmission ended.

Riker did a double-take and looked at Vale. "Did a Klingon captain just quote Abraham Lincoln to me?"

Vale chuckled. "I don't know." Then she remembered the

message Riker had taken. "Anything you'd like to share?" she asked cautiously.

"Yes," the admiral said, remembering. "Is *Aventine* still on?"

"*Right here,*" Dax said. "*Admiral, do you want us to help* Gorkon *mop up? I know you'll want to investigate below, in case the Unsung did visit here.*"

"We'll handle that. There's a special assignment from Command—and we'll need *Aventine*'s speed." He shook his head, incredulous as he reflected. "I'm not sure I can even begin to explain what it is . . ."

Seventeen

Kahless had at last completed his tailoring. Worf had to admit that it was work well done: unicolor warrior's garb, perfectly functional if not a perfect fit. The emperor had chosen to make that alcove with the flat boulder his home. Worf had billeted himself outside the rock, between Kahless and everyone else. Doubt and discord continued to roil the Unsung; while no one had made a menacing move toward either of them since that terrible moment in *Chu'charq*'s mess hall, Worf accepted the possibility that minds could change.

He and Kahless were taking a late evening meal together, recalling the incidents that had brought them back together. Worf had a battle to tell of, in his escape from Thane; Kahless recounted his outsmarting of the tricksters.

And then there was an uncomfortable matter for Klingons—an experience that, to Worf's surprise, they had both shared.

"What was the ailment you say you had, Worf?"

"*Tharkak'ra*," Worf said. "It is an exile sickness. I caught it aboard *Rodak*." He frowned. "I am ashamed as a Klingon to say it laid me low."

Kahless punched his hand with his fist. "I think I had it, inside the hull. For two days I lay on a heat manifold, sweating and near death." His eyes went wide with realization. "I thought it was from lack of bloodwine. If I had known it was a simple sickness that had felled me, I would have cut my own weak throat."

"It strikes all Klingon adults who spend time on Thane," Worf said. "Perhaps it is better to consider it a rite of passage."

"Hmph." Kahless looked away for a moment, and then his face grew serious. "You know, Worf, with the exception of what that fiend gave me, I have not had a drop of wine since Gamaral."

"How do you feel?"

"Thirsty." Kahless laughed. "I do not miss it. Drink should be used to celebrate battles. Sitting out there on Cygnet IV all those years, I drank barrels I did not deserve."

Worf did not think it wise to comment, but inwardly he was glad to hear the confession. Kahless changed the subject, asking him about a suicide from that afternoon.

Much of the unrest in the cave had come from arguments started or finished by Harch, who continued to seek an aggressive end to the story of the Unsung. Following his mentor Zokar's death, it seemed he had lived for little else. But someone else, apparently, had even less to live for. A fortyish member of the Unsung who had ventured farther back into the cave system had thrown himself into one of the fiery vents.

Worf related the story as he had heard it. "He had been speaking of doing so before, in grief over learning that Kruge had not returned from the dead. By plunging into the flames, he said he followed the true Kruge into death."

Kahless put down his bowl and shook his head. "These are the remains of a world turned upside down, Worf."

"These people have been ill used," Worf replied. "Do not misunderstand. What they have done is unconscionable, unforgivable. I have told you what I learned about the massacre of the sentries at Spirits' Forge, done at this Cross person's command. Valandris told me the story. It matches the massacre at Gamaral in dishonor." He shook his head. "And yet I see these people as they have lived, I see their children, and I think that if things had been different, it might not have come to this. They might have resisted the false Kruge."

"Admit it, Worf. They were poorly led."

"I am not sure how much to blame Potok. I saw the report Ambassador Spock made a hundred years ago. The general was trying to keep his people together, hoping to shepherd them through discommendation. A sentence," Worf added with distaste, "that may have been undeserved, from what I understand. I know what it is like to be dishonored due to political machinations—but I suffered alone. Potok took responsibility for hundreds." He took a deep breath. "How might any Klingon have responded in such a place?"

"You would have done better," Kahless said, looking kindly on him. "I may be the clone of Kahless, but you, my friend, have been an even better example of his teachings at times."

Worf shook his head, unwilling to accept the praise. "You are the rightful heir, Emperor."

"I was grown in a lab. I have no more claim to moral authority than does any Klingon," Kahless said, his eyes distant. "You have the greater deeds." He looked at his bowl, unfinished. "Certainly in these last years, as I grew fat in my solitude, my thinking grew flabby too. I was wrong to live alone. I see that now."

"Emperor, belief is like a blade. It grows dull when it is not used."

"Cross used our beliefs as a blade against our people—but so did Potok. Whatever he intended, Potok appears to have destroyed any hope his people might—"

Worf saw Kahless look up. The commander turned to see Valandris approaching along with three others. One he recognized as Hemtara, the mathematical thinker from *Chu'charq*'s bridge crew. Another was Dublak, who had been so shaken earlier on seeing Kahless's return from the dead.

The fourth was little Sarken, lingering behind Valandris.

Worf and Kahless stood. "What do you want?" the emperor asked.

"We would like to know more," Valandris said.

"More?"

"I read a book at Spirits' Forge," she said. "In it, you—the real Kahless, I mean—said to leave nothing until tomorrow."

Kahless paused, clearly thinking on how to respond. "That is correct. It is wrong to sit and wait, to quarrel and wish—as your people have been doing. A true Klingon sees the right path and takes it, whatever comes."

"What if we do not know the right path?" Hemtara asked.

"There are times when it will be impossible to tell," Kahless said. "You must accept this. You already know that any path taken halfheartedly is bound to be the wrong one."

Valandris let out a sigh. "Kahless, when we committed to Kruge's way, he said a similar thing to us to get us to work his will. We devoted ourselves to it, fully and with our lives. Yet you and Worf have said *that* was the wrong path." She looked at him searchingly. "What would have guided us?"

"The other tenets," Kahless said, "and your true Klingon heart. Worf told me that you regretted your ambush at Gamaral. Is this so?"

"I do," Valandris said, straightening.

"If you had never known the teachings of Kahless the Unforgettable, how did you come to that feeling?"

Valandris considered for a moment. "I . . . do not know. I just felt it." Her brow furrowed. "It wasn't like in hunting, where we pounce on a mindless thing. It just feels—"

"Like your opponent deserves better," Dublak said. He looked down.

Kahless studied them and nodded. He focused on Sarken. "How would you put it, child?"

She chewed her lip as she thought for a moment. "It is not good to do a bad thing."

Kahless laughed, loudly and heartily—and this time, somehow, the sound did echo, drawing the attention of others. "You put it well," the clone said. "But our people would say *batlhHa' vangIu'taHvIS quv chavbe'lu'*."

One does not achieve honor while acting dishonorably. But that, Worf thought, was not the important thing that Kahless had said. No, the words that had put a spark in the faces of the emperor's listeners were spoken earlier.

Our people.

Kahless scaled the flattened boulder that had been his makeshift worktable and stood, facing the rest. Glancing to his left, Worf saw that beyond the dormant birds-of-prey, night had fallen outside the cave opening. But the dinner was done and the fires were burning. There were songs to sing and stories to tell.

Eighteen

The armored workers filing past Shift looked alike. She appeared no different, of course, in her Breen armor. They paid her no mind as they marched toward the prep center, where they would augment their suits with propulsion units allowing them to work in the zero gravity of the shipyards.

Their gait was so uniform, their manner so controlled, that an unindoctrinated observer might consider them automata. To Shift's eyes they were anything but mindless robots. They were heroic, driven, unified. Breen, pledged together to the advancement of the Confederacy and the spread of its values. She rejoiced to hear again the sound she had long missed: the low buzz of many Breen vocoders in use at once. Normally, they spoke only when necessary and always in advancement of their common cause.

Yet this day was different, one long anticipated by the workers who had labored for years in secret inside the asteroid orbiting Jolva Ree. Today the Breen were arming the secret attack fleet they had been building for the Holy Order of Kinshaya. Finished months earlier, the spherical *Fervent*-class warships had sat waiting to be deployed. Their completion, and the chance that they might now be used, was owed entirely to Shift.

Back during her first visit to the Breen facility hidden deep in Kinshaya territory nearly four years earlier,

Thot Roje had been facing the demise of his greatest project and with it, his career. The backlash following the Niamlar Circle Massacre on Janalwa had made the battlespheres Roje was building for the Kinshaya useless; the new ecumenical administration under the reformist Yeffir had shown little interest in continuing hostilities with the Klingons—or with anyone else. And while the Kinshaya did not abandon their alliance with the Breen through the Typhon Pact, the new Episcopate had made it clear it was going to keep the Confederacy at arm's length.

But Jolva Ree had not been shut down. Shift had convinced Roje to keep the project going while he launched a parallel effort to undermine the new Kinshaya authorities. Having joined the Breen and completed her training, Shift had assisted. Unlike many Breen, she felt comfortable operating without armor, and did so on numerous missions to Janalwa. Orion traders were not uncommon sights on Kinshaya worlds; Shift had visited under several different names and guises, offering secret material assistance to Ykredna, the former Pontifex Maxima. She had also opened back channels to Kinshaya military personnel.

Those efforts had borne fruit. After just a year—including bribes, blackmail, and the odd assassination—Shift and her comrades in the intelligence service had brought the two powers closer together than they had been when the Breen troops were openly operating in the capital. A subtler form of domination had begun.

Yet one thing had eluded the Breen. The expansionist policies of the Holy Order had been a relatively recent development, coinciding with the race's conquest of the Kreel and its subsequent alliance with the Pact. Pontifex Maxima

Yeffir, while weakened, would never wage war just on the Breen's say-so. The Kinshaya might do something less risky on their own stupid impulses, but they would not become sacrificial pawns in a Breen power game. They required a shove of a particular kind—an idea that had struck Shift during her conference with Roje and Domo Pran during their exit from Klingon space.

The worker processional finally past, she crossed the hall to a docking tube. Within moments, Shift was aboard her sometime home for the past year, *Blackstone*. The difference, however, was startling. Gone were the operators, huddled over their command interfaces in the illusion control center; in their place were several Breen laborers carting immense data processing units. Thot Roje was here, as was the underling who had of late become his nemesis.

"Welcome, Chot Shift," Roje said. *"You have not met Chot Dayn?"*

"Everyone knows of Chot Dayn," she replied. "You have done much to make our people more efficient."

"Not nearly enough," Dayn said. *"Waste is rampant across the Confederacy. And it festers far from our borders too."*

She did not have to guess what Dayn was referring to. It was an open secret that the logistical specialist had been sent by the domo to shut down work at the asteroid and break everything down for scrap. She also assumed he was Amoniri.

"The face of the Breen" was supposed to be a great equalizer, and in general it had been for her. Regardless, newer members could not help speculating what sort of being was inside their neighbor's armor. True, they weren't *supposed* to; that defeated the whole idea. But Shift had discovered a number of behavioral tells. Fenrisal, like Roje, tended to be sly. Silwaan, cautious. The Amoniri, bossy. No, she was not supposed to notice things like that—but to the Breen way of thinking, this was also a deficiency of others. They were failing to project Breen-ness, for want of a better term.

Chot Dayn was as insufferable as they came. He looked around at *Blackstone*'s command center—eerily empty without the truthcrafters. *"At the domo's command, I directed the workers in your absence to commence final preparations for the fleet,"* he said, *"and many of our Spetzkar special operations forces are on their way here. But I fail to see how this vessel will make a difference, Thot Roje. It hardly seems worth all the trouble."*

"You have only seen part of it," Roje said. He turned to face a rounded bulkhead. *"Behind this wall lies the heart of the ship's functions, the key to its operation—once we access it."*

Chot Dayn raised his hands in frustration. *"Why do you wait? Bring torches and open it, then."*

"That would destroy its workings," Shift said. "The imaging chamber is the heart of *Blackstone*'s illusion-generation system, the critical link between the vessel's computer processors and the emitter atop the hull. There is a key to activate it."

"A key! Do you have it?" Dayn asked.

"I have never seen it used. But I know who has it." She looked back. "Perfect timing," she said, watching Gaw slouch in, flanked by Breen guards.

"Is that you in there, Shifty?" Gaw asked, looking her over. "You know I don't understand what you're saying."

She turned to Roje. "I must speak to him in Federation Standard."

"Go ahead," the spymaster said.

"By all means," Dayn piped in, crossing his arms in boredom. *"We have already waited years."*

With a spoken command, Shift made an adjustment to her vocoder. "You understand me now?"

Gaw nodded. He looked over at the Breen bringing in the new equipment. Two more entered carrying sizable loops of ODN cable. "I guess you guys are serious."

"We need to activate the imaging chamber, like we discussed."

Gaw nodded. "Yeah, I guess you usually saw the imaging chamber open because you were with Cross. We'd shut it down by the time you found us in the comet tail."

"We need to get inside, Gaw."

The Ferengi sighed. "I need my pince-nez," he said, pointing to the bridge of his nose. "My little glasses."

"You can see well enough without them," Shift said. "Stop wasting time."

"You don't understand. They're the key." He pointed to a knickknack atop his workstation—a little orb that threw off multicolored light when spun on its magnetic base. "And I'll need that."

Huh, Shift thought. She had played with the widget herself over the past year. She took it from its stand while Roje ordered that Gaw's personal effects be delivered to the command center. After a few minutes, while Chot Dayn stood around grousing about his time being wasted, a Breen arrived carrying the glasses.

Gaw gestured for them, and then asked Shift to come near. "Set the orb on top of that," he said, indicating the console nearest the curved wall. While she did as asked, he rubbed the lenses of the pince-nez on his sleeve. "All truth-crafter ships have their own ways to unlock the imaging chamber. Sometimes it's a magic word. Sometimes it's sound. Sometimes it's light." He blew on the glasses. "Give that a spin, dearie."

With a whisk of her gloved fingers, Shift put the orb into whirling motion, sending random rays of rainbow light into the air near it. Gaw approached with his glasses between his thumb and forefinger and moved them back and forth before the orb. The lenses caught the light, redirecting it to the curved bulkhead—which immediately began rotating, revealing the brightly lit chamber inside. At the same time, the darkened screens in the command center surrounding the Breen came to life.

"I didn't even see a sensor," Shift said.

"Yeah, we're good. The real Harry Blackstone did a lot of tricks with lights and colors, so that's what we went with," Gaw said, looking down at his glasses in his palm. He shook his head sadly. "I never thought I would show that to outsiders."

Thot Roje stepped over and quickly seized the pince-nez from the surprised Ferengi's hand. He took the orb and handed it to a technician. *"Analyze this and duplicate our own method."*

"Now this," Shift said, holding out her hand to show the bookmark from the *Annals* volume.

Gaw's head hung low. "You know I can get in trouble with the Circle for this."

"You're already in trouble," she said. "And so is Cross."

He shrugged. "I get it, I get it." He took the ribbon from her, stepped inside the chamber, and fed it into a slot. Then he stepped back outside and gestured to the new data cores. "I told you we'd need more processing power. Those won't be enough."

"There's a dozen more just like them upstairs in Cross's penthouse. I got rid of the bed," she said with some satisfaction. "All connected to the trunk ODN line."

"Take a walk to the bridge, then," Gaw said, settling in at his control station. "If this works, you're about to see a show."

The Breen did as he instructed, and they saw what he promised. Even Chot Dayn was convinced. *"Contact Domo Pran,"* Roje said. *"Operation Proxy Warlord is a go."*

Nineteen

"The better question, Captain, is what *I* can do for *you*."

That, Chen thought in the turbolift, was what she could've said back on the bridge when Picard asked her if there was anything he could do for her. All manner of responses had popped into her head since she'd left the bridge, ranging from the simple—"I'd like an assignment, sir"—to the inappropriate: "Why, yes, Captain. You can deal me back into the game, so I'm not wasting my time."

Holding her tongue wasn't in Chen's nature. For a half-Vulcan she was frank and vocal. But there was a time and place to campaign for assignments, and it wasn't on the bridge. Especially not when half the crew likewise felt left on the shelf.

Yet Chen believed she had a particular beef. Over the course of the Unsung crisis the contact specialist had gone from being a critical player to an extra. At Gamaral, she had been at the center of the action, repelling the Unsung who had boarded *Enterprise*. She had taken an important role in the investigation, drawing on her knowledge of the House of Kruge and the members who had been killed during the *may'qochvan* commemoration. That had led the captain to keep her on the bridge during the desperate race to Thane in the previous month. She had faced down the Unsung in person and lived. That experience was important.

After Worf returned from Thane, however, Chen's profiling work on the Unsung lost much of its value. There was no longer any doubt who they were, and what they were about; the commander had learned the exiles' story in detail during his imprisonment. It fit with what Starfleet knew about the fate of Commander Kruge's staff and with Ambassador Spock's hundred-year-old report on his meeting with General Potok. That mystery had been solved.

The remaining unknown—locating the Unsung—was a question more amenable to La Forge's technological skills. The rudimentary behavioral model Chen had built based on the Unsung's previous actions was invalid with the death of their puppet master. Now the rump remains of the squadron could go anywhere or nowhere—if it even stuck together. Predicting their movements had become more a matter of projecting where they *could* go, rather than where they would go.

The lieutenant emerged on an upper deck and made for an observation lounge that seldom saw use: one of her favorite spots for unwinding while off duty. Seated in a high-backed chair, she glanced out at whatever comet *Enterprise* was trailing and took out her padd.

Catching up on news was of little comfort. There was the fruitless search since Ghora Janto and the worrisome reports of Klingon-on-Klingon violence inspired by fear of the Unsung. Reports of numerous incidents of hostility by Klingons toward Starfleet, including several outright lapses in peaceful cooperation involving people who supposedly answered to the Empire. Martok's control, one of her favorite analysts suggested, lessened every time Lord Korgh spoke.

She thought turning to events outside the Empire would make her feel better. A series of reports from Rashtag, the capital city of the Kinshaya homeworld Janalwa, did the opposite. The Holy Order, in the middle of its Year of Prayer, was in upheaval. Four years earlier, secular forces had put an end to religious rule following a massacre abetted by the Episcopate's Breen allies; the resulting backlash had cost Ykredna, the ruling Pontifex Maxima, her office.

Chen had advised the dissidents on behalf of Starfleet, later helping them to bring their changes to fruition. It had been one of her finer moments in the service: helping to transform a society for the better. Yet for four years she had watched helplessly as the reforms had eroded, one by one.

While no longer maintaining garrisons on Janalwa, the Breen had managed to salvage some of their influence over the Kinshaya government through their economic and military connections. The Episcopate had been in power too long, its roots were too deeply intertwined with the mechanisms of society. Yeffir, the once-jailed leader of the reform movement, had been elevated to head the church— whereupon she was trapped ruling over a combative group of entrenched Matriarchs who saw that she never got anything done and who then blamed her publicly for the inaction.

The latest bit of news, however, took Chen's breath away. The first free elections for the new secular government had finally occurred—scheduled in the middle of the Year of Prayer. Aged and traditionalist voters had chosen as their leader none other than Ykredna, the defrocked former pontiff, running on a platform of military strength and reinstitution of the inquisition. The race, the report said, had been close—until news of the rampaging Klingon cult tipped the balance. Klingons were the mortal enemies of the Kinshaya—and the Unsung, who had nearly harmed the Order's envoy to the H'atorian Conference, had become a political goldmine for the onetime Pontifex Maxima.

Still . . .

". . . *Ykredna?*" Chen said aloud as she put down the padd in disgust. "What the hell is wrong with you people?"

"Is there a problem, Lieutenant?"

Chen turned her chair to see someone standing quietly by the port, his hands clasped. "Commander Tuvok. I'm sorry—I didn't hear you enter."

"I was coming to meditate. *Houdini* is a fascinating vessel, but it is cramped. There is little privacy."

She rose. "If you want privacy now, sir, I could—"

"Please remain." The Vulcan looked weary, but willing to talk. "I repeat my question: Is there a problem?"

Chen looked back at the padd on the table. "I was catching up on the Kinshaya."

Tuvok nodded. "I read of the work you did with the Devotionalists to bring about reform. It was admirable."

"Fat lot of good it did. They're falling back into their old ways. And the Unsung crisis has been fuel for the fire."

"You must not judge yourself too harshly," Tuvok said. "There is often an arc to history, and the actions of one are not always enough to turn it. But it is a start."

"Sir, weren't you one of the earlier Starfleet visitors to Kinshaya space?"

"That is correct. *Excelsior* visited the original Kinshaya capital, Yongolor, many years before the Klingons devastated it."

"Were they just as frustrating to deal with then?"

Tuvok raised an eyebrow. She could imagine he was puzzled by a Vulcan who had chosen to embrace emotion, rather then Surak's teachings. "I formed no impressions of them. I remained in orbit. But I consulted with Curzon Dax, the Federation's envoy to the Kinshaya. I also had the opportunity to study the reports of Captain Sulu and his contact specialists."

"I remember seeing a summary of the report. The Kinshaya were being manipulated by outsiders. Someone tried to make them think one of their deities had returned."

"Niamlar," Tuvok provided. "It was reflecting on that experience that inspired me to study what Object Thirteen was doing. We now know it was the *Blackstone*—and it is reasonable to infer that the tricksters *Excelsior* encountered were using similar capabilities."

Chen looked outside at *Houdini*. "Has anyone interviewed the original operator of that ship?"

"Ardra? There is little point. No one in her crew has broken confidence during years of imprisonment. It is a matter of honor to them."

Honor among con artists, Chen mused. *I guess you can find it anywhere.*

"Did the people of Yongolor ever learn that they were being manipulated?"

"It was not our place to inform them," Tuvok said. "There was concern that the responsible party could have been a Kinshaya. If so, that would make it an internal matter, outside our purview."

"Wasn't it ultimately about a robbery?"

"Yes—and that is why Captain Sulu intervened to stop it and drive off the tricksters. His reasoning was that they were most likely from offworld."

"If he concluded that, why didn't he tell the Kinshaya?"

"Their society is built on faith. Captain Sulu judged that revealing that information might have unexpected and far-reaching ramifications. Ambassador Dax also felt that such information might not be welcome or believed coming from the Federation—especially since the illusionists departed, leaving no trace of their visit. At worst, Starfleet might have been blamed for the Niamlar con."

"I could see the Kinshaya doing that, sadly."

Tuvok studied her. "You seem distressed, Lieutenant."

"It's just that I really thought our efforts would take hold. It's frustrating to see them vanishing."

"May I ask if you were raised Vulcan?"

She looked at him, a little surprised by the question. "My mother raised me. She was human. But I know of our culture."

"I ask because peace is intrinsic to Surak's teachings—and when it is disturbed, it is more than a political setback. You are experiencing what has happened as a personal failure."

"Yeah, kind of." Chen tended not to give her Vulcan half a lot of thought, but Tuvok had hit on something. "I feel like I'm watching them throw something priceless away."

"Understanding, reason, and logic lead to peace—even for the Kinshaya."

She chuckled. "That's easier said than—"

Tuvok's combadge chirped. *"Captain Picard to Commander Tuvok."*

"Yes, Captain?"

"Please report to the bridge. Our comet scans have detected something."

"Right away." He tapped his badge. "We will have to continue this conversation another time."

"Thank you, sir."

Tuvok reached the doorway and paused to look back. "Keep studying the Kinshaya, Lieutenant. If the Unsung have shown us anything, it is that trouble often grows in the gardens we neglect."

Twenty

The exiles spoke with Kahless long into the evenings and started again early in the mornings—and because Cabeus rotated so quickly, Valandris felt she scarcely slept at all. But she would not have slumbered even had the planet existed in permanent night. As long as Kahless had the energy to speak, she had the will to listen.

The group surrounding the clone was always different, walking around with him both inside and some distance outside the cave opening. Valandris had been nervous about their being detected, but Kahless had told her that fear was the enemy of all Klingons—and that fear of the unseen was the worst of all. She knew he meant existential dreads, but as the hours went on, the forces hunting for the Unsung felt ever more distant.

Inside the cave, beside *Klongat*, Kahless pointed to the letters marked on the hull and explained the ancient origin of each glyph. Children who had lived on the vessels thrilled to hear that each was named after a different animal of Qo'noS. *Klongat*, the stalker with razor claws and an even sharper temper. *Krencha*, a monstrous reptile that crawled about. *Cob'lat*, an immense furred beast with fangs. And *Chu'charq*, the great conqueror of lands locked in ice.

Each one suggested things strange and mysterious to those who had grown up in the wilds of Thane. There was a larger universe out there, created not as a gift to the Klingons, but as something for them to take. A challenge, from birth to death. Sarken, who had taken to clinging near either Worf or Valandris, bounced with excitement.

Valandris usually saw Worf lingering on the perimeter, watching silently. He had stood by whenever his emperor tired of speaking, or needed support in a discussion; but the former rarely happened. Occasionally he shot Valandris a look of wry satisfaction. Any fears he had about Kahless's reticence were clearly fading.

But it had not been enough, was not enough for Kahless simply to tell his listeners about Klingon history and the ways of warriors. He also quizzed the exiles about themselves and their lives. Here, Worf participated more, clearly thinking it was something that needed to be done.

"You call yourselves the Unsung," Kahless said as he stood beneath the wing of *Klongat*. "Yet as constructed, the word makes no sense. Speak it." Seated on the cave floor before him, his listeners did as he asked. "That is incorrect," Kahless said. He pointed at Valandris. "You. Say it like a Klingon."

Valandris's eyes widened as she searched for something to say. "I don't know how. We were given the term by Lord Kruge." She corrected herself: "I mean Buxtus Cross."

"Who was no Klingon. There are many ways to coin a new word or phrase in our tongue, but not all fit the spirit or the thought." Kahless paced, gesticulating as he spoke. "Are you referring to a warrior the singers have forgotten? *lulIjpu' bomwI'pu'.* Or perhaps a warrior whom no one has composed an opera for: *ghe'naQDaj qonta' pagh.*"

Worf, leaning against one of the landing struts, said, "The term Cross used was in their announcement: *Hew HutlhwI'pu'.*"

"Ah," Kahless said. "Those without statues. No, I would never use such a term for you."

"Why not?" Valandris asked.

"Have you done anything to deserve the statues in the first place?"

"I—" Valandris frowned. "*The Empire* would not think so."

"Nor would anyone," Kahless said. "The sculptor certainly would not. No, that is not how I would speak your name."

"Indeed," Worf said, "it is not what Klingons have been calling you."

Valandris rolled her eyes. "I am not sure I want to know."

"It is nothing obscene," Worf replied. "They call you *DachwI'pu'*—the absent ones."

"I don't understand," Hemtara said. "I thought *Dach* meant to let your mind wander. To be an absent-minded person."

"That is slang," Kahless said, "which has come about in recent generations. Kahless the Unforgettable would have chosen different words. If you mean to lose focus, use *buSHa'*, or perhaps *qImHa'*. But *Dach* in itself means to be absent—and in the context of *Subpu' vaSDaq Dach* there should be no ambiguity."

Valandris repeated the words slowly. "*Subpu' vaSDaq Dach.* 'They are absent in the Hall of Heroes.'" Those surrounding her repeated it.

"That is exactly the term the Empire is using to refer to you," Worf said. "You are the *DachwI'pu'.*"

The exiles tried on the name. Dublak, an older Unsung who had been among the most despondent before joining Kahless's talks, asked, "Where is the Hall of Heroes?"

"On Qo'noS. But that is not the only thing implicit in the term," Kahless said. "Yes, the name means those alive have deemed you unworthy of songs and statues. But it also suggests the true stamp: that the Unforgettable has found you unworthy of Sto-Vo-Kor."

No one said anything for a moment. Then a high-pitched voice broke the silence. "Why should we want to go to Sto-Vo-Kor?" Sarken asked from beside Valandris. "Is it a better place?"

Kahless smiled broadly and chuckled. "Ah, is it. It is the reward all Klingons seek, that which lies at the end of the stream traveled by the Barge of the Dead. It is a place where the hunt never ends."

"That sounds like where we lived," Valandris said. She shook her head. "Kruge took us away, made us destroy it."

Kahless's smile disappeared. "I do not understand. Why did you value this Kruge so much, when you had never known the real man? You are all far too young."

"For decades there was an old couple who taught children of Kruge, on Potok's behalf," Dublak said. "A warrior and his mate. They died a few years ago." The Klingon paused. "I am told they were my grandparents."

Kahless's eyes narrowed. " 'You are told . . . '? You do not know?"

"I knew, but they had no relationship with me. They taught me of Kruge. That is all."

Kahless's gaze darted to Worf, who responded with a knowing look. "Dublak," Worf asked, "were they part of the original group that was discommendated with General Potok?"

"Yes." Weltern, whose delivery was so near that she attended only seated sessions, spoke up. "They knew Kruge, had served under him. They would have followed him anywhere, done anything for him. Their stories about him kept us alive. They're half the reason why we're all here today."

"What is the other half?"

Dublak looked down. "They were responsible for that too. They were Potok's escorts when he boarded James Kirk's *Enterprise*."

"When Potok's freighters were stranded in the Briar Patch?" Worf asked.

"That's right," Valandris said. "When they realized whose ship they were on, they did as they should have—they attacked. But rather than die in combat, they were taken prisoner. That is the story, at least."

Worf glanced at Kahless. "Spock's report said that Potok's visit to *Enterprise* began with a brawl. It landed him and two others in the brig."

Kahless looked back with concern. "Potok's officers had just been defeated at Gamaral—and had been denied death by combat. You are telling me the Federation did the same to them?"

"It is not Starfleet's way," Worf said.

"It is the Klingon way." Kahless looked to Dublak. "Did they express shame, indignity?"

Dublak looked up. "They did, Kahless. Kirk even visited them while they were being held, taunting them from behind the safety of a force field." He shook his head. "But they did not seek vengeance once they were free."

"Potok had ordered them not to act," Worf said. "He was their leader."

"*Kruge* was their leader, dead or alive," Kahless said. "You know very well, Worf, that they would have felt a responsibility to kill Kirk and anyone who protected him."

"Kirk was an honorable human," Worf said. "He killed Commander Kruge in fair combat. 'An honorable death requires no vengeance.'"

"Did Dublak's grandparents know it was honorable, Worf? Did they see the fight?"

"No. But Spock knew—and he said in his report he told Potok."

"If Potok told my grandparents that, I do not think they truly believed him," Dublak said. "All they remembered years later—all they said, after Potok was old and going blind—was that when he was handed the chance to slay Kirk in combat, he walked away. He walked away, and my grandparents followed."

"Down into the abyss where there is no reward." Kahless shook his head. "I begin to understand. You would not have known what passing on such a chance would have meant to your grandparents. But they—and those exiled with them—would have." He looked out across his group of listeners. "The people who settled on Thane may not have been condemned for any dishonorable act they committed. But they felt they had acted dishonorably and that they deserved their fate. And that tainted their every decision when it came to their offspring." He looked across the gathering, where many heads were now bowed. "Your community was damned from the start."

Weltern looked plaintively at the emperor. "You see, now, why we embraced Kruge so completely. He was the only person the elders ever spoke highly of," she said. Her face grew pained, and she winced. Suppressing it, she continued in a higher pitch, "He gave us names. And freedom."

Kahless looked at her with concern. "What is the matter?"

"Nothing," Weltern said, rubbing her belly. "My time is near."

He laughed. "That is not nothing."

"It is for *our* people," Valandris replied. "One more person born into discommendation. Dublak just said it. The only reason we knew parentage at all was for biological purposes—and to keep track of how long our lines were condemned." She gestured to the girl beside her. "Sarken only knew her father well because Tharas defied convention to spend time with her. He is gone now."

Kahless put up his hand before him. "No. Your father is with you always."

A hush fell over the group. Kahless looked out to the darkness beyond the cave opening. "That is enough for today. Now we sleep."

As he retreated to his alcove, Valandris rose—and thought about her own parents. Long dead, they had eluded her as successfully as any animal she had ever hunted on Thane. Yet now, they were squarely in her mind's eye, just as she had seen them, the one day she ever saw them together.

She lingered for a moment, contemplating what it meant. Then she dispelled the unbidden image and joined Sarken in helping Weltern stand.

Twenty-one

"**C**heer up, Gaw," Shift said, her Breen vocoder not altering her words. "You get to do what you do best again—and it beats every alternative."

The Ferengi sagged before his terminal, his station in the illusion control center now minus his light-emitting knick-knack. *Blackstone* was under way again and as crowded as Shift had ever seen it. Gaw was surrounded once more by all his technicians—save 1110 and 1111, the Bynars captured by Starfleet. There were Breen playing watchdog everywhere, and the additional computers in the center made it difficult to walk freely.

Which was fine, because the Breen didn't want the truth-crafters going anywhere.

"You got what you wanted," he said morosely. "We're all here. Truthcrafters don't crack—but you guys press pretty hard."

"You should be happy," Shift said. "We haven't asked you to spill your precious secrets about how the ship really works."

It wasn't for a lack of interest, Shift knew—or intent. There simply hadn't been time. Thot Roje was certain the operation had to go forward immediately, before Korgh's tower of lies started to collapse. But she was certain the Breen would eventually find out all about *Blackstone* and how to replicate it.

She just wasn't going to tell Gaw that—or that Cross was dead. "Look on me as just another practitioner. I have some people I want to trick. You're helping me."

"Truthcrafters pick their own practitioners, Shift." Gaw glared at her. No *dearie* this time, she noticed. "I want to know about Buxtus."

"I told you, he's not in good shape. But we're helping him. Just do your job."

Blackstone lurched, startling all the truthcrafters aboard—already a jumpy bunch. "There, we're under way." Shift patted Gaw on the back. "I'll see you in a while."

"I'll be counting the minutes," Gaw grumbled.

Shift reset her vocoder and walked forward to the bridge. Thot Roje was in the center seat, issuing instructions not just to the Breen around him, but also to those aboard the *Fervent*-class Kinshaya battlespheres parked inside the hollowed asteroid.

"*Squadron, activate all engines,*" Roje said over his helmet's comm. Shift guessed his voice was feeding out to the massive spheres, all of which were coming to life. "*Prepare to exit station.*"

"*Check-in with Spetzkar special operations forces completed,*" said Chot Dayn from a nearby station. There were no Kinshaya aboard the ships; skeleton crews of the Breen's finest were crewing—for the moment. "*All vessels report perfect functioning. I am hardly surprised. You had months and months to practice start-up and nothing else.*"

Shift glared at Dayn, knowing he could not see her icy expression. Yes, the Kinshaya ships had sat unused for a long time, but the day had finally come—thanks to her. Why couldn't he be happy?

Roje outranked Dayn and gave him the attention he deserved: none. "*Make sure everyone in the squadron understands the order of operations,*" he commanded. "*Helm, take us out.*"

Ahead, the space doors parted, allowing *Blackstone* to exit. Once clear by several kilometers, the ship halted. Aft sensors gave Roje a visual on the squadron as it left the asteroid. Thirty-one battlespheres, as formidable as any force the Kinshaya had lately fielded. It was even one of their holy numbers.

"A great day," Roje said. The line was barely audible, and Shift wondered whether he intended for his vocoder to catch it. The Breen, she had learned, were intensely private. That was hardly surprising, given the steps they took not to be understood by outsiders and the premium they placed on looking identical. There was another reason for discretion: because Breen were measured by performance and loyalty, many of her fellow citizens were constantly looking over one another's shoulders, judging. She hadn't spent much time in the Confederacy proper, but she'd had a devilishly hard time getting to know any of her fellow Breen well.

Roje had been different. Maybe it was because she rescued the intel chief years earlier; perhaps it was because he saw her as clay with which to craft not just the ideal agent, but the ideal Breen. He had shared his motivations. An agent provocateur for the Breen in the Dominion War, Roje had performed heroic acts of mischief across the Alpha Quadrant—until a change in the alliance's fortunes sent him to Cardassia. There, cadres of Breen agents he had trained for years were thrown against the Cardassian Liberation Front—and then, Cardassian civilians.

It had been a far bloodier business than Roje had imagined it would be. Most of his companions died. In the unkindest cut, the Founder suddenly called the whole thing off. Roje had scrambled to escape Cardassia Prime, not trusting a treaty to protect his exit. The effect on him was profound. He had never lost his disdain for Pran—now domo—whom he blamed. And he had sworn many times to Shift that he would never leave his agents in the lurch.

He had done right by her, standing by, patiently waiting for news—and appearing just when she needed to be extracted from *Ark of G'boj*. Shift was glad to return his loyalty with an operation that had the potential to save his career.

"*Squadron, engage cloaks,*" Roje commanded.

Outside, the giant globes vanished from view. The Breen had obtained the cloaking devices from the Romulans, who knew nothing about the Kinshaya ships, much less their devices' deployment aboard them. That was intentional: Roje wanted the Kinshaya to be the Breen's client, not the Romulans'.

Shift looked at the screens on the bridge. The same tracking systems that had allowed *Blackstone* to track the Phantom Wing while cloaked—thanks to Odrok's hack of the birds-of-prey's stealth positioning systems—were now allowing the Breen aboard the illusion ship to follow the movements of the Kinshaya warships.

"*Our crews report everything functioning normally,*" Dayn said.

"*Make sure they are certain of the sequence of events,*" Roje said. He looked back at the chot. "*Are you?*"

"*I know the plan,*" Dayn replied. "*To the extent that any being can follow something born of madness. I cannot believe the domo approved it.*"

I'm going to enjoy shutting you up, Shift thought. She looked to her friend and superior. "*The truthcrafters are pre-pared, Thot Roje. And so am I.*"

"*Thank you, Chot Shift. It is good to have such supportive help.*" Roje shot a passing glance at Dayn. "*Take your posi-tions. Helm, engage our cloaking device and set a course for Janalwa. Let's make history.*"

Twenty-two

Picard had been anticipating Cometary Body Atogra-1066, although not because there was anything important about it. Rather, by reaching the year of the Norman Invasion, he had a helpful mnemonic to remember where in the search they were. There were still many candidate comets to examine, sadly: it was his fondest hope they would run out before he reached the French Revolution.

Nothing had appeared to be unusual about the cometary body, a dirty snowball outgassing as it approached its sun. Rather, Dina Elfiki's analysis had found something unusual about 1066's tail.

"There is an irregularity in the dust trail left by the comet," she said as Tuvok arrived on the bridge. "Grains escaping the nucleus should follow a dispersal pattern that varies depending on the solar wind and conditions on the body. But in this comet, we've detected an irregularity that can't be explained by natural causes."

Tuvok stepped over to the science station. "It appears that something following along behind the comet deflected the dust outward for a period in a uniform manner." His eyes narrowed. "A wake caused by the shields of a starship."

"Someone was following the comet, but is no longer," Picard said. "Theories?"

Tuvok was still considering. "Lieutenant, nothing unexpected has been found on the comet?"

"Nothing at all," the science officer said.

From the security station, Aneta Šmrhová spoke. "Captain, there is one interesting thing about it. The comet is large enough to hide behind."

"*Blackstone*," Tuvok concluded. He considered the sequence of events. "I theorize the fire it took from *Jarin* damaged the ship and its cloaking device. If her shields still worked, the comet's tail would have offered a temporary haven while it underwent repairs."

"Further evidence they did come this way," Picard said. "When did they depart?"

"It couldn't have been too long ago," Elfiki said. "The trail would have dissipated. I can project a range of times."

"Make it so." He turned to Glinn Dygan. "When you have it, contact the Klingon Defense Force. Find out if anyone else was near this area at that time and if they detected anything."

"Aye, Captain."

Picard invited Tuvok and Šmrhová to join him in his ready room. Once all were seated there, he brought up on his computer the image of Buxtus Cross, their only solid link to *Blackstone*. His eyes scanned the lengthy report. "Lieutenant, has Starfleet been able to find anyone else who knew this person?"

"From his youth, plenty," Šmrhová said. "He made quite an impression. And we know a lot about his Starfleet time. He fits the profile of someone attracted to con artistry."

"A thespian too." Yes, Picard could see a trade like Ardra's appealing to Cross. "The last person to see him was a Starfleet legal advocate," Picard read. "Emil Yorta." He paused. "I don't see an interview with him."

"He's not in the service anymore. I've been trying to find him."

"We should certainly like to speak with him," Picard

said. "Commander Tuvok, what do you make of this situation? You've operated *Houdini*—and you were present at Cragg's Cloud. Can you understand what the *Blackstone* operators would be doing and thinking?"

Tuvok thought for a moment. "I must preface by saying that any conjecture is based on our theory about why *Blackstone* was in the nebula."

"Understood. Continue."

"We know from Commander La Forge's research that *Blackstone* was present at Thane and H'atoria when the Unsung were. Cross admitted having knowledge of them, including the ability to track them. We also have confirmed from forensic evidence that the Unsung were aboard the *Ark of G'boj*, having participated in a battle with her Klingon crew."

Šmrhová added, "We've found Klingon blood and score marks from disruptors. Also, trace elements from materials used in Unsung battle gear, matching what we found in *Enterprise*'s transporter rooms and on Gamaral."

"A discarded pouch was also discovered," Tuvok added. "It contained the same foodstuffs found by *Titan* at Spirits' Forge."

"The Phantom Wing was at Ghora Janto while *Blackstone* was at Cragg's Cloud." Picard said. "So they must have split up immediately afterward."

"Yes," Tuvok said. "Cross and *Blackstone* were in the nebula specifically to rob *Ark of G'boj*, judging from what we saw on the Bynars' data collection devices. They were taking inventory."

"Which brings us to the moment we lost touch with *Blackstone*," Picard said.

"Here my conjecture begins," Tuvok said. "The *Blackstone* crew was caught unawares by the attack of the *Jarin*. Cross certainly did not see it coming. It is also logical that whoever destroyed *Jarin* was not a *Blackstone* ally—otherwise, they would have used that force to reclaim the treasure on *Ark of G'boj.*"

Picard's eyes narrowed. "A third party involved." He looked out the port at the comet tail. "*Blackstone* may have been in there hiding from *them,* rather than the Klingons."

"A possibility."

Picard rubbed his forehead. "Now we're also searching for Object *Fourteen*?"

"I do not know if the *Jarin* attacker was cloaked, Captain. The fire that destroyed the bird-of-prey came from a position within the nebular cloud. The cloud was opaque."

"Noted." Picard looked to his screen. "So from *Blackstone* we have Cross, the Bynars, and this person." He advanced the image on his display to show a depiction of an Orion woman. "Cross's assassin, whom he called Shift. Her dossier is far less complete than his, I see."

"*Ark of G'boj* didn't have surveillance sensors on the bridge, so that image is based on our observations," Šmrhová said. "No hits in our databases."

"Orions," Picard said, musing with his fingers on his chin. "We were wondering how the Unsung knew which pirate targets to strike." He gestured to the screen. "Could she be our connection?"

"It is possible," Tuvok said. "It is also possible that she could be aligned with the ship that destroyed *Jarin.* She did not seem surprised by its arrival."

"What would her motive be for killing Cross?" Picard asked. "What secret was she protecting? Is it the same one as the Bynars'?"

"Cross was about to tell us how to find the Unsung. A reason finding *Blackstone* is imperative. It may have that capability too."

The captain took a deep breath. The silence was broken by the chirp of his combadge. "Picard."

"Glinn Dygan, Captain. The Klingon Defense Force has just responded to our inquiry. They detected no vessels in the vicinity of Atogra during the time the suspect vessel was hiding in the comet tail," Dygan said. *"They had no ships in the area."*

The captain sighed. *That would have been too easy.*

"But there is something that was nearby, sir. A Breen ship."

Picard asked, "Breen?"

"Aye, Captain. The Gorkon *reported an encounter with one of the Breen searchers, a* Reikin-*class fast-attack warship named* Sustax. *It appeared to be lingering in the Cabeus system."*

"Where is the *Sustax* now?"

"The ship lacked its required Klingon escort. Gorkon *accompanied the* Sustax *to the border."*

"Stand by, Glinn." Picard looked to Tuvok and Šmrhová. "If the Breen detected *Blackstone*, what are the odds they would tell us?"

"They are not a helpful nation." Tuvok contemplated for a moment—and raised an eyebrow. "It is curious they would be off on their own—and I am unaware of anything near Cabeus that would merit their attention."

"Perhaps the better question," Picard said, "is that if the Breen detected anything at all, what would be the odds they would tell the Klingons?"

"Approaching zero," Šmrhová said. "Their participation in this search has smacked of opportunism. I wouldn't put it past them to offer to rearm the Unsung's ships for them, so long as they harass the Empire."

Picard's jaw clenched. He'd suspected that the Unsung needed help to do what they had done, but a state sponsor hadn't occurred to him. They had struck at the Romulans, and the diplomats on H'atoria. The Breen had escaped unscathed.

Too far a leap. He settled for a shorter one. "Maybe they did find something—something that they wanted to keep to themselves. Let's go take a look at Cabeus. I've seen enough comets for one lifetime."

Twenty-three

Weltern's time was nearer than anyone had expected. Kahless had temporarily suspended his late evening teachings as the exiles gathered around the Klingon woman, assisting in her impending delivery.

Chu'charq was repaired and running. Weltern could have chosen its sickbay for her labor. But the Unsung had lived decades in the natural setting of Thane and thought nothing of the birth taking place on the rock floor of the cave. The only nod to comfort was in the fact that they had placed her near the opening, where the air was better.

Kahless wondered if the exiles had ever been aware of how good a life they had had on Thane. Many Klingons, he knew, would long to live in such a setting, free to hunt unlimited game, relieved of the demands of interstellar empire. But then he remembered all the things that had been taken away from them.

Worf was worried, judging from his expression as he approached Kahless from one of the birds-of-prey. "I have a dilemma," the commander said.

"Let me guess," Kahless replied with a wry smile. "You have been asked to help deliver the child."

"I have done that before," Worf said with a barely perceptible shudder. "It was not what I was expecting." He stepped closer to speak confidentially. "Valandris wants me to double-check the work on the dilithium crystals aboard *Chu'charq* and other vessels when the time comes. I am not sure what to do."

Kahless nodded, understanding. "You fear to unleash these people once more into the galaxy."

"Your teachings have been welcomed by many, but not all." Worf nodded in the direction of the corner of the cavern where the bellicose Harch and his cronies stalked and smoldered. They had avoided Kahless's talks—and, surprisingly, even the personal combat exercises the clone had led in the middle of the cavern floor.

Those had been an idea of Worf's, and they had brought more exiles into Kahless's gatherings. Young and old had responded, joining the ranks for exercises and mock duels. Only Harch and his bitter friends remained aloof—barely hiding their thoughts as they eyed the ships while repairs progressed.

"The false Kruge had a year to indoctrinate the exiles," Worf said. "You have had far less time in which to undo it."

"It is worse than that. We are having to undo a hundred years of Potok's wrongheaded approach." Kahless took a deep breath and let it out. "I am reaching them. But you are correct. If we would depart, I must reach them all."

"And if I attempt to use the ships' systems to broadcast our presence," Worf said, "your efforts will be for nothing—and they may all be killed." He frowned. "I cannot slow down the recrystallization process to give you more time. But if necessary I can sabotage some portion—"

"These people have been sabotaged enough." Kahless passed Worf. "Go back to the ships and continue the work. I will leap into the fire." He looked back. "Er—not in the way that other Klingon did."

With that, Kahless strode purposefully toward the objectors. Seven of them, including five males ranging from fifteen to forty, stalked about a flaming gas vent, mouthing their frustrations. In the middle was black-haired Harch, who spotted the emperor and spat on the ground.

"Go away, clone, before we kill you again. We aren't interested in your tall tales!" Harch gestured to the blade strapped to his upper arm—a *d'k tahg*, from the ships' stores. "Begone!"

"I have come to sharpen that blade for you," Kahless said. "It grows dull."

Harch yanked the blade from its scabbard and waved it about, slicing the air as his companions cheered. "I could sharpen it in your skull!"

Kahless was unmoved. "That is not the blade I meant. I refer to your mind." He smiled, baring his fanged teeth. "Yours is dull and unable to cut water."

Harch blinked as one struck in the face by an unseen object. Then he lunged with the weapon. Kahless slammed the palms of his hands against the younger Klingon's extended wrist and stopped its motion, just as the tip of the blade neared his chest. Then he grabbed Harch's wrist and twisted, even as he brought a knee up into his attacker's ribcage. The dagger clattered to the cave floor. Seeing Harch's companions moving toward him, Kahless shoved his off-balance assailant backward. Harch collided with the advancing Klingons, causing those in the lead to stumble.

Out of the corner of his eye, Kahless saw Valandris rushing up, disruptor in hand, followed by several others who had been gathering near the impending birth. Kahless waved them off. "Back! This whelp is mine!"

Upright again, Harch spied his dagger at Kahless's feet— and looked up to see that the emperor was holding his own blade.

"What do you wait for, killer? Come for it!" Kahless's eyes

darted down to the knife below and back to Harch. "You have slaughtered doddering nobles and valiant Sentries alike. How can you fear a Klingon grown from a drop of blood?"

Harch stood, seething—and suddenly aware of all those watching: his friends, for certain, but also many new observers, flanking Valandris. Kahless worried for a moment the two groups would have at each other. But Harch dusted himself off and took a step back. "I have killed you already, clone. There's no use doing it again."

"I will tell you what there is no use for," Kahless said. "Stomping around, threatening to fly off and unload your torpedoes at random, just to end in destruction. Our people have a saying, 'Fools die young.'"

"I am not so young," Harch said, beating his chest. "Tell us what we have to live for. Tell us!"

Kahless started to open his mouth—when a scream came from across the cavern. By the second one, it was clear what was happening. "*That* is what you live for, besides battle. You live to father a child."

Valandris stepped beside the clone. "You do not understand, Kahless. He *is* fathering one," she said, peering at Harch. "Right now. Aren't you?"

Harch said nothing. His companions looked at him as he fumed.

"That's right, Harch. Weltern told me about you two. I thought she was lowering herself with an oaf like you—all of Zokar's cronies lacked minds of their own. But our people aren't very good at having standards."

"I am the father," Harch snapped. "What of it?"

Kahless scowled. This behavior didn't make any sense. "You mean *you* are that woman's mate—and you are hanging about here grousing? Today, while your child is born? You should be celebrating."

"I bring only more shame to the child," Harch said, refusing to look in the direction of the birthing. Slowly, the fire seemed to go out of him. "I am three generations from discommendation. Weltern is four. So her child takes a step backward, because of me."

"According to Potok's rules!" Valandris said. "Why care about his practices now?"

"Practices that shattered families," Worf said, appearing behind Kahless. Attracted by the commotion, he stepped to the left side of the emperor. "But this child must have been conceived while you were all serving Kruge, not Potok. You must have hoped things would be different."

"That Kruge was a liar," Harch snapped. "You told us so!"

"So you go back to considering yourself unworthy of a name," Kahless said. "Potok is dead, Harch. And I tell you that if you do seek to build a new life—a Klingon life—there is no better time to start than on such a day as today." He stared at the hothead. "You can die a fool—or found the House of Harch."

"I do not understand," one of Harch's companions said. "A discommendated Klingon has no house."

"You are never lost," Worf said. "I was discommendated. I have my house. There is hope."

Shaking, Harch opened his clenched teeth to let out a deep breath. Then he shook his head. "Not for me," he said, turning. "Never for me." Harch looked to his companions—and seeing no support, he began walking, foot after trudging foot, toward the nearest pillar of fire.

An infant's cry resounded across the atrium. Kahless, hearing it and seeing that Harch was paying no mind, declared, "Morath's bones, I have had enough!" The clone charged across the cave floor. Grabbing Harch by the back collar of his tunic, he twirled the despondent Klingon around and shoved him across the cave floor.

"You will see," Kahless yelled. "You will not die before you see!"

Kahless pushed Harch through an opening in the crowd around the panting Weltern. Raneer, *Chu'charq*'s helm operator, lifted up a dripping, naked, and writhing babe. The child's bony crown caught the light. "Weltern's child," Raneer announced. "It is male."

"It is more than that," Kahless said, nudging Harch. "It is your *son*."

Harch stood, spellbound. For a moment, Kahless seemed concerned at letting the Klingon, who had been so despondent a moment before and incendiary before that, touch the child. But those worries vanished when he saw how Harch looked on the infant.

On the ground, Weltern looked up at him. It took her a few moments to register his presence—and when she did, it puzzled her. She could only ask, "What do you think of that?"

For his part, Harch could only get out, "I . . . do not know what to say."

"Neither do I," she replied.

"I have the words," Kahless said, watching Harch take the child from Raneer. " 'Your blood.' "

" *jIH dok*," Harch repeated.

Kahless looked down to Weltern. " 'Our blood,' " he said.

"*maj dok*," she said. They did not need to hear the rest from Kahless. "*Tlinghan jIH*," they said.

I am a Klingon.

"The House of Harch is begun," Kahless said. "Honor may come or it may not. But one is always of his house."

As Harch stood mystified by his mewling son, Kahless took the new father's shoulder and pointed outside. "Take him beneath the stars. Tell them that he is a Klingon and that they are his for the taking."

Harch lifted the squealing baby over his head and did exactly that. A procession of the Unsung followed him outside, trailed by an entranced Valandris. Worf shot Kahless a look of admiration he would always treasure. Only Weltern remained, and Kahless lifted her so she could watch. She was Klingon and would be ready to skin a *targ* in an hour, but for now she needed his help.

For the first time since his retirement, Kahless knew his purpose. The Unsung did not need another leader, telling them what to do or whom to be. They needed only a guide to help them find the path from the darkness.

Kahless the Unforgettable would take care of leading deserving souls to Sto-Vo-Kor, as he always had. It would be the mission of Kahless the clone to help them deserve it.

ACT TWO

THE SIDE OF ANGELS

2386

"In trust I have found treason."

—*Elizabeth I*

Twenty-four

A miracle occurred, as it did every day. Over the slums of eastern Rashtag, capital city of the homeworld of the Holy Order of Kinshaya, Janalwa's star emerged round and whole. It was a circle, a circle of light—and while the Kinshaya were not sun worshippers, they did revere the circle beyond all other things.

Yeffir came just before dawn every day to the balcony garden to revel in this moment. Aged and infirm, the Kinshaya female took solace in the fact that the circle could be found everywhere—even looking over the houses of the poor, whom she had tried so hard to help.

So many hopes. So many failures. Life was a circle. An opportunity, missed, could always be counted on to come around again.

She just did not know how many more times she would be there to take it. Yeffir stood unevenly on the cold stones of the patio, feeling the arthritis in the four-fingered hands at the ends of her forelegs. Her leathery wings, so magnificent in her youth, frayed at the edges; useless for flight, they served to insulate her long form against the crisp morning breeze.

In a slow, sometimes painful canter, she took her daily constitutional around the balcony, which wrapped far around this smaller dome of the Cathedral of State. Rounding the building, she saw Niamlar Circle to the west, the geographic and spiritual heart of the city. Kinshaya were already on the plaza, meditating and praying—and there were also merchants selling and educators teaching. Once, the latter two groups would never have been permitted to gather there; it would have been considered a sacrilege.

But there had come that terrible day four years earlier when the Kinshaya Inquisitors—with Breen thugs at their side—had fired into a crowd of protestors on the circle, defiling the holy shape with the blood of innocents. Yeffir had not been present. An itinerant preacher not affiliated with the Episcopate, she had been jailed for leading the Devotionalist movement, seeking to turn the Kinshaya away from dreams of conquest and toward peace. None of the many tortures they had subjected Yeffir to had given her the pain she suffered when she heard about her murdered followers.

The horrors of the Niamlar Circle Massacre had been broadcast across the known galaxy, prompting a chain of events that still made Yeffir dizzy to consider. She had been freed and the Breen banished. Ykredna, the manipulative Pontifex Maxima, had been deposed; that was better. The Matriarchs had put forward Yeffir, who had never been in their hierarchy, to serve as Ykredna's replacement. She had been stunned and honored—and overwhelmed by the sheer love the people had shown her.

She had accepted, only later realizing that she had been put forward as a figurehead to forestall a battle between high church officials, none of whom felt they could win public support in that charged atmosphere.

She had done a few things. The Inquisitorial Palace, across the plaza, had been emptied and turned over to Vicar General Tepesor, who was taking steps to make it the seat of a secular government. Thousands of religious and political prisoners had gone free. She had also started to wind down weapons production; the Episcopate's control of the military complex was deep-rooted.

Yet zealots remained in every walk of life, slowing progress. On the extreme, a group of hardliners had seized warships two years earlier in a vain attempt to reclaim what they felt they had lost. It had taken the Federation ship *Enterprise* to thwart them, the Starfleet ship on which T'Ryssa Chen, ally of the Devotionalists, served. But the more insidious threat came from within. It was not enough that retrograde thinkers constantly undermined her, or that ridiculous bodies like the Office of Infidel Relations continued to function as always. No. Ykredna herself had wheedled her way into the chief position in the new secular bureaucracy.

It was Ykredna who was destined to be the cloud over this day. Yeffir had known of the upcoming meeting for days and dreaded it. It was to have been a sign of progress: the new vicar general crossing Niamlar Circle to pay her first official call on the Pontifex Maxima. A blessing would be given, and all would be right. Only it was Ykredna that Yeffir, looking down, saw leading a proud processional of Kinshaya toward the domes of the holy church.

Many brave and peace-loving Kinshaya had died to get the woman out of the Cathedral of State. Nevertheless, it was Kinshaya who had voted to allow her to return—in this, the Year of Prayer, no less. It was not right.

"Pontifex?" asked a young acolyte from the doorway to the balcony. "It is time."

Angels and spirits, give me strength, Yeffir thought. *And the wisdom to tolerate peaceably those with whom I do not agree.* With doleful eyes, she turned and repaired inside.

The former Pontifex Maxima spent more than an hour telling the current Pontifex Maxima about her own cathedral.

That was well enough, Yeffir had thought, and not the tiresome rant she was expecting. Younger than her by some years, Ykredna seemed to have taken her recent election to a secular seat as an excuse to dandify her wings with golden tassels and a fresh set of tattoos. Yeffir felt plain in comparison, yet she had no doubt which look was more favorable to the people.

It was not until they reached the Yongolor Rotunda, beneath the largest dome of the structure, that Ykredna had started in on the subjects Yeffir was expecting to hear about. No one entered the room without invitation, and so the former Pontifex was sure she had a captive audience without distraction.

"'*Aya*, and you know this is a re-creation of the interior of the Temple of the Gods on Yongolor, our late and wondrous homeworld, before the demon Klingons that *you* refuse to exterminate laid waste to it."

Yeffir simply nodded. Of course she knew what the room was; the building had been hers to run for four years. And she could not deny that she had not exterminated the Klingons. She had no desire to do such a thing.

"'*Aya*, and it was in that place ninety-three years ago that the Great Niamlar manifested, warning the unfaithful that not to war on the Klingons, as you have, is the greatest of sins."

"I am aware of the story."

"No story, if by story you mean a myth. Scores of faithful saw Niamlar the Wondrous—for whom we have named our circle. Niamlar the Warlike, who is said to have captured the devil-father Kahless and swallowed him whole."

"I know this." Yeffir gave a glance to the ceiling, where an ornately detailed painting of Niamlar's mysterious manifestation encircled the gap left by the cupola. It remained one of the more puzzling mysteries of their faith. She sighed and looked down at Ykredna.

"Niamlar appeared in a Year of Prayer demanding slaughter, but the people were weak and failed her, and she departed. You know, Pontifex, that every thirty-first year we celebrate a Year of Prayer, in honor of the thirty-one greater gods of the pantheon?"

"I know, for I am the head of the church," Yeffir replied, not bothering to hide the impatience in her voice.

"And you know that ninety-three is thrice thirty-one, and that there are three circles to be found in the etheric structure of the cosmos, and three prophets who found them?"

"And three doors to this room." Yeffir wondered how fast her old legs could get her to one.

"'*Aya*," Ykredna said, "these are signs that to win Niamlar's return, you must this year support an increase in attack fleet production of—"

"Three percent, correct?"

"I was going to say *ninety-three*." Ykredna's muzzle turned upward. "It is written."

"What? Where?"

"In the very fabric of the cosmos."

Yeffir's mind boggled. "I will not recommend doubling the size of our arsenal. Not when the poor starve."

"The poor will serve on our new ships and feast on the spoils of infidel civilizations. We will enslave the remaining Kreel—and erase the demon Klingons, once and for all!"

"I will not do so."

"Then I will not leave," Ykredna said, sitting down.

Yeffir blinked, her eyes tired. "You are just going to sit there?"

"Your Devotionalists used such peaceful means to get their way years ago," Ykredna said. "As the people's vicar general, I can do the same." With that, she bowed her head and started chanting mantras.

Yeffir stared for several moments. She had expected a lot of things from Ykredna, but this was not one of them. Should she call the other Matriarchs, to get the vicar general out? What was the procedure when such madness befell?

At last, she decided Ykredna was doing no harm and headed toward the exit. "I will not disturb your prayers," Yeffir called back. "Perhaps when I return we can—"

"*I have returned!*" boomed a voice from behind, producing a sonic wave that nearly knocked Yeffir off her feet. The Pontifex, ears ringing, turned to find the last thing she had ever expected to see, seated within a blazing fire at the center of the rotunda.

Niamlar!

Twenty-five

The murals, Yeffir thought, did not do Niamlar justice. Nor did the recordings from the previous century, which she alone in her pontifical role had been allowed to see; electronic images of the gods were forbidden to the masses, who might seek to disprove them using nonspiritual means. Viewing the records of past visitations from the archives had been her first duties as Pontifex Maxima. She assumed the practice was intended to instill the church leader with additional fervor based on a certainty that the gods existed.

But images could not replicate the quaking of the marbled floor under Yeffir's feet as the shining dragon stomped about on Kinshaya legs several meters long. Ten meters from steam-spouting snout to the tip of her serpentine tail, Niamlar bounded angrily about the rotunda.

"*I am Server and Protector. Shield and lance of the Kinshaya, guardian against the great demons. Where are my worshippers?*" the colossal beast hissed. "*Where? Where?*"

"*Aya*, I am here, Great One!" Ykredna cried. She was still on the floor, but had completely prostrated herself, putting her neck to the marble. She refused to open her eyes. "I knew you would return!"

"*And what are you?*" Niamlar said, facing Yeffir. The Kinshaya felt the heat from the giant's foul breath; it made the hairs on her back stand on end. "*What do you pretend to be?*"

Yeffir's left foreleg collapsed, putting her down on one knee. Fear? Respect? Weakness? She did not know why she knelt, but she tried to face the shining Niamlar as she responded. "*'Aya,* I am Yeffir, Great One. I am Pontifex Maxima, your mortal agent."

Niamlar abruptly lurched forward, causing Yeffir to shrink. The creature's forked nose sniffed at her. "*You are a Devotionalist and a heretic, unfit to lead my church. You are aged, cowardly. You have made my people a disappointment.*"

"I was Pontifex, Niamlar!" Ykredna dared to look up. "I was always your servant—and will be again. Tell me what you would have us do—and I will do it." She shuddered. "Just spare the Kinshaya who adore you!"

Niamlar stomped again and again, so hard Yeffir feared the ceiling would collapse. But then her motion ceased. "*I came once before and found you wanting.*"

"You will not, now," Ykredna said. She stood—wobbly at first, and then straight and strong. "This is a new capital world, with a new church—and a circle that bears your name. Command us as you would."

A beat, while Niamlar considered. "*I offered to destroy the Klingon devil-master Kahless when I last visited—but you failed to impress me with your offerings.*"

"You want offerings?" Yeffir asked. "Niamlar, our people are impoverished—"

"*Silence!*" Niamlar's tail pounded against the far wall. "*The Klingons created a clone of Kahless—this I know. I also know he was slain by their treacherous own—as devils will do. Judgment has fallen on them; their so-called Empire writhes in agony. The seat of the enemy is beset with tribulations.*"

"*'Aya,*" Ykredna said, "they are distracted, weakened."

"*This time it is you who will destroy the devils. I will accept no small rocks, no single worlds. I have foreseen that the entire frontier will be denuded, left open for liberation. If you would save your people from destruction, my new Pontifex, you will reclaim the territories taken by the infernal Commander Kruge more than a hundred years past.*" Niamlar's eyes blazed hot. "*And you will level his provincial capital, as his people leveled ours.*"

Horrified, Yeffir stood. Striking the Empire now? And Ketorix, industrial arsenal of the Klingon frontier? "Forgive me, Niamlar—"

"*I will not.*"

"—but we lack the personnel for such a war."

Ykredna snorted. "That is what she thinks, Niamlar. Revolutionary forces loyal to me have been in hiding on Janalwa, waiting for the opportunity to serve. They simply lack the ships."

Yeffir gawked at Ykredna. It was an admission of something she had long suspected: the force that Picard had thwarted had indeed been Ykredna's—and she knew how to summon them.

The news seemed to please Niamlar. "*You are wise, Ykredna—a prophet, surely, to prepare so well. I restore you as Pontifex Maxima.*"

"You cannot do that," Yeffir said, trembling. "The Episcopate is a worldly organ, and you but one of the kingly powers."

"*Are the others of my kind here?*" Niamlar's tremendous head looked about. "*No.*"

"'*Aya*, Niamlar," Ykredna said. "Your word is law." She faced Yeffir. "You will support her too—or suffer worse than the tortures we subjected you to in the past."

Yeffir shook her head. None of it made any sense—but she knew one thing for certain. "There can be no strike against the Klingons. The attack fleets are too few."

"That is your fault," Ykredna said. "You and your heinous movement."

"Ours is the common people," Yeffir said, barely concealing her shock and misery in the moment. "Devoted to traditional worship and peace with our neighbors."

"You complete and utter fool. Niamlar is a god of war! Your weakness endangers us all." Ykredna turned and beseeched the monster. "If you will spare us, O Mighty, we can build them up again in time."

"All our hopes, dashed," Yeffir said. Grasping at anything, she added, "Our allies in the Typhon Pact would never support such an operation."

"*Wrong,*" Niamlar declared. "*You have allies, tried and true, whom I have dispatched as sentinels to your aid. They have stood loyally with you before, on the circle that bears my name, doing the church's work.*"

Yeffir blinked. "What—*the Breen?*" She couldn't believe it. "You cannot mean they are your messengers. They do not follow our religion—or any, that I know of."

"*I am Niamlar. Can I not use lesser beings as tools to put you on the path?*" Niamlar made a circuit of the rotunda. "*They have been engaged by me to help you deliver a rebuke to the Klingons. No—the Rebuke.*"

Ykredna was breathless with excitement. "What form shall this rebuke take?"

"*Walk outside. And when I return in an hour's time, I expect to see your generals here before me.*" With that, Niamlar vanished.

Yeffir felt dizzy, winded. She barely heard when, as she was passing out of the rotunda with Ykredna, a messenger approached with news of proximity alarms from the planetary defense systems. And she was speechless when, on the balcony where she had started her day, she looked over Niamlar Circle to see the cluster of black *Fervent*-class warships, decloaking one after another to the astonishment of the Kinshaya below.

Ykredna lifted her head high to the heavens, which were quickly filling with deadly hardware. "It is truly the Rebuke," she said. "And my people will deliver it."

BLACKSTONE
ORBITING JANALWA

Shift stepped off the transporter pad as invigorated as she had ever felt in her life. Gone was her Breen armor; she wore a jumpsuit to allow free movement. And she had needed it as she had inhabited the being of Niamlar.

"What did I look like?" she asked as Gaw was marched in. "I could tell they were amazed. It *felt* amazing."

"It looked it," Gaw said, still a little dazzled. "You're inhabiting a Jilaan original. Nobody did it better than her truthcrafters."

"And that whole character was encoded on the book-mark," she said, taking a towel to her face. "Astounding. The motions were just so strange—I could see the parts of my body moving. I felt like a giant!"

"It's the extra processors that help. Jilaan figured out a way to map four legs, wings, a head, and a tail to your physical movements—and I still don't know how she got the whole stink-breath thing to work." He sighed. "What great times those must have been."

She slapped him on the shoulder. "We're making more," she said.

Chot Dayn and Thot Roje entered. She could see Dayn recoiling from her armorless appearance—but Roje paid it no mind. After altering his helmet's output so Shift, bare-headed, could understand him, he spoke. *"Sensors indicate Kinshaya are already gathering, waiting for your next appearance. There are also reports that Ykredna's supporters are coming forward to greet our warships. The coup is real."*

Shift smiled. "What did *you* think, Chot? A waste of effort?"

Dayn squawked something incomprehensible and headed back to the bridge.

Roje chuckled. *"A good first act. You must convince them to board quickly, to escape detection—or word will get back to the Klingons."*

"I will—after I put the other part to this in motion."

"I look forward to it." Satisfied, Roje departed.

Gaw looked around at the changes the Breen had made to his precious ship and shook his head. "I'm not sure about any of this. You're starting a war."

Shift smirked. "What's your problem? You helped Cross talk a bunch of Klingon exiles into going on a killing spree."

"Yeah, but that was for a fortune."

"And this is for freedom. Yours—and Cross's. You'd better put aside your reservations, my friend."

He watched her coolly. "I'm not so sure we're friends anymore."

"Believe me, you'd better keep the ones you have." She reached into her pocket and located a handheld communicator. "We'll send Niamlar down again in a while. I have to go make a very important call . . ."

Twenty-six

Tragg had worked at the palace most of the evening. As leader of planetary defense, his main command was elsewhere in the compound—but Korgh thought it important that his youngest son spend at least a few hours a day with him. It might not be too late to put a mark on the young man's character after all.

Korgh had set Tragg up in the first of the offices lining the long hall. It had once been assigned to the old letch Lord Udakh, whose last time in it was reportedly at the start of the century, and that for a tryst. He figured Tragg might make better use of it, if only marginally.

Korgh had sat inside with him going over the little that needed to be done for the protection of Ketorix; mostly increases in policing to prevent any more Unsung-inspired incidents. Korgh certainly no longer needed a pipeline of discommendated individuals; most had been arrested or sent packing. Rooting out such filth would make Tragg look good to his new underlings.

Then their attention had turned to preparing for the *chavmajta*: shoring up support and finding more High Council members to join his walkout. Korgh had no intention of asking anyone who might leak his plan to Riker or Martok. Surprise was paramount.

It appeared that Worf's whelp had taken the responsibility for preparing for the ritual on the Federation side. Riker was on the hunt, with *Titan* and his other Starfleet ships, scouring the dankest corners of the Empire for any sign of what remained of the Phantom Wing. So much time had passed since Ghora Janto that Korgh began to hope that the exiles had left the Empire or immolated themselves. Either would be fine with him. If he succeeded against Martok before they resurfaced, he could make sure the general public never heard any of the facts behind their creation.

Tragg entered. Korgh looked up from his padd. "Did you find out what that sound was?"

"A communicator," Tragg said. "It was in a box, in Lord J'borr's old office." He scratched the side of his head. "I didn't think he ever came here."

"Never mind. Do you have it?"

"I do not."

"I will see to it," Korgh said, rising. "Go and fetch me a bottle of bloodwine—one from the storeroom below. I would drink before bed."

"You should have servants, Father. You are lord now."

"I did not raise you to be a spendthrift. Go."

Korgh watched Tragg vanish down the hall before making his way to J'borr's office, the former nerve center Odrok had maintained. Inside, he shut the door behind him and saw the comm unit buzzing away on the desk beside the box.

It was one of the encrypted communicators he had used to contact Buxtus Cross. A dead man, according to the Federation.

With trepidation, he reached for it and activated it. "Yes?"

"There you are," responded a female voice. It sounded familiar. *"Finally!"*

"Who is this?"

"It's your high priestess, Lord Korgh. It's N'Keera."

"My—?"

"Shift, you fool. Buxtus Cross's apprentice."

The Orion? He had been told she had killed Cross, but that she had been beamed off—by the *Blackstone*, he presumed. A loose end that needed tying off—or cutting. "Where are you?"

"Like I'm going to tell you. You tricked us already, remember?"

"The Federation says you killed Cross. Why did you do that?"

"Come on, don't pretend you never wanted to. He got on my nerves."

That, Korgh could accept. "The Unsung. Do you know where they are?"

"You mean you don't?"

"I asked first."

"What do I care about them? We did a job for you—and you rooked us," she said. *"But you're going to pay now, or I'll have quite the story to tell."*

"Blackmail?" Korgh snorted. "Jilaan would never have approved of such a thing. The Circle is supposed to be beyond that."

"It's beyond our honor, you mean?" Shift laughed. *"That's rich. You Klingons are all about honor—yet you hired us to deceive and slaughter. What would your fellow High Council members think of that? We're the only reason you're on the council in the first place!"*

Korgh's heart pounded. "Untrue," he said, fearful of being entrapped. He had provided the special communicator Shift was using; it should have shut down in the presence of a recording device. Still, he did not know who else was present beside her. He had to proceed slowly. "I understand you are upset. Speak reasonably, and I will try to address your concerns in a fair manner."

"Fair—like with the homing device you put aboard Ark of

G'boj. *Very clever. Then you sent that bird-of-prey after us—while it lasted.*"

Korgh's eyes lit with rage. "It was *you* that destroyed *Jarin*? You killed my grandson?"

"*Maybe we did and maybe we didn't.*"

"The ships of the Circle of Jilaan carry no armaments! It is against all the codes of their—"

"*Again with the honor. Try to accept that in a hundred years, things might have changed.*"

"Then you admit it!"

"*I admit nothing,*" Shift said. "*I know how you Klingons think. If you got it into your teeth that I killed your precious man-child, you'd never let it go—and we would never be able to make a deal.*"

Korgh smoldered. He listened for noise out in the hall. Hearing none, he checked the door to make sure it was closed. "What is this deal?"

"*I'm running Cross's crew now—and what we do isn't any less expensive. Prices have gone up, in fact, because of all your messing around.*"

"Your price!" His teeth clenched.

"*Two treasure ships. I want a spare Ark of G'boj for pain and suffering.*"

"*Two—?*" Korgh's expression turned sour. "How did you suffer, Orion?"

"*I spent a year on safari with your crazy exiles—none of whom had ever learned how to bathe.*" She paused. "*You're going to send the ships to . . . what's the name of that place nearby? Oh, yes.* Balduk."

"Balduk?" It was at the tip of an arm of Klingon territory curling far around the Romulan Neutral Zone—about as isolated from the center of imperial power as any subject system got. "That . . . is far away," he said cautiously.

"*I'm not doing this any closer. You were able to involve the Klingon Defense Force in your trap for the Unsung at Ghora Janto because it was a military installation. There's nothing like that to defend at Balduk.*"

He nodded. Whoever Shift really was, she knew the Empire.

"*I can't see you getting the full military to come along without the chancellor asking what it's all about. If you pretend the Unsung are there, he'll want to know how you know.*" She laughed. "*No, I expect you to send some kind of muscle after us, old man. But out there, every direction but one is away from the Empire. If I don't like what I see, we're gone.*"

Korgh frowned and considered her statement. "You will be there personally?"

"*I wouldn't miss it. Your people are going to stand by as my people check out the ships—and make sure they have no hidden homing devices or explosives. And they're going to watch as we warp away.*"

"What do I get in return?"

"*One year.*"

"A year?"

"*One year in which I go away, remain silent, don't bother you at all,*" Shift said. "*I just spent a year working for you without pay. I'll give you that for free. But in the future, our silence is sold by subscription.*"

Korgh nearly crushed the communicator in his hand. "You would suck my blood dry, parasite!"

"*Relax. It won't be your money you're spending by then, if I know you. You've launched yourself from obscurity to the High Council in the space of a month. I'm certain that given a year, you'll have the assets of the whole Empire to work with . . . Chancellor.*"

Korgh froze. "Why do you call me that?"

"Because I'm betting there's only one way you can go to get out of the jam you're in—and it happens to be the direction you were already going." She chuckled. *"So, Qapla', my good friend. We are all in it for your success. See you at Balduk. And if we don't—it'll be a short lordship."*

The communicator went dark. Korgh stared at it in a rage—and then dashed it against the wall. It broke to pieces.

He was grinding the remains of it with his boot when he heard footsteps outside the door in the hallway. He quickly kicked the debris under the desk and opened the door. Tragg was outside, dutifully bearing a bottle.

"Father, what is it? You look as though you have seen Molor himself."

Feeling his chest, Korgh realized for the first time how heavily he was breathing. "Something has happened."

Tragg put the bottle on the floor and grasped for Korgh's arm, to keep him standing. "What has happened?"

Korgh struggled to find his focus—and locked eyes with his son. "Contact your brother. I need the House of Kruge's home defense fleet mobilized immediately for an expedition."

"An expedition?" Tragg looked at him as if he were going mad. "Father, the fleet cannot leave our holdings."

"There is no time—and no choice." Recovering, he charged up the hall, Tragg in tow. "There is a situation that needs addressing, once and for all!"

Twenty-seven

CABEUS

For a group of people without a chain of command, the Unsung had always moved with a swiftness that surprised Worf. Such was the way of a community that was, at its roots, a hunting colony. He had seen how quickly the fauna could turn against the residents on Thane. As soon as the recrystallization work was done, the exiles had acted quickly to decamp from the floor of the Cabeus cavern and return to their ships. Once they decided to do something, they wasted no time.

On several previous stops, the Unsung had made efforts to minimize traces of their presence. Not now. Something fundamental had changed with the birth of Harch and Weltern's child. Previous infants born to the exiles had been cause for sadness. While the newborn was genealogically far from a restoration of honor—seven generations was the Klingon rule—Kahless's discourses had put things in a new light.

What the emperor had said was not new. Worf had even said it once to his brother, Kurn. "We cannot regain honor by acting dishonorably." But Kahless had deconstructed that sentiment, which held within it the notion that the dis-commendated *could* act honorably—and thus their behavior mattered. Yes, fellow Klingons might consider them non-entities. The exiles might even be barred from Sto-Vo-Kor. But what they did mattered—which implied that they had to matter too.

The Unsung had decided to reveal themselves to the

Empire and accept the consequences. It was a path Kahless had favored, but the idea had come from Valandris. The surviving Unsung had endorsed it. That, Worf thought, was important. They needed to decide for themselves.

As he passed through *Chu'charq*, Worf saw the new mother and son. Weltern was speaking with Valandris, seeking the younger woman's advice. Valandris's responsibilities in the group had grown. The exiles might look to Kahless for spiritual direction, but Valandris, organizer of so many hunts, would make sure they got where they needed to go.

"Let me speak with Worf. I will contact you soon with a destination," Valandris said. "*Qapla'*," she added, half a smile forming as she tried the term on.

"*Qapla'*." Weltern gave her gurgling bundle a squeeze and headed aft.

"Their child still has no name?" Worf asked.

"No. But it is not the same as it was during Potok's time." Valandris looked at mother and child receding into the distance and nodded thoughtfully. "The elders would have denied us names for our entire lives—and the same for our children, no matter how we lived. This child *will* have a name; he is of the House of Harch. But first Harch and Weltern intend to seek adversity, as Kahless says, so the name they give him will have honor."

Worf liked the notion. *The emperor had finessed that well.* Kahless had squelched the child being named after himself. Both parents felt they should never again deify a charismatic leader. This put the emphasis on the Unsung's actions.

A topic that still concerned him. "I saw that Harch has taken station aboard *Krencha*'s bridge. Does Weltern go to join him?"

"She commanded *Latorkh*, he operated *Rodak*'s helm. *Krencha* lost crew at Ghora Janto. It makes sense." Valandris's smile dissipated. "It will also be a check against him, should the old reflexes return. I have the rest of the children aboard *Chu'charq*. I do not doubt the others' interest in Kahless and the ancient ways—"

"But if we meet the wrong sort of reception, that could change." Grimly, Worf nodded. "I concur. I had told Kahless earlier that we should travel aboard *Krencha*, just in case."

"That makes sense." She grinned. "I will miss having you as a passenger—even an unwilling one."

They walked into main engineering, where Kahless stood with several of the exiles around one of the reactors. Looking between his listeners, he noticed Worf and Valandris approach. "Ah," he said. "I was just telling of how the true Kahless and Lukara took on the five hundred at Qam'Chee."

"An excellent story," Worf said. As he had so often over recent days, the commander marveled at how ably the clone had picked the right stories. The tale of Kahless the Unforgettable and the woman who would become his mate reinforced the value of family, something the emperor had emphasized since the birth of Weltern's son. It also included, as its moral, not waiting to do a difficult thing.

Valandris and the Unsung had decided to take a most difficult path. "How far can we go?" she asked Hemtara.

"The dilithium crystals continue to meet the specifications laid out in the tutorial," Hemtara replied, gesturing to a padd by a console. "All four vessels are functioning normally—but it's not clear how many operational hours we'll get. The tutorial did not say."

Worf nodded. "Those who provided you the birds-of-prey wanted you to be able to survive some eventualities, but didn't expect you to be a permanent force. Hence the bombs on board." He gestured to the padd. "You said that voice belongs to an aged Klingon woman—the engineer who came to train you? You remember nothing else of her?"

"She was as old as our elders," Hemtara said. "You said the House of Kruge built these ships. Could she have been one of the original engineers?"

"Perhaps. But Lord Korgh informed us he knew of no one alive who could have been involved on the Phantom Wing project. Of course, he also said he had no idea the project existed before this year."

Kahless scowled. "Find that woman, Worf, and you will find the people responsible. For Cross, his tricksters, everything."

Valandris took a deep breath. "We will let the Empire figure it out. But the time has come to decide. You said it would be unwise to simply announce ourselves, Worf. What would you do?"

Worf scratched his beard. "I have given this much thought. We could seek out the *Enterprise* or one of the Starfleet vessels. You would have a better chance of surrendering without bloodshed. It would begin to redress the harm you did at Gamaral."

Valandris frowned. "We did the greater harm to the House of Kruge. Cross sent us to kill their nobles. And wasn't H'atoria one of the house's worlds?"

Worf froze. What she was saying was true, but he hadn't considered it before.

"These are the house's ships," Hemtara said. "We should return them."

"Which would have been the will of the true Kruge," Dublak said from the back of the gathering. He gestured about the ship around them. "The weapons would be returned to his house."

Stained with the blood of his kin, Worf thought. He didn't like this direction at all. "They will not welcome you," he said. "The fleet protecting Ketorix is strong and likely on alert. They will destroy you as soon as you decloak." He paused. "But Kahless would be able to announce our presence—"

"He is no hostage, to be traded for our safety," Valandris said. "We will not hide behind anyone. It isn't Klingon." She asked Kahless, "Is it?"

Solemnly, Kahless said, "No."

Worf appealed to him. "Emperor, this is unwise. It is believed you are dead, at their hands. Many warriors are on edge, and after Ghora Janto there are more dead to avenge. They *will* retaliate."

Kahless shook his head. "They seek the difficult path, as Klingons should. To walk to the very gates of those they have offended and declare responsibility? It is something the Unforgettable would have done."

Silence fell across main engineering.

At last, Worf spoke. "It was the House of Kruge that had your people condemned a century ago—during a different time, under a different chancellor. Perhaps Chancellor Martok and the High Council will respect this gesture." His eyes narrowed. "But I would increase the odds that the exiles would survive the meeting. All the children are aboard *Chu'charq*, so Kahless should remain here as well. You may not wish to hide behind another, Valandris, but it is right that they should have someone with which to stand."

Hemtara looked to Valandris. "We *would* be revealing that Kahless is with us at some point, if they let us live that long."

Valandris nodded. "If they see him when they board, they might spare the young."

"I will stay as well," Worf said.

Kahless shook his head. "Worf, you told me you wanted us aboard *Krencha*'s bridge, in case—"

"We will not separate again. I am honor bound to defend you."

"A Klingon defends himself," Kahless said, cracking a smile. "But if this is to be one of the great moments in Klingon honor, there is no other's company I would rather have."

Twenty-eight

"**W**e've just picked up Starfleet's special delivery as ordered," Dax said. On the screen on Admiral Riker's desk in his sector command center, the captain rolled her eyes. *"My crew would like me to tell you that if this was your idea of making nice after the whole Takedown thing, it leaves a lot to be desired."*

Riker laughed. "They didn't actually say that, did they?"

"Would I lie to an admiral?"

"Rendezvous with *Enterprise*. It may be a waste of time—but on the off chance that it isn't, time is of the essence."

"We could do this even faster if they can meet us partway."

"Done." Riker leaned forward. "Captain, that's one more I owe you."

"Maybe you'd better hold off on the accounting until this mission is over," Dax said with mock seriousness. Then she smiled. *"We're on it.* Aventine *out."*

Riker rose from his chair—and bumped one of the four padds on his desk. It fell to the deck with a thump. He knelt to pick it up. More than one padd was superfluous, but his multitasking had grown to such a degree that even with a staff to help, he was having trouble keeping it all straight.

The hunt for the Unsung. The upcoming *chavmajta*. Starfleet Command's latest flight of fancy, on which he had dispatched *Aventine*. And now something very odd indeed was happening with the Klingon Empire—or, rather, a particular section of it.

Walking from his office into the operations center, he saw Ssura and several others poring over the mystery. It wasn't Starfleet's business to keep tabs on Klingon vessels, military or civilian—and certainly not inside the Empire's own territory. But the quest to find the Unsung meant everybody was looking at everything—and Starfleet's vessels had reported that more than a dozen Klingon warships had put out from the frontier territories administered by the House of Kruge. All had suddenly departed, with no destination announced.

"There goes another," his Caitian assistant reported. He pointed a furry finger at one of the panels in the center displaying the locations of various vessels. "That's *Udakh*, out of Narendra."

"You're sure they've gone to warp?" Riker asked. "Not just cloaked?"

"Some of these ships don't even have cloaks," Ssura replied. "They're definitely leaving. And here's the kicker: it looks like most of them are home guard ships."

Riker gawked. "Why would they pull their defensive units at a time like this?" He looked at the star map. "Has Lord Korgh's office told us anything? Have they found the Unsung?"

That would fit, Riker thought. Korgh's son Lorath had somehow tripped over the plans of the Unsung and set a trap at Ghora Janto. He had told Riker about it in advance. How had Lorath learned about the Phantom Wing's plans? That explanation, the general had taken to his grave.

"Starfleet Intelligence reports that Lord Korgh's second-born, Tengor, was recently put in charge of the home fleet," Ssura said. "His flagship just departed."

"Maybe that's what it is. They've got another lead they're not telling us about." *It sure is fishy*, Riker thought. But then, he could easily imagine Korgh wanting his family to hog all the credit for nailing the remaining renegade ships.

"Can we ask the chancellor?" Ssura asked. "Home guard vessels aren't always under the command of the Defense Force. But one would hope Martok knows what they're doing."

"Maybe." Riker paused, entertaining another thought. He touched a control on the star map interface, widening the focus to bring in other parts of the Empire. "Are any of the other houses scrambling vessels? Any of Korgh's allies?"

"We don't have that information. But I can make inquiries."

"Do so, quietly. Korgh doesn't seem the sort to share, not like his late son. If his allies are on the move and it's not the Unsung . . ." Riker did not finish the statement. A move by Korgh and his allies against Martok and Qo'noS seemed unlikely in the extreme. Klingon regimes were constantly in danger of military overthrow, but the new lord was playing the political game so well he hardly needed a coup.

The lieutenant had caught his drift. "If they are moving against the chancellor, do we warn him?" Ssura asked, worried. "I remember during their civil war, we had to be careful about intervening."

"Let's hope it doesn't come to that," Riker said, knowing full well he would try to help Martok and hang the consequences. "In the meantime, let's assume they've got a lead on the Unsung. Find out where they're headed."

U.S.S. ENTERPRISE
CABEUS

The explorers of the fifteenth century on Earth had gone looking for a route to China and discovered the New World instead. *Enterprise*'s quest to discover why the Breen ship

Sustax had lingered in the Cabeus system had not yielded any signs of the *Blackstone*. However, sensor sweeps had found something else: evidence that several birds-of-prey had been there. It wasn't the Northwest Passage, but the *Enterprise* would explore it.

His security chief, Aneta Šmrhová, had been following any possible lead, no matter how slim, with a singular passion. When the captain and Doctor Crusher entered the transporter room, they found only Ensign Jaero, looking rather haggard, waiting. He had an evidence-collection case in one hand. "Lieutenant Šmrhová is already on the surface," Jaero said.

"Very well," Picard and Doctor Crusher joined the ensign on the transporter platform. "Energize."

The ensign's work previously had been critical to the discovery of the underground starship factory on Gamaral. Earlier that day, one of Šmrhová's endless scans had possibly detected something on Cabeus that simply didn't belong. Picard wondered if Šmrhová had badgered the Tellarite ensign into agreeing with her assessment that the cave needed to be checked out.

It wasn't long, however, before Picard realized that her persistence had paid off.

"Here, sir," Jaero said in the cave. With his tricorder open and scanning, he set down the case and opened it, revealing several stacked petri dishes. With great care, he scraped a fine shiny powder from the ground into one.

"Illium-629," he said, running his tricorder over the material. "A byproduct of decrystallized dilithium. Relatively inert, yet detectable by our long-range sensors." He studied the tricorder's readings. "It looks purposefully deposited, perhaps by individuals unsure that it was safe. Chemical markers suggest it was removed from a warp core reactor within the last seven days."

"You're certain this material could not occur naturally?" Picard asked.

"There is no dilithium on this planet, Captain. The Klingon mining surveys are quite complete—and our studies corroborate that."

"Which would make this planet a good place to hide, if you happened to know that," the captain said. It wasn't clear to Picard how the Unsung *could* have known, but any doubt about their presence here was quickly disappearing. He watched as Šmrhová and Crusher scanned the inside of the cave. Both women had done more work with forensic evidence during the Unsung crisis than they had in a long time: tedious, painstaking work. The doctor seemed enervated, enjoying the mystery. The lieutenant wore a determined expression as she strode over to him.

"Landing gear imprints," Šmrhová said. "Birds-of-prey, looks like four."

"And we are seeking four," Picard said.

"The footpads matched with the marks found elsewhere. It looks like the Unsung were here for quite a while. We're finding evidence of campsites by the gaseous fissures."

Crusher had even better news. "There are hairs and dead skin cells all over the place. They were here for some time— and may only have left in the last twelve hours. I think we just missed them, Captain."

Picard considered the timeline. "I'm wondering if the Breen ship had detected them, but chose not to share that with Captain Klag."

"Why?" Šmrhová asked.

"I don't know. Maybe it's a complete coincidence," Picard said. "But we've suspected all along the Unsung had someone's help—and if they're recrystallizing dilithium, that's further evidence. That isn't something the exiles would have figured out on their own." He turned to Crusher. "Assemble a team. Begin data collection and DNA typing. Compare the material found with what was left at Spirits' Forge. Make sure this is the Unsung and not just some group of squatters."

"Squatters with birds-of-prey?" The security officer pressed him. "I'm not sure we need further proof, sir."

"That . . . is not the only reason to do the analysis," Picard said cautiously.

Šmrhová studied him and for the first time in days smiled. "You're hoping to find evidence Worf was with them?"

"Hope springs eternal, Lieutenant."

Picard stared into the cave and wondered aloud, "We know the *Blackstone* was nearby. Could the illusionists have made another attempt to impersonate Kruge, luring the Unsung here? Could they still be in the area?"

"Commander Tuvok is running the detection protocol he developed and La Forge reports *Houdini*'s sensors would know if *Blackstone* was in the system and projecting," Šmrhová said. "So no illusions—but they could be cloaked."

"Ready to strike again—perhaps even at us." It seemed they were once again just behind the Phantom Wing, forever doomed to keep chasing—

His combadge chirped. *"Captain, priority message from Starfleet Command,"* announced Glinn Dygan. *"We are to rendezvous with* Aventine, *all possible speed."*

The captain looked at Šmrhová. Her face went sour and she mouthed, *What?*

"Glinn," Picard said, "make them aware we have new evidence—and are on the Unsung's trail."

"I took the liberty, sir. Orders stand, all possible speed."

Šmrhová looked back around at the cave, her frustration evident. "Sir, let me stay." She frowned. "I can investigate. Leave me a runabout. You just *can't*—"

Realizing what she had said, the lieutenant went silent.

"Doctor, would you and Ensign Jaero take the samples back to *Enterprise*?" Picard asked.

The two complied—and Picard waited until the hum of the transporter faded. Šmrhová stood at attention waiting to take her medicine. She had been running herself—and anyone she thought could help her find the Unsung—ragged.

"Lieutenant," he said, "I *know* you were not at fault for Gamaral. Worf knew the risk, as did you when you volunteered. Aneta, I need you to listen to me: *you are not at fault.*"

"Sir, I should have—"

"That's an order. No more."

"Yes, sir." She breathed deep and inhaled. "Thank you, sir. Any idea what could be so important, Captain?"

"I haven't a guess," he said. *But if it's another wild-goose chase, you won't be the only person upset.*

Twenty-nine

"**N**othing *still?*" Korgh asked from the hallway as he looked into his youngest son's new office.

"Father, you must relax," Tragg said from behind his desk as Korgh stormed in. "This thing will kill you."

"I am not an old man, to be felled by a bit of bad news. This is a military operation. I want a status report!"

Tragg shrugged. "They're still at warp. I do not know what more I can say."

The task force had been hastily assembled. Commander Tengor had rounded up as many warships as could reasonably be spared from Ketorix, Narendra, and other House of Kruge systems. Even H'atoria and Ghora Janto, whose garrison commanders had understandably complained, given their past targeting by the Unsung. No one knew it was Korgh himself who had sent the cultists there. Korgh could not concern himself with the Unsung now. Shift and her blackguards had to be obliterated.

Tragg, in his new role as general of the ground forces, had contributed hundreds of warriors. They were hidden inside the two treasure ships that Korgh had dispatched along with Tengor's task force. Baffles had been installed to block any life-sign readings. Tengor would allow Shift's people to beam aboard the vessels, and then he would massacre them. The rest of his flotilla would find *Blackstone* and destroy it. It was so simple even Tengor could not foul it up.

"Our best warriors are with them," Tragg said. "You can relax." He peered across the desk at Korgh. "But I wish you would tell me more about these people we are going after."

"In time," Korgh said. "For now, know that all depends on their destruction."

Tragg accepted that without further argument. "I am concerned about our orbital defenses," he said. "Let me contact General Kersh. She could be recalled from the Unsung search for home defense."

"Do *not* involve her," Korgh snapped. He had no intention of allowing his rival to nose around wondering why he had sent his forces to Balduk. Korgh had no time for the irrational worries of Tragg, who just days before had no planetary security responsibilities at all. "Recall ships from our frontier outposts, if you feel you must." He charged out into the hallway. "And keep trying to contact Tengor!"

KINSHAYA BATTLESPHERE *FERVENT-ONE*
APPROACHING NO'VAR OUTPOST, KLINGON SPACE

"*'Aya*, outsider-ally and Niamlar-sentinel," the gray-faced cleric said. "The truth comes to you."

Standing in the command well of the *Fervent*-class battlesphere—Kinshaya loved their decorations but had little use for chairs—Thot Roje watched the many-bangled quadruped approach. While he had already adjusted his helmet to respond in the Kinshaya language, making proper respect to a bishop of the Episcopate was more complicated than he had time for. "What news?"

"Our crusaders are restless in their quarters," Bishop Labarya reported. "They know we have crossed the threshold into Klingon space and long to harrow the evil pit."

"Tell them their patience will soon be rewarded."

Roje's certainly had been. Years building the fleet, staring at the possibility that the vessels might never be used. Countless hours seeing that the interiors of the ships were designed exactly to the tastes of the Kinshaya; the Breen had gone all in, building the ornate domed cathedral-like bridges they preferred. Millions of Kinshaya *noreg* spent in secret support for Ykredna's hardliners, all of which would have come to naught if she never retook power from the apostates.

And then, suddenly, success. He owed it all to Shift. Who could have guessed that all it took to prod the Kinshaya back to war was a scheme concocted nearly a century earlier by interstellar grifters who fancied themselves magicians? Only Shift had. She and Chot Dayn remained in the Janalwa system, Dayn looking on in bewilderment as she coordinated planetary affairs in the guise of a god. Ykredna had been restored to power, but the true coup was Shift's. For the moment, Niamlar ruled for the Breen.

What had followed, Thot Roje believed, was one of the fastest offensives ever assembled and launched in the history of interstellar warfare. Roje had transferred his flag from *Blackstone* to *Fervent-One,* where the Spetzkar troops working the bridge's operations pits made room for Ykredna's military loyalists. The plan they executed was off-the-shelf, concocted for the *Fervent* fleet by Breen strategists should there ever be another Klingon civil war. Less than twenty-four hours after the Breen guided the battlespheres into the skies over Rashtag, the fleet was on its way. The Kinshaya were calling the offensive the Rebuke, a term Shift's Niamlar character had coined.

The vessels were deploying all along the Kinshaya border

with the Klingon Empire—and beyond it, their cloaking devices enabling them to slip past opposition.

Not that there was much to bypass. The Klingons had allowed Breen ships to travel their space openly in the ostensible search for the Unsung. The fools never realized that the Breen were reporting back ship positions and defensive emplacements. So Roje knew that many of the patrol ships were off on the search, and many of the House of Kruge home guard ships, which administered this region, had departed.

It was not a civil war that denuded the frontier defenses, but another of Shift's brainstorms. She had sent a message to Lord Korgh, diverting his attention to faraway Balduk. The door had been left open—and Roje owed it all to Shift.

She had saved him from the Orions, and now Shift was saving his career. Trust did not come easily for a Breen, particularly one who worked in intelligence. Roje's disastrous experience on Cardassia at the conclusion of the Dominion War had soured him on ever depending on others. But it was nearly impossible for any Breen to make progress in the Confederacy without allies, and Shift had been both loyal and intrepid, a rare combination.

Chot Shift was a treasure. Roje swore that when his mission succeeded—when the Klingon Empire was both truncated and alienated from the Federation—he would see that she was rewarded. And his resources might be limitless, if their efforts resulted in the addition of a *de facto* Breen colony in the Beta Quadrant, populated and defended by Kinshaya but controlled by the Confederacy. They might even make him the new domo. That would serve Pran right for how things went at Cardassia. He wondered how Shift might like to have his job as intelligence chief. Roje was sure she would impress. From slave to thot in just a few years: What better example could there be of the opportunities the Confederacy offered sentient beings?

Roje looked up at the massive status screen, improbably situated between two stained-glass displays. Represented were six attack battlespheres of his squadron, all currently cloaked and advancing toward No'Var Outpost, one of the House of Kruge's outermost holdings. He already knew from intel reports the Empire had an early warning communications station that was guarded by a debris field and the Klingon battle cruiser *D'pach*.

It would make an excellent first test for the Rebuke and its mixed crews of Breen and Kinshaya. It was fortunate for the Breen that the *Fervent*-class's operations centers were designed for use by the bipedal Kreel as well as by the Kinshaya. Roje didn't think it wise to let the Kinshaya run the mission all by themselves. He didn't doubt their devotion; just their good sense.

"*'Aya*, and the demons speak their vile tongue via subspace," a Kinshaya officer declared from one of the control interfaces. "Let us decloak and destroy them."

"Hold," Roje ordered. "We cannot lose surprise this soon. Intercept their transmission."

One of his Breen officers activated a control, bringing up an audio feed from the *D'pach*. The broadcast was on one of the encrypted Klingon Defense Force channels; obtaining the decryption key had been one of the recent triumphs of Breen espionage. Kinshaya brayed and squealed in existential anguish as the words of an accursed Klingon rang through their flying temple of war.

"—*don't care what Lord Korgh says. I answer to General*

Kersh—and she's off hunting the cultists. And I'm not leaving my post. Tell them Commander Thagon, at least, has sense!"

"Alert all vessels," Roje said. "Forward three ships, assume position nearest the outpost. Everyone else, follow our lead. In approximately five minutes, I will give the signal. Target communications arrays as soon as you decloak."

Roje looked back at the bishop. "Do your people consider it a sin to kill the unwary?"

"Not demons," Labarya said.

Thirty

❝ —*Commander Thagon, at least, has sense!*❞

In listening to the intercepted transmission, Worf made use of yet another feature on the Phantom Wing ships, presumably provided to the Unsung by their mysterious patrons. The official codes had already been entered into its comm system permitting those aboard to listen to Klingon Defense Force channels. Not to transmit, he noted; "Kruge" would not have wanted them to have that ability. Valandris's people had relied upon information from the feed several times in scouting their targets.

This time, their purpose in listening was different. No'Var Outpost was still hundreds of thousands of kilometers ahead, floating in an asteroid field. Worf could just make out the battle cruiser beyond on the magnified screen. He knew from the intercepted audio that it was *D'pach*, and he knew the outpost. He had visited it scant months earlier during the Takedown Incident. Worf considered that only one ship was garrisoned here to be a stroke of luck. A smaller welcoming party would be less likely to try to wipe out the exiles.

The four remaining ships of the Phantom Wing had traced a course dipping into and out of Klingon space; ironically, partially along the free-flight corridor Admiral Riker had wanted to establish at the H'atorian Conference. The thought had been to minimize chances of detection before they could surrender, as planned, on Ketorix.

While the ships' reinvigorated dilithium crystals had worked fine, *Cob'lat*'s antimatter storage system had thrown off alarms several times, forcing the entire squadron to stop while still cloaked. The Unsung would not leave any of the birds-of-prey behind. While *Cob'lat*'s engineering team was still working on the issue, Worf and Valandris met to discuss turning the Phantom Wing over to Klingon forces somewhere else.

"General Kersh administers this station," Worf said. The Unsung all knew of her; the fake Kruge had made a villain of Kersh, and they had faced her at Spirits' Forge. "She is tough, but fair. Yielding to her would be honorable."

Valandris and her companions barely concealed their disappointment at the small distant bodies on the screen. "It is not Ketorix," she said. "We would not be speaking to the lord of the house."

"Kersh is a member of the house—granddaughter of J'borr, whom you slew. It would be appropriate to make restitution to her." He glanced over at Kahless, who watched with curiosity. "And she is more likely to let the children live. You know from the other transmissions that most commanders would shoot on sight."

"You heard what Thagon said," Valandris argued. "Kersh isn't even here. What do we do, sit and wait for her?"

Worf looked back at the comm system. He had not heard any reports detailing exactly where Kersh was—but he was reluctant to give the exiles the chance to change their minds. "If you decloak with shields down and hail them, Thagon will call Kersh to the station."

"Will there be anyone left alive when she arrives?" Dublak asked.

Discussions broke out between members of *Chu'charq*'s

bridge crew over what to do. Exasperated, Worf listened to the Defense Force transmissions, hoping some indication of Kersh would magically appear. It did not.

Amid the hubbub, Kahless stepped over to Worf and spoke confidentially. "You seek to end this sooner."

"You have done wonders with them," Worf said, looking at the others. "But with delay, things could unravel. I trust Kersh to do right. Korgh lied about his identity for years, claiming to be Galdor to remain close to his house. However noble his intentions, I question his choice of means."

Kahless watched the exiles. "I will support—"

"Look!" Raneer cried. In the distance, black orbs materialized around *D'pach* and the floating outpost. They were spherical starships, which spat disruptor fire at the targets they surrounded.

For a sickening moment, Worf—not registering what he was looking at—worried that the other Unsung birds-of-prey had decloaked and struck. But the other vessels were alongside, according to the stealth positioning system, right where they should be.

The strikes on *D'pach* had another impact on *Chu'charq*'s bridge. They could see, but they could also hear the crash of static replacing the carrier signal from Thagon's still-open channel. The decloaked spheres' surprise was apparently absolute; the outpost commander had never said anything. His battle cruiser exploded under a repeated fusillade— while only a few moments later, No'Var Outpost was shattered by repeated barrages.

Then the attack ended, almost as soon as it started. The spheres vanished, two by two.

"What was *that*?" Valandris said, gawking at the main screen.

Worf was as stunned as anyone. They were too far from the scene to act—but they were still under cloak and could investigate without danger. He pointed to Raneer. "Take us there. There may be survivors!"

Valandris looked at him—and then nodded to her young friend. "Do it." Raneer touched a control, and *Chu'charq* lurched. "Tell *Klongat* and *Krencha* to follow," Valandris added. "And remain cloaked!"

KINSHAYA BATTLESPHERE *FERVENT-ONE*

The Kinshaya continued to cheer, shrieking in that irritating way of theirs. Thot Roje had already decreased the volume on his helmet speakers once. He had long contended the Kinshaya were constitutionally unworthy to be members of the Breen Confederacy; they were barely functional as allies. The genius of Shift's idea, he felt, was turning them into true puppets. They deserved no better, just based on their behavior on the bridge now.

"Silence your followers," he told the bishop.

"We have purged this place of evil," Labarya said, her useless wings flapping in excitement. "Why do you not sing, Breen?"

"Because this is a single military outpost. We are after greater game." He looked to one of his officers for some competence. "Did they send any warning signal?"

"No, Thot Roje," the Spetzkar officer said. *"We struck perfectly. Should we scour the remnants for recording devices that might have seen us?"*

"Unnecessary. By the time anyone comes to investigate, the whole Empire will know where we are." He crossed his arms and looked to the strategic map. "Onward."

Phantom Wing Vessel *Chu'charq*

Chu'charq and its flanking vessels had required little time to reach the site of the attack. As soon as they were in range and scanned for life signs on both targets, hope vanished just as quickly.

"Who were they?" Kahless asked, stomping about in a growing rage. "Who would strike in this manner?"

"There should be a way to review the sensor feed," Hemtara said. A few moments later, she found the control she was looking for—and the events repeated on the main viewscreen, with further magnification.

"Freeze image." Worf studied the orbs. "Kinshaya warships." He had not seen that particular class before, but the profile fit nothing else. The hull color and size might be new, but the weapons were mounted in typical Kinshaya fashion.

"Are they at war?" Valandris asked. "I saw them at that conference of yours."

"There has been no mention of it." Worf had been monitoring the comms for hours for information on how the Unsung would be received. "This is a sneak attack."

Kahless walked amid the exiles, who stood staring first at the motionless image—and then at the destruction outside. The scene changed to a live view. Klingon corpses could clearly be seen amid the wreckage. The Empire had towed rocks to the outpost's orbital neighborhood to better protect it; this new debris field was just as artificial, but far more chilling to behold.

"You see," Kahless said, "this is what it is to witness an ambush. You heard no announcement from the Kinshaya. This was no victory, but the act of cowards."

Valandris breathed heavy as she looked out. "We—we have to do something."

"They're cloaked just like us," Hemtara said.

Valandris headed for one of the control interfaces. "We'll flush them out," she said, touching a control. "Decloaking."

"No, wait!" Worf said, hurrying to her position. But she had already raised shields by then—and after a few moments, it appeared no one had noticed them. "They must have left."

Reluctantly, Valandris asked, "What do we do? The Empire will think *we* did this."

"You seek to avoid blame?" Kahless asked, an eyebrow tilted.

"I seek to warn them. But they will never listen—not to us. Not after what we have done." She looked to the Emperor. "*You* could warn them, though. You and Worf."

Worf looked at the comm system, whose limitations he had recently come to better understand. "We can receive on the Defense Force bands, but it appears we are only able to transmit locally. There is no one left to hail."

Valandris rubbed her bony forehead. "I forgot. We were only ever able to call back to Thane while we were on operations for the imposter. I never considered calling anyone else."

Worf remembered the network of repeater stations, now destroyed, leading to the Briar Patch and the Unsung's erstwhile master. It was another way of controlling what they could and couldn't do. While Buxtus Cross was dead, the checks he imposed still thwarted them.

Frustration setting in, Worf listened to the feed from the

Klingon Defense Force, mentioning ship movements. One in particular caught his attention.

"What are you doing?" Valandris asked as he sat and pulled up the star map on another screen.

"Finish *Cob'lat*'s repairs. There *is* someone we can reach—who will listen."

Thirty-one

Alone in the void. It was a natural state for starships; their function was traversing vast distances populated by nothing whatsoever. *Enterprise* and *Houdini* had arrived first at their rendezvous point with *Aventine*—an unexpected prospect given the other vessel's immense speed—and sat motionless in a patch of Klingon space far from any star.

Chen saw nothing whatsoever outside the observation lounge port. Since her conversation with Tuvok, she had spent several of her off-hours here, contemplating the things she'd discussed. Vulcan meditation still seemed like an alien and unnecessary practice to her—but she couldn't dispute that being here relaxed her, allowing her to focus on the larger issues.

One of them was the Holy Order of the Kinshaya. Janalwa had gone relatively mute, a highly irregular thing for a people who couldn't keep from evangelizing. Her padd displayed only a handful of news items. They came from the Episcopate and were bizarre even by Kinshaya standards. Regularly scheduled agricultural reports appeared as expected, but now spoke in rapturous terms about the most mundane things. The taproot harvest had come in three percent higher, proof that the gods were alive and walked Janalwa, where their feet produced miracles whenever they touched the soil.

A three-percent miracle, Chen thought. The gods must favor taproots, but not by a lot. She set the padd on the table behind her.

Exhaling, Chen looked out at the emptiness—and found

it reflected in her being. Ennui aboard *Enterprise* had been replaced by confusion following the ship's mysterious orders away from the one lead it had found on Cabeus. Chen felt useless and out of the loop. Now that mood was spreading, threatening even to engulf the captain. He was close to losing his temper over Starfleet's unwillingness to explain their strange redirection.

Chen tried to focus for several moments on the blackness before giving up. She shook her head. "Sorry, Tuvok," she said to the air. "I don't see what you get out of this." She rose and reached for her padd—

—which buzzed, indicating a message. Examining the device, she saw the missive had been sent some time earlier from one of the Devotionalist friends she had made on Janalwa. Multiple attempts at delivery had been made, prodding at the Holy Order's firewall in hopes of reaching her. One, finally, had gotten through.

The message contained no words, written or spoken. The Episcopate's automated censors would have stopped that immediately. What it did contain was nineteen seconds of shaky imagery, taken by a tricorder.

She recognized the location. The subject, however, was something else.

The doors opened. Tuvok stepped through. "It is agreeable to see you, Lieutenant Chen. Have you been meditating?"

"No." She offered Tuvok the padd. "Tell me what you think of this . . ."

A quiet family dinner had been a rarity for Picard in the days since the Unsung crisis had started. The delay in *Aventine*'s arrival had given him a chance to eat with René, who was nearly five. And a chance for him and his wife to discuss something other than their disappointment at being ordered away from Cabeus.

Still the subject crept in, despite both their efforts to avoid it. "It's occurred to me there might be some genetic material deposited on the illium," Crusher said. "Someone had to have dumped that material out of the birds-of-prey."

Picard nodded. That was the only sample they'd had time to collect before returning. "By all means, have a look."

"Are you looking for Number One?" René asked, using the term he'd always heard his father use for Worf.

"We are looking for quite a few things right now," Picard said. He managed a smile. "But yes, Worf is one of them. Many of our friends have been lost before, and have been found."

Picard and Crusher managed to stay off the subject of *Enterprise* and its mission until they had put René to bed. For a few hours after that, the two did their best to avoid talking of Klingons, illusionists, and missing friends before retiring.

The break from reality ended when the captain's combadge chirped. He looked at his wife and sighed as he found the badge where he had left it on his bedstand. "Yes?"

"Bridge, Captain. Aventine has just arrived."

"Hail them. And route it to my quarters."

He dressed quickly and stepped out to his desk. Onscreen, Sam Bowers appeared. "We were expecting you sooner, Commander," Picard said.

"Sorry, Captain. We had a little trouble with our passengers." Bowers smirked. *"Well, really just one. Captain Dax will be delivering them to you personally."*

"Acknowledged," he said. "I'll meet them there."

Crusher appeared in the doorway, already back in uniform. "Still a mystery?"

"I'll see what it is. Stay here."

"Oh, no," she said. "I'd love to see what was so important we couldn't spend five more minutes on Cabeus."

Picard acquiesced easily, as he shared the feeling. They were waiting when two figures materialized.

Ezri Dax was one. Beside her was a rumpled man in his seventies wearing a lavender greatcoat that had seen better days.

"Captain," Picard said.

"Captain," Dax replied. She looked about, a little startled.

"Is something the matter?" Crusher asked.

"There were supposed to be three of us."

"*Aventine* reports the third person asked for some delay before they energized," reported the transporter chief.

"Typical," Dax said, shuddering perceptibly. She turned to the man next to her and helped him off the transporter pad. "Captain, I'd like to present Mister Emil Yorta, a public defender at the Thionoga Detention Center—the place we've just come from."

Picard advanced toward the pair. "I know your name, sir. They tell me you were the last person to see Buxtus Cross."

From under bushy white eyebrows, Yorta winced. "That, ah . . . was a long time ago."

"Is that the reason you're here? Because he was your client?" Picard asked as he shook Yorta's hand.

"No, it's because of my other client." Yorta pulled Picard closer, turning him away from the transporter pads. He spoke in a low whisper. "She, ah . . . talks about you a *lot*."

"*She—?*"

Before Picard could ask anything else, a glowing figure materialized behind him on the transporter pad. Picard froze as he heard a buttery voice he had done his best to forget. "Why, *hello*, Jean-Luc. Such a pleasure to see you again."

Beverly's stunned reaction was all the confirmation he needed of what he already had guessed. Reluctantly, he turned. "Hello, Ardra. Welcome back to *Enterprise*."

Thirty-two

Picard had seen many prisoners board *Enterprise*. Some were sullen, others defiant. But not one had looked as Ardra did. Imperious, majestic—and not at all like someone who had been incarcerated for nineteen years.

Silver threads in her sleek ebon gown made her appear to shimmer as she walked down from the transporter pad; under a towering crown of curly black hair, she looked as if she'd stepped off a chessboard. Bone structures flared upward above her dark eyes, creating the illusion that her eyebrows were always arched. *Perfect.* Her manner had always seemed to him to range from mocking arrogance to impetuousness.

He had never discovered her real name, nor her species. But he knew she was not his favorite person.

Unfortunately, he had always seemed to be hers. "This is truly a reunion long overdue," she cooed, wafting across the deck to him. She reached out for his hands—and when he did not offer them, she proceeded to place hers on his chest. "I should hate you for what you've done to me. But I knew the fates would bring us back together."

Picard edged away from her and cleared his throat. He gestured toward Beverly. "You remember Beverly Crusher, my chief medical officer—"

"And his wife," Crusher added.

"Oh," Ardra said, looking the doctor over and deciding not to offer her hand. Instead, she put her fingers beneath the captain's chin. "I thought you'd have preferred that counselor of yours."

Picard grimaced. Nineteen years earlier on *Enterprise*-D, Ardra had impersonated Deanna Troi while trying to seduce him. He gave her an icy look. "What are you doing here, Ardra?"

The illusionist held his gaze for a moment—and then withdrew her hand. "Your Starfleet asked for my help," she said, sashaying across the transporter room. "I told them I would only give it to you, personally, and only if I could surprise you," she said, pausing to look pointedly back. "I may still bear a grudge."

Picard looked to Dax for an explanation. She confirmed what Ardra had said. "She told Starfleet she would only talk to you, Captain," Dax said. "Admiral Riker dispatched us to Thionoga to bring her to you."

"Captain Dax has been the most *wonderful* host," Ardra said, voice dripping with syrupy malice. "*Aventine* is surely the most luxurious ship in the fleet."

"She refused to go anywhere unless we fashioned new clothes for her. Not replicated," Dax said. "Fortunately we have an ensign in engineering with skills."

"I'm sorry I was delayed in transporting over," Ardra said, "but I couldn't do without my favorite perfume. I—" She paused, laying eyes on the new arrival in the doorway. "Who have we here?"

"Commander Tuvok," Picard said. He stepped over toward the Vulcan, hoping that would prevent his incorrigible guest from pawing him. "I would have you meet Ardra, the owner of the vessel you have been studying."

Ardra's sweet smile became a frown. "I saw my ship outside. Have you been messing about on it?"

"The term I would use is *research*. Your ship is unharmed." Tuvok looked past her. "I am here because I have business with Captain Dax."

Dax nearly leaped at the opportunity to leave. "If you don't need me, Captain—"

"Thank you very much, Captain." As Dax and Tuvok departed, Picard looked at Ardra's companion. "Mister Yorta, why are the two of you here?"

Yorta shuffled to Ardra's side. Together they were as mismatched a pair as Picard had ever seen. "My client has information connecting to inquiries Starfleet has made," the lawyer said. "Our arrangement with Starfleet was that her participation would be kept in the strictest confidence. She has a professional reputation to maintain in her community."

"What community?" Picard asked.

Ardra tilted her head and gave a *tsk* sound. "Magicians do not tell their secrets, Jean-Luc. And we do not tell on one another."

Picard's eyes narrowed, and he looked at Yorta. "Cross. This is about Buxtus Cross."

"Cross is indeed why *I* was first contacted," Yorta said. "My brief, regrettable meeting with him. Ardra does have something to say about that individual." He fished in his pocket for a padd. "But what got our attention was when Starfleet investigators circulated the picture of this woman." He turned the padd about and displayed for Picard the computer-generated image of an Orion female.

"Shift," Picard said. "Cross's murderer."

"His apprentice, I suspect," Ardra said. "I know her well. Or as well as you could ever know your cellmate."

"Your—?" Picard looked back at Beverly, who seemed similarly shocked.

Ardra affected an impish smile, turned, and stepped back onto the transporter pad. "I'm sorry you weren't happier to see me, *Captain Picard*. Perhaps if I return to Thionoga, some other old friend will invite me—say, to dinner?"

"We've already eaten," Crusher said, not in the least impressed.

Picard gave her a pained smile that said that the needs of the service would have to come first. "I'll see if we can arrange something for our guests. But then, Ardra, you will tell us what you know."

"I can do better than tell you. I can *show* you." Ardra raised a dark eyebrow.

Ezri Dax felt a serious moment of déjà vu as she sat in one of the quarters *Enterprise* afforded visiting officers and dignitaries. Curzon Dax had been in similar quarters in *Excelsior* ninety-three years earlier when a young Ensign Tuvok had presented his theories about the visitation of the goddess Niamlar to the Kinshaya on Yongolor.

This time, Tuvok was accompanied by Lieutenant T'Ryssa Chen, *Enterprise*'s first-contact officer. If the meeting had, heretofore, seemed familiar to Dax, the image that Chen put onto the quarters' display screen took it to another level.

"Whoa," she said. "The Great Niamlar. That brings back memories."

"I thought it might," Chen said.

The imagery—several seconds worth—depicted the great dragon just as Dax remembered it. "That's an angle I never saw. Where'd you get this?"

"It was supplied to the lieutenant by one of her contacts in the Devotionalist movement," Tuvok said.

"Interesting," she said. "I didn't know there was any imagery captured on Yongolor, apart from what Sulu recorded."

Tuvok and Chen looked at each other. The Vulcan explained, "Captain, this is not from Yongolor ninety-three years ago. It is from Janalwa—*earlier this week*."

Dax's eyes went huge. "Niamlar's *back*?"

"Or a facsimile."

The Trill stared at the images. "Tuvok, that is *exactly* the creature I saw in the temple on Janalwa. Nothing is different. Only the background has changed."

"That was my conclusion also. I only have summary data," Tuvok said. "I have sent a request to Memory Alpha to obtain Captain Sulu's full scans. However, based on our mutual recollections, I think it is safe to conclude that whoever created the illusion is back."

"Could Niamlar be like the Bajoran Prophets and really exist?"

"Illogical. That chance seems remote."

Chen was spellbound by their conversation. Snapping out of it, she asked, "You think it's possible that the same scam is being run a century apart?"

"Certainly." Tuvok gestured to the observation port, outside which *Houdini* floated. "Ardra was active twenty years ago, and there is evidence that her ship is older than that. If Niamlar is a computer-generated holo-construct like the others *Houdini* generates, that same illusion could be repeated at a later time."

"But to what end?" Chen asked. "Another robbery?"

Tuvok tilted his head, concentrating. "Perhaps. But to have it happen in such close physical and temporal proximity to the Kruge impersonation raises many questions."

Dax stared at them both—and then back at the image of Niamlar, god of war. "I think we'd better get some answers."

Picard's second meal of the night had been far less enjoyable than the first. Beverly had declined to join them, going back to bed. But Ardra was wide awake, and he had to find out what she knew—even if it meant having to fend off alternating flirtations and angry barbs about having cost her the last nineteen years of freedom.

He wasn't surprised that her appearance had little changed since their first meeting. Illusion was Ardra's business, and just as she had kept the alias she was using when she was captured, she kept the same look. But he was just as certain that this look was, like everything else about her, false. As the dinner wore on, he grew increasingly convinced that the entire meeting was a scam.

The captain had said so when Yorta had suggested they adjourn to, of all places, the holodeck. The lawyer entered a program from his padd into the archway and stood ready to execute it.

"I would like it stated for the record, Captain Picard, that my client has come forward willingly to assist the Federation. By showing you this," Yorta said, "we expect to see a material change in Ardra's condition."

"There it is," Picard said. He'd been certain all along that Ardra had not suddenly decided to join the side of the angels. "The original charges against her were made by the Ventaxians. They would be the ones to appeal to for leniency, not Starfleet."

"But the sentence for her crimes on Ventax II has long since expired," Yorta said.

"One of which involved the theft of *Houdini* from a Federation impound facility subsequent to her Ventaxian arrest," Picard said. "Piracy is no small matter. She is serving extensions to her sentence because of her several escapes."

"I just knew you were going to bring up Shanzibar," Ardra said. "That was just a trifle. Besides, if we're going to talk about theft, what have you people been doing with my vessel? You're messing around with things you don't understand—again!"

"We used *Houdini* to spare the Ventaxians a life of miserable servitude. You were impersonating—"

"Not just impersonating," she said with a sly grin.

"—a god in order to extort the produce of an entire world. We were not going to let that happen."

She shook her head. "And that, my dear Jean-Luc, is why Starfleet is such a dreadful bore. You have no respect for a well-cast illusion."

"I do." Picard looked around at the black grid of the holodeck. "This is a place for illusions. The illusions here entertain, even inform." He looked to Yorta. "This will inform the Federation, you say?"

"I believe it will," the lawyer said.

Picard regarded Yorta. "I trust you." He looked to Ardra. "I trust *him*," he said, making it clear whom he did not trust. "I agree to enter into a negotiation about what we might be able to do on your behalf—*after* I see this."

"Enter—?" Ardra shook her head. "Forget negotiations, Picard. I want a deal *now*."

"You have just heard it."

Standing by at the arch, Yorta looked to Ardra. She shrugged. "Starship captains can be *so* difficult," she said. "Go ahead, Emil. Run the program."

Thirty-three

Picard did not understand how a space station could be dank—much less, a holographic one. And yet somehow, Thionoga Detention Center managed to adapt the feeling of a Victorian-era gaol into a modern setting.

Everything looked old, shabby, and used-up. Including the occupants, members of various species who shambled around with shackle-like control mechanisms around their wrists—or whatever limbs they had that suited. Picard stood in line with Yorta, waiting to get into a mess hall whose name, he could already see, was a double entendre.

"You're saying this holographic program is based on a security recording from two years ago?" Picard asked. "It hardly looks like it belongs in this century."

"Thionoga is a place out of time," Yorta said. "It's part of the wreckage of the corrections experiments of the 2200s. It was a joint undertaking between the Federation and a number of nonaligned systems near the old Klingon Neutral Zone. The idea was to cross-fertilize different cultures' methods of rehabilitation, in the hopes of achieving better results."

"Did it?"

"No. Since the Federation didn't have absolute say over the place, the penal colony became a stagnant pool, a place for the partner systems to dump the unrepentant. No efforts were made here to reform."

Picard looked at the prisoners near him in line—a mix of sad faces and psychopaths; victims and predators. They were not reacting to him. As part of this holographic reconstruction, the other characters were simply doing as they had done at the time of the recording.

Apparently Thionoga spied on everyone, for he could hear every conversation he got close to. Most discussions were of violence or misery.

"I find it remarkable," he told Yorta, "that the Federation would still choose to be involved with this place."

"It isn't. The Federation stopped sending people here in 2375 after a commission investigated. All Federation prisoners were removed from the facility—but there are several dozen people like Ardra who face separate charges from Thionoga's operators, arising from their stays there. That's why I left the defender's office—I've been working on getting people moved, one case at a time."

It looked to Picard like a noble cause, even if he remained dubious about Ardra. He saw her now: two of her. The holographic Ardra of 2384, looking surprisingly radiant given the circumstances and the drab gray clothing the offenders were allowed. She was holding court at a table with two other female convicts. Meanwhile, the true Ardra—as if there was anything about her that was true—was sitting leisurely atop one of the counters, idly tossing holographic forks and spoons against the back of the head of a mammoth Nausicaan guard with a bandage on his nose. The hologram paid her no mind.

Picard realized very quickly why he was being shown the recording. There was a young Orion woman at the table beside the holo Ardra, huddling close to the convicted fraudster and talking covertly. She matched the description given by Tuvok and Šmrhová. "Shift, I presume."

"I knew her as Vella," the real Ardra said. "When Emil showed me her image—right after telling me he'd been asked about Cross—I was certain it was her."

Picard nodded. "You must let me show this image to our officers who saw Shift."

"Very well," Yorta said. He consulted his padd. "Vella— her only known name, probably an alias—had been sent to Thionoga for killing a Kinshaya dignitary. A member of the new Devotionalist administration, it says here, who had been traveling to a religious retreat in nonaligned space."

"Does it mention a motive?"

"No. Robbery, one suspects."

Ardra laughed. "If I remember Vella, the Kinshaya probably looked at her wrong." She looked over at the holographic Orion. "That woman didn't suffer fools gladly."

Picard watched the holographic Ardra and "Vella" at the table together. Vella alternated between wariness when others were nearby, and rapt attention as she listened to the illusionist. The latter accounted for more time, as other prisoners seemed to give Vella a wide berth.

"You appear to have taken her under your wing," Picard said as he watched the spellbound Orion listening to the holo Ardra.

"Spend enough time in prison and you can find yourself in the company of some of the most tiresome windbags," Ardra said. "Vella was a woman after my own heart, smart and sophisticated, for what she was."

"And that was?"

"Hard to tell. She didn't say much about herself. And she certainly didn't let anyone belittle her."

"There is a report," Yorta said, "of Vella breaking a guard's nose with a cafeteria tray." He consulted his padd. "I don't seem to find any holographic record of that."

"I remember it," Ardra said with a broad smile. "I was there. It was this guy," she said, pointing to the holographic Nausicaan she had been taunting. "That character was always with the hands. He deserved it."

Noting that only one other person was at the table, Picard took the opportunity to get closer.

"This is the part we want you to listen in on," the lawyer said.

When the captain sat at the table, the holographic Ardra was in mid-spiel. "If you are interested in this path, my dear, you must know: it is by invitation only. The truthcrafters choose what practitioners they work with. And the practitioners choose their apprentices."

"Truthcrafters?" Picard said. He looked to the real Ardra. "Your allies who were aboard *Houdini*."

"Yes, yes." She waved dismissively. "Listen."

"Where do I find them?" Vella asked her friend.

"The Circle holds convocations every year," the holo Ardra responded. "This time next month you would find them celebrating in a particular bar on Sherman's Planet." She lowered her voice. "But I would be cautious. Some of today's practitioners have no scruples. Take Buxtus Cross, who visited me once—a little Betazoid monster. He's the worst of the new lot. He would do absolutely anything."

Yorta visibly went queasy at the name.

"But wherever I find a practitioner," the Orion asked, "I will find a truthcrafter ship?"

"Mmm," the holo Ardra said. "If you are looking for work on that side of things, darling, I do not think you have the skills. It's highly technical. But you would be allowed to see a ship once you became an apprentice."

Picard watched as Vella studied the holo Ardra. "Could you take me on as your own apprentice, Ardra?"

The holographic woman laughed. "I have no ship and no crew. Blame Jean-Luc Picard for that."

"I still do," the real Ardra piped in.

Picard looked up. "This is how Shift discovered the people aboard *Blackstone*. And Buxtus Cross."

Ardra sighed. "She was looking for trouble."

"She found it," Picard said. He listened to the holos talk about the Circle of Jilaan—a new name to him—and its proud traditions. Until Tuvok and La Forge's discovery of *Blackstone*, he had never imagined Ardra was part of a larger community.

Then the captain paid closer attention to the third person at the table, a female who seemed by far the oldest person in the room. She sat quietly eating—yet it was clear she was hearing everything. "This Klingon woman. What was she charged with?"

"Piracy," Yorta said.

Picard raised an eyebrow. "She seems . . . advanced in years for such a profession."

Ardra chuckled. "Anyone can be anything, Jean-Luc." She hopped down from the counter and strolled up to the table.

Yorta consulted his padd. "She called herself Heghtar. She had hired a group of mercenaries to take a Cardassian transport. When they were captured, they gave her location up."

"What was the transport carrying?" Picard asked.

"It was, ah . . . weapons and explosives," Yorta said. "A lot of remote detonation equipment too. She never said why she wanted it."

Ardra put her arms on the unnoticing Heghtar's shoulders. "Little old Klingon woman, wanting all that. I expect I'll be just as ambitious at that age—I never grow old, of course. I am eternal."

"You were friends?" Picard asked.

"I've known gargoyles that talked more. She always looked cursed—like she was living a life that someone else had forced her into. But she had connections like you wouldn't believe. She could get lines on things that no scrounger in Thionoga could."

Yorta nodded. "Including the materials used in an escape attempt for the three."

The real Ardra's expression soured. "Yes, that. I created the perfect holographic illusion with the equipment Heghtar smuggled in—put all the guards on the wrong track. But we discovered the escape pod only held two. Vella took my place beside Heghtar just as the guards arrived."

Picard looked at her. "She betrayed you?"

"Heghtar had accomplices in a freighter ready to beam the occupants out of the escape pod. Vella must have figured the old woman had to go along to make it work. But then she stole my spot."

"My client pleaded guilty to the escape attempt," Yorta said. "I believe it was her . . . sixteenth?"

"Details," Ardra said. She glared at the Orion. "You'd think after all I taught her, she would show a little respect."

"I suspect loyalty among thieves is hard to come by," Picard said as the holographic projection, having reached its end, froze. "When my people encountered Shift, she had just killed Cross. We suspect the two of them may have engineered a massive deception, creating the violent Klingon cult known as the Unsung."

Yorta looked at his client, startled. "So *that's* what this is all about! Starfleet had been so mysterious, asking about Cross." He turned back to Picard. "It makes more sense now."

Ardra stared at the immobile image of Vella. "So she looked him up after all. I knew Cross had hooked up with Gaw's crew aboard *Blackstone*. Does she still have the ship?"

"We don't know," Picard said, standing up from the table. "We haven't been able to find either of them."

"Oh, she knows where it is," Ardra said. "She's smarter than anyone thinks." She pursed her lips. "I should have been more careful."

Yorta worked a control on his padd. "Captain, I can give you Thionoga's biometric information on Vella—or Shift, as you call her."

Picard looked at the frozen trio at the table. "Do you have the same for Heghtar?"

"I do."

"Provide that as well. A Klingon connection could shed a lot of light on this."

Ardra stepped toward the captain. "Now we will discuss the terms of my release."

"Release?" Picard shook his head. "I don't know if I can manage that. But your cooperation will be considered."

"Come now, Jean-Luc. I've told you all I know. You don't need me anymore." She reached out for his collar and tugged it. "At least not as an informant. We both know you'll always need me." She winked at him.

Picard suppressed a shudder and called for the holodeck's arch. He was about to tell the computer to end the program when the doors opened. He looked out to see Tuvok, Chen, and Dax standing there. Picard gestured to the room. "Welcome to Thionoga. A very enlightening place."

"I think we may have found something else that will interest you, Captain." Tuvok addressed Ardra. "And you, as well."

Thirty-four

"That little scamp," Ardra said as she stood staring at the image of Niamlar before the Kinshaya. "Vella, Shift, whatever you call her. I call her a thief."

The observation lounge was packed. It was not Picard's practice to invite prisoners—or their attorneys—to senior staff briefings. The room was made fuller yet by the addition of Dax, Tuvok, and Doctor Aggadak from *Houdini*. Doctor Crusher, working on a lead, was absent. The imagery Chen had been sent from Janalwa was momentous, and the captain suspected Ardra could speak to it in a way that no one else could.

"You call her a thief," Picard said, "because you believe this is another larceny attempt? Or because you believe Shift stole *Blackstone* to make it happen?"

"That's not it at all," Ardra said, pointing back at the image hovering over the table. "That's one of Jilaan's greatest creations."

"You have mentioned this Jilaan before. She was another of your so-called practitioners?"

"She was the last Illusionist Magnus, in whose honor the Circle is named." Ardra got a faraway look in her eyes. "I was her last apprentice."

"Jilaan is dead?" Picard asked.

"Magicians never die," Ardra said. "They just disappear."

"Buxtus Cross is in our morgue," Šmrhová offered.

"He doesn't count. He was a sociopath out for a cheap thrill—an embarrassment to the order."

"You sought to enslave a planet," Picard said.

"But I didn't kill anyone." She looked back at the images.

"And I didn't go about stealing other people's ideas. Jilaan cast this illusion nearly a century ago."

"It was ninety-three years, to be more precise," Tuvok said.

"I was there," Dax said. "I saw it."

"And yet you look so young." Ardra smiled primly at her. "No, I knew of it from the *Annals*—our Circle's records. Jilaan herself even told me of it. I don't know how our Orion friend found out about it." Ardra put her finger on her lips and thought. "Unless she found it in the *Annals*. It's possible she talked Cross into showing her his copies." She shook her head. "What a fool he must have been."

La Forge was piecing things together. "How do you know that's Shift creating that illusion—or *Blackstone*? There are at least two of these ships out there. How many more exist?"

"I'm not telling you that," Ardra replied tartly. "But I can tell from Niamlar's movements that she's being portrayed by an amateur. She's tromping around like clowns in a horse suit. Jilaan never saw the day she looked that bad." Ardra's eyes flicked to the back of the room. "Er—who is this person back there and why is she so animated?"

Picard looked to see his Nausicaan guest fidgeting with excitement. "Doctor Aggadak, who has been caring for *Houdini* during your incarceration." The captain had already noticed that Aggadak had not been able to take her eyes off Ardra. "Doctor, do you have something to contribute?"

"Sorry," Aggadak said. "I just got excited that there might be more of these ships out there." The Nausicaan fixed her eyes on Ardra. "It's so good to finally meet you. You are a legend."

"It's always nice to meet one's fans," Ardra said, adding

coolly, "Such as they are." She returned her attention to the image. "No, it's one thing to create a tribute to one of Jilaan's performances—that's why the code is provided. Or even to use the same creation in support of another, larger illusion. That's accepted practice. But to run the exact same ploy is unworthy of the Circle."

"*Is* it the exact ploy?" Dax asked. "Do we know if there have been any demands for financial tribute on Janalwa?"

Chen straightened in her chair. "Starfleet Intelligence is in the dark. Except for official channels, all media in the Holy Order have gone completely silent. Worshippers are being allowed into the Cathedral of State by invitation only now—mostly supporters of the hardliners. I think my friend must have been the last Devotionalist to get in there. I haven't been able to get back in touch."

Picard clasped his hands on the table. He had played Dixon Hill many times; the past few weeks had given him far too many opportunities to play detective. "Let us look at these incidents. We have the *Blackstone*, used in an attempt to defraud a group of Klingon exiles into believing that an ancient hero had returned. We believe material gain was at least partially involved—given the *Ark of G'boj*—but clearly there were also acts of murder with political ramifications."

Picard studied the writhing image. "We have an attempt to defraud the Kinshaya with an illusion of their god of war. The Kinshaya, whose official Shift was convicted of murdering, and who are often manipulated by the Breen." He glanced around the table. "What if Shift is some kind of secret agent, whose friendship with Ardra was all about finding out how to get control of a truthcrafter ship?"

He was speaking while deep in thought, the words flowing as he considered the angles. "Is it possible the Breen could have found *Blackstone* and conveyed it out of the Empire, to use it to manipulate the Kinshaya? Could the *Blackstone* have made it from Atogra to Janalwa? Is there enough time?"

La Forge nodded. "If *Blackstone* has the same warp drive as *Houdini*, plenty of time. It's easier than assuming there was a third illusion-generating ship involved."

"There isn't," Ardra said. "No one in the Circle would disrespect Jilaan like this."

"How can you be sure?" Dax's eyes narrowed. "You've been in prison for nineteen years."

"I have my resources." Ardra found an empty chair by the wall and sat next to her attorney.

Quiet fell across the room. Picard kept turning over the elements in his head. The Klingons. The Unsung. The Kinshaya. And somewhere in there, the Breen. He felt tantalizingly close to something—but what?

Ardra's advocate finally broke the silence. "This is all very interesting," Yorta said, "and I'm pleased my client could advise you. But I'm not sure there's anything else we can assist Starfleet with."

Picard's eyes narrowed. "This is the second time the Kinshaya have been tricked. We don't know to what end but if it is connected to the Kruge trickery, we can assume it's a bad one. Should we tell the Kinshaya of the hoax?"

"They wouldn't believe us," Chen said.

La Forge snapped his fingers. "Ventax II. We used *Houdini* once before to show that Ardra was a fraud."

"Watch your language," Ardra said from her place by the wall. She gave him an icy smile.

The engineer continued, "What if we took *Houdini* there and fought fire with fire? Fake fire, I mean."

"Creating our own character to countermand whatever instructions the false Niamlar is giving?" Picard asked. He mused over the concept. "I'm not sure how I feel about that. It would compound the victimization—and would be seen as an incredible sacrilege if it were ever found out. We can assume that Shift is already using the Kinshaya's religion against them for some reason, just as Jilaan did for financial gain. I would not do the same, even for a good cause."

"Captain Sulu had some of the same concerns at Yongolor," Tuvok said. "He determined that we should thwart whoever was transmitting the imagery. But he did so in such a way that their faith was not shaken."

"Do we have the ability to jam their illusion transmissions, as Captain Sulu threatened?"

"Not that I know of," Tuvok said. "We never had the chance to try aboard *Excelsior*. We merely threatened."

A gasp came from Ardra's direction. *"A bluff?"* She shook her head in amazement. "Why, you little Starfleet scoundrels. Jilaan said our people were running about in a panic after that!"

"Will Riker would say we are a card-playing people," Picard said. Then something else occurred to him. "But what if we didn't tell the Kinshaya they were being tricked—but simply made it obvious that that was the case?"

Tuvok's brow furrowed. "Please elucidate, Captain."

"We cast our own illusion, right in the same space as Niamlar. And then we show how the trick is done."

Ardra put up her hands. "Oh, no! We *never* do that. Jean-Luc, that is the cardinal rule."

"But a rule has already been broken, or so you say. If your order has any standards, they have certainly been violated." He looked to Tuvok and La Forge. "Would you be able to take *Houdini* to Janalwa—cloaked—and do exactly that?"

La Forge cleared his throat. "I'm not sure we have the capability to show the Kinshaya anything as convincing as that." He gestured to Niamlar. "We only have access to the few characters who were in the system when Ardra was arrested."

"That's because you've never found my archives, with the *Annals*," Ardra said. "And you never will."

"Not without your help." Picard studied the defiant illusionist. "Mister Yorta, I'm willing to pledge that Starfleet will do everything possible to change your client's situation, should she help us to undo the mischief that a ship of her Circle has done."

Ardra spoke up. "Now, wait a second—"

Yorta waved her off. "What does that offer mean, Captain? Are we talking freedom?"

Picard looked at her and swallowed hard. "Yes, if possible."

"And *Houdini* restored to me?" Ardra asked.

"That's for Starfleet to decide. But I will personally speak for your liberation."

Yorta looked at his client, who conferred with him in agitated whispers.

Picard cut the discussions short. "My offer is firm, Ardra. It will not change. You will render assistance to Commander La Forge and his team as they find necessary. You will seek to undo the harm that we suspect Shift may be doing with *Blackstone*. We might be able to locate Shift and resolve major questions in the Unsung matter."

Ardra shook her head. "I'm not sure I really want to—"

"No?" Picard rose from his seat at the head of the table. "Very well," he said, picking up his padd. He looked to La Forge. "The plan for *Houdini* is approved. Assemble a team and do what you can—without her help."

Ardra gripped her armrests. "Jean-Luc, you must see reason!"

"I do see. You told me earlier that you are eternal. If losing the past nineteen years of your life has had no meaning for you, I can't see why you would object to going back. Lieutenant Šmrhová, take her to the brig. Adjourned."

Thirty-five

*O*ne thing about dealing with more than one crisis at a
time, Riker thought: *after a certain point, you don't
feel the weight of each additional calamity.* The human mind
could only process so much. Logically, he understood his
difficulties were being compounded, but he only felt the
burden of whatever he was grappling with.

Switching focus from one crisis to another offered
relief—even, perversely, when the other problem was bigger. If he needed to take a break from *Titan*'s search for the
Unsung—an investigation being received with increasing
antagonism by the Klingons—he went to his *chavmajta*
preparations. Failure of the *chavmajta* would be cataclysmic
and would most assuredly lead to his losing his commission,
but at least it took his mind off scouring space for cloaked
ships.

Riker stared at the pile of padds. The presentation dealing with the most recent events was on the topmost one. The
challenge seemed insurmountable. He had to put things in
the best light, while also standing ready to defend Starfleet's
actions. The frustration he felt while observing on the bridge
had crept into his office.

He swept up his padd, deciding the best thing to do was
to work on the bridge. Deanna vacated her seat, allowing
him to sit. Vale had merely nodded to him, not objecting,
possibly figuring that it was an improvement over his standing and literally looking over her shoulder. The first officer,

Dalit Sarai, had initially looked concerned, but that had faded when it became clear that Riker's focus was solely on his padd.

It felt better to be here, hearing and seeing the search going on as he worked. And if he felt somewhat self-conscious in Troi's chair, he knew she was not far away. It wasn't as though they required an empath's talents to read the receptions they were getting from the Klingons, anyway: hostility was hostility.

Titan was currently in the Pheben system, an active area for miners working for the House of Kruge. Ironically, it had been where Riker had served in the officer exchange program with the *I.K.S. Pagh* with Klag. Earlier at Theta Thoridor, Klag had been the last friendly Klingon *Titan* had encountered. Here at Pheben, *Titan* had been attempting to run down yet another Unsung lead when several independent mining vessels had approached.

"No threat," Keru said. "But they are blocking our approach."

"Five ships," Sarai said.

"Full stop," Vale ordered. "Hail the one in front of us."

"You are not welcome in this place," declared the crusty Klingon prospector who appeared on the main viewscreen. *"For years I sold to the Kruge family. Starfleet let the Unsung gut them at Gamaral!"*

"Captain, we are trying to find them," Vale said in her most patient voice. "This system hasn't been searched yet, and we have a report—"

"Tell the Defense Force!"

"We have. We'd be happy to talk to the home guard ship in this system. But we can't locate them."

"They were gone when we arrived," the miner said. *"It is*

time for you to leave too. Get out of Klingon space!" The transmission ended, cut off from the other side.

Vale looked to Riker. "This is an important mining system. Why would they leave it—"

Keru interrupted, "New contact, arrival from warp," he said. "Klingon battle cruiser. Captain, it's the *Gur'rok.*"

"General Kersh," Riker said under his breath. Kersh, who had started out hostile to Riker before the Unsung crisis began, had only grown more irritated with him in the days since. Their every encounter had been a misery, and he wasn't expecting this one would be any better.

"Titan," the general said on hailing, not bothering to hide her distaste. Then she saw who was sitting next to the captain. *"And our favorite admiral. When we started getting messages from miners of an intruder in this system, I expected the Unsung. You are not welcome."*

"We're just following a lead. Same as you, General," Vale said.

"I should rephrase. You are welcome no more. Our forces here can—"

Kersh stopped, midstatement, as the audio was cut. Several Klingons could be seen conferring with the general. When she looked up again, her cool resentment had been replaced by genuine wrath. *"There is supposed to be a battle cruiser in this system—with three birds-of-prey!"*

"The miners tell us they suddenly left," Vale said.

"Suddenly left?" Kersh's eyes blazed with rage. *"A Klingon would never abandon his post!"*

"Ask them yourself," Vale said.

"Did they see them leave?"

"General—"

Kersh shook her head, her anger boiling over. *"This is the limit. I have been getting word of home guard ships missing from their posts, with no flight plans filed and no orders to leave from the Defense Force."*

Riker turned to Vale. She gestured for him to deal with General Kersh. *"More ships are missing?"* he asked.

The sound of his voice set Kersh off. *"Yes, more ships! I have also lost contact with D'pach, at the No'Var Outpost. The outpost itself is also not responding."* She leered at him. *"You remember that place, Riker?"*

"Of course. You haven't let me forget it." The Takedown Incident would forever be under Kersh's skin. "Have they reported in to Qo'noS?"

"They haven't reported to anyone! I've tried rerouting one of the ships from H'atoria—but it's left station, too!" She glared at him. *"That was the site of another of your triumphs, wasn't it?"*

Riker stood, straightening his uniform. "General, what are you insinuating? That we had something to do with their departure?"

"If they left." Kersh's volume lowered, but her tone grew more ominous. *"My most loyal warrior is stationed at No'var. Thagon would never abandon his post. You should know: you faced him once before!"* Kersh glowered, suspicion forming. *"And now I find you here and our forces missing. I ask you again—where are the ships garrisoned at Pheben?"*

Riker thought for a moment. "This system is infested with subatomic bacteria that devour starship hulls. Perhaps that—"

"The Empire has known about the organism for more than twenty years," Kersh said. *"Every ship here uses decontamination protocols."*

"I know. *Enterprise* helped one of your ships deal with the problem."

"We do not need your help!" Kersh shouted. The transmis-

sion ended—and the image on the screen was replaced by the *Gur'rok*, now nose to nose with *Titan*.

From behind, Keru reported, "The mining ships are moving away. *Gur'rok* has just raised her shields."

"*What?*" Riker looked back at the security officer in astonishment. "Hail her."

"Mister Keru, do it," Vale said, her focus on her armrest controls. *Titan* had been in full-blown interstellar incidents before. Any false move could have profound consequences.

"Audio only," Keru said.

"General Kersh, this is Admiral Riker."

"*You will leave this system while we investigate.*"

"*Titan* is here at the chancellor's invitation. The Khitomer Accords allow us to be here."

"*The Accords be damned,*" Kersh said.

U.S.S. *Enterprise*
Deep Space

"Lieutenant Šmrhová is bringing her up," Picard said.

He had figured Ardra out, almost to the minute. She had lasted exactly through one replicated meal in the brig. While he had no doubt it was better than the fare offered at Thionoga, eating it behind a force field had reminded Ardra of what she was going back to.

The *Houdini* task force was in his ready room. La Forge, Tuvok, and Aggadak representing those who knew how to work *Houdini*—and Chen and Dax, to advise on how best to influence the Kinshaya.

"We shouldn't start our illusion until we find out what Niamlar has been telling the Kinshaya," Chen said. "We might have to have Ardra respond to it in our counter."

"This isn't a magic competition," Picard said. "We demystify this particular meddler's trick and capture Shift. Once the Kinshaya know about her, I believe she would rather turn herself over to Starfleet."

"We would have a better chance of catching her with a starship," La Forge said with resignation. "But we can't pull ships away from the Unsung search."

"Speaking of, I'd better get back to it," Dax said. She stood. "My job here is done. I've told you all I can remember of what Curzon saw. I wish you all luck—chasing wizards and dragons sounds like more fun."

"Thank you for bringing us Ardra, Captain." Picard could not quite believe he had said those words. He rose. "The rest of you continue working here. Ezri, I'll see you out."

When Picard and Dax walked out onto the bridge, Šmrhová was just stepping out of the turbolift with Ardra and her lawyer. Ardra looked little worse for her brief incarceration, yet she smiled curtly as the security chief removed her manacles. "Thank you ever so much," she said.

Picard and Dax approached the trio. "I understand we've come to terms," he said.

"I could never say no to you," Ardra replied.

"You understand you're not getting the *Houdini* back—you're just getting to use it," Picard said. "And it will require you to do something you've said you will never do—something you and your people have gone to jail to avoid." Picard studied her. "Are you willing to help us?"

"Oh, I'll go," Ardra said. "Not because you want me to, Jean-Luc—although you are still darling. And not to save the Kinshaya, or the Klingons, or the whoevers. I won't even do it to get out of prison." Her lip stiffened. "I'll do it to teach that little worm a lesson. No one tramples on the legend of Jilaan."

"Very well, then." Picard turned and shook hands with Dax. "I wish you the best of luck in your—"

Ensign Balidemaj called out from tactical. "Vessels decloaking, ten kilometers ahead!" Every pair of eyes on the bridge turned toward the main viewscreen. "Two—no, four birds-of-prey!"

"Shields." Picard stepped over to his command chair. They were in Klingon space, and the appearance of birds-of-prey, decloaking, wasn't unusual. But something about *four*—

"Vessels match the configuration of the Phantom Wing ships seen at Ghora Janto," Balidemaj said. "It's the Unsung."

"Red alert!" Out of the corner of his eye, Picard saw his *Houdini* task force emerge from the ready room. La Forge dashed to the first officer's post beside the captain.

"Phantom Wing shields are up," Šmrhová declared, taking her station. "Disruptors are not charged."

Dygan looked up from ops. "They're hailing, Captain."

"On-screen," Picard ordered. It was not the Unsung's practice to hail. But as surprising as that was, nothing could have prepared him for the figure who appeared on the viewscreen.

"Greetings, Captain Picard. I have returned."

Kahless!

Thirty-six

The truthcrafters, Ardra had bragged, were capable of convincing anyone they had seen anything. That was on Picard's mind when he saw Kahless, victim of the assassins on Thane, and Commander Worf, missing since H'atoria. They stood on a Phantom Wing bridge surrounded by Unsung.

"La Forge?" Picard asked without averting his gaze.

"No signals from an illusion projection unit. They're real."

Kahless wore a sort of clothing Picard had never seen before; it looked handmade. Worf was still in his uniform, soiled and tattered. They were flanking a young Klingon woman, in the garb of the Unsung, seated in the bird-of-prey's command chair.

The scene left him tongue-tied. "Emperor" was all he could get out. He heard Dax activate her combadge, ordering. *"Aventine, if you're seeing this—stand by."*

The Klingon woman spoke. *"I am Valandris of the Unsung, who struck Gamaral and H'atoria. We have stepped into the open to stand for the acts we have committed."* Picard could tell she spoke with an unusual Klingon accent. *"But there is something else."*

"Commander Worf," Picard said, "how did you find us?" It was the first question he could think to ask.

"Your flight plan was reported in a Klingon Defense Force dispatch we intercepted," Worf said. *"Captain—"*

"We must tell you of what we have seen," Kahless said. *"The Kinshaya have invaded the Empire. They strike from black orbs with the ability to cloak. They have already destroyed No'Var Outpost."*

Picard looked flummoxed.

Dygan was already checking. "The Empire just now circulated a report. Loss of contact with the station and its battle cruiser, Captain. They're not sure if it isn't a communications failure."

"*It is no failure,*" Valandris said. "*We saw the dead.*"

Worf said, "*We are sending you our sensor records, so you can spread the warning.*"

Picard left his chair and stepped up to Dygan's station. The imagery came in.

"I don't know the class, Captain, but they're definitely Kinshaya," Dygan said.

Šmrhová added, "Sir, if they have six . . ."

Then they likely have more. Picard was already on his way back to his seat, ordering, "Get me Starfleet Command—and Qo'noS."

U.S.S. TITAN
PHEBEN SYSTEM

Riker stood before the viewscreen, staring down Kersh. "We don't have to do this dance, General. I know I've disappointed you in the past—but I'm here, now, trying to do right by a friend. A friend and an ally."

"*I don't fire warning shots, Admiral. I want you out of this system. I'm not your friend and I'm certainly not your—*" The audio was suddenly cut.

"Sir!" Ethan Kyzak blurted.

Riker looked at him. "What?"

"*Enterprise* has a priority-one message for you," Kyzak said. "My board here just lit up like wildfire. You've also got a priority-one message from Starfleet Command and from the Klingon Defense Force."

Riker looked up at the main viewscreen, where a Klingon was delivering a message to Kersh. "I guess we're both in trouble," he said, forcing a smile.

"Let's take the *Enterprise* first," Riker ordered.

"Captain Picard reports that he's just found the Unsung," Kyzak said, his voice rising in pitch. "Emperor Kahless and Commander Worf are alive. The Kinshaya have launched a raid on the Empire. He recommends we immediately go to—"

"Red alert!" Vale called out.

They'd avoided provoking the *Gur'rok*—but *Titan*'s crew responded immediately to the command, raising shields. Riker looked up at the viewscreen, concerned that Kersh would misunderstand—but he could tell from her expression that she had gotten the same message.

The same impossible, befuddling message, with news both wonderful and terrifying. The hunt was over and his friends were alive—and the Empire was now at war.

The facts had no time to sink in. The commanders of four colossal Kinshaya battlespheres chose that moment to decloak and open fire.

KINSHAYA BATTLESPHERE *FERVENT-ONE*
ORBITING KETORIX PRIME

The Breen had few oaths, but Roje found one to swear anyway.

Wave after wave of the Rebuke had moved across the Klingon border, taking station in systems long coveted by the Kinshaya. Narendra. H'atoria. Pheben. And most importantly, Ketorix, industrial capital of the House of Kruge—and ancestral home of that late commander, who had so vexed the Kinshaya and whose name they still feared.

That fear was to have been conquered today, once and for all—and it would have been. The test run against the No'Var Outpost had been successful; the Breen had counted on a certain interval before news of the place's destruction went out. But the defenders were aware now, precious minutes before the general attack was to have begun. Roje didn't understand why. No other ships had been on their sensors at No'Var. Who possibly could have sent out the warning?

No matter, he thought. He could hear the hordes of Kinshaya below decks, pounding their feet, ready to be transported down to Ketorix to begin their attack. They would sever the territory of the House of Kruge from the Klingon Empire and destroy one of its most important armorers in one swift, crushing blow.

"Commanders in other systems are moving in," Bishop Labarya said. "We await your blessing, Breen-ally."

"Commence general operations," Roje ordered.

"The infidels will be ended. Niamlar guide us."

House of Kruge Industrial Compound
Ketorix Prime

"They're not here," Tengor reported.

"What do you mean?" Korgh asked. He rubbed his eyes. Exhausted, he had fallen asleep in his office, waiting for Tengor's call. "Who's not here?"

"The people you said we would find at Balduk, Father. They're not here. Should we return?"

Feeling his muscles cramp as he straightened in his chair,

Korgh clasped his hands together and gritted his teeth. He couldn't believe he had to explain it again. "The fugitives' ship will be under cloak, Tengor. They will see your force and decloak. Then you will strike." He tried to think of what else Shift might try. "Or if they should somehow transport directly from their cloaked vessel to our transports, you will kill the boarders—and then detonate torpedoes in the nearby area until their ship is revealed."

"Well, they're not decloaking. I've got a huge number of ships here, Father—and the captains are all restless. How long do we wait?"

"As long as it takes. You tell them they serve me. End transmission!"

Korgh shook his head. He had waited and waited—for *that*?

He rose, feeling numbness in his leg. His blood circulation had been cut off due to his odd posture dozing in the chair. Korgh limped across the room to the window and drew back the curtain. He started to shield his eyes, knowing already he had slept until nearly noon waiting for his moron of a son to—

A blaze of light blinded him—and a second later, a shockwave struck the building, shattering the window and throwing the old man backward. Clamorous sound reverberated through the structure.

On his knees, Korgh coughed and clawed at his eyes, trying to sweep away any grains of debris. The transparent aluminum in the pane had snapped into large chunks, not pulverizing—but there was other dust in the blast. His eyes adjusting, he crawled toward the gaping aperture and saw a blazing crater where one of his factories had been. Sirens blared.

He felt someone touch his back. "Father!"

Korgh remained by the window, now perilously open to the ground far below. "What—what—?"

Tragg pulled him away from the brink. "All the alarms are going off across the planet," the younger Klingon said. "Ketorix is under attack!"

In that instant, Korgh, who as a young man had never gotten to fight the battle he wanted, realized that war had instead come to him.

ACT THREE

THE LINE OF FIRE

2386

"Khrushchev reminds me of the hunter who has picked a place on the wall to hang the tiger's skin long before he has caught the tiger. This tiger has other ideas."

—*John F. Kennedy*

Thirty-seven

Shift could not see it, but she could hear it: the sound of jubilation, of a promise kept. The bells of the great church echoed through the structure, growing louder every time someone opened a door to the outside. Whenever that happened, she could also hear the roar from Ykredna's supporters, gathered out on the circle.

The cheers were for a guaranteed victory; a bloody retribution long owed to the infidel Klingon Empire. They were for the restoration of ecumenical rule, after a disastrous flirtation with liberalization under the Devotionalists. And most of all, they were for her, or rather, for the character she was playing.

Shift found it invigorating. For the first time, she truly understood the appeal that the Circle's kind of impersonation had for Cross. The Breen had given her the power to escape her past life by putting on a mask. The truthcrafters could make her appear as anyone at all.

It was easy to get carried away. But she would not, because Shift was a professional, and because she understood the other game that was being played. The Kinshaya were cheering, yes, but they had no idea who the triumph really belonged to. It would be the Breen Confederacy that would reap the spoils.

Ornamented with flashier regalia than ever, Pontifex Maxima Ykredna marched into the rotunda and made her respects to the Great Niamlar. Shift's creature form responded with a flourish of wings.

"'*Aya*, O Divine One," Ykredna said. Guards entered behind her, prodding along the former Pontifex, blindfolded. "I have brought the heretic Yeffir before you, Great Niamlar, that she might be judged. Devour her as you did the Klingon heathen brought before you on Yongolor so long ago."

Shift caught her breath as she saw what had been done to the old female. Where feathers had been remained only broken quills, and her fur was caked with grime. Yeffir's head hung low—but when she lifted it, she spoke with a spirit unbroken. "I do not recognize your dominion, Niamlar. There are other gods, gentler and wise. To surrender to violence is to lose."

"*Hear the words you use*," Shift said. "*Surrender. Loss. You wither in shame.*" As Niamlar, she stamped about the marbled floor. "*Leave the apostate bound here—alive, her eyes open that she may suffer as she witnesses the triumphs she would have denied my children.*"

"We will do as you say." Ykredna turned, reared up on her hind legs, and slapped Yeffir's face with her right hand. "Speak your treason no more."

Shift watched as Ykredna's toughs chained Yeffir off to the side and ripped away the blindfold. The Orion-turned-Breen was glad the Kinshaya had gone for it. There had been a way in Jilaan's original Niamlar illusion design for her character to seemingly kill another; it had been done to Korgh, way back when. By the *Blackstone* using a transporter beam on the victim, Shift could give the impression she was incinerating someone.

But no preparations had been made to use the tactic, and she didn't want to spring it on Gaw's truthcrafters. The last thing she needed was to attempt something and fail.

She heard a tone in her earpiece. A full status report was

in from the Empire; it was time to return to *Blackstone* to receive it. As Niamlar, she declared, "*I go to the astral plane to support our brave and patriotic friends. No true believers will fall this day.*"

Ykredna looked up, startled. "Will . . . I mean, *when* will you return, Great Niamlar?"

Shift wasn't surprised by the question. The members of the Episcopate had been edgy all along about her suddenly disappearing, as Jilaan's Niamlar had done so many years ago. Particularly Ykredna, who had so much on the line—especially now that most of her most militant followers were off fighting with the Rebuke. But Shift wasn't going for long. "*I will return and give you an accounting of the victories in my name. Let the bells ring across all our worlds. The time for the Holy Order is ended. This Year of Prayer will be remembered as the year you became the Holy Empire!*"

The ethereal-looking flames rose up around her—and in a flash, Shift was back aboard the *Blackstone*. Smiling and out of breath, she toweled off a layer of sweat. She didn't know how Jilaan's programmers had managed to make their hologram generate heat, but she certainly felt it, even in her Breen-designed jumpsuit.

Four minutes later, she was back in the cooling comfort of her Breen armor—and presentable for her colleagues on the bridge. Chot Dayn looked back at her from his status displays. "*You should have had the Kinshaya put Yeffir to death. It would have been more efficient. She could give us trouble in the future.*"

She had been wondering what he would criticize this time. Dayn had not seen the project he could not micromanage. "Yeffir is powerless. She serves a greater purpose as an example."

"*You fear to kill?*"

"Not at all," Shift said. *Try me sometime, you insufferable boor.* Fortunately, the subject was easily changed. "You called me with an update?"

"The Rebuke, as you call it, has just been unleashed across multiple sectors." Dayn gestured to the blinking circular icons in several locations on his star map. Vessels appeared with the symbol of their respective forces, be they Klingon, Starfleet, Romulan, or Breen. Most were scattered across the Beta Quadrant, with few near the theaters of war. A Klingon cluster appeared frozen way out at Balduk. *"Attacks are under way."*

Shift was startled. She looked at the time. "This was earlier than we'd planned. Did someone discover the test strike at No'Var?"

"No one could have. Our searcher vessels in the Empire did not report noticing anyone headed that way." Dayn crossed his arms. *"At least thus far, we have not had to include our search ships in the attack."*

"Roje wanted to leave that as a last resort," Shift said. The longer the Breen could be seen as innocent bystanders, the better. In the meantime, the fact that every Breen searcher had a Klingon escort meant that the Confederacy already knew the location of many of the Empire's ships.

Shift couldn't have been more pleased—and Dayn's grudging acceptance that the plan was working was a delicious bonus. The domo's snitch, so long a critic of Roje, was realizing which way the wind was blowing.

"There is the potential here to redraw the map of the Beta Quadrant," Dayn said. *"With your illusions, the Kinshaya become our slaves, even as the Kreel are theirs."*

"And their territory, ours to use as we see fit."

Dayn made a wide two-handed gesture indicating a broad area of the map. *"Between the Order's original territory and the new conquests, the Confederacy could hold a massive swath of the Beta Quadrant."* He pointed. *"We effectively create a rearguard threat to the Federation."*

"Who are friendless in the region thanks to the Unsung," Shift added. "Do you still doubt this stratagem, Chot Dayn?"

"It has moved too fast," Dayn said. *"Given more time, we could have assembled a larger force—brought more of the liberators and other Kinshaya warships into it."*

"Surprise would've been lost," Shift said. "Between the disarray caused by the Unsung and Korgh's redirection of his home fleets, our best chance is now."

Dayn shook his head. *"By all reports Korgh was ascendant in the Empire. You could have blackmailed him at a later time."*

"When? After the Unsung were found, and the Klingon vessels were all back on station? Or after all his lies were found out? We had to act. Your master, the domo, understood."

"The domo is master to all of us, Chot Shift."

"Of course, Chot Dayn. Good luck to you."

I despise you, she thought as she walked from the bridge into the illusion control center. Bureaucratic backbiting had been the one thing Shift had never liked about the Confederacy. Her operations, whether on Janalwa or Thane, had provided respites. Even Thionoga, where she had been inserted as a prisoner a little more than two years earlier in an attempt to either recruit Ardra for the Breen or to learn where truthcrafters could be found.

That fact she had recently shared with Gaw, in between her sessions as Niamlar. It came up again as she spoke with him now.

"I still can't believe you really knew the lady," Gaw said. "It makes sense. I should have known you just didn't show up at the bar on Sherman's Planet looking for a drink." He looked at her. "I guess you really are a better practitioner than Cross."

"Thank you," she said, and meant it. Gaw had always treated her decently, and she admired the respect he paid his trade. "Are you still offended by what we're doing?"

"It's different, that's for sure. Nobody's ever used truth-crafters in the name of a state before." Gaw removed his recently-returned pince-nez for a quick polish. "Oh, sure, we *mess* with states all the time—we take them over and cash in. But that's playing around compared to what you guys are pulling." He stared at her. "How long do we have to do this?"

"That's beyond my station to know," she said. *Indefinitely* was not a word she wanted to use with him. "Just know that it's working."

"Good. Any word on Buxtus?"

"He's improving. He said he wishes he were here and for you to keep up the good work."

Shift patted the Ferengi on the shoulder and headed off to rest before her next performance. Even a god deserved a break.

Thirty-eight

The entire galaxy, it seemed to Korgh, had gone mad.

Since the House of Kruge chose it for its administrative base, Ketorix Prime had never seen a hostile act by a foreign power. It had even been spared in the Borg Invasion. Certainly, it was far enough from the frontier that the Kinshaya would never approach it.

And yet at least five Kinshaya battlespheres were in orbit over Ketorix, as near as Korgh could tell from reports. Maybe more, but certainly not less—such was the confusion caused by the wretches' attacks on the satellite defense platforms and their repeated and ongoing bombardments of the surface. The blast that had taken out his window appeared to come from a bomb targeting his headquarters; the Kinshaya had just been a few hundred meters off.

After extracting Korgh from the ruins of his office, Tragg had called the home guard, which had belatedly activated the defensive energy shield over the city. Korgh, meanwhile, had a very brief—and extremely pointed—subspace conversation with his other son. Tengor, who had never fathomed why he was being sent to Balduk in the first place, mawkishly swore to return and save the house's holdings. But it would take time before his forces could arrive. Korgh knew they could not be counted upon. The Klingons at Ketorix would have to make a stand.

Rebuffed by his father's refusal to leave, Tragg had transported across the compound to the military garrison to consult with his underlings. Korgh spent the time as calmly as he could, changing into his uniform and donning a disruptor. He then stepped out into the atrium, where he went to choose a *bat'leth* of importance from the family's war museum. It would be a historic day, one way or another.

He grew increasingly frustrated as he heard explosions outside, either against the shield or outside its protective zone. Shift had deceived him, clearly—but how in the name of Gre'thor had she managed to sell him out to the Kinshaya? Jilaan had tricked those dunces easily decades before; they were no tactical geniuses. How would they even have the sense to mount such a broad surprise invasion, much less the hardware?

He found the *bat'leth* he wanted—one wielded by Kruge himself against the Kinshaya—frustratingly out of reach. The lights were low and he wasn't going to fumble about looking for the stepstool. In the end, he settled on the commemorative *mek'leth* from the ceremony at Gamaral. It galled him to fight a defense with the names of Kruge's other heirs etched upon it, but he couldn't be choosy now. It might even add to his story.

The glows from a large number of transporter effects caught his eye, and Korgh turned to face the new arrivals. It was Tragg, alongside a dozen warriors from the home guard.

"News?"

"Our ground forces are spreading out across the area," Tragg said. "I am so new to the office I have never had the chance to drill them. I'm not certain exactly how they're deployed." He gestured to the other warriors. "This detachment is for you, here at the headquarters. I joined them— there was no sense guarding an empty barracks."

Battlesphere disruptors fired from orbit struck the shields

outside, sounding like thunder. "What word from the Defense Force?"

Tragg's expression turned dour. "We do not know. That first barrage before we activated the shields destroyed our main communication station. We are trying to get through by other means."

"What was the last our people heard?"

"Most of the Defense Force ships were in other sectors, searching for the Unsung. The few that weren't are likely already engaged. Kersh is at Pheben. I haven't heard what's happened in the other sectors."

"More glory for us," Korgh said, straightening. Surely, he thought, even if Narendra fell, someone would arrive at Ketorix in time—and the possibility of reinforcements invigorated him. He pointed to the closest two warriors. "There is broadcast equipment in the alcove outside my office. Bring it. I will address the worlds under our banner. Commercial and personal ships can be used against the invaders." He turned toward the massive statue of Kruge slaying the Kinshaya. "I will speak in front of that. It will put steel into our citizens' bones."

U.S.S. TITAN
PHEBEN SYSTEM

These people know what they're doing, Riker thought as a barrage to *Titan*'s shields shook the vessel. He braced himself against the doorframe to the ready room he had just exited. Another impact struck just as he was ready to start moving again.

Vale looked back between commands. "I'd find a safe place to watch the fireworks, sir."

"Just headed for the balcony seats," he said, taking advantage of a momentary break in the action to hurry up the steps of the command well toward the master systems display where an open chair awaited. Troi was back in her usual counselor's seat, where he had been when the shooting started; he'd left to get a fuller status report from Starfleet Command.

"It's happening all across the frontier sectors," Riker said, straining to be heard over the din. "Kinshaya battlespheres of a new class—just like these—striking multiple targets."

"Then I won't take it personally," Vale said. "Alter course, one-two-five mark six-six!"

Titan banked hard, swinging around one of the Kinshaya battlespheres. Positioning wasn't of much use against a spherical opponent that had weapons emplacements evenly distributed across its surface—but there were four Kinshaya warships on the scene, and by moving, *Titan* could keep at least one vessel always in another's eclipse.

General Kersh had resisted hails asking to coordinate their actions against the Kinshaya—and *Gur'rok*'s shields had paid the price for it. "We keep trying to take some heat off the Klingon battle cruiser," Vale reported, "but then the Kinshaya chase down mining ships."

"I trust your judgment," Riker said, and he did. The Klingon mining ships that had attempted to bar them from the Pheben system had scattered willy-nilly, and whenever *Titan* and *Gur'rok* weren't double-teamed, the unoccupied Kinshaya had used the small ships for target practice. *Titan* had been forced to attract as much enemy attention as it could.

As they swooped past another ebon globe, Vale asked, "Counselor, what are they thinking over there? Besides the obvious?"

"I sense what you'd expect," Troi said. "Exaltation, excitement. Religious fervor." She paused, her brow wrinkling as she struggled to concentrate amid the chaos. "And something else. There's a calmer presence there, more focused. A different sort of mind, different emotions."

"That could be the difference between the Kinshaya and their Kreel slaves," Sarai suggested.

"I'm not sure which is dominant. I think they both believe they are."

Riker studied the display behind him, trying to make sense of the storm of information coming in. "The Defense Force has rearguard units in motion, Captain. But for now we're on our own."

He looked back to see *Gur'rok* fighting off its attackers, still heedless of any of *Titan*'s hails. Starfleet's rift with the Klingons was real and visible right outside the ship. Riker could not imagine Pheben was the only place it was having an effect.

His effort to preserve the Accords had failed. And both Federation and Empire would suffer.

PHANTOM WING VESSEL *CHU'CHARQ*
DEEP SPACE

Valandris didn't know much about the Federation, but she had already determined that its members certainly talked a lot. There had been the conference on H'atoria, intended to be *all* talk—where, when she was disguised as a Sentry, Starfleet Admiral Riker had apologized at length to her for something. She still wasn't sure what that had been all about.

After the Phantom Wing revealed itself to *Enterprise* and the other ship—*Aventine*, Worf called it—Valandris had been ready for anything. Instead, in the minutes following

Kahless's warning about the Kinshaya, the Starfleet captains had retreated from the viewscreen, off to confer with their superiors. It made no sense to her. If the people of Thane stopped to discuss every wild animal that charged the camp, they would quickly find themselves that day's meal.

"It is necessary," Worf had said. "There are many choices before them."

"Kahless the Unforgettable says we should never hesitate."

That had prompted laughter from the emperor. "Kahless the Clone says that he who strikes blindly cuts only himself."

So the Starfleeters had talked, seemingly satisfied that Worf and Kahless were safe, and that while the two were aboard *Chu'charq*, the Unsung meant no harm. Time was not lost, as La Forge, now seated in the captain's chair during Picard's absence, explained the purpose of the third vessel nearby.

"So *that* is how it was done," Worf said. He had recognized the ship called *Houdini* earlier, and also a woman named Ardra, standing on *Enterprise*'s bridge, who had apparently owned the small craft. "Buxtus Cross created his Kruge illusions with such a ship."

Valandris still had trouble believing it. "Are you telling me a ship like that was cloaked above Thane for all of last year?"

"And it was following the Phantom Wing wherever you saw Kruge," La Forge said.

She could not fathom how any spacecraft could create so convincing an illusion. She had spent countless hours with Kruge. But then, much outside preparation had gone into providing them with the birds-of-prey in the first place. Anything was possible.

While they waited for the captains' answer, Worf had decided that his colleagues should see a certain bit of evidence. Sarken appeared with it, entering onto the bridge with a padd in an open box. "It's from that room no one ever went inside," Sarken said. "I only touched it at the edges, Worf, like you said."

"Thank you, Sarken." Worf lifted the box in his hands and held it so the observers on *Enterprise* could see it. "Commander La Forge, this padd is one of dozens the Unsung found aboard every Phantom Wing vessel. It is a tutorial on running the ships—narrated, in places, by whoever was responsible for providing the exiles with the starships."

La Forge looked at it with eagerness. *"We'd certainly like to see that. But we'll both need to drop our shields before you can—"*

Valandris made a gesture to Hemtara—and an instant later, the box disappeared from Worf's hands and rematerialized on the deck in front of the engineer. *"Oh,"* La Forge said. *"I'd almost forgotten about that little trick. Thanks—this'll help us figure out more about who was deceiving you and why. And it could help with the Kinshaya."*

"What do you mean?" Valandris asked.

"We think the same ship that tricked you might have prompted the Kinshaya attack," La Forge replied. *"Maybe even the same way—by impersonating one of their deities."*

"Kruge was no deity—just a mortal, whose face and reputation were used," Kahless said. "Cross intended to do the same with me. It appears the blackguards have moved to other deceptions. Shameful."

"I saw the destruction they caused at the Klingon outpost," Valandris declared. "Even if such people were misled into attacking, they must still be stopped."

She looked to her side and noticed Worf's satisfied expression.

"What?" she asked.

"Nothing." But the look on his face did not change.

Thirty-nine

Picard's face was ashen when he and Dax emerged from his ready room onto the bridge. The Unsung, so recently enemies, had been proven correct. When Starfleet Command spread the word about the Kinshaya attack on No'Var Outpost, the Holy Order had responded by revealing its ships everywhere and launching attacks.

But both captains feared the alert had come too late.

"Reports continue to come in," Picard said. "The Kinshaya are striking at worlds all across the frontier—including Ketorix, the administrative capital of the House of Kruge. No warning. None—but yours," he said, gesturing to the Klingons on screen.

"The beginning of an interstellar war," Worf said.

"From what we've been told," Dax said, "the Kinshaya are deploying forces we did not know they had, including ships of a design we previously have not seen. It doesn't seem to be all of the Typhon Pact powers—at least so far."

"The Romulans seem shocked," Picard said. "The Breen . . . who can tell? What I do know is that we have new orders."

Dax asked, "Are you listening, Sam?"

"Never left," Bowers said over an open channel.

Picard turned to face the Klingons on the viewscreen. "Under Starfleet's instructions, our two starships are to accept the Unsung's surrender."

"It is not surrender," Kahless said. *"That is not the Klingon way. But neither is striking from the darkness and fleeing. The*

*Unsung will no longer do that. They stand behind their acts.
They will hide no longer."*

Hearing the emperor's words, Picard wondered whether
Cross was the only magician the exiles had met. "Very well.
The Unsung will face Klingon judgment at the appropriate
time. We will distribute their numbers between our brigs
and disable the Phantom Wing. Then we are to leave immediately for the fronts."

"Fronts?" La Forge asked.

Picard explained, "*Enterprise* and *Aventine* are by far
the closest Starfleet vessels to two worlds currently under
attack—Narendra III and Ketorix Prime. Both, for some
reason, are stripped of their patrol ships."

"Command wants us to split up," Dax said. "It's our
choice which worlds we go toward."

"I have chosen Narendra III," Picard said. "Another
Enterprise fought until the bitter end to protect that planet.
Starfleet has given us ten minutes to transfer the Unsung—
but then we must go."

Tuvok, standing in the aft with Chen, Ardra, and Yorta,
stepped down into the command well. "Captain, what
about *Houdini* and our plan to end the Niamlar deception?"

"On hold, Commander, indefinitely," Picard said. "I
explained as much as I could to Admiral Akaar while we
were waiting for our assignments. Command feels that the
Houdini is too slow to reach Janalwa in time to be helpful. By the time you arrived and surveyed the situation,
the Kinshaya could be dug in. I agreed that we should not
lose our senior officers before what is likely to be a pitched
battle." He looked back to Ardra and her lawyer. "Starfleet
also regarded as remote the possibility that our new 'partner'
would honestly contribute anything."

"I think I'm offended," Ardra said. "But if you believe I'm

tagging along as you run off to war, you're mistaken. Give me a shuttle, so I can get away from this madhouse."

"Request denied." Picard noticed she didn't say anything about going back to prison. "Let's start those transfers." He moved toward his chair, which La Forge vacated.

Before either sat down, the engineer spoke up. "Captain." Picard looked at him. "Commander?"

"Captain, *Houdini* isn't fast enough on its own to reach Janalwa. But it could be tractored by the *Aventine*."

Tuvok stepped forward to La Forge's side. "The Borg once tractored *Voyager* through warp. *Titan* assisted the Romulans in towing the Vanguard colony—"

"I know the examples," Picard said. "*Aventine* has a slipstream drive, another matter entirely." He looked back to Dax. "Has any ship that size ever been tractored by a vessel using a slipstream drive?"

"No." Her brow furrowed. "But it could be possible. We'd have to watch the tractor beam—and the *Houdini* would have to be manned, standing by to use thrusters. "

His excitement for the idea building, La Forge stated, "We can do it, Captain."

Picard saw Šmrhová frown at tactical. "I don't get it," she said. "How can both ships go sauntering into Kinshaya space without sending up an alarm? *Houdini* has a cloaking device, not *Aventine*."

"You weren't aboard the *Enterprise* at Ventax," La Forge said. "*Houdini* has the ability to extend its cloaking field a considerable distance away."

Picard thought back. Yes, that had been one of Ardra's more impressive tricks—one of her few that had not required *Houdini*'s illusion projection systems. She had caused *Enterprise* to disappear—or seemed to, by the use of *Houdini*'s cloaking device.

"We just do it again," La Forge said. "We have *Houdini* enter Kinshaya space with its cloak shrouding *Aventine.* Then she stays with us while we get into position over Janalwa."

"Use of a cloaking device aboard a Federation vessel is a violation of the Treaty of Algeron," Picard said.

"*Houdini* is not a Federation vessel," La Forge said.

"Perhaps," Tuvok said, "we require the services of a legal expert."

All eyes turned to Yorta.

"I do criminal law," the older man said, shuffling uncomfortably under the attention. "But you needn't consult me. Not when you have one of the negotiators on the treaty here." He looked to Ezri. "Curzon Dax worked on several of the treaty drafts, if I'm not mistaken."

"Our crew shouldn't have even been using the cloaking device aboard *Houdini* when they were chasing *Blackstone*," Dax said. "It was a Federation-commandeered ship."

"But it wouldn't be in this case." Ardra stepped forward. "*Houdini* is my ship. If you want me to set foot on it, you'd better believe I'm captain. You would be my passengers." She looked to Dax. "And our cloaking of your ship would be my responsibility."

"Thin ice," Picard said. "If the Romulans learn about it and protest—" He stopped himself. "I suppose that will all depend on whether the Kinshaya have gone off without the approval of the Typhon Pact." He shook his head. "But even if we were to agree, two worlds remain in danger. I cannot defend both of them with one ship."

"*You have five,*" Valandris said.

The officers turned to face the main viewscreen. The Klingons had been silent during the discussion, but now Valandris stood. "*I do not understand all that you have discussed,*" she said. "*It was our people's desire to go to Ketorix to stand before those we offended. The Phantom Wing will go in* Aventine's *stead.*"

Picard regarded the Unsung. "This is a major undertaking. You know how you will be received."

"*If we are greeted by Klingons, we will take what comes. But if we are met by Kinshaya, we will make them regret they were ever born.*"

Beside her, Worf nodded. "*Captain, the remaining four ships are the equal to one of ours. If* Aventine *has a mission that could end the conflict altogether, the Phantom Wing could take its place.*"

Picard's eyes narrowed. "Emperor?"

Kahless spread his hands before the Unsung visible in the background. "*I vouch for these people, Picard. They are not who Cross tried to turn them into. Give them the chance to be the warriors they were meant to be.*"

Picard could not suppress an amazed smile. "I suspect there is a story behind this that will be fascinating to hear. But you know my orders: I am duty-bound to bring you in. You must understand—"

Valandris sat back down and touched a control on her armrest. "*We will do as I said, Captain Picard. Good-bye.*"

The image on the viewscreen vanished to be replaced by the sight of the four birds-of-prey. Picard watched as they disappeared under cloak, one by one.

Šmrhová asked, "Captain, orders?" After a moment, she appealed to him again. "They still have Commander Worf and Kahless. We can stop them."

He studied the darkness on screen—and a determined expression formed. "We know where they're going. With luck we can *all* reach our destinations in time."

Forty

"The next time we leave for a long mission," Sam Bowers said as the turbolift doors opened, "we should schedule an additional month just to be briefed on what's happened since we've been gone."

Stepping with her first officer into main engineering, Dax knew exactly what he meant. Days earlier, she had convened a lengthy briefing following her initial conference with Tuvok to bring her crew up to speed about the Unsung. This time it was to explain the capabilities of *Houdini* and *Aventine*'s intended role in taking it to Janalwa—

—and, *oh yes*, the small matter of the Kinshaya invasion of Klingon space. There had been some murmured objections, as she had expected, to the Unsung defending Ketorix rather than *Aventine*, but Command had quickly approved the slipstream-tow plan. It only served to reinforce that drastic measures were necessary.

She and Bowers had just gotten an update from the chancellor's office, which tried very hard to convey the impression they were still in control. Pheben was seeing a pitched battle between starships and the Kinshaya, but no landings had yet taken place. Of Narendra III, it was known that Klingon satellite defense forces were putting up a valiant fight. Nothing was known of Ketorix at all.

"The Romulans are condemning the Kinshaya and pulling their Unsung search ships out," Bowers said. "If it's a Typhon Pact attack, it makes no sense at all."

"Which is why it's worth our trying to cut the Gordian knot," she said.

The captain's presence caught the attention of the officers around an engineering table. Mikaela Leishman, *Aventine*'s chief engineer, was meeting with La Forge and Tuvok on the tractor beam problem.

"Status, Mikaela?" Dax asked. "Did I promise too much?"

"No, as it happens, slipstream towing was one of my side projects," the human woman said. "I've been looking for a chance to test some ideas out."

"Glad to deliver," Dax said. "How soon can we get under way? *Enterprise* has been gone for two hours."

"I think," La Forge said, looking up from the numbers he was rechecking, "that Commander Tuvok and I have the *Houdini* side of things nailed down. I'll be coordinating with Lieutenant Leishman's tractor beam control. Tuvok will handle the cloaking. Doctor Aggadak is on the *Houdini* with Ardra and the *Enterprise*'s engineering task force preparing for what we have planned for Janalwa."

"Sounds crowded," Dax mused. With *Enterprise* going into battle, Picard had told Šmrhová that her place was on the bridge. *Aventine*'s security chief, Lonnoc Kedair, had taken her place on *Houdini*, watching over their convict-turned-ally Ardra. "Tell Ardra her lawyer says hello from sickbay, and that he'll confer with her just as soon as he feels better. I don't think the man was expecting to head deep into hostile territory."

"You'd think in criminal law he's gone into some rough neighborhoods," Bowers said. "I'll get back to the bridge and set course, Captain."

"We'll get everyone situated and give you the word," Leishman said to Dax. She turned to the visitors. "Good luck, Commanders. I hope we didn't get a decimal point wrong."

Phantom Wing Vessel *Chu'charq*
En Route to Ketorix Prime

The Phantom Wing was in warp space again, headed for its original objective. Worf could not forget the surprised expression on his captain's face when Valandris had cut the transmission. The commander had not objected to her move when he had the chance; Captain Picard would be within his rights to consider Worf's failure an insubordinate act.

Yet Worf knew that Kahless and Valandris were correct. So often over the previous weeks, the exiles had taken him places against his will. This trip to Ketorix, he supported fully. The Unsung returning to face those they had wronged was one thing. For them to want to intercede against the Kinshaya was unexpected—and purely, absolutely Klingon. They had to be allowed to see it through.

The squadron raced, under cloak, across the Empire that the Unsung had so recently stalked with malevolent intent. Kahless was in the mess hall, speaking to the nearly four-dozen children who were aboard *Chu'charq*. They had never displayed any anxiety before the Unsung's other battles, and now they reveled in the clone's fantastic tales of ancient heroism. The exiles had only ever heard cautionary tales from their elders. Before a storyteller of Kahless's talent, young and old alike were transfixed.

Not that *Chu'charq*'s nineteen adults were all in the audience. A few were, of course; most of the others were at their stations. Worf had seen one listener depart early. He found her far forward in the darkened ready room, her legs crossed as she sat on the deck looking out the port at the streaming stars going past.

Whether she saw his reflection in the port or heard his footsteps, Worf did not know—but she spoke without turning her head. "Are all these stars part of the Empire, Worf?"

"Here, yes," he said as he stepped farther into the room. "Not all have worlds. But Klingons count them as part of their dominion, their birthright."

"I had no birthright," she said, still spellbound. "We had nebulae in the sky over Thane, and stars. But nobody told us they could belong to us." He took a seat nearby, and she looked back at him. "I lived in a crater on a small world, Worf—secluded and far from anywhere. Those who ruled my people did their best to strip us of all pride, to make us feel small."

Worf simply listened.

"Yet even before the fake Kruge arrived," she said, "my friends and I tried to make something ours. Through the hunt, we lived a larger life. I was Valandris, before I had a name. And if I could have hunted stars for my own, I would have."

"You knew you were a Klingon," Worf said softly. "No matter what they did to you. No matter what your ancestors did. You did not need Kruge to tell you this—nor me, nor even Kahless." He looked keenly at her in the starlight. "You have a birthright, Valandris. You all did."

She turned away, shaking her head. "It all seems so big. Hearing your Picard talk of empires and pacts—I'm not sure any of us are ready for your world." She chuckled. "Presuming anyone lets us in."

"And presuming we live through tomorrow. It will sort itself out."

Brought back to immediate concerns, Valandris stood and turned. "We have a problem," she said, pacing the room. "I received a hail. The child—Harch and Weltern's son—has taken ill."

Worf raised an eyebrow. "What is wrong?"

"Infantile *tharkak'ra*," she said. "It is not life threatening, but it requires full-time care, and we cannot spare either Harch or Weltern from *Krencha*."

"I could transport over so that one of them could care for the child," Worf said.

"You could, but you would be better aboard *Cob'lat*," she said. She took a seat across from him. "They are still having technical problems that require more than a year's experience and a tutorial on a padd."

"I can do this."

"I have suggested to Weltern that they beam the boy aboard *Chu'charq* at our next stop," Valandris said. "Sarken and her friends can care for him better than his parents can."

"That makes sense."

"I would like Kahless aboard *Klongat*."

Worf frowned. "He does not have experience operating one of these vessels." *Though he has seen plenty of the inside of one*, Worf thought.

"*Klongat*'s crew is the youngest. Beroc and Bardoc, the brothers . . . they know what they are doing, but it would be better to have his leadership."

"I cannot see Kahless denying you. *You* are a true leader, Valandris."

"I am mildly amused that you think so, especially given the number of times I have tried to kill you." She allowed a smile. "What kind of person was your mate?"

"Alexander's mother was highly intelligent—much better with diplomacy than I have ever been. He takes that side of his character from her, I think." He looked toward the port as he recalled Jadzia. "There was another. She was a great warrior, and wise. They are both dead."

"You will not take another mate?"

"I feel my life is full," he said, looking back at her, "for now."

"I know exactly what you mean." She rose and headed for the door. "Get some sleep, Worf, son of Mogh. For soon we fight."

Forty-one

Picard's and Crusher's duty shifts usually coincided; scheduling was one of the perks of command. But Ardra's arrival had put Picard out of synch with his wife. Therefore, their quarters were empty when he returned for a couple of hours' rest before the battle that awaited the *Enterprise* at Narendra III. When he woke, Picard found she had left a message asking him to join her in sickbay.

"I don't have much time," Picard said, somewhat refreshed as he entered her office. "Narendra III looms."

"I know," Crusher said. "I think you'll find this worth your time." She led him out to her lab, where several screens displayed information above a table that included various sealed petri dishes. The first several were marked CABEUS.

"If you are going to say that you found that Commander Worf was on Cabeus," he teased her, "I can tell you . . ."

She smiled. "Yes, we even heard that down here in sickbay. This is about something else." She handed him a petri dish filled with powder.

"What am I looking at?" he asked.

"I studied the deposits of illium-629," Crusher said. "Klingon birds-of-prey have four crystals mounted outside the warp core, which are held in place by control arms. When they begin to decrystallize, as must have happened, the illium collects in the basin of an external plug cap, safely outside the reactor."

He examined the dish. "That's what the Unsung dumped in the cave."

"Yes—but not just that. I found microscopic remnants of keratin in the illium. It came from Klingon fingernails. I suspect the plug cap must have been emptied by someone before, who manually scraped the inside to clean it." She brought up an image of a DNA chain on one screen. "Fingernail cells aren't the best quality for sequencing, but they're tough, and they last."

"These seem to have done so," Picard said as he read. "This sample appears to be at least five years old."

"From the previous cleaning, I suppose. The same person seems to have been maintaining all the ships—we found traces in all four deposits."

"Five years," Picard mused. "I don't think it could have come from any of the Unsung. That's before they had the ships. And they seemed fearful of the byproduct. I doubt they would have scraped the caps with their bare hands."

"Here's what else is special." Crusher handed him another dish.

He didn't need any help with this one. "Hair."

"This is from the Mount Qel'pec debris on Gamaral."

"The hangar where the Phantom Wing was built?" *Enterprise*'s engineers had located the remnants of construction equipment, but little else. "Are you telling me this follicle survived a hundred years?" Picard knew from his archaeology training that mummies had been found with hair, but that was under conditions where specific preservative steps had been taken.

"Microbes tend to like keratin less," Crusher said, "and in the collapsed hangar, there was no exposure to soil—only stone. We found this sandwiched between two slabs with no exposure to the air." She changed the display on a second screen. It depicted a broken helical chain of DNA. "Klingon hair tends to be made of stern stuff."

Like the rest of them, Picard thought. "It's only a fragment."

"But enough to confirm a 99.99 percent match with the Cabeus sample. The Klingon woman—I was able to determine that much—who left this hair in the hangar a century ago was aboard the Phantom Wing ships again five years ago." Crusher raised her finger. "And that's not all." A touch of the interface brought up an identical DNA sequence on the third screen—as well as the image of an elderly Klingon female. One Picard had seen before.

"Heghtar! Ardra and Shift's companion from Thionoga."

"Emil Yorta provided the prison's dossiers."

Picard's eyes narrowed. "I'm assuming Heghtar isn't her name. Do the Klingons have any information on her?"

"The Empire has a very small biometric database. Starfleet has some data on recent Klingon travelers; none appear to be related. But I haven't even gotten to the best part yet."

She led him into the hallway outside the isolation ward—where through the window, Picard could see gowned technicians examining a padd. "The Unsung's," he said. "The one with the woman's voice."

"That's right. Fingerprints on the device and the voiceprint match what was in Thionoga's records. Whoever Heghtar is, she is the missing link between when the Phantom Wing was built and getting them to the exiles on Thane."

Picard smiled as he considered the connections. "And she is also the connection with Shift and the illusionists."

"We have evidence leading to this woman. Means and opportunity. We just need motive. And her, of course."

The captain assumed she wasn't with the Unsung now; Worf would have said if she was. But it was more to go on than they'd had before. He was delighted, enough so that for the moment the weight of the impending battle lifted.

He stepped closer to Beverly and whispered, "Narendra nears. I have a Klingon planet to save."

"Jean-Luc, you say the sweetest things."

Not bothering to check on who was around, Picard kissed his wife. Then he chuckled and looked at her. "Beverly, are you telling me that we've chased these birds-of-prey and that damn illusion ship all across the Klingon Empire—and that you may have figured it all out with a hair, a fingernail, and a padd?"

Smiling gently, Crusher adjusted his uniform. "Good luck against the Kinshaya. I know you'll keep us safe. You always do."

Kinshaya Battlesphere *Fervent-One* Over Ketorix Prime

"*—if you are Klingon, take to the skies in whatever you have. Freighters. Scout ships. Anything with an engine and weapons. Rise to the challenge, and defend our valiant house in this, our greatest hour . . .*"

"*They are an hour away from being exterminated,*" one of Thot Roje's Breen companions said as the message concluded.

The image of Korgh, standing defiantly before his offensive Kruge statue and calling his people to action, had set off no end of furious stomping and wailing from the Kinshaya in the command pits. Roje saw it for what it was: a sign of weakness, a plea for help. Anyone could make a hopeless defense sound heroic—but in the end, it would still be hopeless.

Roje looked ahead to see the battle raging outside. Some Klingons had apparently already followed the orders of their corrupt excuse for a lord: a ragtag wave of construction vehicles, personnel shuttles, and cargo haulers were in orbit, firing their pathetic weapons. The disruptor fire either missed the black orbs altogether or glanced harmlessly off their shields.

"Wipe them out," Bishop Labarya declared, sparing Roje a flowery festival of descriptors for a change. *Fervent-One's* gunners did as commanded, wreaking fiery carnage against the volunteer flotilla.

"*Fervent-Five has located a power plant outside the perimeter of the defensive shield,*" Roje's lieutenant said.

"Even Klingons are not stupid enough to power a shield with an unprotected source," Roje said.

"*No, but now that the area has crossed the terminator into night, sensor readings suggest it is likely on the same grid. If it can be destroyed, there will be a momentary drop in power output in the industrial compound as the system compensates.*"

"We will concentrate our fire on the shield at that moment." Roje nodded with satisfaction. He was not a military leader in the sense the Klingons had them; his command was limited to intelligence and special operations. But the Battle of Ketorix Prime was just a part of one of the largest intelligence operations in recent Breen history, and Roje thought that his generalship had been above military standards.

He turned to the bishop. "Alert your shock troops. They transport to the surface on my command. Leave nothing alive."

Forty-two

Tuvok's career had taken him into security and counter-espionage, but his interest in science, his original specialty aboard *Excelsior*, had never waned. Assisting La Forge with the complicated computations required to help *Houdini* keep in *Aventine*'s slipstream without shearing apart had been stimulating. As a prototype, *Aventine* was able to perform many different missions while simultaneously exploring scientific questions. It reminded Tuvok of his experiences helping to design the *Delta Flyer* while aboard *Voyager*.

Slipstream travel was faster than standard warp and looked different; following along in *Aventine*'s wake made the starship appear to be flying directly into a blazing sun. He and his fellow Starfleet officers had focused on the readings on their screens, making sure *Houdini* didn't get out of line.

Tuvok passed into the illusion control center, where Ardra sat in a broad-backed chair, appearing to hold court for Doctor Aggadak, T'Ryssa Chen, some of *Enterprise*'s engineers, and a bemused Lonnoc Kedair. The chair, he knew, had come from her quarters above. However, he did not know where she had gotten her new rose-colored gown. Tuvok thought she looked like a character from a playing card. Her hair was bound up high, forming a natural crown.

She noticed him. "I have a bone to pick with you, Commander. My ship is in considerable disarray."

"It has been in storage for many years," Tuvok said, "kept by Doctor Aggadak."

"She has done well," Ardra said, nodding to the Nausicaan. "It's you Starfleet people who've been living aboard for the past few days. You straighten things that should be crooked, and disturb things that should be straight."

"We required a working starship. It could not be left as a shrine."

Ardra waved her hand dismissively. "I knew you wouldn't understand. Jilaan always said, 'Never let anyone backstage.'"

"What can you tell us about Jilaan?" Tuvok asked. "Your circle is named for her. Why does she merit such reverence?"

Ardra looked up as she spoke. "She was the epitome of class. She was Napean—they're empathic, you know. She took pride in making the people she fooled feel good about it."

"She intended to rob the Kinshaya," Kedair said. "I've read the report. That's class?"

"Tosh." Ardra's nose pinched as she regarded the Takaran security chief. "She was taking part in a fair transaction. The Episcopate was running a business, living off the labors of their people, selling spiritual experiences for a tithe. Jilaan and the crew of the *Zamloch* gave them an experience like they'd never had before."

"One they never asked for," Tuvok countered.

"Oh, my Vulcan friend, I don't doubt that they profited from it." Ardra smirked. "Their kind always finds a way."

Consulting her padd, Chen nodded. "According to the records from the time, donations to the Episcopate spiked fivefold following the visit of 'Niamlar.' Pontifex Urawak used the possibility that Niamlar might return as a way to drum up contributions."

"You see?" Ardra said. "Everyone was happy."

"Not the people who gave the money," Kedair said.

"Nonsense. If it wasn't Niamlar there would have been another reason."

Tuvok got to the question he had wanted to ask. "You said Jilaan was Napean. Cross was Betazoid. You are not human, yet the names of your ships recall entertainers from Earth's history. What is the connection?"

"To honor the first Illusionist Magnus, who started the Circle long before Jilaan." Ardra looked at Chen, explaining, "Humans had a time when your imaginations were beyond your technical means. You compensated by developing technologies to create illusions—almost to the exclusion of advancing science! It was a suitable analogy for what we do. Some of our earliest practitioners were Xyrillians, but we all use the human motifs."

Tuvok nodded, quietly satisfied that she had given him a hint to the origin of the technology. Xyrillian holo-chambers predated the Federation's. He wanted to learn more, but the mission came first. "We have successfully entered slipstream, Doctor Aggadak. Are you prepared to generate Ardra's illusion?"

"It'll be a pleasure." Aggadak's gruff persona had melted in the presence of the captain of her favorite relic starship. "Ardra told me it would require extra data processing, so I had Lieutenant Leishman tuck new data cores into one of the offices." She respectfully told Ardra, "We didn't move anything."

"I'm not concerned. *Houdini*'s a much newer vessel than *Blackstone* if that's what we're facing. What you've installed should be enough." Ardra smiled primly and hopped from her chair. "That's that."

Kedair was startled by her sudden move. "Where are you going?"

"To rest. It will be darling to be back in my own bed."

"Wait," Chen said. "Don't you have to program your illusion?"

Ardra pointed to her head. "It's all right here." She disappeared up the steps, leaving a confused Starfleet crew behind her.

Kedair looked to Tuvok. "Sir, do you think she's being straight with us?"

"If she is not, we will be forced to use one of the programs in the library." The Vulcan shook his head. Fek'lhr, the Klingon devil, was one of the characters in the system, but *Houdini* had made him appear as a devil already once and he had no interest in masquerading again. Tuvok was equally certain it would not go over well with the Kinshaya.

U.S.S. ENTERPRISE
APPROACHING NARENDRA III

Forty-two years ago, the *U.S.S. Enterprise*-C under Captain Rachel Garrett had come to the aid of the Klingon colony at Narendra III. Four Romulan warbirds launched a sneak attack on the blue-green world. The outpost fell, and Garrett's ship was destroyed—but not before the *Enterprise* put in a valorous effort.

That Pyrrhic victory had become a historic moment for the Federation's relationship with the Klingon Empire. Had it not been for the *Enterprise*-C's honorable sacrifice impressing the Klingons, many believed the Federation might eventually have slid into war with the Empire. Picard was sure Captain Garrett's feat would be one of the key moments when Martok and Riker presented their defense of the special relationship at the *chavmajta*—presuming that event ever happened.

Four attacking ships were again above Narendra III. The planet, resettled and repopulated, was home to millions. Their orbital defenders had just given their last when the *Enterprise*-E came screaming out of warp.

"They haven't started planetary bombardment," Šmrhová said as she eyed the four colossal orbs, drawing closer to the planet through the clouds of debris that had once been the orbital defense stations. Antispacecraft disruptor blasts, appearing as minuscule red needles at this range, lanced upward from the surface. "I'm not detecting any sensor sweeps in our direction."

"Let's get their attention," Picard said. "Photon torpedoes, dispersal pattern sierra." He pounded his fist gently on his armrest. "This one's for Rachel Garrett and *Enterprise*."

Forty-three

"Where's Ardra?" Commander La Forge said as he entered the illusion control center. "We're nearly to Janalwa. We threw our cloak over *Aventine* as soon as we entered Kinshayan space—and we're about to drop out of slipstream."

Kedair rolled her eyes. She gestured to the spiral staircase. "She went to change clothes again."

La Forge checked the truthcrafter stations. Everyone—including Corinne Clipet, who had been along since *Houdini*'s first flight from Starbase 24 to study the ship's workings—was seated and waiting for something, anything, to do.

La Forge's combadge activated. *"Aventine* to *Houdini,"* Dax said. *"Five minutes to slipstream exit. You ready?"*

"Stand by, *Aventine,"* La Forge said. He gave an imploring look to Tuvok, who stood next to the staircase.

Taking the railing in hand, the Vulcan looked upward. "Ardra, your presence is required."

Nothing.

The two commanders looked around the room—and fixed their eyes on Chen, who was up and moving. "Excuse me, sirs." Chen set foot on the bottom step and called, "Ten seconds to curtain!"

La Forge heard rustling above, and then saw black heels and a swirl of skirts as Ardra descended. Her hair was still up as before, but she was wearing yet another outfit, presumably from her own stash. Reaching the deck, she adjusted the hem of her dress. "Sorry. I was seeing what still fit." She glanced at La Forge and winked. "It's like I never went away."

"Ardra, we're running out of time," he said. "You were supposed to come up with an illusion to counter *Blackstone*."

"What, that?" she asked idly as she checked her nails. "I have that taken care of."

Tuvok raised an eyebrow at La Forge, and then asked, "Is there a database of illusions aboard we haven't been able to find?"

"Oh, no." Ardra glanced back at the cylindrical imaging chamber, open since La Forge, Tuvok, and Aggadak discovered it. "You shouldn't even have found as much as you did. I have everything upstairs."

"Up in your bedroom?" La Forge asked.

"No, my sweet."

Tuvok felt his control slipping. Calmly he asked, "Do you have mental powers we are unaware of? An ability to interface with computers?"

She smiled and touched his sleeve. "And they say Vulcans don't have imaginations."

"Who says that?" Chen asked.

"I do." Ardra sighed. "Hold on," she said, walking to the counter next to where Kedair was standing. "This'll be just a second."

"Three minutes!" called Aggadak from the bridge.

"You don't hurry an artist." Ardra looked at her hands, leaned over, and plunged her fingers into her hair. Working the black follicles, she freed a surprisingly long and extremely thin ribbon that had been keeping her hair up.

As La Forge approached the counter, he focused on the decoration, which seemed to get longer and longer as she worked her hands through it. After a moment, he began to perceive that it was not one long ribbon at all, but many lengths, all of different colors and tenuously connected.

La Forge reached for one. At his touch, it detached from the others.

"Not that one," Ardra said. She took it back and went searching for another. Finally, she lifted up a single shimmering ribbon and brought it before her eyes, just centimeters away. "Aha! *The Mystical Manifestations of Jilaan before the Kinshaya, 2293*," she said reverently. "I know it by heart."

"A ribbon?" Kedair asked.

"It's a bookmark," Ardra said, "for a book your people never found because I had the sense to hide my copies of the *Annals* where even *you* couldn't find them." She passed the shining band to La Forge. "Here."

"Microfilaments," he said, staring at it. "There's data on here."

"Mmm," Ardra answered. She took the many other ribbons, rubbed them together in her hands quickly—and whether through sleight of hand or technology, they reformed into a single strand. She began putting her hair up again with it. "It was the one thing they let me keep at Thionoga. I guess they thought it was too small for me to harm anyone with, including myself. It came in handy when I had projection equipment smuggled in for my escape attempts."

Tuvok's eyes narrowed as he worked it out. "The character Jilaan created is on that ribbon?"

"Don't just spoil it for everyone," she replied. She gestured to La Forge. "Go. In the imaging chamber, feed that into the slot."

La Forge started to move. Then he looked back. "Which slot?"

Ardra looked at the overhead, disgusted. "The one marked MEMORY'S MYSTIC BAND."

When Tuvok looked puzzled, Chen spoke up. "*Alice's Adventures in Wonderland*," she said, smiling. "*That* one, I read."

Inside the chamber, La Forge inserted the end of the filament inside the reader, which hungrily gobbled the rest of it from him. A gong sounded from somewhere—and outside in the control center, displays over the stations suddenly came alive.

Ardra looked around with satisfaction. "My compliments to the doctor. Everything still works. It's just the rest of you that leave coffee mugs lying around." She straightened her refixed hair. "Well, I'm off," she said, starting to walk.

"Wait a minute," Kedair said, barring her exit. "Where are you going?"

"Why, to the transporter room. You heard them, Lieutenant. It's showtime."

Kedair glared at Ardra's hair. The ribbon, somewhere in there, could no longer be seen. "I know about all your escape attempts. I'm not going to have to worry about you running off down there, am I?"

"Another time, perhaps. But I don't happen to know anyone in Kinshaya space," Ardra said. "Besides, I have a promise from Jean-Luc Picard. He is many things—but he also happens to be astoundingly, cloyingly, painfully honest. His word's magic, in my book."

"You won't be alone in any event," La Forge said.

"What do you mean?" Ardra asked, startled.

"Our supporting cast calls for a diplomat," Tuvok said. "And we have someone in mind for the role."

U.S.S. Titan
PHEBEN SYSTEM

"*Enterprise* has arrived at Narendra III and has engaged," Kyzak announced from ops. "Four Kinshaya battlespheres."

"What, did they get a special rate on these things?" Vale asked. "I'd wish him luck, but we're dealing with four of our own."

"He's too busy to listen," Riker said as he studied the system map. He was weary. *Titan* had spent several hours engaged against the Kinshaya without help from *Gur'rok*, which was following its own strategy. Neither had done significant damage to the black spheres, in part because it had been impossible to focus on just one.

The same dynamic had prevented the Kinshaya from making landings. Pheben III was a farmworld; Pheben IV, a processing center for many of the ores of the region. Pheben V was the homeworld of the multitentacled Pheben species, one of the many conquered peoples who labored for the Empire. The fact that the system contained several planets that were not only habitable but also productive had no doubt placed it high on the list of Kinshaya targets. It had also bought the residents of each planet time, because of how the Kinshaya fought.

Whoever was commanding the Holy Order's squadron seemed unwilling to send a single battlesphere off on its own, lest it find itself double-teamed by *Gur'rok* and *Titan*. The fact that he and Kersh had not spoken was thankfully unknown to the Kinshaya. The battlespheres would pair off and head for Pheben III and IV, or III and V, or IV and V—allowing *Titan* to harry one group and *Gur'rok* to chase the other. That required no cooperation. It had resulted in an inconclusive engagement that stretched on, with no end in sight.

"It's not a battle," Sarai said. "It's a logic problem."

"Wish we had Tuvok here." Riker instantly realized what he'd said. The admiral caught a backward glance from the first officer in the next moment. Sarai had been installed in the post over Tuvok. Sarai, Tuvok, Troi, Ra-Havreii: four commanders was a lot of brass even for an admiral's flag-ship.

"New contact," Keru said.

"Friend or foe?" Vale asked.

"You tell me, Captain. It's Breen."

Riker blinked. "There should be a Klingon escort with it."

Keru shook his head. "Negative, Admiral. Breen warship is flying solo."

"The Breen ship seems to be observing," Sarai said. "Taking stock."

"Hail it," Vale ordered. Then she looked back at Riker. "Should I ask, 'Whose side are you on?' "

Kyzak said, "I wouldn't worry about it, Captain. They're not responding."

Typical, Riker thought.

Titan banked hard as two of the Kinshaya battlespheres veered off together, heading toward Pheben IV. Vale ordered the starship to follow.

"Aspect change on the Breen," Keru announced. The Breen vessel could be seen up close, on the main viewscreen, darting into *Titan*'s path and slowing its progress against the Kinshaya.

"What do they think they're doing?" Vale asked. "Weapons?"

"No, and shields are not up," Keru said. "They just won't get out of the way." The warship continued to weave back and forth, forcing *Titan* farther and farther from its optimal pursuit path.

"Passive assistance," Riker said. "They've picked a side without firing a shot. Captain, try to get past the Breen without opening another front."

Forty-four

Few things Korgh had experienced were eerier than existence beneath an energy shield under bombardment from space. Disruptor blasts struck with mighty flashes that coruscated across and along the lines of the invisible protective field—making for the most peculiar effects when observed by Korgh looking through the skylight in the atrium. No nocturnal weather event on Ketorix had ever looked as strange—or frightening.

Reports had placed Kinshaya assault forces already on the ground outside the defensive energy dome. Tragg had made his office the command center for the ground troops rushing to engage the enemy. Korgh had opened one after another of the offices he'd intended for his heirs so that other warriors could use the computers inside to check on the whereabouts of Tengor and the Klingon Defense Force. When another warrior asked him to unlock J'borr's office—Odrok's former Unsung command center—Korgh had redirected him to the next office in line. It had been a bitter reminder, and it left an acid taste in his mouth.

All that remained for Korgh was to pace circuits of the torch-lit atrium, *mek'leth* in hand, alternating glances between the family's trophies and the intermittent flashes from above. He had maintained this place for fifty years, all the while envying and hating those who held the house. He had not had time to have all the portraits of Kruge's feckless heirs removed. Every flash of light from above drew his eyes to another, standing in their ridiculous heroic poses. *Udakh. J'borr. A'chav. Kiv'ota.* Fools, all—every one, murdered by Korgh and his minions. With each blast, they seemed to taunt him.

You do not belong, they said. *Kruge never adopted you. He took the Phantom Wing from Gamaral without telling you. You were never his son!*

Korgh snarled in anger—a sound that startled the four warriors standing guard in the spooky atrium. The lord turned away from the walls and moved toward the center of the atrium, beneath the statue of Kruge battling the Kinshaya. Clutching his *mek'leth* hard, he looked up at Kruge's graven face, a visage he trusted and knew. Knew well enough to engineer the perfect impersonation of the commander, for his own ends. Disruptor-lightning flashed again and again beyond the skylights, backlighting the head of Kruge's statue and giving the icon's face an otherworldly grimace.

The blasts above came ever faster. Korgh could not take his eyes off Kruge's face—and in his ringing ears the old man heard the voice of the commander he once knew, saying words that chilled him to the bone:

You used my face and name!

You are a disappointment, without honor!

You were never my son. And you are no Klingon!

Korgh went to one knee, shut his eyes tightly, and screamed, "No!"

Outside, another flash: the biggest yet, a light so bright he saw it through his eyelids. Korgh felt the shockwave pummeling downward, as if a hammer had struck the whole complex. He heard the crash of glass and the pained yells of warriors.

The sound still reverberated through his skull when

Korgh opened his eyes and saw what had happened. The skylights had blown out, their shards injuring all the warriors and blinding one; only Korgh's position beneath Kruge and the Kinshaya statue had protected him. Portions of the ceiling between the panes had given way, raining down debris. Through the gaping hole, he saw directly into Ketorix's night sky—where large orbs of death could be seen descending.

So horrid was the scene above that Korgh barely noticed Tragg arriving. "Father," his youngest said, "the Kinshaya have destroyed the shield over the compound!"

"I know," Korgh said, gripping his *mek'leth* and rising. The bombardments had stopped in the immediate area, and he knew why. His face looked grim in the torchlight. "Prepare."

KINSHAYA BATTLESPHERE *FERVENT-ONE*
OVER KETORIX PRIME

"*Fervent-Three*, descend. *Fervent-Four*, descend."

All was going exactly as planned. The Kinshaya were far from the best shock troops Thot Roje could imagine; they were an undisciplined lot. Ykredna's partisans were a mixture of regular military and religious fanatics, and for every serious-looking fighter, there were two decorated as if on parade.

The armor the Kinshaya wore was formidable, and he could easily imagine them stampeding in the streets below, disruptors blazing as they ran down hapless Klingons. Yet during his inspection of Labarya's troops, Roje had seen many who had spent more time on painting their armor than on understanding how to hold their weapons.

The best had already beamed down and were closing in, now that the energy shield was defunct. They would form a perimeter, trapping the Klingons as the battlespheres descended over the cityscape, becoming platforms dealing death. Then they would beam down the remainder of their troops as an occupation force.

"Fervent-Three *reports the Kruge family's industrial head-quarters is in visual range,"* his lieutenant said.

Roje repeated it to Labarya, who responded, "Do not destroy the devil's home. It must be a spoil, to be taken by our forces and sanctified by his blood."

"Very well," Roje replied. "Pass it on to the ground assault teams."

He looked quickly at his displays reporting the situation at other locations. Kruge's home guard fleet had yet to return—a wonder, Shift was—and only a few Klingon Defense Force ships had reached other worlds. But the picture was not entirely positive. *Enterprise* had somehow lucked onto the assault on Narendra III and was hotly contesting the planet—while several Breen warships had been forced to abandon their pretense of searching for the Unsung in order to interfere with the defenders at Pheben and elsewhere. The domo had strictly forbidden Breen forces from openly engaging with the Klingons and their Federation ally, but they were in it now.

Within the hour, Roje estimated Ketorix Prime would be wrapped up. The Breen Confederacy would have, through the Kinshaya, a secure foothold in what had been Klingon territory. "There's nothing else to do up here," he declared. "Prepare to descend on my—"

"Proximity alert!" his lieutenant said. *"A bird-of-prey decloaking!"*

Roje's snout wrinkled inside his helmet. This wasn't completely unexpected; there had to be some Klingon Defense Force ships close to the sector when the warning went out. Before he could order the ship targeted, *Fervent-One* received a hail.

Puzzling.

"Put it up," he commanded, "but don't let them see the bridge."

His lieutenant cast the image onto one of the towering polygonal panels that doubled as a stained-glass pane when not in use. It was a Klingon woman, surrounded by others of her kind. *"I am Valandris,"* she declared. *"I announce myself as your enemy."*

Kinshaya in the operations pits howled to see her. *"Another bird-of-prey decloaking off to port!"* Roje heard.

There was another hail—and the Breen controller sent the image to an adjacent pane. A Klingon male and female spoke. *"We are Harch and Weltern of the Unsung—descendants of the discommendated of Gamaral. We announce ourselves as your enemy."*

The Unsung? Roje couldn't fathom the development—and was still more startled when a third bird-of-prey decloaked to starboard.

This hail brought more Klingons on screen—including, at center, one he knew. *"I am Worf, son of Mogh, of Starfleet on the Unsung ship* Cob'lat." A slight grin crossed his face. *"You already know what I am."*

The announcement of a fourth bird-of-prey, to *Fervent-One*'s rear, found Roje numb with confusion—which only deepened when he saw the figure at the center of the fourth group. It was the Klingon emperor, the sight of whom sent the Kinshaya, already rattled, into paroxysms. Shift had told Roje that Cross had kept the alcoholic wretch alive, but under no circumstances would he have ever predicted that

Kahless—or Worf for that matter—could make common cause with the exiles.

Yet there they were. Together—and surrounding *Fervent-One.*

"These people's forebears sought to preserve the holdings of Commander Kruge," Kahless said, showing his teeth. *"Their children have come here to complete their mission. And you have come here to die!"*

Forty-five

Niamlar sat in silvery repose as Kinshaya worshippers filed past, paying their respects. Many were allies of Ykredna's old order, most of them aged; the young had gone off to fight. Another group comprised members of the state bureaucracy, which the new Pontifex wanted to infuse with as much fear of the church as possible. Ykredna led both bodies now, and as long as Shift's god of war was at her back, her political power was absolute.

Shift had been informed that the Devotionalists were in flight, hunted by the newly reconstituted Inquisitors. A few had gotten in long enough to get a look at her, but as far as the authorities knew, none had shared what they'd seen. The Breen expected that word would eventually go beyond Janalwa about the returned god, but by that time the military operation would be successfully concluded. She might be able to play the role indefinitely—

—which, Shift was beginning to realize, was a mixed blessing. The continuous procession of prayers, requests, and confessions of the Kinshaya increasingly made her long to be back aboard the *Blackstone*. Not one interesting individual had come to see her since the battle began. Shift had not tired of godhood; rather, she had begun to hope for a better class of worshippers.

But she had done her job, commanding all who came before her to commit their hearts, resources, and children to the war against the Klingons and to Niamlar's chosen sentinels, the Breen. While the Episcopate's taboo against broadcasting images of their gods meant that she had to work by word of mouth, that had suited the Confederacy's plans. The domo had not wanted to show too much to the galaxy and certainly did not want the Breen's connection known. Shift understood; Korgh, for his own reasons, had been careful not to show the fake Kruge in the Unsung's proclamation. Sometimes it was better to keep things mysterious.

Ykredna was in the middle of introducing some sports figure of no consequence when the Pontifex suddenly screeched. Snapped to attention, Shift saw the glowing effect of three bipedal individuals being transported into this haven for the four-legged.

The three wore Starfleet uniforms. One, petite with short dark hair and the freckling of a Trill, was flanked on one side by a taller woman with longer black hair. Shift did not recognize either of them, but she remembered the male Vulcan from her near-capture aboard *Ark of G'boj*. He held a phaser, as did the taller woman; both appeared to be acting as guards for the Trill, who stepped forward.

"Intruders," Ykredna yelled. "Infidels! How dare you enter this place?"

"Sorry to barge in like this," the Trill announced as the Kinshaya worshippers scuttled behind a concerned line of guards. "I'm Ezri Dax, captain of the *Starship Aventine*. This is Commander Tuvok, tactical officer from *Titan*—and Lieutenant T'Ryssa Chen from the *Enterprise*. A lot to remember, but in Starfleet, we try to get everyone involved."

Yeffir, still chained to a pillar, asked, "Chen, my friend, is it truly you?"

"It is, Your Holiness," Chen said. She eyed the guards. "I'll be with you as soon as I can."

"*She* is not Pontifex," Ykredna declared. "*You* should not be here! This is a holy place!"

Ezri Dax stepped up to Niamlar. "I saw a temple just like this on Yongolor. I don't expect you'd remember that." She smiled. "I've changed since then."

The Trill gazed up at Shift's illusory character. "But *you* certainly haven't changed." She shook her head in admiration. "Niamlar, Niamlar. Just like Curzon saw. Only your message this time was different. We heard you. You've been sending the Kinshaya off to war."

Shift remembered the name Curzon from the *Annals* and Jilaan's illusion, but could not recall the specifics. "*You violate my sanctum*," Shift said. "*Begone, vermin, lest I cast you into the abyss.*"

Dax looked around. "I don't see any abyss."

"I think our giant friend is saying this place isn't big enough for the two of you," Chen said.

Tuvok looked up and around. "The dimensions of this room appear adequate." He gestured to the opposite side of the rotunda, where a sizable clearing had opened where worshippers had been. "In fact, I calculate that the area is large enough for two beings of Niamlar's dimensions."

"Really?" Dax said, looking at the space. With an impish grin, she turned back to face Shift. "I'll tell you what. Let's find out." She clapped her hands together. "*Abracadabra!*"

Light and sound erupted from the open space. Flames blossomed from the marbled floor, generating a mini–mushroom cloud that licked the ceiling above. Electricity arced back and forth across the billowing formation—which then seemed to come alive, releasing a horrific scream from a mouth that did not exist. And then it did, as the features of a colossal being took shape.

A being that looked just like Shift's Niamlar character.

Well, maybe not *just* like, Shift realized as she watched the monstrosity stomp around, beating its wings. This Niamlar had more definition, more detail than her illusion did—and for a moment, Shift wondered if she had offended the real god.

And then she remembered that was crazy. "*Identify yourself,*" Shift demanded.

"*I am Niamlar,*" the new dragon replied. "*Niamlar as she was meant to be seen, Niamlar as she was meant to be portrayed.*"

Portrayed? Shift looked around to see that the Kinshaya who had not fled had dropped to the floor at the sound of the new Niamlar's voice. A voice that sounded far more ethereal, far more otherworldly than Shift's. Even Ykredna had prostrated herself.

The visiting giant swished her tail around. "*Yes, you see the Great Niamlar, one of the greatest creations of Jilaan, she who worked miracles with molecules, who took light and gave it form.*"

Jilaan? Shift gulped. She wanted to contact *Blackstone* and the truthcrafters, to find out what was going on—but that wasn't an option. "*I know this name Jilaan,*" her character said cautiously. "*She was mortal, and is gone.*"

"*Her works live on,*" the other Niamlar said. "*You should know. You're one of them.*"

Shift leered with suspicion—an expression, she knew, that must look odd coming from her giant doppelgänger. If this was a trick by Gaw, it surely wasn't funny—but she couldn't imagine that it was. *Blackstone*'s processors were straining just to make one Niamlar seem material. Two dragons were quite beyond its capacities.

"*You speak nonsense,*" Shift finally said. "*My children, I created this shadow-self to teach you not to trust those who would mislead you.*"

"That's not going to work," Dax shouted, which she needed to do in this conversation between titans. "Why don't you tell them the truth?"

Shift froze. She considered triggering her transporter recall and vanishing back to the *Blackstone*—but she was terrified of what the interlopers would say, and how it might impact her scheme. She was going to have to ride this out—and hope that someone in orbit had noticed what was going on. Even a god could use guidance from above.

BLACKSTONE

ORBITING JANALWA

Gaw took his glasses off and stared at his screen, not believing what he was seeing. He could hear a low buzz from his fellow truthcrafters—the ones who had knuckled under to the Breen's demands.

The only people in the illusion control center who hadn't yet noticed what was going on below were the Breen guards responsible for keeping an eye on the technicians. In what Gaw knew to be the way of guards, they had tuned out the peculiar things they'd seen on the truthcrafters' screens. The plan belonged to Shift and Thot Roje, and one more dragon appearing made little difference to them.

What the other Niamlar had said, however, had caught Gaw's interest. His and that of his headset-wearing colleagues.

Jilaan.

Seeing Chot Dayn enter—he only recognized the Breen

because none of the other armored creatures carried themselves with such haughtiness—Gaw issued a command that moved the angle from the sensor feed on all his colleagues' screens upward, taking the Starfleet officers out of view. Dayn appeared behind him and spoke in words that Gaw could understand. *"Why are there two Niamlars on screen?"*

"Shift wanted to do a trick to impress the rubes. It's a simple mirror-image routine with a randomizer on the limb movements. It's pretty technical."

Dayn lingered for a moment—but then another Breen entered from the bridge, letting loose with a series of squawks. For a moment, Gaw assumed that the people up front had somehow learned about what was going on. When Chot Dayn turned purposefully away, Gaw asked, "Going so soon?"

"Spare me your babble. I have a war to check on."

He was checking on it in a hurry, the Ferengi noted; the Breen was back on the bridge in seconds. Something must have happened, but the Breen hadn't realized something was going on down on Janalwa.

Gaw looked to his companions and put his finger to his lips. *Let's just see where this goes . . .*

Forty-six

"**F**ire all weapons!"

Had anyone told Valandris just weeks before that she would be orbiting the Kruge family compound, she would have assumed that she was the aggressor, going to reclaim the headquarters for her Fallen Lord. Instead, she was assaulting a massive Kinshaya battlesphere—one of two still in orbit, protecting the four descending to the factory center.

Valandris had insisted that they not attack while cloaked, a decision that Kahless and Worf endorsed in spite of the disadvantage. But the Unsung were not the rustics that the false Kruge had conned. Every exile aboard was a veteran of the conflicts over Gamaral and H'atoria, and at Ghora Janto. They knew their way around a battle. By contrast, the ungainly Kinshaya battlespheres seemed slow on the response.

"*This is* Cob'lat *to all ships,*" Worf said over the comm. His bird-of-prey had gone in first for a low-level run, just skimming the surface of the nearest battlesphere's shields. "*The shields are weakest directly beneath the ships' south poles, where the landing thrusters are mounted. The disruptors on the surrounding ring fire outward, not down.*"

"Message understood," Valandris said, commanding Raneer to bank *Chu'charq* from its present course and begin an attack run on the second orbiting battlesphere. The only Kinshaya she had ever met, on H'atoria, she hadn't liked at all. This would be a pleasure, whether she survived the attack or not.

KINSHAYA BATTLESPHERE *FERVENT-ONE*
OVER KETORIX PRIME

"Close with *Fervent-Six*," Roje ordered. "Put the birds-of-prey in our crossfire!"

His crew belatedly complied as the battlesphere's shields were buffeted by another photon torpedo. Facing their first real opposition, Roje realized that his team of Breen and Kinshaya personnel was performing less than optimally. The Spetzkar were more adept at individual combat than ship-to-ship warfare—and they were working a class of starship that, while not alien to them, had been designed with someone else in mind.

The Kinshaya were highly excitable and prone to mistakes. They were all over the map. It had been a concern that Chot Dayn had raised repeatedly. Moving fast to blackmail Korgh into diverting his defenses, the Breen had been obliged to accept whatever forces Ykredna sent, and there had been no time to meld them into coherent crews.

"We cannot establish a crossfire, Thot Roje," his lieutenant reported. *"The birds-of-prey are staying away from the zone between our ships."*

Worf's influence, Roje thought. *He knows better.*

But the other Unsung vessels were dealing damage too. For the past several weeks, the Phantom Wing had been the scourge of the Klingon Empire, humiliating Starfleet to boot. Roje had never expected to face them. The Unsung were always part of Korgh's plans, according to Shift, and they were evidence that he wanted destroyed. The remains of the squadron had disappeared for days, and Roje had assumed they had gone to ground.

What were they doing here, fighting *for* Korgh? What wizardry could Kahless and Worf possibly have worked to make that happen? It beggared belief. The discommendated Klingons were nothing, worse than nothing. Why would they ever fight for an empire that loathed them?

Klingons make no sense, Roje thought. He looked for something to hold on to as another bird-of-prey started its attack run.

Phantom Wing Vessel Cob'lat
Over Ketorix Prime

The bird-of-prey's disruptors spoke again, and the Kinshaya paid. The perfect shape of the battlesphere was no more, a jagged gash blazing beneath its equator.

Worf clapped the armrest of his command chair and offered his congratulations to the twin brothers. He had not known Beroc and Bardoc on Thane, but as helmsman and gunner under his tutelage they had quickly proven a lethal combination. They whooped at their success and prepared for a run on the other battlesphere in orbit.

Worf's concerns went beyond the foes outside. *Krencha*, Weltern and Harch's ship, had taken a bad hit and was venting into space as it made wider loops around the targets.

"The fires are bad," Weltern said over the comm. The *Cob'lat* had lost visuals. Worf could hear the rumblings of internal explosions aboard *Krencha*.

"Let us beam you aboard," Valandris called from *Chu'charq*.

"We will not flee from the fight," Harch piped in. *"We have something else in mind."*

That concerned Worf, who remembered that Harch had served with Zokar, who had rammed a Klingon battle cruiser in a suicide run. "Harch, their shields are still up," he transmitted. "Do not act foolishly."

"Do not fear, Worf. We will not end in that way," Weltern said. *"But if we face death, we do so as a family."* A pause. *"Tell our son our names."*

The transmission ended.

Before Worf could establish contact with *Cob'lat,* he saw *Klongat,* where Kahless served, losing acceleration. Reduced to thrusters, it might not be much use in space—but there were other targets it could still challenge: the four battlespheres already in Ketorix's atmosphere, firing on the citizens below. And that was where the true need was. Only the Unsung's lives were at risk in orbit; the real threat was on the planet.

That is where we should be, Worf thought. He hailed *Chu'charq.* "Valandris, we must descend," he said. "The hunting is better."

"You know what I like," she said. *"But* Chu'charq *will remain with* Krencha, *to protect you from these fiends in orbit during your descent. You and Kahless will have all the fun."*

Worf realized the state of *Krencha* must be dire. Valandris, in defending the wounded, had become the leader the Unsung so longed for.

"ghIj qet jaghmeyjaj," Worf said. *May your enemies run with fear.*

House of Kruge Industrial Compound
Ketorix Prime

Help had arrived!

One of the other warriors in the atrium had seen them

first through the holes in the roof: two birds-of-prey rocketing downward through the clouds to engage the Kinshaya. Exultant, Korgh and Tragg hurried to his ruined office, where they hoped to have a better vantage point.

From the gaping hole that had once been the exterior wall to Korgh's office, father and son watched the running battle between the two birds-of-prey and the battlesphere. For the longest time, they had resembled carrion birds challenging a moon—with as much chance of success.

Then the odds changed. In descent mode, the Kinshaya ship's braking flaps folded outward like petals, increasing the surface area that was not armored. The birds-of-prey took full advantage, firing disruptors at the exposed area. The battlesphere was landing blows in response—but it was clear that the vessels were more formidable in orbit.

For a moment, it looked as though the battlesphere might try to escape to space. But several moments after ignition, a thruster shook loose from its moorings, sending the vehicle on a spiraling trip that ended in the darkness beyond the city. Flames erupted across that part of the landscape.

"Yes!" Tragg yelled over the sounds of explosion.

"It is only one," Korgh said, focusing on the birds-of-prey, which were moving on to their next victim. "Who are these warriors? Has Tengor returned?"

"I do not know, Father." Tragg held his communicator, which had grown increasingly useless over the past hour. "There is conflicting information coming from all around. Someone said they are the Unsung!"

Korgh couldn't believe his ears. The heat of battle generated much misinformation. The fools were out in force tonight. But Kinshaya blood had at last been shed. "I have to return to the atrium," Korgh said. "I must send another broadcast to rally the people now that help has come!"

KINSHAYA BATTLESPHERE *FERVENT-ONE*
ABOVE KETORIX

"We have done it! We have done it!"

Roje looked to the bishop with annoyance. The two battlespheres in orbit had combined fire to destroy one of the remaining two birds-of-prey still in space. *Krencha*, the Klingons had called it in their transmissions. The destruction of the Klingon vessel had prompted a celebration by Labarya and her companions, who chanted and swayed as if the battle were over.

"*Focus*," Roje implored. There was still a bird-of-prey out there—by far, the most effective one of the four. *Chu'charq*. And down in Ketorix's skies, *Fervent-Three* had just been destroyed, with *Fervent-Five* now under reported attack. This was no time for revelry.

"*Something is wrong with* Fervent-Six," Roje's lieutenant said.

The other battlesphere in orbit was no longer firing—and the remaining bird-of-prey was avoiding it.

It dawned on Roje why.

"*Fervent-Six*, this is Thot Roje," he called out over the comm. "*Fervent-Six*, have you been boarded?"

There was no response from the other ship at first—and then, sounds of chaos and tumult.

"That's disruptor fire," Labarya said, the gaiety clearly over. "And those are Kinshaya screams!" She looked at Roje in panic. "How could they be boarded? Their shields are up!"

"The Phantom Wing vessels can beam through shields," Roje said, arms feeling limp. "Everybody knows that." But he had forgotten. Yes, *Krencha* had been destroyed. But clearly, first, its crew had beamed onto *Fervent-Six*. And they were now killing everyone they could find on the bridge.

Perhaps the competence problem wasn't limited to his crew, Roje thought. Perhaps he wasn't a great general after all.

More wails came across the comm, even as *Chu'charq* renewed its attacks on *Fervent-One* with greater force. Labarya was frantic. "The Klingon cancer has infected the other vessel," the bishop said. "You must fire on it!"

"We will not," Roje replied. He was flabbergasted. Yes, many of the troops aboard had been beamed down already, but there were still other personnel to consider. "Our people are on it. *Your* people are on it!"

"What of it? We would not give the demons the pleasure of making an abattoir of one of our holy vessels. It was Niamlar who in ancient times said to kill the wounded, for they are lacking in devotion!"

"Your 'holy vessel' was sitting in my shipyard for *four years* waiting for you," Roje said. "And I am not going to fire on it because your *war god* tells me—"

Roje was not going to fire—but in one of the nearby command pits running *Fervent-One*'s disruptor banks, the Kinshaya at the controls listened to their bishop rather than their Breen ally. Over the panicked squawks of the Breen, the flagship unloaded on its companion vessel. With the shields of the battlesphere already damaged, their blasts cut through and dealt *Fervent-Six* a mortal blow.

The Breen spymaster stood gawking at the carnage on the display. "What did you just do?" he screamed at the Kinshaya.

Before the bishop could answer for them, a figure appeared on the main viewscreen—the same Klingon woman who had hailed him. Only now her eyes were fixed and wide with anger and shock. *"My blood was on that ship,"* Valandris said.

"My people too," Roje said, knowing that only his crew could hear it.

She punched a control on her armrest. *"I am coming for you. Run."*

Forty-seven

A debate between dragons was a thing to see. That is what many of the Kinshaya in the cathedral had apparently decided, overcoming their fears to gather in the rotunda. Shift noticed that at least three Kinshaya were holding up devices either recording or broadcasting the encounter; such was strictly forbidden, but the regime's guards were paying no notice. In fact, one of the offenders *was* a guard. The scene was too fantastic.

The new Niamlar had just put on a show for the crowd. First she had twisted and turned, moving her wings and tail in ways that Shift still hadn't figured out how to do. Then she had blown a cloud of smoke into the air above her. As it settled, it showered her with sparks that gave her enormous form an eldritch glow. When it faded, the new Niamlar's hide had changed from silver to gold.

The Kinshaya stamped in seeming approval. Lieutenant Chen took the opportunity to check on Yeffir, chained to a pillar off to the side. *"Don't free the heretic,"* Shift warned. *"Get away from her, or I will smite you both!"*

"Come now," the Golden Niamlar said. *"We both know that you don't have the ability to do that. You're all talk—and while we're at it, we should chat about your vocabulary. Your 'ancient god' talk is by way of a second-rate holo-novel."* The creature lifted her head proudly to the heights. *"A true practitioner researches her role, sometimes for a year or more. You sound as if you picked this up over a weekend."*

"I believe that is exactly what happened," Tuvok said.

Chen spoke to her friend. "Yeffir, when did this Niamlar first appear?"

"A few days ago," the chained Kinshaya said, her voice gravelly. "She heralded the arrival of the Breen, and the ships they said they built for us."

"The plot thickens," Dax said. "We saw the Breen officers out on the plaza, but we assumed that was because Ykredna was back in power. But it's something else, isn't it?" She gave Shift a canny look. "Jilaan came to extort for herself. *But you came for the Breen.*"

"*I am a god, one of the thirty-one!*" Shift declared, beating her imaginary wings.

"*Spare us,*" her golden counterpart said.

The Vulcan, deep in thought over the revelations, spoke up. "The *Blackstone* was saved from the Klingons at Cragg's Cloud by an unseen attacker—and later a lone Breen ship was in the region between that location and the Klingon border." He turned to look at Shift. "I suspect the Breen destroyed *Jarin*—and conveyed the cloaked *Blackstone* to Kinshaya space for the purpose of deception."

Dax's eyes went to the floor as she contemplated something. "Wait. Does that mean that the Breen were behind impersonating Kruge too? The Breen created the Unsung?"

"*No!*" Shift blurted, before realizing she had broken character—and, possibly, given away the game. She tried to get back on track. "*Why do you vex my people with your prattle?*"

"I would like to know what this *Blackstone* is," one of the Kinshaya near Ykredna said. "What do they mean, Great Niamlar?"

"*Until this counterfeit is gone, I will answer no more,*" Shift said.

"*Oh, she won't answer,*" the Golden Niamlar said, nearly

purring the final word. "*But this one was always there with the questions. That's all she ever did—pumping me for information about the Circle and my powers.*"

Shift froze. "*Buxtus?*" she asked. *It wasn't possible!* No one answered her—and the silence enraged her. She had stabbed Buxtus Cross, left the arrogant little snot bleeding to death on the deck of *Ark of G'boj*. Sensors had confirmed he was dead.

And yet, didn't Cross live in the realm of illusion?

"*You—you can't be Buxtus,*" she said. "*He's dead! I know! I—*"

She went silent—but Tuvok finished her sentence. "You were going to say that you would know because you killed him. I witnessed it." He turned to the Kinshaya. "Buxtus Cross was an illusionist who deceived the population of entire planets. With her words, I conclude that the individual behind your war god is Shift, his apprentice."

"*Apprentice, my eye. She's a thief,*" the Golden Niamlar said. "*She may have stolen knowledge from Buxtus Cross, but she stole it from me first.*" The serpent twirled around so that her head was facing Shift's. "*Isn't that right, cellmate? Tell them about it, Vella!*"

Shift blinked. "*Ardra?*"

BLACKSTONE
ORBITING JANALWA

Ardra!

Gaw put his fist against his teeth and stared. He and his colleagues had managed to keep their Breen minders from seeing the Starfleet officers on their screens, and they had all heard what had just been said below in their earpieces.

Cross was dead. Not convalescing back at the Breen base,

but probably in a Starfleet morgue. And Shift, loving, sweet Shift, had put him there. She had killed him—and lied about it, to get Gaw and his companions to do her bidding.

Even more startling, the other Niamlar was Ardra, one of his idols. He had been looking to connect with her when he found Cross instead. Unbelievably, Starfleet appeared to have brought her to Janalwa. Possibilities raced through his mind. The Federation had *Houdini*; everybody knew that. Had Ardra made a deal?

And was there room in the deal for anyone else?

He looked furtively around at the Breen. They were animated, heading back and forth between the illusion control center and the bridge. It wasn't about what was happening in the cathedral, he surmised, but about something else. The war, perhaps. That gave him a chance.

The Breen minder saw him looking about and squawked.

"All right, buddy, all right. I'll get back to work." *You bet I will*, he thought, as he began composing the first of a series of private messages to his colleagues. He had some quick work to do.

CATHEDRAL OF STATE
JANALWA

Ezri Dax watched the two "gods" circling each other. Initially surprised that Shift hadn't beamed out when the hard questioning began, the captain realized Shift's Niamlar had no choice but to stay and rebut her accusers. Departing would clear the stage, so to speak, for Ardra and the Starfleet officers to sway the Kinshaya.

But it wasn't clear they needed additional swaying. "You are a fraud," Yeffir said, unchained by Chen. "You are a Breen trick!"

"*Not by the Breen—but for them,*" Ardra-Niamlar said. "*Shall we show them what we can do, my old friend? Perhaps show them how we instill fear.*"

A flash of light filled the rotunda—and moments later, the golden dragon was replaced by a fearsome-looking Klingon male. All about, the Kinshaya shrieked—but when he opened his mouth, his voice was far from the booming one Niamlar had used. It was Klingon—but it was also soothing. "Don't exert yourselves, my friends," the warrior said. "This is just another design of Jilaan's, from her appearance in your temple long ago."

Ykredna, who had been petrified, gestured to the mural on the ceiling. "Yes! He is Kahless, the abomination who appeared to Pontifex Urawak!"

"Yes—and no." With a snap of the Klingon's fingers, he transformed into Ardra. "He was an illusion then, just as Niamlar was." Her bearing regal, she walked before the Kinshaya and turned to face Shift's character. "This being is artificial as well, generated by a cloaked vessel in orbit."

"The *Blackstone*," Tuvok said.

Ykredna stepped before the remaining Niamlar and eyed her critically. "Is this true? Do you transform as they do?"

"*No. I am eternal.*"

"What she means is that her truthcrafters haven't had time to bring another character online for her," Ardra said.

The dragon stared at her, its expression almost sullen. "*You said your people pledged never to reveal their secrets.*"

"You're not one of my people. And now that it's been used twice, I think even the Great Lady would say that this trick has expired."

Dax crossed her arms. "What will it be, Shift? You don't seem to be in control of the situation anymore."

"*That's what you think.*" Niamlar rose to her full towering height. "*I have tolerated this whimsy long enough. I command that you arrest these heathens.*"

Ykredna looked at the Kinshaya surrounding her and sensed the mood. "I am not sure what to do, Your Grace."

"*You will act, or I will return now to the ether. And when I come back, it will be with my chosen Breen sentinels, who will do what my supposed faithful will not!*"

The Kinshaya did not react to her words. Rather, all of them were looking at the dragon's head.

"*What? What now?*"

"You . . ." Yeffir looked up, mystified. "There is something on your head."

Dax moved around to get a better view. The image of Niamlar had indeed changed. Atop the creature's silvery crown sat a blue headpiece with white lettering. "Okay, that *is* strange," Dax admitted. "Your god is wearing a baseball cap."

"What is that?" Ykredna demanded, pointing. "What is written there?"

Niamlar stopped moving—and all were able to read:

SAVE US
32,560 KM DIRECTLY ABOVE

Ardra saw it and laughed. "Gaw, is that you up there? I'm surprised you would work for this charlatan."

Really? Dax thought.

The characters on the lower line transformed into a different set of numbers. "And what is *that*?" Yeffir asked.

Dax knew, but she could hardly believe it herself. "That would be the harmonic resonance frequency for a cloaking field." She knew the *Houdini* was watching, but she tapped her combadge for good measure. "*Aventine*, this is Dax . . ."

Forty-eight

*E*nterprise pitched and rolled as it skimmed the upper atmosphere of Narendra III. The starship had made so many close approaches to the world that Picard felt as though he were teaching a Starfleet Academy course on the topic.

Picard's challenge differed from the one facing Admiral Riker, whose battle in the Pheben system was still ongoing. The four Kinshaya vessels at Narendra III were up against a planet that had been invaded before and whose colonists were protected by heavy ground-to-space weaponry emplacements. The invaders' approach, once the orbital defense platforms were down, had been to lob torpedoes from afar, hoping to score hits without risk.

Picard had faced a choice. *Enterprise* could make sure that no battlesphere could take potshots with impunity. Or it could act as a secondary ground defense system for Narendra III, intercepting incoming fire with its shields and weapons.

His crew had given him the option of doing both. They had coordinated their efforts to offer Narendra the best defense a lone starship could deliver. Flight Controller Faur had managed repeated hair-raising passes between the Kinshaya and the planet, while Taro Trinell, in main engineering, had constantly shaped and reoriented *Enterprise*'s shields to provide maximum protection for the ground and ship alike. Aneta Šmrhová at tactical had the unenviable job of keeping track of the activities of four essentially identical battlespheres—and while the main computer had tagged each of the Kinshaya ships with special nomenclature, keeping track of their activities was a dizzying proposition. Yet Šmrhová had done that and more, intercepting all but the most errant torpedoes with *Enterprise*'s phasers—and even getting in a few shots at the Kinshaya.

"Any word on the Klingons, Glinn?" he asked for what felt like the umpteenth time.

"They're on the way, Captain."

Same answer as before. Picard shook his head and held on for another run.

House of Kruge Industrial Compound
Ketorix Prime

Ketorix was in flames. The center of manufacturing power for Commander Kruge, who had conquered so many Kinshaya worlds long ago, was now falling to that loathsome species. There was no way to sugarcoat it. Two of the battlespheres had managed to land intact, disgorging their siege equipment and galloping masses of armed Kinshaya into the fire-lit night.

One of the two birds-of-prey whose exploits he had earlier thrilled to had been damaged; it went down somewhere near the compound. Whether it was destroyed or not, he did not know. Its companion vessel had not been seen for several minutes.

Most of the members of Tragg's detachment had gone downstairs to battle Kinshaya storming the ground floor. Before the sensor mounted firmly to the wall so he could broadcast unattended, Korgh transmitted yet another message from in front of the statue in the now open-air atrium.

"We will continue to fight as Klingons. Our descendants will never forget the name of Ketorix."

Weary, he trudged away from the statue. To one side, Tragg pointed to the transmitting device, noting that it was still activated. Korgh waved his hand. "Let the world see us—if anyone watched."

Tragg looked at the other warriors—a group of frightened youngsters with less experience than their commander. He took his father aside and spoke to him in the darkest shadows. "We will not win. But we can die as Klingons."

"No!" Korgh growled. Enough energy had returned to him for that. "I mean, yes, we should fight. But I will not go down so easily—not when we have just claimed this house."

"What other path is there?" Tragg asked.

Korgh tried to think. "Yes," he said. "The basement of this building. There is a tunnel out under the exercise yard to an underground hangar. It has the family's old shuttle—they rarely used it."

Tragg nodded. "The Kinshaya would not know it was there."

Korgh's eyes narrowed. "We could rearm, regroup—and return."

"Is there another lift in the building?"

"None that goes there." Korgh looked down the long hall with its line of offices. "But there is a hidden staircase just inside the door to this level. We could bypass the battle below. Kinshaya do not care for stairs." He chuckled. It felt good to laugh at anything.

"We are going down the hall," Tragg said to his warriors. "Lead the way—but be prepared. As soon as they get anyone on this level, they can provide targeting information for their transporters."

It was a useful piece of information. But Korgh feared his youngest son's prowess might have shown itself too late.

PHANTOM WING VESSEL *COB'LAT*

"I am here, my friend," Kahless said to Worf as he entered the bridge. Several consoles on *Cob'lat*'s command deck were on fire, much like other parts of the ship he had seen on the way from the transporter room. In midair over Ketorix, the bird-of-prey was laying down suppressive fire against the invaders on the ground, and the parked battle-spheres were exacting a steep price for the act.

"I live," Kahless said, "though it surprises me."

"I apologize for not letting you go down with *Klongat*," Worf said. "But we need every warrior!"

"There are better ways to die than crashing into a boot factory. All those you transported appreciate it."

"Their respite will not be long. I have found something," Worf said. He pointed to a monitor across the bridge. "Lord Korgh has been broadcasting from the house headquarters—that taller building inside the compound."

Kahless studied the display. Amid static and darkness, he could see several armed Klingons in motion. "They are holding out there?"

"For some time, and he has been rallying the planet's people all the while."

Kahless made a fist. "Such devotion must be rewarded."

One of the twin brothers—the clone had never learned to tell between them—looked back at him. "There is no place near there to put down, Kahless. The Kinshaya control the surrounding surface."

"Then deliverance shall come from the sky!"

Forty-nine

Gaw looked with satisfaction at his work, and then yelped as a pair of strong gloved hands grabbed at his shoulders. His minder had seen the cap atop Shift's character's head. Yanked from his chair, the Ferengi protested all the way as he was shoved toward the bridge.

On the bridge, he saw that something had already gotten up Chot Dayn's nose—or in his armored snout. Gaw had a pretty good idea what it was. The displays showing the progress of the invasion indicated several fewer Kinshaya orbs than Gaw had seen the last time he had been allowed on the bridge. As he stood there, another blinked and disappeared. Electronic gobbledygook passed between Gaw's minder and the chot.

Dayn faced him and assumed a hostile posture. *"What have you done?"* he said in words the Ferengi could understand. *"What is happening with Shift?"*

Before he could think up a response, another Breen officer entered with a report. Dayn was clearly startled. *"Starfleet officers? In the temple?"*

Violently, he shoved Gaw, knocking the technician against the bulkhead. Gaw slid to the deck—which, the Ferengi realized, was not a bad place to be. For from his position looking forward, he could see the two vessels decloaking outside *Blackstone*. A ship much like his—and a large, sleek Federation starship.

Gaw was the only one braced when the photon torpedo detonated just above the hull. Lights went out on the bridge, and the world went spinning. Once his eyes adjusted and he regained his bearings, he saw the Breen scattered about, still dazed.

The ship's comm system came alive, broadcasting a male human voice. *"This is Commander Bowers of the* U.S.S. Aventine. *You will surrender your vessel immediately. Prepare to be boarded."*

Much of the bridge looked intact to Gaw, but outside he could see a spiral trail of debris—including, he recognized, large sections of *Blackstone*'s dorsal mast.

The illusion projector.

His heart sank. *Blackstone* would make no more magic. Chot Dayn, getting to his feet, appeared to have no illusions either. He squawked a command—and seconds later he and several of his companions transported away.

CATHEDRAL OF STATE
JANALWA

From Dax's perspective, she knew the moment her orders had been carried out. The captain did not know exactly what had transpired, but she had just seen Niamlar transform into a very startled Orion woman. "Shift, I presume."

Tuvok and Chen hurried across the floor of the rotunda to her. He pointed his phaser at her—and unwilling to risk her escaping, grabbed her arm. She resisted, but could not get away.

She was wearing a jumpsuit that Dax had seen before; it was worn beneath Breen armor. Shift was sweating profusely. Chen turned the woman's other arm to expose the

Breen symbol on the sleeve. She and Tuvok turned Shift so that the Kinshaya could see.

"It is true," Yeffir said, genuinely astonished. "The Breen have sent us to war on a lie!"

"Do you have anything to say to these people?" Dax said.

Shift glowered at the captain, her lips tightly sealed.

"How about to me?" Ardra asked, strolling forward in casual triumph. "You and Heghtar abandoned me. Did she help arrange the business with the Klingon cult, after you met Cross? Such mischief for one so old—and one so young."

"I have nothing to say to you," Shift said, a snarl on her face. "You people in the Circle use your abilities for nothing, only to enrich yourselves. You're an offense to equality. You're worse than useless."

Dax's combadge chirped. "Go."

"This is Lieutenant Kedair. Captain, my strike force has taken Blackstone—*along with a number of Breen warriors who chose to surrender. We also have some very relieved technicians."*

"Send them straight to the brig. Is she spaceworthy?"

"Yes, but the illusion generator hardware appears destroyed."

"Duplicate all the databanks and do an evidence sweep." Dax looked back at the Kinshaya. "I want you to put the *Blackstone* down in the plaza, outside the cathedral. Dax out."

"Captain, you are bringing it here?" Tuvok asked.

"That's right." The captain turned and faced the Kinshaya. "We could have used our own illusionist to order you to stop your war with the Klingons," she said as she walked in front of them. "But then we'd be treating you with no more respect than the Breen did."

The Trill pointed to the western exit. "I invite each and

every Kinshaya to go take a look at that thing—and to view whatever images were taken of what happened here today. I think you'll find it's in your interest." She clasped her hands behind her. "I also think you'll find it's in your interest to recall your people from the Klingon Empire. I don't think you would have gone to war on your own."

Ykredna found herself the focus of many angry Kinshaya eyes. She was shaking. "Even if that was not Niamlar," she said, "we still have our beliefs! The Klingons are monsters, devils!"

"Everyone has beliefs," Dax said. "I believe there are people who do evil. Devils can belong to any species, not just Klingons."

Shift let loose with a sardonic laugh. "Klingon devils? I could tell you quite a lot about one I know—"

And she might have, if it were not for the transporter effect that suddenly materialized around her, separating her from Tuvok's grasp. The last thing Dax saw on the woman's face before she was spirited away was a look of utter surprise.

"Unfortunate that this keeps happening," Tuvok said, almost allowing his frustration to show.

BREEN SHUTTLE
ORBITING JANALWA

Shift materialized in the darkened rear of a small excursion craft. As she caught her breath, she realized two Breen officers were there beside her. Without her helmet and its interface, she could not identify them.

But she had no trouble recognizing Chot Dayn when they escorted her to the forward compartment. She knew the figure in the passenger seat from the dismissive way he crossed his arms and tilted his head whenever he looked at her.

"Your face offends me," he said so she could understand.

"My helmet is aboard the *Blackstone*."

"Everything about you offends me," Dayn said. *"You novice, you child—you of the wild schemes and ideas. You sold the domo on this nonsense—and it has come to nothing!"*

Looking forward, Shift could see the damaged *Blackstone* sitting beside the *Aventine*. The Kinshaya patrol vessels in orbit were giving the Starfleet vessel a wide berth. Off to the other side of *Aventine* she could see another vessel, nearly *Blackstone*'s twin.

So that was how they did it, she thought.

"I have recalled all Breen on Janalwa to their safe houses and ships," Dayn said. *"We do not have the forces here to contest the Starfleet vessel, should they choose to seize the government buildings or the communications links with the attack fleet. And I do not trust the Kinshaya to support us."*

"They supported us long enough. The plan did everything it was supposed to," Shift declared. Hunkering down now was pointless. She had to attack. "Thot Roje by now has conquered all of the House of Kruge's territory. How long the Kinshaya cooperate is of no concern. We have wounded the Empire."

"Things were not going so well at our last report—which is why I had this shuttle standing by to reclaim key personnel." Dayn stared at her. *"You are not key personnel anymore. But the domo would not want you in enemy hands."*

"We will see what Thot Roje has to say about my position," Shift said icily, "and yours."

Before Dayn could respond, a clarion sounded. Shift saw it was an incoming message from *Fervent-One*. "Now you will see," she said, slipping past Dayn and activating the viewer.

The face that appeared on the screen was, indeed,

Roje's—yet that was just the start of the horror. His helmet was off, and a gloved hand gripped the fur between his ears.

His throat had been cut.

The owner of the hand moved backward and appeared in the frame with him. Shift, who had gasped before on seeing her friend, inhaled hard again.

Valandris.

"Your leader here was trying to call you, Breen, to tell you of his great success in repelling the boarders of the Unsung."

Chot Dayn looked at Shift—and then back at the fearsome warrior on screen.

"Your offensive has stalled. His part, anyway." Valandris's eyes narrowed with recognition as she studied her listeners. *"An Orion woman.* Enterprise *said such a person was with the pretenders who portrayed Kruge and N'Keera. Would you know of this?"*

Shift's throat went dry. She could not respond.

"Remain silent, then. And if you meet her, tell her—no one crosses a Klingon and lives." She cast the blood-matted corpse to the deck and cut the transmission.

Fifty

"*Greetings, Picard. I hope you left some scraps for us.*"

Picard had seldom been so relieved to receive a hail. The *Enterprise* had held off the battlespheres for what had seemed like an eternity, expending a fair portion of its complement of photon torpedoes. One of the massive orbs had even been sent limping away after Šmrhová had scored repeated hits on the same location—a difficult task considering how easily the ships rotated their damaged portions out of harm's way. Yet while they had stemmed the tide, there was no way a single ship could turn it.

Gorkon's arrival was most welcome—despite the fact that the battle cruiser appeared to have taken some worrisome damage. "We are glad to see you, Captain Klag. What is your condition?"

"*Furious,*" Klag said on audio. "*The damned fool Breen search ship we were escorting tried to block us as we were about to enter warp.*"

That did not surprise Picard, who had received reports of similar incidents. "Their condition?"

"*Looking for a new way home. It explains our delay.*"

"We are glad to have you here." The captain looked back at a drained Šmrhová and smiled. "Shall we begin?"

They *had* begun—only just—when one after another, the battlespheres stopped firing.

"*What is this?*" Klag transmitted. "*Fifteen seconds of a fair fight and they quit?*" He swore in aggravation.

Picard stared at the viewscreen, somewhat befuddled by the novel sight of space that wasn't crisscrossed by deadly Kinshaya ordnance. "Hail them, Glinn."

After consulting his interface, the Cardassian reported, "No answer, sir."

"Captain," Lieutenant Elfiki said, "sensors are detecting disruptor fire."

"Where?"

"The disruptor fire is *aboard* the ships," she said. "At least two of them."

Picard sat down, puzzled. He hailed *Gorkon*. "Captain, there seems to be a disagreement as to whether to continue."

"*There can be no disagreement between us, Captain.*" *Gorkon* was still quite distant but had not stopped hurling torpedoes since arriving in system. "*You and I will fight on until the stars burn out.*"

"The Kinshaya are in disagreement."

"*Hmph.*" Klag could be heard giving a command, and *Gorkon* stopped firing. "*I would say our arrival had this effect,*" Klag said. "*But the Kinshaya are not so smart—especially when it comes to my people.*"

Dygan said, "Captain, priority one being rerouted by Command to all vessels in Klingon space. It's the *Aventine*."

ORE-PROCESSING CENTER
PHEBEN IV

"*—and the Holy Order has issued a general stand-down and withdrawal order while the Matriarchs empanel a group of inquiry,*" Captain Dax said. "*They outnumber the Breen aboard the battlespheres, so I expect any disagreements won't last long.*"

Standing in the wreckage-strewn barracks of Pheben IV's

largest ore-processing facility, Riker looked at the belea-
guered *Titan* security team and responded. "That tracks
with what we've seen here, Captain Dax. Most of the ground
invaders transported out and left. Thanks for the hail."

*"I figured you'd want the full story. I'll touch base with you
in a couple of hours about wrapping up here."*

"Sounds like you're on top of it." He grinned. "Keep this
up and you'll make admiral."

"I thought you were trying to get on my good side. Dax out."

Riker had been allowed to visit the processing plant only
after the fireworks had ended. His inspection had shown him
the remnants of a pitched battle, one that had been joined
when *Titan* and *Gur'rok* finally evaded nuisance Breen ships
to reach Pheben IV. With the battlespheres disgorging Kinshaya assault troops, the two starships had beamed teams
to critical points in the facility—and ultimately had saved
most of the Pheben laborers from being massacred.

Lieutenant Kyzak looked up from the phaser he had been
tinkering with. "Sounds like a horse is coming," he said.

"Good ear." Riker noted the direction of the galloping
sounds—and was startled to see a lone Kinshaya, unarmed
and shed of its barding, bolting through the barracks like a
thing afire. Behind it charged several Klingons, armed with
disruptor rifles and *bat'leth*s.

"Hold," Riker said, appealing for the pursuers to stop.
"Didn't you hear?"

General Kersh entered the room, following her warriors.
Spotting Riker blocking their path, her expression soured.
"Everywhere I go."

"I was just making sure your people had heard about the
Kinshaya pullback."

"We have heard," she said, standoffish. "They are making
sure that particular Kinshaya has heard about it."

Riker looked back at the young Kinshaya, cowering behind a locker. "I don't think fighting him will be honorable."

Kersh stared at the Kinshaya—and then looked at Riker for a long moment. She shook her head, seemingly bewildered by the recent sequence of events. "Riker, sometimes I think you know our ways better than we do."

She stared at him and contemplated. "Before the attack, I had been about to strike your ship."

"I remember."

"Had I done so in my rage, it would have been the end of the Accords."

He stepped toward her. "It's not the end, for either of us. Look at it another way. A new era has begun." Riker straightened and shouted in his best Klingon: "*tagh may'qochvan!*"

Kersh stared at him in wonder—and then smiled as she realized the implications of what Riker had said. She turned to her companions. "*tagh may'qochvan! net Sovjaj!*" she said. "The *may'qochvan* begins—let it be known!"

As the warriors and the security officers cheered, Kyzak sidled up to the admiral. "What does it mean?" he asked.

Kersh heard and answered. "The *may'qochvan* is a time of truce, of celebration, between rivals who have joined to defeat a common enemy."

Riker nodded. "The nobles of the House of Kruge, for all their faults, decided to let their *may'qochvan* continue for a hundred years—a century of peace." He smiled and offered his hand to Kersh. "Let's see if the Federation and the Empire can top that record."

Fifty-one

Had there been any major change in the status of the war, Korgh knew there was no way anyone in the darkness of the tower would have learned of it. Certainly the Kinshaya had not reacted as if help had arrived for the besieged Klingons of Ketorix. They continued to emerge from the turbolift—and yes, even the stairwell—to charge down the long hall, challenging Korgh and his escorts.

They had numbered five when they started—Korgh, Tragg, and three young warriors. Two of them had fallen, and now the third was in a desperate fight with not one, but three Kinshaya. Tragg, his right shoulder bleeding from a gash, pulled at Korgh's uniform. "Father, we must fall back!"

Korgh would not leave the young defender—but one of the Kinshaya ran the warrior through with a lance, gutting him. Tragg yanked his father back into the atrium just in time to avoid a spray of disruptor fire.

Together they ran back toward Kruge's statue, black and ominous in the darkness. The torches had long since gone out; the red haze from the flames of the city lit the space where the skylights had been. Reaching the far side of the statue, Korgh stumbled, causing father and son to strike the floor together.

While down, Tragg looked back between the rear legs of Kruge's graven Kinshaya victim—and saw the thing that Korgh only heard, bumping along the floor toward them. "*Grenade!*"

Tragg covered his father's body as a sphere of destruction filled the atrium. The base of the statue deflected the brunt of the energy, but could not fully protect the Klingons from the sonic assault and the blazing heat.

And then, just as Korgh thought he would never hear or see again, he heard a sickening crack—and looked up to see the nightmare shape of Kruge and the Kinshaya falling toward him. He seized his motionless son and rolled, just as more than a thousand kilograms of statue came smashing down onto the floor.

Gasping for air in the rubble, the old man clawed at the debris in the darkness. Feeling heat-scarred flesh, he struggled to uncover Tragg. The brunt of the collapse had missed both of them, but Tragg's left leg beneath the knee was crushed.

Through the smoke, he saw the Kinshaya disruptor bolts begin again. Scrambling over the wreckage, he found a *bat'leth*, shaken off the wall in the chaos. *Kruge's.* That would do. He clambered over the top of Tragg's body and raised the *bat'leth* in defense as the Kinshaya charged, weapons before them. There were three—no, more. Korgh tried to hold his ground, but there were so many. He dropped his weapon and wailed. *"Kahless, help me!"*

Disruptor fire lanced over his head from behind, tearing into the Kinshaya and slowing their advance. Someone passed on his left—another on his right. There were two figures in the darkness, both engaging the Kinshaya with *mek'leth*s. They chopped at the invaders, driving them back. His body covering his son's, Korgh stared spellbound, wondering who his saviors were. Had Tengor's people finally arrived?

Another Kinshaya fell. One of the Klingons turned back to look at him. "Are you all right, my lord?"

"W-Worf?"

Korgh was still trying to process the fact when a lone Kinshaya charged from the hall that led to his quarters. Rifle drawn, he brought it to bear on Korgh, preparing for what would be a point-blank shot. The other Klingon turned and hurled his *mek'leth* with such force that when it struck the neck of the galloping villain, the Kinshaya's whole body was flung several meters backward.

Korgh looked back at the body in astonishment—and then at the warrior who strode over to reclaim his weapon from the corpse. Korgh could not make his mouth move.

The Klingon looked back at him and grinned. "Yes, yes. I am Kahless, and I have returned. I think that is what you were going to say."

Korgh's eyes widened—and he thought himself mad. He collapsed over his son's still-breathing but otherwise motionless form. He wept. "*Do not judge me, Kahless!*"

"Here, here," Kahless said, approaching and climbing over the debris to reach him. "Do not fear, brave grandfather. You have done well."

Worf, satisfied that the attack was done, clambered toward Korgh and Tragg. "This warrior needs medical attention," he said of the prone figure.

"He is my son," Korgh said. He looked back and forth between the Klingons helping him up. "Kahless? Worf?"

Worf nodded. "It is the emperor. You must not have heard yet—the emperor was never slain."

"Never slain!"

Kahless growled. "Yes, I was kept alive by a Betazoid trickster named Cross—he who impersonated Kruge and created the Unsung. Cross is dead. I am not."

Korgh's lip trembled as Worf studied Tragg's wounds. He looked into space. "Did—did Cross say who put him up to that?"

Kahless looked at Worf as if the question was unexpected. "No," the clone said.

Dizzy with the news he had not been found out, Korgh looked up—and saw a bird-of-prey hovering overhead through the shattered skylights.

"It is *Chu'charq*," Worf said. "We saw your office had been blown open. She beamed us into it."

"I wanted to land *Cob'lat* on your roof," Kahless said, "but its damage was too great, and it had to be abandoned. There is but one ship left of the Phantom Wing."

"The Phantom Wing," Korgh parroted. "Yes." He stood up, mindless of the tattered and torched state of his uniform.

"The battle beyond seems to have stopped. Victory is ours." Kahless pointed up to the bird-of-prey. "We will get your son aid. Rest now."

"I—I must attend to my house," Korgh said.

Worf and Kahless looked at each other—and at the mess the atrium had become. "Clean another day, Lord Korgh," Worf said. "We do not know if hostilities will start again."

"I must attend to my house."

Korgh found a path around the debris and dead bodies and into the long hallway. There, through the darkness and down the hidden staircase, he made his way to the shuttle. There was only one person who could save him and his house now, and he had little time to reach her.

FINALE

THE WORK OF AGES

2386

"The work, my friend, is peace. More than an end of this war—an end to the beginnings of all wars."

—*Franklin Delano Roosevelt,*
undelivered address for April 13, 1945,
the day after he died

Fifty-two

Korgh's frantic flight to the capital had been littered with difficulties right from the start. The secret shuttlebay in the Ketorix compound was beneath a courtyard strewn with debris from the Kinshaya attack; the doors had resisted opening. Escaping had required putting the thrusters to full throttle and forcing the exit, a dangerous maneuver in such a small space.

Anguish had followed as Korgh ascended and saw what the Kinshaya had done to his beloved compound. For fifty years as *gin'tak*, he had rebuilt and modernized the factories, bringing the House of Kruge back from irrelevancy and making a better life for hundreds of thousands. The sight of so much of his work in ruins pained him utterly, and he had struggled not to dwell on it. Warriors died and buildings fell. His cause had to live on.

Korgh's next problem had come upon achieving orbit, when the skies—initially empty but for the smoldering husk of a Kinshaya battlesphere—suddenly grew crowded. A Klingon Defense Force squadron arrived from warp, followed thirty seconds later by Tengor and his flotilla of home guard vessels. In the race to save Ketorix, Korgh's pathetic middle son had come in dead last.

The sight of Korgh's shuttle—the only thing in motion—had drawn the attention of the Defense Force battle cruisers, which hailed demanding that he halt. Having no time to linger and identify himself, Korgh went immediately to warp, course-correcting later on.

The isolation of the long flight had given him time to brood—and to plan. Things had changed, and were changing, even as he made his way across the Empire.

Reports revealed something he'd forgotten: he had not cut off his final broadcast from the atrium. The wall-mounted sensor had remained active, somehow surviving the devastation of the grenade blast. Klingons everywhere had seen his and Tragg's desperate dash back into the museum, and the statue-toppling blast that had followed; they had also witnessed the triumphant return of the Emperor Kahless, soon surrounded in the scene by the handful of surviving adult members of the Unsung.

The exiles reportedly had come to stand behind their deeds before the leader of the house, but Korgh had gone and Tragg was unconscious. The last he had heard was that the Unsung were in the hands of the Defense Force. Tragg's condition concerned Korgh, but it was more important that neither Kahless nor the Unsung seemed to have connected Buxtus Cross to him.

A lengthy classified report sent to him from the chancellor's office was another mixed bag. The *Blackstone* had been captured in Kinshaya space, having played a role in prompting the invasion; the report did not detail how it had been captured, but clearly it had never gone anywhere near Balduk. However, neither the vessel nor its truthcrafters had yielded any information about who hired them to create the Unsung. At least Cross had been as good as his word on that. Only Cross and the contemptible Shift had ever known Korgh's name.

Shift, the report held, had vanished—presumably spirited away by her Breen collaborators. Korgh tasted bile when he saw that phrase. How long, he wondered, had the Orion woman been in their employ? Long enough to destroy his grandson's starship, likely, and to arrange their nefarious invasion scheme. She had simultaneously tricked Korgh into diverting his home guard and the Kinshaya into attacking. His masterstroke had been a hundred years in the making; hers had been hatched in far less time.

The good news was that Shift was gone and, at least thus far, the Breen had gone silent following their implication in the failed incursion. The Romulans were openly furious with their Typhon Pact ally. The Klingon Empire was busy driving out Breen "searchers" on pain of death. Korgh swore he would not give Shift and the Breen the chance to exploit him again. He had to make his vulnerability irrelevant.

He had found Qo'noS in a state of pure jubilation when he landed. Some glee was because of the successful defense; while Ketorix took the brunt of the assault and Pheben IV had seen significant industrial damage, the toll in other systems had been limited to orbital emplacements. But Klingons loved a story, and no one could resist the tale of Kahless, back from the dead to lead the Unsung from their pit of shame on a quest to drive the Kinshaya away.

The euphoric mood was part of the reason Korgh had chosen a remote landing site on Qolkat's estate. There was no benefit to his speaking about the events; no message of his could compete with that. Besides, any claim he might make to a heroic stand on Ketorix could lead to questions about why he had ordered his forces away in the first place.

Lord Qolkat was full of news, all of it bad. The accursed Starfleet vessels *Enterprise* and *Titan* having acted heroically, Martok and Riker considered their positions strengthened. The two had announced that the *chavmajta,* postponed during the emergency, was to be held later in the week, after

Riker made his return. It would even come before any judgment of the Unsung. Work on the Federation consulate was being stepped up, with additional Klingon laborers being hired to finish the job. There was no lack of applicants, Qolkat had said. The Federation had friends again in the First City.

Korgh had immediately convened a meeting of his High Council allies at Qolkat's estate. He had sought to stiffen their spines, to keep them onboard for his *chavmajta* walkout. Ultimately, he had been forced to offer several of the house's holdings, lesser places untouched by the Kinshaya, in trade for their support. Satevech and Grotek had asked for so much that he wondered if they had Ferengi blood. Who had ever heard of getting control of a star system in exchange for standing up and walking out a door?

Yet he knew that if he succeeded, none of that would matter. All the star systems of the Empire would be his. It could be done—with the help of the one person who had supported him the longest.

Disguising himself, Korgh used the personal transporter in Qolkat's home—a luxury of the very rich—to beam into a run-down neighborhood in the Old Quarter. There was no time to walk there, and his bruises from the battle would have made it agony. Deposited in the alleyway beside a familiar hovel, he entered and scaled the stairs, his muscles crying at every step.

He found the door partially open. He looked inside and called out. "Odrok?"

There was no answer.

Korgh's breath quickened. His accomplice for the past century had departed after their last argument on Ketorix, swearing never to return. She had left his thoughts since then; he had assumed she would go back to her residence on

Qo'noS to drink herself to death. But he needed her now—and pushing the creaking door all the way open, he worried that he had arrived too late.

Odrok appeared from around the corner. Looking haggard, she carried an armload of drained bloodwine bottles. Korgh couldn't tell if they were empties from today or a long time ago, but she seemed sober enough when she spoke. "I am not surprised to find you here."

"Yes," he said, shutting the door behind him. "Much has happened."

"Tell me no more." She trudged past him to the window and dumped the bottles outside. Korgh heard them shatter on the pavement.

"They say that Tragg is on the mend." He shuffled awkwardly. "I cannot be with him, of course."

She looked back at him, eyes tired. "What do you want, Korgh?"

No "my lord," he thought. There was nothing to do but get to the point. "I have a job for you," he said, crossing the room.

"I figured as much."

He stepped to the window and pointed across town. "I need you inside the Federation Consulate."

She looked blankly in the direction he was pointing. "I cannot see how," she said, turning away to resume her cleaning. "You remember the takeover of the original embassy by Klahb, the rebel group, a few years ago. Security has increased since."

He looked back at her and managed a grin. "The Federation Consulate has invited Klingon workers in to finish the auditorium in time for this week's *chavmajta*. Qolkat's house has connections—and he owes me favors. You can be one of those selected."

"To do what?"

He looked through the door to her bedroom—and to the mirror that doubled both as a secret transmitter and the door to a hidden closet. "I know you have explosives and remote detonation equipment. Before Martok and Riker speak, my allies and I will walk out. No one else should leave the stage alive."

No emotion crossed her face as she listened. She shook her head. "It has come to this?"

"I have been pushed to it."

The Klingon woman let out a sigh. She rubbed her wrinkled chin. "Why should I do this deed?"

Korgh managed to avoid grimacing. It gnawed at him, but there was no other way. He stepped toward her with an embarrassed smile. "Do this," he said, "and I will take you as my mate, as you once asked. You will head the House of Kruge with me, Odrok—just as you had hoped to do with my mentor long ago."

Her eyes narrowed. "You lie. You said you would never do this."

"I have tried to succeed without you these last days, and I have failed." He quickly took her hand. It trembled—from lack of drink, he imagined. He steadied it with his other hand. "You have been the one with me all these years, Odrok. You took me to the Phantom Wing. You learned how to find the Circle of Jilaan. You put me in touch with Shift and Cross. You helped make the Unsung and my ascension happen. It is right that our final years be spent together—in triumph."

Odrok looked at their clasped hands for a long moment. Then she turned her head so her gaze was on the bedroom and its secret closet. Finally, she pulled her hand away and asked, "How is it to be done?"

"This is the name of Qolkat's man," he said, placing a small card on her table. "I am told the stage and podium will be the last things to go in. You will join the workers installing the sensor package as a senior inspector. With your knowledge, that should be easy—and I know you have ways of concealing what you bring in. You will then hide the explosive in an opportune location."

"Who will have the trigger?"

"You will. Watch the broadcast of the event from here. Once we have left, when Riker or Martok begins to speak, that will be your cue. Count twenty seconds and detonate."

She looked at him. "Will you want your own defeat switch, should the plan need to change?"

"Of course. Leave it in the dead drop near the Great Hall." He put his hands on her frail shoulders. "You always think of everything—*Lady Korgh*."

She pushed his arms away, strode toward the door, and opened it. "Go. I have work to do now and do not want you here."

That is fine with me, Korgh thought as he exited. *Just get it done.*

Fifty-three

Valandris looked out the port at the First City and marveled. She was surrounded by excited children—and indeed felt as a child herself, seeing the Klingon capital for the first time. On this flight, she was merely a passenger on *Chu'charq*, a ship she had come to consider her own.

Kahless had insisted on returning to Qo'noS *only* in the company of the Unsung, something that the authorities had grudgingly agreed to. The most expedient method involved traveling aboard *Chu'charq*, where forty-six children—plus one infant—already had billets. Klingon Defense Force officers manned the bridge stations and walked the halls as sentries; all were easily identifiable not just by their uniforms, but also their facial protectors, suggested by Worf as a way to keep them from catching *tharkak'ra*.

"The Klingons finally confront the Unsung," Kahless had joked, "and it is the Empire's warriors who must wear the masks!"

Worf had added at a different moment that with Kahless aboard, *Chu'charq* was technically *qeylIS wa'*, the designated imperial transport. After a hundred years, the last surviving ship of the Phantom Wing had finally made it into official service—at the top.

Humor had otherwise been sparse for much of the flight. Beyond the fact that none of the exiles knew what the future held for them, only thirteen adults, counting Valandris, had survived the assault at Ketorix. All who had been attached to *Krencha* had been lost when the battlesphere they boarded was destroyed. Several of *Chu'charq*'s crew, including Dublak, had died boarding the ship of the Breen leader. Of the two crews that had fought in the surface action, only five Klingons had survived the fight, including Kahless, Worf, and Bardoc.

Sixty remained of a population of three hundred. Four in five, gone forever. The statistic took Valandris's breath away.

The only thing that brought it back was the children, all of whom had been saved by her preparations—and her dogged will to make sure that *Chu'charq* emerged whole. The youngsters in her ready room squealed with delight as they caught their first sight of the Great Hall.

"Do you see it, Valandris?" Sarken asked. "It's bigger than our whole village!"

"It must be, to keep all the animals outside," she said. Weeks earlier, Valandris would have said "inside"—or something else even more acerbic. But she didn't feel that way now. It *was* something to see, Valandris thought, majestic and impressive, the symbol of a people who knew they had something to be proud of.

Chu'charq's respectful flight past it reminded her of the future that was at hand. Valandris stepped out into the hallway, where one of the guards glanced at her. Worf and Kahless had guaranteed the Unsung's honorable behavior; both had been imprisoned repeatedly on the vessel and had no intention of inflicting that experience on anyone they trusted. Yet their keepers were ever present, and she understood why. The Unsung had killed too many.

The strange thing, however, was that the masked Klingons seemed strangely conflicted over whether to look directly at their charges. It had taken her a while to remember that they were still dishonorable nonentities, no matter what they had done. How did one watch what one would not deign to look at? It was how the discommendated had metastasized into a threat in the first place—not just on Thane, but throughout the Empire. Valandris still felt something about the practice had to change.

Feeling the vessel land, she made her way to the lowest deck. There, in the cargo hold, she could hear Worf and Kahless halfway down the open landing ramp, conferring for a long time with people she could not see. When they re-ascended, two visitors followed them.

One, a Klingon a few years younger than she was, threw himself into a happy embrace with Worf. The young man then looked to her—and in that instant, she saw his father in his cranial ridges. "I am Alexander," he said, "Federation ambassador to Qo'noS."

The discommendated child, redeemed. "I greet you, Alexander, son of Worf. I am Valandris."

The human guest stepped up, saying, "I spoke with you on H'atoria, didn't I?" Admiral Riker searched her eyes for a glimmer of recognition. "You were wearing a face mask then."

"Yes, and the ambassador should take one," she said. "I fear we have transported a disease from Thane."

"The ship is under quarantine here until our authorities can study the problem," Worf said. "It also gives the Empire time to decide what to do with you."

"Have no fear," Kahless said. "I have just sent word to Chancellor Martok that I will not leave your company until your case is heard."

"Emperor, your people would celebrate your arrival," Alexander said, taking a mask. "You would deny them that?"

"My people have denied the exiles aboard this ship to the detriment of all," Kahless said. "The Unsung have said they will stand behind their acts. I will stand with them."

Riker appeared impressed by Kahless's commitment. "Emperor, you must have had an interesting time getting to know them."

"'A week can hold a century for one who seizes life,'" Valandris said.

Kahless laughed. "That saying is one of mine. A good one."

Riker smiled. "Well, the ambassador and I have a century to fit into my *chavmajta* presentation tomorrow. The past few days have given us some great deeds to close with. We'd better get back to it."

Worf reported to his admiral. "I understand *Titan* brought you here, sir. I am ready to return to service," he said. "Is there a way for me to get to *Enterprise*?"

The corner of Riker's mouth crinkled upward. "I think you've earned some time off, Commander. Enjoy the city. Eat some *gagh*." He turned and started down the ramp, before pausing to look back. "You might come by the consulate later. We have a little something we're cooking up that you may be interested in."

BREEN SHIPYARD
JOLVA REE

Shift had watched them work all day, and while she could not understand what Chot Dayn and his three colleagues were saying, she knew what they were up to. They were planting bombs.

The secret construction facility inside the asteroid orbiting Jolva Ree had generated a mighty force of Kinshaya battlespheres—but those were gone. A few had made it back to Janalwa, but most had suffered various fates in

Klingon space. The Klingons, Starfleet, and the Unsung had destroyed several. Breen officers rejecting the Kinshaya stand-down order had in some cases faced violent mutinies, resulting in both sides abandoning ship. Other Breen had self-destructed their battlespheres rather than risk capture by the Klingons.

The result was that the shipyard at Jolva Ree was a barren womb. Its children were gone. All had come to nothing. It had all been a waste—and Chot Dayn despised waste above all things.

He had refused to provide Shift with a new helmet; he no longer considered her Breen. None were available aboard the station, for the entire population had either been part of the ill-fated Rebuke or had fled following news of the reversal. Dayn had taken it upon himself to see that the station was destroyed, lest the Confederacy be compromised further by its discovery.

The anger expressed by the other Typhon Pact partners was enough for the domo to deal with, and the Breen would certainly never use Jolva Ree again. They were no longer welcome in the territory of the Holy Order of the Kinshaya. Chot Dayn had heard the "special relationship" was done, and there was some question as to whether the Kinshaya would remain in the Typhon Pact. It appeared that the Devotionalists would put Yeffir back in charge. The one-time Breen ally, Ykredna, had fled, her hardliner supporters decimated in battle and her reputation in ruins.

Shift knew what that felt like. She sat, locked in what had been Thot Roje's private office, watching the progress outside the window that overlooked the shipyard. The Orion preferred to look out there. Everything around the office reminded her of her dead friend, the first person to accept her as an intelligent being. Dayn had already destroyed the computer in the room, and his companions had done likewise across the station. Should anything survive the asteroid's destruction, a data search would yield nothing.

She doubted anything would survive—especially after hearing Dayn speak upon his return. *"We have used all the remaining antimatter mines,"* he said, setting his filter so she could understand his voice. *"Finally, there is a case where Thot Roje's overaggressive inventory practices have actually helped."*

She did not laugh at his excuse for a joke. "Your companions are back aboard the shuttle?"

"Outside the asteroid, awaiting my command to transport me out. I wanted to give you a choice, though you do not deserve it. You may return to the Confederacy as our prisoner to stand trial for the wasteful disaster you have wrought."

She stared at him. "The other option?"

"Remain here and die in the explosion. It might ultimately be less painful for you—and I consider it the better choice for efficiency's sake. Our order will be saved the expense of your punishment." He turned and faced the window so that he could see the empty station. *"But looking at it in the context of all that you have squandered, it is a marginal expense either way. Frankly, Shift, you are nothing."*

It was the one thing never to say to her. Her eyes narrowed as she looked at his armored back.

Fifty-four

K orgh hated to admit it, but the Federation understood how to make Klingons feel welcome.

It would have been very easy for the designers of the assembly room of the expanded consulate to create something that would have seemed patronizing. Duplicating the main room of the Great Hall in miniature, for example, would have been easy—but also offensive. Setting up a Federation conference area with a bowl of *gagh* on each table likewise would have seemed heavy-handed.

But the consulate's auditorium had been designed to be inclusive. It sat beneath a high arching roof, with a window wall of transparent aluminum at the short end behind the rostrum through which the majestic Hall of Heroes could be seen. There were no soft human chairs for the audience. Instead, the spectator area extended back in a semicircle from the stage on a series of nested steps of differing elevations, giving listeners the option of sitting should a speech drone on too long.

The rest was austere and reverent. The banners of the Federation and the Klingon Empire flanked the stage, with braziers behind. When meetings were in session and fires were lit, the names of honored dead from cooperative Klingon/Federation efforts could be seen inscribed on the soaring arcs of the ceiling. Somehow, the designers had crafted the names so some glowed more, and then others. The inattentive listener could sit all day reading names of heroes lost.

Much of the work was credited to Lieutenant Xaatix, Starfleet's protocol expert. Korgh remembered the reports from Spirits' Forge, where the Ovirian had thwarted one of his plans. That would not happen this time. He had seen Odrok go to work in the consulate with her kit; he had seen her exit without it. According to the indicator on the device she had left for him, the bomb was live and just beneath the floor panels of the rostrum. Its detonation should kill not only the speakers, but a fair number of those High Council members in the room who did not support him—a number that he feared was growing, as more came to light about how the House of Kruge failed to defend itself. He would kill them, and they would deserve it.

Standing with Qolkat as the other High Council members entered, Korgh studied the individuals on stage. There was Riker with his lap dog Alexander; both were conferring with Martok. Scanning the platform, he saw that several of Martok's cronies were up there. Melk, Tanor, Klag: the usual suspects. But it was the Starfleet contingent that interested him. Picard, he recognized—but there were more.

He asked Qolkat.

"The Federation has sent several Starfleet vessels here today to drum up support," Qolkat said. "*Titan*—her Captain Christine Vale is there. *Enterprise*, obviously. *Aventine*, I believe: that is Captain Ezri Dax."

Korgh frowned. He had not heard of *Aventine* fighting any battles against the Kinshaya.

He heard a cheer erupt from those around him. Craning his neck, he saw Worf entering. His role in the defense of Ketorix was known, and parts of his story about the Unsung had gotten out. As yet, Worf was the only person to emerge from the quarantined *Chu'charq*, where efforts to eliminate the *tharkak'ra* virus were apparently close to success.

Many tried to speak with him as Worf made his way down through the hall.

"They will surely put him on stage," Korgh said. "Mascot for the Accords."

But Worf stopped near the dais only long enough to pay his respects. He then retreated to a position in the middle of the audience, pausing only once to make eye contact with Korgh. The look was a strange one, Korgh thought: more watchful than friendly or hostile. It was over in a second.

"The chancellor has agreed to give the Unsung a trial," Qolkat said. "You should expect to see Worf there too."

Korgh shook his head. As soon as he was chancellor, he would quash that idea and have the Unsung immediately put to death. It was not that he feared they knew anything that could implicate him. Rather, they would be his patsies for the bombing of the consulate, a way to redirect any suspicions following his convenient exit from the auditorium. The Federation had given the exiles haven; its Starfleet had let them attack and escape repeatedly. He would accuse the Federation of plotting to decapitate the Klingon regime, its plan all along, by allowing the assassins it had cultivated—and which Worf had brought to Qo'noS—into its facility.

As his second act he would void the Khitomer Accords. War with the Federation would come when he was ready, and when he had chosen which allies he desired. Commander Kruge would approve of the end, if not all of the means.

Looking back to the stage, he noticed a new arrival on stage chatting with Riker. "Why is General Kersh here? I did not tell her to come."

"She answers not to you, but the Defense Force," Qolkat said. "And they answer to Martok."

Korgh steamed—but in the next second, he was delighted

to realize that yet another rival would go down. He smiled. Even this quickly concocted plan, conceived in desperation, had the touch of genius.

A gong sounded. "*Qapla'*," Qolkat whispered.

Korgh made his way down to the stage to say his piece. Ascending the steps to the platform, he gave only a glance to his opponents, gathered together on either side of the stage.

"As you know," he said before the podium, "I called this *chavmajta* to demand that the Federation justify its continued alliance with the Empire. Many of you also know that my own house suffered an invasion from one of our most loathed enemies. An invasion successfully repelled!"

Cheers rose from the councilors. It was time to make the turn. He gripped the sides of the podium, and his tone grew grave. "You may have heard that Starfleet contributed to the defense of my family's territory. To this, I can only say what my adoptive father always told me, 'Never trust the Federation.' They have been negotiating for a free-flight corridor, so that trash like the Breen and the Kinshaya could traverse our space unaccompanied. We now see what they would do if they had that power." He clapped the surface before him in time with his words. "The Federation would *add* and *add* and *add* to its members, constraining our growth in every direction—until, having strangled the fighting will of our people, they would invite us to join their group, wiping out what it is to be Klingon."

He raised his hands. "No. We have trusted them before—and paid for it with our dearest blood. And I ask you to join me in refusing to listen to their lies!"

Korgh stormed off the rostrum and made his way up the jagged path leading between the listeners and the exit. He caught sight of Worf, glowering at him as he went. Purposefully, he did not look to see who was following—and in the cacophony of raised voices, he could not tell whether there were cheers for him. But he could sense he was being followed, and reaching the banquet area outside, he looked back to see that a dozen councilors had joined him.

Korgh then saw Martok move to the podium. The chancellor began speaking, starting to tell of the fruits of the Accords. "You have heard the words of an angry old dullard," he said. "In response, let me tell you of the sacrifice an *Enterprise* captain made at Narendra III years ago—and how another was prepared to do so again this very week!"

That was the cue. Korgh turned in the doorway and passed between his allies. Now in the lead, he continued walking forward between the tables, trying not to appear conscious of the thing that was coming. Hearing the explosion behind him was almost a relief. He made a show of stumbling forward, as if surprised by the noise. And he joined his supporters, whose alarm was genuine as they did not know what was planned, in hurrying to the entrance of the assembly area. He looked in expectantly . . .

. . . and saw that only the front portion of the stage had been blown open. Smoke poured from beneath the platform—while atop, the Federation and Klingon personnel scrambled about. Martok knelt beside the opening, puzzled, and drew forth the shattered remnants of a device, its transceiver still attached.

The bomb was a dud!

In the crowd, Worf made his way to the aisle, tapping his combadge and commanding the Federation guards. "Seal the facility," Worf yelled. "Locate the personnel records of those who worked on the stage. Check the sensors to see where the signal came from. Find who did this!"

Korgh quickly turned, eyes wide. As Federation guards hurried into the room to respond, he looked about for Qolkat or one of his other supporters. They had scattered, perhaps fearful their departure would be connected with the blast. They had only known about the walkout, after all; following a successful assassination, he would have given them cover by blaming the Unsung. But now he had more than them to be concerned about. He turned and hurried away before the doors could be closed.

Korgh's mind raced. He had seen part of the bomb casing, intact. It had to have some trace of Odrok on it somewhere; she was too rushed to be careful. And then there was the detonation transmission. The thing would be found out.

Outside, he hurried into a secluded alleyway. He would have to go where he had intended to go afterward all along, and do the thing he had always intended to do.

Fifty-five

Korgh still had access to Qolkat's personal transporter, whose site-to-site settings he had preprogrammed to take him to only one place. He used it—and emerged from behind Odrok's building, pausing only to toss the now-useless defeat switch onto the street. He ground it to tiny pieces beneath his heel, near the glass from several of her broken bottles.

The lord felt pain in every step as he hurried too fast up the stairs. The door was not open this time, but he forced it. In the bedroom, he found Odrok in exactly the condition he expected: collapsed across her bed, drunk. More bottles told the tale: apparently she was not out of liquor after all. She had botched the operation, one final time.

His fury rose. He wanted to strangle her—but caution, as ever, prevailed. He remembered what he had planned. He would take care of her—and then the materials she had hidden in the storage area.

"Odrok, Odrok," he said to her motionless form. He let out an exasperated sigh. "After we were successful, I was going to bring you the best bottle of bloodwine money could buy—not this swill you've been drinking." From the folds of his robe, he located a hypospray. "We would have shared it—a toast to our future."

Breathing fast, he sat the woman upright on the bed. "Then I was going to give you something else," he said. Using one hand to steady her, he brought the hypospray between them. "Severance for one hundred years. Too bad. Too bad for us both." He moved the device closer to her neck—

—and saw her eyes open wide. Wide, full of fury, as her frail hands grabbed his wrists. She squeezed, forcing him to drop the hypospray—and kept squeezing, snapping his bones and causing him to yell in shock and agony. Then she smashed her bony forehead against his, stunning him.

She stood, still holding his hands and shaking the heavier Klingon like a child's doll. Nose bleeding, head pounding, Korgh looked at Odrok in panic. She was acting with the strength of someone a third her age and twice her size. "You liar!" she yelled. "You traitor!"

She released his hands and grabbed the sides of his skull, starting to apply crushing pressure. His head turned, Korgh's eyes bulged—and then he saw it. The hidden door behind Odrok's mirror opened. It was the room where she kept her tools of espionage. Admiral Riker emerged from that place of darkness. He hurried inside and grabbed the old woman's hands. "Stop! You want him alive." He struggled to save Korgh. "Stop, Martok!"

Odrok froze, her angry eyes fixed on Korgh's panicked ones—and a second later, a flash of light replaced the old woman with the Klingon chancellor. Martok growled loudly and cast Korgh to the floor.

Dazed, bewildered, Korgh looked up to see the real Odrok enter the room from the hiding space. Riker asked her, "Odrok, do you confirm that Lord Korgh hired you to assassinate the chancellor?"

"Yes," she said, almost hissing the word as she looked at him. "It is just as I said when I called you, Riker. He did this—and much more."

Korgh looked back at her, not comprehending. "You, Odrok? You arranged this?"

"Yes, Korgh. Me, Odrok." She pointed to the chancellor. "Martok was using the same tools your hired killers used in creating the Unsung."

Wincing at the pain in his wrists, Korgh got to his knees and shook his head. He didn't know how much the others knew—and while that was the case, he decided he wasn't going to admit to anything. "Tools? What tools? I don't know what you mean."

Riker growled in disgust. "Stop spinning, Korgh."

His eyes narrowing, Korgh thought it might help to seem cooperative. "Wait. Are you referring to the illusion-generation vessel I read about in the report?" He pretended to think. "Yes . . . the *Blackstone*. I was informed that no longer functioned."

"That information was correct." Jean-Luc Picard entered the bedroom—as well as the Trill captain Korgh had seen earlier. "Sorry we're late," he said to the others. "There was only so much space in the closet, so we transported to the street."

"And Worf?" Martok asked.

"He is on stage now, explaining what happened." Picard looked down at Korgh. "As I was saying—it was not the *Blackstone* that cast the image of Odrok, but the *Houdini*, thanks to Captain Dax."

Dax bowed. "The folks in orbit have been pretty busy. They modeled Odrok so Martok could impersonate her. The Martok you saw on stage was a very unusual person named Ardra, whom I would like to get off my ship as soon as possible."

Picard flashed Dax a grin before his expression turned serious. "The bomb was an illusion generated by our friends aboard the *Houdini*, with the assistance of the *Blackstone* truthcrafter crew. They were eager to help out and reduce their possible sentences."

"We have not even begun to consider yours," Martok said. He glared menacingly down at Korgh. "I despise deception. But Riker said I should do this to find where deception truly hid. And now I know."

Weary, spent, Korgh looked back at Odrok. "This is madness," he said. "A fantasy. Why would you believe her? *Her*—"

"A drunk?" Odrok asked. Her face filled with revulsion. "Tell him."

"You were excellent at covering your tracks, keeping at arm's length from your transactions," Picard said. "But there were three Federation starships with very good crews involved. They found a shadow walking through all the events connected with the Unsung: the Phantom Wing's creation, its dilithium maintenance, training of its pilots, and even the theft of the Hunters' transporter technology. When we learned that Ardra and Shift had a Klingon cellmate on Thionoga, the shadow took form." Picard looked to the woman. "She operated under many names—but she had to be the connecting element between the truthcrafters and the Unsung."

"When Odrok contacted us," Riker said, "we knew immediately who we had. We also knew we had to act fast. *Aventine* was coming with *Houdini* as evidence in the Unsung's trial. I just asked Captain Dax to get here a little sooner."

"Such a tale, such a production." His acid tongue recovered, Korgh asked, "And why, pray tell, Picard, are *you* here?"

The captain looked keenly at him, barely hiding his scorn. "You took advantage of my trust—and my crew's hospitality. I wouldn't miss this for the world."

A Vulcan appeared in the doorway behind the two captains. "Excuse me, sirs. *Houdini* reports that its sensors have recorded all events in this room since Lord Korgh entered. This part of the evidentiary chain is intact."

"Lord Korgh, I'd like you to meet Commander Tuvok," Riker said. "He's *our* shadow. He's been after the truth the whole time."

Korgh struggled to stand up. "I am sure it is satisfying to you all to prattle on. This is nothing but nonsense, created by the Federation to frame an enemy of their favored chancellor. If those filthy Unsung can have their day, I will certainly have mine."

Martok grabbed Korgh roughly by the shoulder and lifted him up. "You will get your day. But I would not count on having many more past that."

Fifty-six

The judge looked down on Worf from his station high above in the shadows of the tribunal box. "This court appreciates your experience, Worf, son of Mogh. There can be no better advocate for the accused than one who witnessed so much."

Worf felt the same way, which was why he had agreed to advocate for the Unsung. "Thank you, Your Honor."

The Unsung's trial necessarily had to precede any action against Lord Korgh, and political necessity required that the old Klingon be judged as quickly as possible. A delay in sharing the astounding story of Korgh's dishonor with the public only served to undermine the Empire. It meant there was no time to brief an advocate on everything Worf knew. He had to act. Years earlier he had failed in pleading for the lives of other Klingons—the renegade Captain Korris and his companions. This time, Worf had to find a way to succeed.

The commander did not know if the coliseum-style court surrounding him was the same one where, decades before, an ancestor of Worf's had infamously defended James Kirk and Leonard McCoy. The First City had suffered massive damage during the Borg Invasion, and many new places had been built. The court certainly felt like a place from out of the past, with its multiple tiers of viewing boxes hewn from rock, rising nearly out of sight.

Harsh light streamed down on Worf—but not on the

accused. They stood in darkness, unworthy of being seen. "Speak now to the status of the defendants," the judge said.

"I contend," Worf said, ignoring the echo, "that the heirs to the House of Kruge did not nobly fight at Gamaral a century ago, and that Chancellor Kesh erred in acceding to their demands to discommendate Kruge's officers. I have submitted my findings in that matter."

"We have them," said one of the other judges in the box. "A contemptible tale. General Kersh, do you contest these charges?"

Kersh emerged from the shadows. As granddaughter of J'borr, she had been the natural choice for prosecutor. Worf knew she would have an interest in defending the reputation of her blood. "The only story I know is the one my family told," she said. "They were long regarded as heroes. I would not see them condemned now on speculation."

Worf turned to face her. "I interviewed all the nobles of the House of Kruge before reaching Gamaral. Not one could accurately describe the battle or the location."

"A hundred years had passed!" she said. "Surely—"

The judge interrupted, "No battle of such importance could be forgotten. We have spoken with the chancellor's historians and deem Worf's contention correct. The victory was not theirs. They should not have taken the officers' honor as their spoils."

Worf pressed his advantage. "The Unsung's conduct in defending the House of Kruge's family compound expunges any stain that might have fallen on the discommendated officers for failing to protect his house from the thieves within the family."

The word *thieves* brought mumbles from the crowd and an acid look from Kersh. It did not seem to distress the judges. "With this, too, we agree," one said. "We expunge the discommendation from those warriors and their descendants. Let the name of General Potok again be spoken."

The audience rumbled, but the justice was not finished. "One condemnation is lifted; another remains to be adjudicated. The defendants must stand for the crimes they have committed. They may yet be discommendated for their own actions."

Worf glanced at the figures behind him in silhouette. "Must they still stand in darkness? Are they not Klingon?"

"Well spoken," said the judge on the right. "Let the accused be seen!"

Light poured down on the prisoners' dock, a waist-high circular enclosure—greatly expanded, for this session, to hold the thirteen surviving adults of the Unsung. Worf saw Valandris, with Hemtara and Raneer from her bridge crew; Bardoc of the twins; Nelkor, the foolish youth; and several others, all of whose personal stories of courage under fire at Ketorix he had learned in preparation for the trial. The children, not accused, were led from designated boxes at ground level to stand quietly behind their elders; Doctor Crusher and a team of Klingon medics had identified and eliminated the *tharkak'ra* virus in the children and on *Chu'charq.*

Those watching roared to see them, these strange Klingons who had rocked the Empire with their deeds. Several of the Unsung looked up and about like trapped animals—but Valandris stood firm, staring directly up at the judge's box.

"I am Valandris," she declared loudly and slowly, pronouncing her words with the accent Kahless had taught them all. "I am Klingon, as are those of my blood here. We stand before you and claim the acts of Gamaral, H'atoria, and Ghora Janto. These and more, against the Orions."

"The Orions are of no consequence to us," the middle judge said. "Speak of the others."

Explaining, Valandris told of the manner in which the exiles had been cut off from Klingon culture. She detailed the arrival of the false Kruge—a tale that Martok had allowed to be told, after Korgh's arrest—and how he had won their allegiance. The story was long, and the judges interrupted several times with questions. But Worf knew she had left nothing out and that her tale, passionately told, was effective.

"If Kruge indeed did live," Worf said when she was finished, "then General Potok and his officers would have owed him allegiance. The response of the officers' descendants to the arrival of the 'Fallen Lord' was Klingon."

"But *they* were not Kruge's officers," Kersh declared, pointing at the defendants. "They were under no obligation to commit dishonorable acts."

"We had no notion of what honor was," Valandris replied. "Until Worf and Kahless showed us."

Worf let that sink in with the justices before bringing up something he had learned from Ardra's attorney. "You have already heard they were never taught the Klingon way," he said. "I submit that, as impersonated by the criminal Buxtus Cross, the false Kruge had such influence that he was able to supplant their judgment with his. The legal term in the Federation is 'diminished capacity.'"

"No meaning in our society," Kersh said.

Before Worf could rebut the general, Valandris spoke. "He did enthrall those of us who had known nothing but despair." She took a deep breath and shook her head. "But as time went on, some of us realized what we were doing was wrong." She looked down. "I did."

Valandris had rendered useless one of Worf's lines of

defense. He was searching for what to say next when an unusual sound rang out through the arena: a baby's cry. The spotlight moved—and all saw Kahless entering the floor.

Having stayed out of sight on *Chu'charq*, the emperor had not been seen publicly since his appearance on the broadcast from the Ketorix compound. When the audience saw him walking in—*with a Klingon infant in his hands!*—pandemonium erupted. Thirty seconds of cheering and applause, during which the judge never gaveled them to order.

"I am sorry for my delay in appearing," Kahless declared. "I was getting advice from my new young friend here on the best way to sharpen a *bat'leth*."

Roaring laughter was the response. Kersh, knowing herself overmatched, receded to the shadows.

"A joke, but only just," Kahless said. "The children of Thane are wonderful hunters. It is a world you must all visit—though I would suggest staying out of sewage pits."

Worf felt enervated by his arrival. "Tell them of the child, Emperor."

"He is the son of Harch and Weltern, two warriors of the Unsung who died protecting Ketorix. Their ship in flames, they boarded a battlesphere and took the bridge, forcing the Kinshaya to destroy their own vessel." Kahless walked with the gurgling child to the dock where the other Unsung stood. "Like the rest of his people, this child was given no name at birth. He waits to see if you find his parents' acts honorable."

"*G'now juk Hol pajhard,*" Kersh said, reemerging. "A son will share in the honors or shame of his father. It is our way."

"Perhaps," Kahless said. "But it strikes me he is quite small to be concerned with these matters." He handed the child to Raneer and then climbed over the railing to join the accused—an act that startled the whole crowd.

A stunned judge said, "You are not accused, Kahless."

"I stand with them."

"I had heard you would take this path," Kersh said. "This is not necessary—though it is a noble act on your part. These people tried to kill you."

"They in fact killed another Klingon, a general whose name may only now be spoken," Kahless said. "On their world, their law applies, not ours. And for my imprisonment, I forgive them."

"And I," Worf said.

"But the other crimes remain," Kersh said. "Gamaral, H'atoria. These must be answered for."

"Indeed," Kahless said, over the baby's mewling. "But my experience with them—and their willingness to accept blame, and to fight for Ketorix, has led me to suggest a different punishment to the chancellor and court."

Worf looked at Kahless, puzzled. They had not discussed it.

"We came here to stand for what we have done," Valandris said. "We will accept what comes."

The middle judge pounded his gavel against the counter. "Sentence will be pronounced—that suggested by the emperor. The children of the exile community, being not in guilt, are to be raised on H'atoria. There, they will join settler families and be raised as Klingon."

The audience buzzed with approval.

The judge moved on. "You thirteen will be relocated to that planet as well," he said. "You are sentenced to duty at Spirits' Forge, where you will take the place of the Sentries you slew and impersonated. There, you will stand guard—and continue to learn from Kahless what honor means, for as long as he sees fit to keep you there."

Worf spun around to look at the emperor. "You are going with them?"

"I am," Kahless said, his voice rising as he spoke. "Let the fortress become a place of pilgrimage for all who seek to understand honor—or who have stepped off its path and seek to find it. Then will it truly be a forge for spirits."

"The sentence is humbly accepted," Valandris said—but her voice could hardly be heard over the cheers. Worf saw that even Kersh was touched—and he could not help but smile. Kahless had found his calling—and the exiles were no longer Unsung. They were Klingon, and would have songs.

The judge called for attention. "There is just one more important matter undone," he said. "There is a child who needs a name."

Holding the infant now, Valandris chuckled. "This is something we had already discussed amongst ourselves," she said as the commander of the group. "To honor the Klingon who not only came back from discommendation, but who led others from it, we present to you all Worf, son of Harch."

There was no quieting the crowd after that.

Fifty-seven

Lord Korgh was a member of the High Council, making his prosecution more complicated. There had been a hearing in the courtroom vacated by the Unsung, a much more somber affair in which the allegations and evidence were made public. As a high official facing grave charges, Korgh had demanded the whole High Council sit for the *meqba'*, or hearing of evidence, in the Great Hall, away from a general audience.

While both of his sons were present, Korgh had asked neither to stand as his second, or *cha'DIch*. Tengor he considered beyond useless, and Tragg was still in pain from his injuries. Korgh was surprised that he could find no one among his council allies to defend him; the cowards feared being connected with his assassination attempt. Qolkat was already being scrutinized. Korgh had finally determined to go on alone, knowing he had always been his own best advocate.

He had listened impatiently for long hours as one Starfleet witness after another presented evidence at Martok's request. Korgh had heard the Klingon investigators and what they had found in the data systems in his ruined Ketorix compound. He had been forced to endure their elaborate reconstruction of his actions since the Battle of Gamaral a hundred years earlier, and his funneling of resources toward what they called "the Unsung project." Korgh had attempted to refute their presentations at every turn. To obfuscate, to confuse, to belittle: anything that would muddy the picture.

Then had come the witnesses associated with the *Blackstone* and its deceptions. The Ferengi truthcrafter, Gaw, had never interacted with Korgh, yet he knew about everything the exiles had been bidden to do. The good news for Korgh was that Gaw was timid and craven in the way of his people, and he came off poorly. His suggestion that the High Council members "should really look into buying some chairs" was, Korgh was certain, a new low for utterances in the Great Hall.

But as outlandish as the technician and the practices he described may have seemed to the council, Gaw's allegation that Lord Korgh had sent *Ark of G'boj* as payoff had been damaging. Worse was his suggestion that the Breen spy, Shift, had blackmailed Korgh into sending away his house's defenders. Korgh had been forced to dance verbally around that.

He had heard the prosecution would bring a star witness, and he had every idea about who it would be. He was not surprised in the least when Odrok walked before the council. He refused to even look at the traitorous wretch as she told the tale of her hundred-year association with him.

It was all true, of course—but every word stabbed. *Such betrayal.*

"You realize," Martok said as she concluded, "that you are complicit in all of his crimes?"

She replied, "That is wrong, Chancellor."

That caught Korgh's attention. He watched her. When she spoke, it was with a passion he had not seen in her in years.

"I began in Commander Kruge's service," she said, "a hundred and ten years ago. He was my liege. I was following his orders when I removed the Phantom Wing from Gamaral.

After his death, Korgh represented to me that he was following Kruge's final wishes."

"But there were no orders telling you to deceive the exiles," Martok said. "There could not have been. There were no exiles while Kruge lived. Where his orders ended, Korgh's began."

"I believed Korgh to be the rightful heir of the family," she said.

"You knew he was not," another councilor interjected. "You arranged with the Unsung to fake his adoption!"

"I knew there was no proof of the rite," Odrok replied. "But I *wanted* to believe it. I wanted to think that I could continue to serve Kruge."

Martok asked Korgh, "You contest this woman's story?"

He laughed. "It is the delusion of a drunkard. Odrok worked for me as a domestic, before I turned her out." He glared at her. "This tale is her attempt at revenge."

"You tried to kill her in her bed!"

"She had called, begging me to visit her after the ceremony. She claimed she was in unbearable pain. She did not merit a warrior's suicide by blade, so I brought her a hypospray to spare her further suffering. I see now it was an attempt by my enemies to entrap me."

He looked at the council members. Some still appeared conflicted. Spreading confusion had sown doubt. There were simpler types, he knew, who would never consider financial records, electronic communications, or forensic data as evidence; they looked only to words spoken and the people behind them. He only had to appear more believable than Odrok to some of them—and he hoped he had succeeded.

Martok addressed her once more. "Have you anything to add?"

"Yes," Odrok said. She faced Korgh for the first time—

and her eyes looked daggers at him. "It has taken me too long to admit this, but Korgh is Kruge's true heir in one thing. Both were willing to use anyone to get what they wanted. Kruge even killed his . . ."

She paused, unable to get the words out. "His lover," she finally said. "He killed a woman named Valkris."

Martok's aide, an official historian, spoke up. "There is no record of such an act. Our investigations only found that Valkris obtained the Genesis data, and that she likely provided it to him."

"She was never seen again," Odrok said. "Korgh would have brought me to the same end as Valkris, once he was through with me." She glared at him. "Perhaps the nobles that claimed the House of Kruge were no heroes. But neither did Korgh deserve it."

Korgh waited. "Are you finished?" When she did not respond, Korgh waved his hand dismissively. "You have here a serial liar, who stalked me for decades. I suggest the entire mad scheme was hers. There is nothing to connect me to the Unsung and nothing to connect me to the Phantom Wing. It is all a fantasy, a frame-up by a desperate chancellor. Do not be fooled."

"You disgust me," Odrok said. She spat in his direction. Then she turned and walked back though the crowd, leaving the chamber.

"Is this all there is?" Korgh asked the High Council. "Lies and misapprehensions? I cannot think you would unanimously accept these tales. Let us bring this to an end—and get back to debating the future of the Empire and its leadership."

"There is one more witness," said a human voice from the back of the room.

Korgh looked back to see Picard entering. The Klingon

snorted. "Let me guess—you have found a thread from my sleeve where it should not be. What else could you know?"

"I am not the witness." Picard faced Martok. "Chancellor, the holographic transmission has been established. The Romulans were most willing to assist."

Korgh blinked. *The Romulans?*

"Project the witness," Martok said once the equipment had been set up.

A life-sized figure materialized in the center of the room where Odrok had stood. Korgh gawked as he saw who it was.

"*I am Ambassador Spock,*" the Vulcan announced. "*I am honored to have the chance to address this assemblage.*"

"Your words are welcome in this place, Ambassador," Martok said.

"*My work on Romulus makes me unable to attend in person, but when I learned of the events in the Empire—and of my possible role in them—I had to speak. I could not do otherwise.*"

Korgh's mouth went dry. His shoulders sagged.

"*I am told that you have all seen the report I filed in 2286, after U.S.S. Enterprise-A's encounter with General Potok's exiles inside the Briar Patch, or Klach D'Kel Brakt. You know of my encounter with them—and with the captain of a bird-of-prey who sought to recruit the refuges.*"

"Do you see that captain here?" Martok said.

The holographic Spock turned, not looking that much older than when Korgh had first encountered him. "*Yes. Lord Korgh is the Klingon I met on the bridge of Potok's freighter. He had been aboard a bird-of-prey he claimed was part of a secret squadron—and he called upon an engineer named Odrok.*"

"What?" Korgh laughed, nerves getting to him. "This—this is madness, a fabrication. That was a hundred years ago."

"*I never forget a face,*" Spock said. "*And as you said to me back then: Vulcans do not lie.*"

Korgh looked around the room. There was no doubt in any of the councilors' faces now. The witness was unimpeachable.

"Thank you, Ambassador," Martok said. "You have been most helpful."

"Before I end transmission, Chancellor, I would like to say two things."

"Of course."

"First, I understand many blame General Potok for his poor choices in running his community. The Klingon I met was a man of introspection—and, I believe, had a strong sense of honor. He did not accept exile because he was guilty of the crime he was accused of. He judged himself and his allies as having failed—and that is why he chose to go. Had I known that the harshness of his views would, in later years, damage the well-being of the exiles and their descendants, I would have advised moderation. But he would not have accepted my counsel."

The hologram looked around the room, as if he were studying the faces of the councilors he could see. *"Second— and more importantly as we approach a century of peace: There are those who say that the accord between the Klingon Empire and the United Federation of Planets is not an equal one. They compare the number of starships or the amount of territory, and find the bargain uneven."* He paused. *"Speaking as someone present at the beginning, I make the following observation: they are correct."*

A rumble of surprise quaked through the hall.

"They are correct," Spock said, *"in that we are not two beings born from the same cell, with identical compositions. We are distinct, with different cultures. We will always maintain our individuality—and we can do so while still remaining partners. Because there is one area in which we can be* exactly *equal: faith. Our faith in you is exactly equal to yours in us.*

When trust is diminished, our prospects together are limited. When we trust one another, no crisis can divide us."

Shaking his head at his fate, Korgh could barely look at the listeners—but he could see they were spellbound.

"Recent events tested your people's faith in the Federation," Spock said. *"We understand why—and take responsibility, just as I do for my own role. But our friendship was never in danger, because of the Federation's faith in the Klingon Empire. Some may have thought the successful resolution too slow, but no one should have doubted it was coming. We are honored to be your friends, and we always will be."*

Shouts of approval came from the councilors and the audience members alike.

"An important legacy has been bequeathed from my generation to yours. Peace is the work of ages. Let us continue working— together."

Fifty-eight

Korgh had been convicted.

While confident of Korgh's guilt, Captain Picard had remained uncertain of the trial's outcome until the message from Ambassador Spock had arrived. The news that the Vulcan had learned of the proceedings and wanted to contribute had changed everything. No Klingon doubted his memory or his trustworthiness. Yes, Picard could see the hand of the Romulans; Spock had been working openly with their Unification movement, and they were aggrieved with Korgh over the near-killing of their ambassador at H'atoria. They would have seen that Spock learned the whole sordid story. But the net result had been positive.

The trials and their verdicts had been followed with interest aboard the *Enterprise*. Korgh's sentencing had been put off until the next afternoon and was closed, for Klingons only. Having returned to *Enterprise*, Picard steeled himself and headed to the conference room near the brig, where he had a legal matter of his own to deal with.

Ardra was there, resplendent in burgundy. She and Gaw chatted as the old friends they were. Also in the room were the other *Blackstone* truthcrafters, happy to be reunited with the Bynars 1110 and 1111. Emil Yorta, the sole lawyer in a roomful of defendants, was a popular person.

Picard stepped to the head of the table. "The Klingon Empire has agreed to allow Starfleet to handle your cases in appreciation for your help in Korgh's capture and conviction."

"Bless you, Captain Picard," Gaw said.

"I have also spoken with the Judge Advocate General about your cooperation. However, the facts are that the truthcrafters were accessories to the murders of the Sentries on H'atoria and played a role in the conspiracy creating the Unsung." He faced Gaw. "You cannot walk away."

Gaw's smile went crooked. "You've got us there."

"Ardra," the captain said, "what you did on Janalwa not only negated what Shift did to those people—but you also unraveled the same fraud performed years earlier by Jilaan."

She looked at him suspiciously. "And?"

"Starfleet has been made aware of a large number of episodes where other—*practitioners*, you call them?—have disrupted societies."

"Oh?" Ardra said innocently. "Where would you have learned that?"

"A series of books found aboard *Blackstone*. The Breen apparently did not have time to remove them."

Ardra turned and scowled at Gaw. "They've got your copies of the *Annals*!"

Gaw shrugged. "What am I supposed to do?"

"What indeed," Picard said. Lieutenant Šmrhová entered and handed him one of the recovered volumes. "I understand that many of your illusions were harmless," he said, opening the book. "But for every one of those, there is an episode where truthcrafters acted to the detriment of a whole civilization." He faced Ardra. "We believe that you can assist in undoing the work of your Circle in Federation space—and of thwarting future attempts."

Discussion broke out between the truthcrafters. Ardra, incredulous, put up one finger and the room fell silent. "Come now, Jean-Luc. Do you *really* think I would work against the Circle?"

"Consider it another way. You've suggested that standards have declined in your order. Starfleet will put you aboard the *Houdini* to spend your sentences working on behalf of the Federation. You would act as a control on the Circle, undoing past harms and preventing excesses." Picard gestured to the book before him. "These recorded episodes suggest your people originally created illusions from a love of the art, not for material gain or to create chaos. This service would bring the Circle back to its traditional path."

"Flying around the galaxy, showing how our tricks were done?" Gaw was animated. "I still can't see why we—" Then Gaw paused. "Wait. Did you say in there you'd be letting us go? No prison?"

"No prison," Picard said. "You would serve your sentence aboard the ship, with Doctor Aggadak and a Federation security team helping you."

"Parole officers," Gaw said. "Going where *you* make us go. Same as the Breen intended for us."

"No," Picard said. "You would be doing it because you owe it to the societies you swindled. And we would not ask to learn your methods. We would just direct where and how you used them."

"It would be . . . an odd kind of community service," Yorta said.

"With the community being all of space." Seeing Gaw and the other truthcrafters giving it serious consideration, Picard closed the book. "That is the offer." Taking the volume beneath his arm, he turned to leave.

Ardra attempted to follow Picard into the hall, but was stopped by Šmrhová. Picard waved her off. He spoke with Ardra alone outside. "Yes?"

"This plan of yours," Ardra said. "*I* didn't do the things

that they did. What I did for you at Janalwa gets me out of prison. We agreed!"

"It gets you out of Thionoga and erases Ventax II." He gestured toward the book in his hand. "What do you suspect Starfleet will find that you have been involved with?" A wry smile crossed his face. "The Mighty Ardra, known under twenty-three aliases in one sector alone?"

She pursed her lips and looked at the book. "You wouldn't know which ones were me."

"I'm confident that your style would shine through."

"Why, thank you," Ardra said, smiling in spite of herself. She stood for a moment, considering. "You know, there hasn't been an Illusionist Magnus since Jilaan. I suppose if I start policing the Circle, that puts me in charge." Her eyes went wide. "They might name it after me."

"The Kinshaya say circles are eternal. There's immortality there."

She chuckled—and regarded him closely. "It *has* been good to see you again. Are you really married, or was that a ruse?"

He eyed her warily. "Really married."

"Well, I should have known you wouldn't lie about—well, anything." Ardra straightened his collar. "Tell your people I'll take the deal."

"Excellent." Picard stepped back from her. "I hope to hear a good report." He turned and started down the hall.

"Let's not wait nineteen years before our next meeting," she called out.

Entering the turbolift, Picard wasn't sure if two decades would be long enough. But he was certain of one thing: however many years passed before he met her again, he knew she would look exactly the same as she did when they first met.

Like magic.

Fifty-nine

"**M**artok's officials talk of restocking the game on some of the nearby islands on H'atoria," Kahless said as he and Worf walked the grounds around the parked *Chu'charq* before dawn. "I expect there will be excursions now and again."

"Another reason for me to visit," Worf said. Day had broken over the military landing grounds, and Defense Force warriors were working alongside the former Unsung—now Sentries—to restock their vessel. Both groups would later board *Chu'charq* to fly to a public site for a ceremonial send-off; it promised to be a madhouse.

"I am surprised to see Starfleet here," Kahless said, nodding in the direction of Admiral Riker and the three captains conferring at the edge of the tarmac. "Will you come to the farewell?"

"*Aventine* will return to its explorations. *Titan* and *Enterprise* will join the honor escort to H'atoria before heading on their way. I am waiting on Korgh's sentencing. I will go to that."

"Yes, there is something you must do," Kahless said. He thought for a moment. "If they require any additional punishment for Korgh, tell them that slaving in sewage pits can be quite invigorating." He chortled.

They stood silently for several moments, looking back at the *Chu'charq* and the mix of warriors and Sentries working together.

At last, Kahless turned and clapped his hand on Worf's shoulder. "I am a Klingon of many words, Worf—most of which came from another, born long ago. But I speak for myself when I say I owe you a debt which I may never be able to repay."

Worf shook his head. "I only sought to do my duty to protect you."

"It is not that. In retirement, the life had gone out of me. I thought the Empire no longer needed me. But I now see," he said, glancing at the workers, "that there will always be those who need help finding the path."

Worf looked at the group—and saw Valandris exit *Chu'charq*'s landing ramp. She looked different. She wore the garb of a Sentry of Spirits' Forge, and the young woman had bound her unruly hair in that group's manner. Valandris saw the two of them and smiled.

Noticing Worf's gaze, Kahless smirked. "A reason for you to visit H'atoria," he said, shaking Worf's shoulder. He departed to speak to the Starfleet officers, chuckling all the way.

Valandris walked up to him, pulling at her collar as she did. "It feels different to wear this for real," she said.

"The duty is a great honor," he said, straightening.

"It is," she said. She looked back at her people. "It is good that the children will be living on the same world with us. I will keep my word to you about Sarken."

"It will do you both good."

Shuffling awkwardly, she spoke without looking at him. "I—I don't know what I expected when I kidnapped you. But I am glad I did. I do not fear the future for my people any longer."

"You have never known fear," he said.

"Yes, I have." She looked at him. "But we killed it." She

put her hand forward, and they clasped forearms. "Thank you, Worf."

"*Qapla'*, Valandris."

With that, she pivoted and started back toward *Chu'charq*. He called after her. "I will visit."

She stopped on the ramp and looked over her shoulder at him. "Bring that son of yours," she said. "Him, I would like to know better." The young woman grinned at Worf before turning and continuing on her way.

Dumbfounded, Worf stared at her—and only then did he realize Admiral Riker and the three captains were watching him. Worf said, "She . . . is interested in *my son*."

"Makes you feel old, doesn't it?" Riker said, barely suppressing a smirk.

"It's all right, Worf," Dax said. "It happens to everyone. Several times, for some of us."

"You know," Vale added cautiously, "he *is* an ambassador."

Flustered, Worf looked to Picard, who generously said nothing. But the captain was smiling.

Riker invited the captains back to the consulate for a farewell breakfast. There, he shared the news he'd received from C-in-C Admiral Akaar. Shift had not been located, but the Breen's involvement in the Rebuke had set back the Confederacy's relations with the Typhon Pact, and its prospects in the Beta Quadrant had been dealt a serious blow.

Chen had just returned from Janalwa; hopes were high that the Kinshaya's behavior might be moderated. An asteroid orbiting Jolva Ree in Holy Order space had exploded for no reason. Starfleet Intelligence suspected it was a consequence of the Breen pulling out of the region. "We may even finally get the free-flight corridor we've been after all this time once this is over," Riker said. There would certainly be fewer contrary voices.

Vale said her good-byes to the other captains and looked to the admiral. "I'll get our ride ready," she said. "We'll await your signal about the sentencing. Maybe we'll all see you tonight at Beale Street," she said, referring to one of *Titan*'s two officer's clubs.

"Maybe Rue Bourbon this time," he replied, naming the other. "I think we're all in a jazzier mood."

She departed—and Picard offered his farewell next. The captain had already scheduled a private dinner aboard *Enterprise* for that evening to thank La Forge and Šmrhorvá for their tireless efforts against the Unsung; now, the admiral supplied some good news to take to them. "The JAG has signed off on your idea for Ardra."

"I know your endorsement helped," Picard said.

"Before the past few days, I wouldn't have thought my word would count for anything."

"You underrate yourself," Picard said. He shook Riker's hand. "I'll see you . . . *someplace else*, I suppose."

"Until then," Riker said, smiling. Picard turned and exited, leaving Dax alone with the admiral.

"I guess I'm off too," the Trill said, starting for the door. "Last to leave, first to get there: that's *Aventine*."

"Captain," Riker said, "thanks again for the save. I know things with us were rough after Takedown. I'm glad we can get past that."

"I've had whole lives that didn't go as planned, Admiral. Trills are big on second chances—and tenth, and twentieth." She smiled. "Looks like there's someone else to see you," Dax said as she headed off.

Tuvok appeared in the doorway. "Am I disturbing you, Admiral?"

"No, we just wrapped up."

Tuvok entered, holding a small pouch in one hand. "With Korgh's sentence being carried out today, I have concluded my work with the Klingon investigators—recovering the items Starfleet would like to examine."

"Thank you, Commander."

"There was one particular item I thought *you* should have," Tuvok said, offering the little bag. "It is no longer needed."

Riker opened the pouch and withdrew a small packet. "Playing cards?"

"They are the ones Buxtus Cross owned," Tuvok said. "The ones that Commander Worf used to signal you from Thane."

Riker read the inscription on the pack. "'A Century of Progress.' The 1933 Chicago World's Fair?"

"Correct," Tuvok said. "A gathering looking toward the future, staged in the middle of an economic depression."

"Hope amidst failure," Riker said, gently opening the pack and withdrawing the cards.

"Given that these led to your identification of the Unsung's homeworld, I speculated that you would like to have them."

"Thanks." Riker gave the cards a riffle. He chuckled. "The ace of clubs is dirty."

"It fell into the mud when Worf fought to save Kahless," Tuvok said. "I further thought you would find them appealing given your interest in the era. Les Paul, Hal Kemp, and Johnny Mercer apparently performed at the exposition. Were you aware of this?"

Riker smiled broadly. "The Paul Whiteman Orchestra opened the show. Whiteman called himself the 'king of jazz'—though purists didn't think that was what he was playing. People have been searching for recordings from the expo forever."

"I regret that I cannot provide those."

"As mementos go, these will do." He put the cards carefully back into the package. "Thank you, Tuvok. We won't be playing poker with these."

"I expected not. As you observed, one of the cards is now marked."

As Riker laughed, Tuvok turned to go. Riker called out, "Hang around for a few hours, Commander. I don't have a gift like this to give you, but there's something that you might like to be a part of . . ."

Sixty

"*Your journey back must have been arduous, Chot Dayn. Enter. Sit.*"

The Breen did as advised. The trip from Jolva Ree had indeed been long and difficult. The path had ended here in the Linnavhava, residence of Domo Pran.

There was no higher place in the Breen Confederacy. And there was no more nervous place for a visitor to be than in the domo's office, across from his desk. Pran sat motionless for long moments before speaking. "*I am told, Dayn, that thanks to your efforts the asteroid was completely destroyed.*"

"Yes, Domo. A colossal waste, but it had to be done. If the Kinshaya's allegiance is in doubt, I judged that we could not allow such a facility to fall into their possession."

"*The right move.*" Pran shook his head. "*It is a shame what happened to Roje, but the battlesphere scheme should have been abandoned with the Kinshaya revolt years ago.*"

"I grant that it was an attempt to salvage something—"

"*Come, Dayn, you need not pretend. You were the most skeptical of Roje—and of his protégé. If you had not been present, I am sure more resources might have been lost.*" The domo stood and paced. "*Chot Shift is dead?*"

"Yes. She knew she was condemned, and refused to waste any more of our resources in her punishment. So she stayed and died aboard Jolva Ree." A pause. "A patriotic choice."

"*Cowardice.*" Domo Pran reached the far wall and looked back. "*I have decided to reorganize the intelligence organization to eliminate Roje's position."* He approached the desk. *"In exchange, I will be adding a new thot to the ranks of the logistical division. You are to have that promotion."*

The domo's guest straightened. "I am honored, Domo. I will make you proud of my performance."

"See that you do."

Later, after the meeting concluded—an hour filled with plans and financial projections—the new thot transported out of the domo's office. In private, back aboard ship, the Breen officer disrobed—and the Orion woman looked at herself in the mirror and considered her names.

T'shantra. Shift. Vella. N'Keera. And now Dayn, her latest identity—and the one taken in the greatest hurry.

After the real Chot Dayn had pronounced her condemned in the facility at Jolva Ree, he had turned his back on her. She pulled the hidden disruptor that Thot Roje had always kept concealed in his desk and stunned him. It had always been a joke between her and her Fenrisal friend; it had been the pistol she had held on him when they had met. He had kept it as a souvenir of their friendship, tucked away in a drawer Dayn had never bothered to search.

She had then stripped her victim—whereupon she realized she had guessed wrong. Under his armor, Chot Dayn was not an Amoniri, as she had suspected—but, in fact, a Silwaan. This was unalloyed good news, because the specialized interior of Amoniri armor would have made it impossible for her to wear. Silwaan were enough like Orions that she had been able to strip off the dead Dayn's armor and take it for herself.

Then, dressed as Dayn and with his identity chip active, she had beamed back to the waiting shuttle for the flight home.

She could have fled at any point. But she was a Breen. Shift still believed in their philosophy. It was the cleverness of her opponents that had outsmarted her, and the weakness of the Breen's Kinshaya allies that had failed Roje. That, and the fact that Dayn was always there to undermine him. She could still serve the Confederacy.

Just as someone else.

T'shantra the slave girl was dead—and now, so too was Shift the Breen secret agent. The promotion would make "Thot Dayn" one of the top logisticians in the government—a position, historically, that had been a launching point for even bigger things. Three domos, that she knew of, had come from their ranks, and there was little wonder why. Their work was difficult in the extreme, managing the accounting and disposition of assets for a sprawling union of star systems.

Thot Dayn put her helmet back on and considered that she did not know the first thing about being a logistician—just as she had not known anything about being an illusionist or a spy.

But she would figure it out.

The Great Hall
Qo'noS

Kahless the Unforgettable had preached "death before chains." In front of the High Council, the order had been reversed: Korgh wore the chains, and he assumed he would momentarily be put to death.

Life had its cruel jokes.

Except for the accursed Worf, Korgh had been spared the sight of more Starfleet personnel sullying the sacred floor of the Great Hall. He did not know why the commander was present. To gloat, probably, at Korgh's downfall. Worf had missed the trial. Whatever indignity came today, the officer would not miss it.

Korgh had come to realize that he hated Worf over all others—even the pusillanimous Martok, still currying favor with the Federation overlords who kept him in power. Worf was the personification of the Accords. Future generations would inherit a weakling Empire subservient to the Federation, if Worf was the sort of Klingon they respected. Kruge had died to prevent that fate—and soon, Korgh was sure, he would too. Even at a hundred twenty, he was too dangerous to keep alive.

He saw his sons present, with their wives, Lorath's pregnant widow, and Korgh's six granddaughters. They were brought in to unnerve him, he was sure; to tempt him into confession, or perhaps hysterics, as he argued against death. He would not give his tormentors that benefit. Neither would his sons fall to their knees, begging for mercy for him. He had not been allowed to talk with them since his conviction, but he was sure they hated his enemies now as much as he did. Tragg and Tengor did not make eye contact. *Good boys*, he thought, to spare their opponents any sign of emotion. Martok and Worf had made a fatal error. Future generations would avenge him and accomplish his dreams.

A gong sounded. Martok, in full ceremonial robes, entered with his aides; he did not sit. Rather, he joined the circle of council members surrounding Korgh.

"This is a dark day," Martok said. "One of our own has committed the most heinous acts. His judgment now falls to us. It begins with the remedy of an error." He called out to the rear of the hall. "General Kersh, come forward!"

Korgh winced as the woman approached and passed into

the circle. The old man had considered this might be coming, but thought it too daring for Martok. *Evidently not.*

"Kersh, daughter of Dakh," Martok said, "granddaughter of J'borr, you were before and are now the heir to the House of Kruge. This council celebrates your efforts to defend your house's holdings at H'atoria and Pheben. You are leader of the house."

"I thank you," Kersh said, bowing her head slightly. She looked to the others. "My house will make you proud. This I swear." She did not look at Korgh at all.

"Take your place, Lady Kersh." Martok watched as the new council member found a place in the circle. Korgh looked away.

"We come to the end," Martok said. "Korgh was spared discommendation along with Kruge's officers a hundred years ago—but with his later acts he has shown he deserves it. It is a fate worse than death. If it has fallen before on those who have not deserved it, we can know that it lands in the right place now."

Guards stepped forward, removed his chains, and withdrew. It was not what Korgh was expecting. *They will keep me alive?*

It was insulting. As if he cared now for their pretty traditions—as if he had *ever* cared. Martok would pay for his lapse in judgment.

"This judgment falls on you and yours for seven generations," Martok said, gesturing to Tragg, Tengor, and their families as he paced around Korgh. "Your honor is hereby—"

"Hold," came a voice from behind the circle.

Martok looked back. "Who speaks?"

"Worf, son of Mogh."

Martok acknowledged him. "Let the son of Mogh speak."

Worf entered the circle. "Hear me, Council. Once, you

did not—because of actions falsely attributed to my father. That has been rectified. But I seek here to address an injustice about to be done. There is no evidence that Tragg and Tengor had any knowledge of Korgh's actions. Nor did their families, which you would condemn along with them."

The circle opened so Worf could address the sons and their families. "Do you disavow Korgh and his acts?"

Korgh saw Tragg and Tengor looking straight at him—and in that moment, the father did not recognize his sons. "We disavow him," they said in unison.

Korgh shook with astonishment. "What are you saying?"

The wives and granddaughters joined the two sons. "We disavow him."

Korgh's face went white.

"You heard them," Worf said to the High Council. "They reject what he did. Discommendation should fall only on Lord Korgh."

The concept set the council abuzz. "I . . . do not know if we have such discretion," Martok said.

"This Council has whatever power it wants," Worf said. He stared down each of them as he walked the floor. "What value are rules, if they create as much injustice as they seek to punish? And what use is a council that hides behind traditions, in order to deny responsibility? That council would be weak and without honor." He stopped and faced Martok. "I know that *you* would never be chancellor of such a body."

Martok's eyes narrowed. He surveyed the council members—and then his eyes fell on the sons and granddaughters of Korgh, their heads bowed in obeisance even as the old man looked up in defiance.

After a moment, he came to a decision. "This council supports the recommendation of Worf, son of Mogh. Perhaps we will revisit this practice in the future. But the shame here began with Korgh's actions. Let it fall entirely upon him."

It was decided. The chancellor approached Korgh and loomed over the old man. "Korgh, son of Torav: Do you know the words you must speak?"

Korgh knew them very well: *tlhIH ghIj jIHyoj.* The first half of the rite of discommendation: "I fear your judgment." But he did not fear any Klingon's judgment, and he would not say the words.

"I dispute your right to stand over me," he said. "I *would* have been the son of Kruge. And your chair should have been mine!"

"*biHnuch!*" Martok cried.

Coward!

The horrid word, mystical in its awfulness, rang out in the hall—and as if moved by magic, first Martok and then the other members of the council crossed their arms and turned their backs on Korgh. So did Worf, who moved with the reluctance of one who had suffered it before.

So, too, did his own family. Korgh saw them turn as one. "My sons . . . ?"

With not a face to be seen, Korgh somehow found the energy to move. He made his way out of the hall.

Sixty-one

Korgh did not notice the ground beneath his feet until he was on the steps outside the Great Hall. The punishment spared him a hundred years earlier had finally come—and everything was lost.

It had taken him a century of scheming to reach the heights he had in the last month. At a hundred and twenty, he surely did not have a century more—and this time, he was truly alone. No Odrok. No supporters.

Not even his sons. They were dead to him, now, following their betrayal. But he was dead to countless others. Ahead of him as he descended foot by trudging foot, a host of Klingons turned their backs upon him. Warriors, strangers, even peasants who had come to the First City to witness the great events of the past few days. They all scorned him.

The sight of so many unworthy people denying him caused his heart to stir. He was Korgh—and he still had his mind. That, and hatred, deep and abiding. It was now all he had—but it had been all he had ever needed.

Yes, he thought, *Martok has made a grave mistake indeed.* Korgh would go into the world, under yet another name, and find new allies, new weapons. And with them, he would bring all of his enemies low.

It would start now. He walked into the street past the turned faces—

—and saw eyes. Human and Vulcan. Admiral Riker, the haughty fool, with Commander Tuvok beside him, holding a phaser. Behind them were several more armed Starfleet security officers.

"What do *you* want?" Korgh turned away, refusing to

give Riker the opportunity to gloat. But the security officers blocked his path.

Riker moved back in front of him. Expressionless, he spoke. "Korgh, son of Torav—"

"Get out of my way!"

"—also known as Galdor. You are under arrest for crimes perpetrated against the United Federation of Planets, including thirty-seven counts of conspiracy to commit murder during the *may'qochvan* celebration on Gamaral, in Federation space. You are further charged with conspiracy to commit fraud against the exiles of Thane, also a Federation territory."

"You must be mad, Riker." Korgh managed a sneer. "You have no authority over me, not here." He pounded his fist against his chest and shouted to the sky. "I am a Klingon!"

Riker leaned in and whispered, "Not anymore."

wa' Dol nIvDaq matay'DI' maQap.

"We succeed together in a greater whole."

Acknowledgments

Worf thought it would take a colossal quest to get Kahless into Sto-Vo-Kor—and taking on this trilogy has at times seemed a monumental quest of my own. A year and a half of my life transpired while I was commuting to the Beta Quadrant, and the fact that the final product reflects what I set out to do owes a great deal to the efforts of many.

First and foremost, thanks go to my editor Margaret Clark, for her boundless patience, invaluable advice, and moral support; as well as to Ed Schlesinger, John Van Citters, and all those who made this work possible. Thanks once again are due Brent Frankenhoff, James Mishler, Robert Peden, and Michael Singleton for their feedback along the way. Marc Okrand's works were again a major source of inspiration. And a Klingon salute to Felix Malmenbeck, who knew it should be *may'qochvan* and not *ma'qochvan*—and who contributed many other suggestions regarding the bits of *tlhIngan Hol* used herein.

My appreciation as usual goes to Meredith Miller, proofreader and number one on my bridge—and especial thanks go to Pocket Books and CBS for allowing me to be part of the fiftieth anniversary year of Gene Roddenberry's creation. I was born the night "A Piece of the Action" first aired, so in a sense, *Star Trek* has been the journey of a lifetime for me; I suspect that's the case for most of you reading. It has been an honor to provide a stop along your own individual *Star Trek* voyages—and as Kahless tells us, there is nothing more important than honor.

Qapla'!

About the Author

John Jackson Miller is the *New York Times* bestselling author of the novels *Star Trek: The Next Generation: Takedown*; *Star Wars: A New Dawn*; *Star Wars: Kenobi*; *Star Wars: Knight Errant*; *Star Wars: Lost Tribe of the Sith—The Collected Stories*; and fifteen *Star Wars* graphic novels, as well as *Overdraft: The Orion Offensive*. He has also written the eNovella *Star Trek: Titan: Absent Enemies*. A comics industry historian and analyst, he has written for franchises including *Halo*, *Conan*, *Iron Man*, *Indiana Jones*, *Mass Effect*, *Planet of the Apes*, and *The Simpsons*. He lives in Wisconsin with his wife, two children, and far too many comic books.